IMC HORIZON CAMPUS
ZION-BENTON TWNS

W9-AZL-999

PRIZE STORIES 1984
The O. Henry Awards

PRIZE STORIES 1984

The O. Henry Awards

EDITED AND WITH
AN INTRODUCTION
BY WILLIAM ABRAHAMS

T 17218
SC
HEN

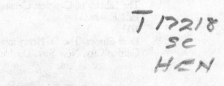

DOUBLEDAY & COMPANY, INC.

GARDEN CITY, NEW YORK

1984

The Library of Congress Cataloged This Serial as
PZ1 Follows:
.011
Prize Stories. The O. Henry awards. 1919–
Garden City, New York, Doubleday [etc.]
    v. 21 cm.

Title varies: 1919–46, O. Henry memorial award prize stories. Stories for 1919–27 were
"chosen by the Society of Arts and Sciences." Editors: 1919–32, B. C. Williams.—1933–
40, Harry Hansen.—1941– Herschel Brickell (with Muriel Fuller, 19 –46)

1. Short stories. I. Williams, Blanche Colton, 1879–1944, ed. II. Hansen, Harry, 1884–
ed. III. Brickell, Herschel, 1889– ed. IV. Society of Arts and Sciences, New York.
    PZ1.011 813.5082
Library of Congress [r50q⁸30] Official

ISBN 0-385-18844-7
Library of Congress Catalog Card Number 21–9372 rev 3*

Copyright © 1984 by Doubleday & Company, Inc.
ALL RIGHTS RESERVED
PRINTED IN THE UNITED STATES OF AMERICA
FIRST EDITION

CONTENTS

PUBLISHER'S NOTE

This volume is the sixty-fourth in the O. Henry Memorial Award series.

In 1918, the Society of Arts and Sciences met to vote upon a monument to the master of the short story, O. Henry. They decided that this memorial should be in the form of two prizes for the best short stories published by American authors in American magazines during the year 1919. From this beginning, the memorial developed into an annual anthology of outstanding short stories by American authors, published, with the exception of the years 1952 and 1953, by Doubleday & Company, Inc.

Blanche Colton Williams, one of the founders of the awards, was editor from 1919 to 1932; Harry Hansen from 1933 to 1940; Herschel Brickell from 1941 to 1951. The annual collection did not appear in 1952 and 1953, when the continuity of the series was interrupted by the death of Herschel Brickell. Paul Engle was editor from 1954 to 1959 with Hanson Martin coeditor in the years 1954 to 1960; Mary Stegner in 1960; Richard Poirier from 1961 to 1966, with assistance from and coeditorship with William Abrahams from 1964 to 1966. William Abrahams became editor of the series in 1967.

In 1970 Doubleday published under Mr. Abrahams' editorship *Fifty Years of the American Short Story,* and in 1981, *Prize Stories of the Seventies.* Both are collections of stories selected from this series.

The stories chosen for this volume were published in the period from the summer of 1982 to the summer of 1983. A list of the magazines consulted appears at the back of the book. The choice of stories and the selection of prize winners are exclusively the responsibility of the editor. Biographical material is based on information provided by the contributors and obtained from standard works of reference.

INTRODUCTION

Rare indeed is the author's collection of stories, being brought out in book form, that does not carry an appropriate acknowledgment to the various magazines in which the stories—all or most of them—first appeared. Even rarer is a book of stories of which none have been previously published. It would seem that without the pedigree or seal of approval that magazine publication represents, gaining for the writer some degree of recognition and the nucleus of an audience, publishers hesitate to take on the very real financial risk, especially as costs keep rising, that goes with bringing out a collection.

Not that a history of prior magazine publication in itself will ensure a book that makes back its cost, let alone a dignified profit. But it does mean, in some cases anyway, that book review editors, encountering a familiar, reassuring litany—something along the lines of "first published in *The New Yorker, Antaeus, Sewanee Review,* and *The Atlantic*" —will pause over the slender volume, often representing years of dedicated work with no more than token rewards, and in a fit of high-minded benevolence decide that the book qualifies for a place in an omnibus review. Rescued from the junk heap, it is allotted, along with four or five or ten other collections, almost as much space as goes routinely to a touted "artistic" novel (the classic of its week) or the ghostwritten autobiography of an important, that is to say temporarily newsworthy, politician.

So the favored collection will make its way to the harassed reviewer who will notice it in a brisk paragraph, singling out perhaps two of the fourteen stories it contains—better that, of course, than to be utterly ignored and sink into oblivion. But space being at a premium, it is unlikely that the reviewer will find room for a grudging little phrase to indicate the provenance of the stories, where they first appeared, and the editors who thought enough of them to bring them into print.

I do not intend to lament yet again the difficulties of publication that confront most writers of short stories; they are too well known to need repetition ("If you have tears, prepare to shed them now"); nor will I linger over the whims, peculiarities, prejudices, and flukes of professional book reviewing. My intention is simply to indicate a fact of literary life to which remarkably little attention is paid in literary histories and works of criticism. Only biographers seem to recognize that between the writing of a work and its publication there are painful experiences for the writer—the quest for acceptance and the eventual appearance of a manuscript in print—that historians and critics glide over as if they never existed.

So far as the short story is concerned, with the exceedingly uncommon exception noted above of a book of hitherto unpublished stories, magazines play, have played, and will continue to play a significantly vital role. If there were no magazines to publish them, short stories as we know and value them—a wonderfully creative form and a significant part of our literature—almost certainly would wither away unseen, or survive through a long decline only by a quaint obstinacy on the part of writers indifferent to publication. (But do such writers exist?)

Granting, then, the indispensability of magazines to the future of the short story, one may properly question their state at present, from the mimeographed pamphlet distributed to three hundred subscribers to the glossiest compendium aimed at a circulation in the millions. What welcome do they accord to stories, and what sort of stories do they want? Not long ago, reading a collection of letters by the distinguished typographer Beatrice L. Warde, written in England during the early years of World War II when the Blitz was at its height, I came unexpectedly upon a sentence that struck me as peculiarly relevant to these questions. "All writing for publication means addressing unknown people in the dark; the writer of books for sale talks (if he's wise) to himself and people pay to eavesdrop; the writer of stories for magazines writes for whatever public is known to like that sort of thing . . ."

Well, Mrs. Warde was writing forty-two years ago, and much has changed, beginning with the world we live in and ending with the stories we write (and read) and the magazines that publish them, though there's a relationship among all three. Excepting certain precisely defined genres—mystery and detective stories, science fiction—for which certain magazines precisely cater (*Omni Magazine*, say, or *Ellery Queen's Mystery Magazine*), can we suggest now, as Mrs. Warde did while the bombs fell about her, that there are magazines whose hospitality a writer can count on for the sort of story he or she wants to write—a story of uncompromising quality, authenticity and individuality, that bears sentence by sentence the unmistakable signature of its author—and whose readers know that *there* is where such stories are to be found.

For convenience's sake, and because the evidence is at hand, I turn to the current collection. It contains twenty stories, chosen from four-teen magazines: two from *The New Yorker;* two from *The Atlantic,* two from *Grand Street;* two from *Antaeus;* two from *Sewanee Review;* two from *TriQuarterly* and one each from *Harper's, Ascent, Shenandoah, Fiction International, The Kenyon Review, Mademoiselle, Mother Jones,* and *The Antioch Review.* Even at a casual glance, one sees how heavily the collection is weighted in favor of the "little" magazines and literary quarterlies. This represents no special prejudice on the editor's part, but an unescapable tilt: quality is where you find it, and you are more likely to find it now in magazines that address themselves to a small audience of discriminating readers whose taste is away from gossip (a kind of creeping *People*-ism now rife in the land) and the short-order read (a kind of creeping *USA*-ism) and who accepts without protest writing that is intelligent, free of stereotypes, and even at times difficult.

This is a relatively new situation: to find the little magazines so dramatically in the ascendant. Only a few years ago a collection of this sort was quite evenly balanced. One took it for granted that there would be stories from *The New Yorker* and *The Atlantic*—properly so—and perhaps from *Esquire* and *McCall's* and *Redbook* and *Cosmopolitan.* But the decline in quality, the lack of interest in encouraging it—so far as the short story is concerned—has become ever more conspicuous and depressing. It is hard to reconcile the *Esquire* of a decade ago with its impressive mix of the famous and the unknown among writers of stories—with the present "new" *Esquire* whose merits, such as they may be, are of an entirely different order.

As for the so-called "women's magazines"—which not so long ago were bravely in search of serious fiction—their decline has been more precipitous and even more lamentable. Ours is an age notable, surely, for the stories written by women—notable alike for their diversity of style and subject matter. I would not hesitate to name Cynthia Ozick, for example, as one of the three greatest living American writers of short fiction. (Only tact restrains me from identifying the other two.) Yet at this very moment, when writers of the stature of Ozick, Gloria Norris, Edith Pearlman, Alice Adams, Melissa Brown Pritchard, Elizabeth Tallent, Perri Klass, Grace Paley, and Helen Norris are actively at work, the women's magazines are sinking, where fiction is concerned, to abysmal depths. Not one of the gifted writers I have listed, with the exception of Perri Klass who appeared in *Mademoiselle* (itself an exception to the generalizations I have been making), was discovered for this collection in the pages of the women's magazines.

The paradox is painful to contemplate. These magazines, self-proclaimed to be in the forefront in their attention to "today's woman"— so brilliant at home and in the office, so interested in interior decoration, microwave cooking, the latest in manners and morals—evidently think their readers too simpleminded to recognize the astonishing achievements, the esthetic sensibility, the wit, the virtuosity of style, the depth of feeling, the grasp of the complexities of contemporary life represented by women writers of our day. The magazines that pass them by are quite simply anachronisms: they belong for all their free-flowing sexuality and pop psychologizing to the 1950s. Dare one suggest that if the women's movement wanted to raise its consciousness to the high level where it belongs, it begin by acquainting women with writers of whom they could justly be proud and whose work they seem not to know at all, rather than worry about the tits-and-ass fiction and photographs that turn up in men's magazines that are themselves superannuated survivors of the 1950s.

We are in the 1980s. Marvelous stories are being written every day and are waiting for publication. *The New Yorker, Grand Street, Antaeus, Sewanee Review* and *The Atlantic* can't attend to them all. It's time for more magazines, newspapers, and foundations to accept this burgeoning reality of our time, one of the few realities that gives us cause for self-congratulation.

—William Abrahams

PRIZE STORIES 1984
The O. Henry Awards

ROSA

CYNTHIA OZICK

Cynthia Ozick is the author of two novels, *The Cannibal Galaxy* and *Trust;* three volumes of short stories, *The Pagan Rabbi, Bloodshed,* and *Levitation;* and *Art & Ardor,* a collection of essays. She is married to Bernard Hallote and is the mother of a college freshman, Rachel.

Rosa Lublin, a madwoman and a scavenger, gave up her store—she smashed it up herself—and moved to Miami. It was a mad thing to do. In Florida she became a dependent. Her niece in New York sent her money and she lived among the elderly, in a dark hole, a single room in a "hotel." There was an ancient dresser-top refrigerator and a one-burner stove. Over in a corner a round oak table brooded on its heavy pedestal, but it was only for drinking tea. Her meals she had elsewhere, in bed or standing at the sink—sometimes toast with a bit of sour cream and half a sardine, or a small can of peas heated in a Pyrex mug. Instead of maid service there was a dumbwaiter on a shrieking pulley. On Tuesdays and Fridays it swallowed her meager bags of garbage. Squads of dying flies blackened the rope. The sheets on her bed were just as black—it was a five-block walk to the laundromat. The streets were a furnace, the sun an executioner. Every day without fail it blazed and blazed, so she stayed in her room and ate two bites of a hard-boiled egg in bed, with a writing board on her knees; she had lately taken to composing letters.

She wrote sometimes in Polish and sometimes in English, but her niece had forgotten Polish; most of the time Rosa wrote to Stella in English. Her English was crude. To her daughter Magda she wrote in the most excellent literary Polish. She wrote on the brittle sheets of abandoned stationery that inexplicably turned up in the cubbyholes of a blistered old desk in the lobby. Or she would ask the Cuban girl in the receptionist's cage for a piece of blank billing paper. Now and then

Copyright © 1983 by Cynthia Ozick. First appeared in *The New Yorker.* Reprinted by permission.

she would find a clean envelope in the lobby bin; she would meticulously rip its seams and lay it out flat: it made a fine white square, the fresh face of a new letter.

The room was littered with these letters. It was hard to get them mailed—the post office was a block farther off than the laundromat, and the hotel lobby's stamp machine had been marked "OUT OF ON DER" for years. There was an oval tin of sardines left open on the sink counter since yesterday. Already it smelled vomitous. She felt she was in hell. "Golden and beautiful Stella," she wrote to her niece. "Where I put myself is in hell. Once I thought the worst was the worst, after that nothing could be the worst. But now I see, even after the worst there's still more." Or she wrote: "Stella, my angel, my dear one, a devil climbs into you and ties up your soul and you don't even know it."

To Magda she wrote: "You have grown into a lioness. You are tawny and you stretch apart your furry toes in all their power. Whoever steals you steals her own death."

Stella had eyes like a small girl's, like a doll's. Round, not big but pretty, bright skin underneath, fine pure skin above, tender eyebrows like rainbows, and lashes as rich as embroidery. She had the face of a little bride. You could not believe from all this beauty, these doll's eyes, these buttercup lips, these baby's cheeks, you could not believe in what harmless containers the bloodsucker comes.

Sometimes Rosa had cannibal dreams about Stella: she was boiling her tongue, her ears, her right hand, such a fat hand with plump fingers, each nail tended and rosy, and so many rings, not modern rings but old-fashioned junkshop rings. Stella liked everything from Rosa's junkshop, everything used, old, lacy with other people's history. To pacify Stella, Rosa called her Dear One, Lovely, Beautiful; she called her Angel; she called her all these things for the sake of peace, but in reality Stella was cold. She had no heart. Stella, already nearly fifty years old, the Angel of Death.

The bed was black, as black as Stella's will. After a while Rosa had no choice, she took a bundle of laundry in a shopping cart and walked to the laundromat. Though it was only ten in the morning, the sun was killing. Florida, why Florida? Because here they were shells like herself, already fried from the sun. All the same she had nothing in common with them. Old ghosts, old socialists: idealists. The Human Race was all they cared for. Retired workers, they went to lectures, they frequented the damp and shadowy little branch library. She saw them walking with Tolstoy under their arms, with Dostoevski. They knew good material. Whatever you wore they would feel between their fingers and give a name to: faille, corduroy, shantung, jersey, worsted, velours, crêpe. She heard them speak of bias, grosgrain, the "season," the "length." Yellow they called mustard. What was pink to everyone else to them was sunset; orange was tangerine; red was hot tomato. They were from the Bronx, from Brooklyn, lost neighborhoods, burned out. A few were from West End Avenue. Once she met a former vegetable-store owner from Columbus Avenue; his store was on Columbus Avenue, his residence not far, on West Seventieth Street, off Central Park. Even in the perpetual garden of Florida, he reminisced about his flowery green heads of romaine lettuce, his glowing strawberries, his sleek avocados.

It seemed to Rosa Lublin that the whole peninsula of Florida was weighted down with regret. Everyone had left behind a real life. Here they had nothing. They were all scarecrows, blown about under the murdering sunball with empty rib cages.

In the laundromat she sat on a cracked wooden bench and watched the round porthole of the washing machine. Inside, the surf of detergent bubbles frothed and slapped her underwear against the pane.

An old man sat crosslegged beside her, fingering a newspaper. She looked over and saw that the headlines were all in Yiddish. In Florida the men were of higher quality than the women. They knew a little more of the world, they read newspapers, they lived for international affairs. Everything that happened in the Israeli Knesset they followed. But the women only recited meals they used to cook in their old lives— kugel, pirogen, latkes, blintzes, herring salad. Mainly the women thought about their hair. They went to hairdressers and came out into the brilliant day with plantlike crowns the color of zinnias. Sea-green paint on the eyelids. One could pity them: they were in love with rumors of their grandchildren, Katie at Bryn Mawr, Jeff at Princeton. To the grandchildren Florida was a slum, to Rosa it was a zoo.

She had no one but her cold niece in Queens, New York.

"Imagine this," the old man next to her said. "Just look, first he has Hitler, then he has Siberia, he's in a camp in Siberia! Next thing he gets away to Sweden, then he comes to New York and he peddles. He's a peddler, by now he's got a wife, he's got kids, so he opens a little store —just a little store, his wife is a sick woman, it's what you call a bargain store—"

"What?" Rosa said.

"A bargain store on Main Street, a place in Westchester, not even the Bronx. And they come in early in the morning, he didn't even hang out his shopping bags yet, robbers, muggers, and they choke him, they finish him off. From Siberia he lives for this day!"

Rosa said nothing.

"An innocent man alone in his store. Be glad you're not up there anymore. On the other hand, here it's no paradise neither. Believe me, when it comes to muggers and stranglers there's no utopia nowhere."

"My machine's finished," Rosa said. "I have to put in the dryer." She knew about newspapers and their evil reports: a newspaper item herself. WOMAN AXES OWN BIZ. Rosa Lublin, 59, owner of a secondhand furniture store on Utica Avenue, Brooklyn, yesterday afternoon deliberately demolished . . . The *News* and the *Post.* A big photograph, Stella standing near with her mouth stretched and her arms wild. In the *Times*, six lines.

"Excuse me, I notice you speak with an accent."

Rosa flushed. "I was born somewhere else, not here."

"I also was born somewhere else. You're a refugee? Berlin?"

"Warsaw."

"I'm also from Warsaw! 1920 I left. 1906 I was born."

"Happy birthday," Rosa said. She began to pull her things out of the washing machine. They were twisted into each other like mixed-up snakes.

"Allow me," said the old man. He put down his paper and helped her untangle. "Imagine this," he said. "Two people from Warsaw meet in Miami, Florida. In 1910 I didn't dream of Miami, Florida."

"My Warsaw isn't your Warsaw," Rosa said.

"As long as your Miami, Florida, is my Miami, Florida." Two whole rows of glinting dentures smiled at her; he was proud to be a flirt. Together they shoved the snarled load into the dryer. Rosa put in two quarters and the thundering hum began. They heard the big snaps on the belt of her dress with the blue stripes, the one that was torn in the armpit, under the left sleeve, clanging against the caldron's metal sides.

"You read Yiddish?" the old man said.

"No."

"You can speak a few words maybe?"

"No." My Warsaw isn't your Warsaw. But she remembered her grandmother's cradle-croonings: her grandmother was from Minsk. *Unter Reyzls vigele shteyt a klor-vays tsigele.* How Rosa's mother despised those sounds! When the drying cycle ended, Rosa noticed that the old man handled the clothes like an expert. She was ashamed for him to touch her underpants. *Under Rosa's cradle there's a clear-white little goat. . . .* But he knew how to find a sleeve, wherever it might be hiding.

"What is it," he asked, "you're bashful?"

"No."

"In Miami, Florida, people are more friendly. What," he said, "you're still afraid? Nazis we ain't got, even Ku Kluxers we ain't got. What kind of person are you, you're still afraid?"

"The kind of person," Rosa said, "is what you see. Thirty-nine years ago I was somebody else."

"Thirty-nine years ago I wasn't so bad myself. I lost my teeth without a single cavity," he bragged. "Everything perfect. Periodontal disease."

"*I* was a chemist almost. A physicist," Rosa said. "You think I wouldn't have been a scientist?" The thieves who took her life! All at once the landscape behind her eyes fell out of control: a bright field flashed; then a certain shadowy corridor leading to the laboratory-supplies closet. The closet opened in her dreams also. Retorts and microscopes were ranged on the shelves. Once, walking there, she was conscious of the coursing of her own ecstasy—her new brown shoes, laced and sober, her white coat, her hair cut short in bangs: a serious person of seventeen, ambitious, responsible, a future Marie Curie! One of her teachers in the high school praised her for what he said was a "literary style"—oh, lost and kidnapped Polish!—and now she wrote and spoke English as helplessly as this old immigrant. From Warsaw! Born 1906! She imagined what bitter ancient alley, dense with stalls, cheap clothes strung on outdoor racks, signs in jargoned Yiddish. Anyhow they called her refugee. The Americans couldn't tell her apart from this fellow with his false teeth and his dewlaps and his rakehell reddish toupee bought God knows when or where—Delancey Street, the lower East Side. A dandy. Warsaw! What did he know? In school she had read Tuwim: such delicacy, such loftiness, such *Polishness*. The Warsaw of her girlhood: a great light: she switched it on, she wanted to live inside her eyes. The curve of the legs of her mother's bureau. The strict leather smell of her father's desk. The white tile tract of the kitchen floor, the big pots breathing, a narrow tower stair next to the attic . . . the house of her girlhood laden with a thousand books. Polish, German, French; her father's Latin books; the shelf of shy literary periodicals her mother's poetry now and then wandered through, in short lines like heated telegrams. Cultivation, old civilization, beauty, history! Surprising turnings of streets, shapes of venerable cottages, lovely aged eaves, unexpected and gossamer turrets, steeples, the gloss, the antiquity! Gardens. Whoever speaks of Paris has never seen Warsaw. Her father, like her mother, mocked at Yiddish; there was not a particle of ghetto left in him, not a grain of rot. Whoever yearns for an aristocratic sensibility, let him switch on the great light of Warsaw.

"Your name?" her companion said.

"Lublin, Rosa."

"A pleasure," he said. "Only why backwards? I'm an application form? Very good. You apply, I accept." He took command of her shopping cart. "Wherever is your home is my direction that I'm going anyhow."

"You forgot to take your laundry," Rosa said.

"Mine I did day before yesterday."

"So why did you come here?"

"I'm devoted to nature. I like the sound of a waterfall. Wherever it's cool it's a pleasure to sit and read my paper."

"What a story!"

"All right, so I go to have a visit with the ladies. Tell me, you like concerts?"

"I like my own room, that's all."

"A lady what wants to be a hermit!"

"I got my own troubles," Rosa said.

"Unload on me."

In the street she plodded beside him dumbly, a led animal. Her shoes were not nice; she should have put on the other ones. The sunlight was smothering—cooked honey dumped on their heads: one lick was good, too much could drown you. She was glad to have someone to pull the cart.

"You got internal warnings about talking to a stranger? If I say my name, no more a stranger. Simon Persky. A third cousin to Shimon Peres, the Israeli politician. I have different famous relatives, plenty of family pride. You ever heard of Betty Bacall, who Humphrey Bogart the movie star was married to, a Jewish girl? Also a distant cousin. I could tell you the whole story of my life experience, beginning with Warsaw. Actually it wasn't Warsaw, it was a little place a few miles out of town. In Warsaw I had uncles."

Rosa said again, "Your Warsaw isn't my Warsaw."

He stopped the cart. "What is this? A song with one stanza? You think I don't know the difference between generations? I'm seventy-one, and you, you're only a girl."

"Fifty-eight." Though in the papers, when they told how she smashed up her store, it came out fifty-nine. Stella's fault, Stella's black will, the Angel of Death's arithmetic.

"You see? I told you! A girl!"

"I'm from an educated family."

"Your English ain't better than what any other refugee talks."

"Why should I learn English? I didn't ask for it, I got nothing to do with it."

"You can't live in the past," he advised. Again the wheels of the cart were squealing. Like a calf, Rosa followed. They were approaching a self-service cafeteria. The smells of eggplant, fried potatoes, mushrooms blew out as if pumped. Rosa read the sign: KOLLINS KOSHER KAMEO: EVERYTHING ON YOUR PLATE AS PRETTY AS A PICTURE: RE-MEMBRANCES OF NEW YORK AND THE PARADISE OF YOUR MATERNAL KITCHEN: DELICIOUS DISHES OF AMBROSIA AND NOSTALGIA: AIR CON-DITIONED THRU-OUT.

"I know the owner," Persky said. "He's a big reader. You want tea?"

"Tea?"

"Not iced. The hotter the better. This is physiology. Come in, you'll cool off. You got some red face, believe me."

Rosa looked in the window. Her bun was loose, strings dangling on either side of the neck. The reflection of a ragged old bird with worn feathers. Skinny, a stork. Her dress was missing a button, but maybe the belt buckle covered this shame. What did she care? She thought of her room, her bed, her radio. She hated conversation.

"I got to get back," she said.

"An appointment?"

"No."

"Then have an appointment with Persky. So come, first tea. If you take with an ice cube, you're involved in a mistake."

They went in and chose a tiny table in a corner—a sticky disc on a wobbly plastic pedestal. "You'll stay, I'll get," Persky said.

She sat and panted. Silverware tapped and clicked all around. No one here but old people. It was like the dining room of a convalescent home. Everyone had canes, dowager's humps, acrylic teeth, shoes cut out for bunions. Everyone wore an open collar showing mottled skin, ferocious clavicles, the wrinkled foundations of wasted breasts. The air-conditioning was on too high; she felt the cooling sweat licking from around her neck down, down her spine into the crevice of her bottom. She was afraid to shift; the chair had a wicker back and a black plastic seat. If she moved even a little, an odor would fly up: urine, salt, old woman's fatigue. She let off panting and shivered. What do I care? I'm used to everything, Florida, New York, it doesn't matter. All the same, she took out two hairpins and caught up the hanging strands; she shoved them into the core of her gray knot and pierced them through. She had no mirror, no comb, no pocketbook; not even a handkerchief. All she had was a Kleenex pushed into her sleeve and some coins in the pocket of her dress.

"I came out only for the laundry," she told Persky. With a groan he set down a loaded tray: two cups of tea, a saucer of lemon slices, a dish of eggplant salad, bread on what looked like a wooden platter but was really plastic, another plastic platter of Danish. "Maybe I didn't bring enough to pay."

"Never mind, you got the company of a rich retired taxpayer. I'm a well-off man. When I get my Social Security, I spit on it."

"What line of business?"

"The same what I see you got one lost. At the waist. Buttons. A shame. That kind's hard to match, as far as I'm concerned we stopped making them around a dozen years ago. Braided buttons is out of style."

"Buttons?" Rosa said.

"Buttons, belts, notions, knick-knacks, costume jewelry. A factory. I thought my son would take it over but he wanted something different. He's a philosopher, so he became a loiterer. Too much education makes fools. I hate to say it, but on account of him I had to sell out. And the girls, whatever the big one wanted, the little one also. The big one found a lawyer, that's what the little one looked for. I got one son-in-law in business for himself, taxes, the other's a youngster, still on Wall Street."

"A nice family," Rosa bit off.

"A loiterer's not so nice. Drink while it's hot. Otherwise it won't reach to your metabolism. You like eggplant salad on top of bread and butter? You got room for it, rest assured. Tell me, you live alone?"

"By myself," Rosa said, and slid her tongue into the tea. Tears came from the heat.

"My son is over thirty, I still support him."

"My niece, forty-nine, not married, she supports me."

"Too old. Otherwise I'd say let's make a match with my son, let her support him too. The best thing is independence. If you're ablebodied, it's a blessing to work." Persky caressed his chest. "I got a bum heart."

Rosa murmured, "I had a business, but I broke it up."

"Bankruptcy?"

"Part with a big hammer," she said meditatively, "part with a piece of construction metal I picked up from the gutter."

"You don't look that strong. Skin and bones."

"You don't believe me? In the papers they said an axe, but where would I get an axe?"

"That's reasonable. Where would you get an axe?" Persky's finger removed an obstruction from under his lower plate. He examined it: an eggplant seed. On the floor near the cart there was something white, a white cloth. Handkerchief. He picked it up and stuffed it in his pants pocket. Then he said, "What kind of business?"

"Antiques. Old furniture. Junk. I had a specialty in antique mirrors. Whatever I had there, I smashed it. See," she said, "*now* you're sorry you started with me!"

"I ain't sorry for nothing," Persky said. "If there's one thing I know to understand, it's mental episodes. I got it my whole life with my wife."

"You're not a widower?"

"In a manner of speaking."

"Where is she?"

"Great Neck, Long Island. A private hospital, it don't cost me peanuts." He said, "She's in a mental condition."

"Serious?"

"It used to be once in a while, now it's a regular thing. She's mixed up that she's somebody else. Television stars. Movie actresses. Different people. Lately my cousin, Betty Bacall. It went to her head."

"Tragic," Rosa said.

"You see? I unloaded on you, now you got to unload on me."

"Whatever I would say, you would be deaf."

"How come you smashed up your business?"

"It was a store. I didn't like who came in it."

"Spanish? Colored?"

"What do I care who came? Whoever came, they were like deaf people. Whatever you explained to them, they didn't understand." Rosa stood up to claim her cart. "It's very fine of you to treat me to the Danish, Mr. Persky. I enjoyed it. Now I got to go."

"I'll walk you."

"No, no, sometimes a person feels to be alone."

"If you're alone too much," Persky said, "you think too much."

"Without a life," Rosa answered, "a person lives where they can. If all they got is thoughts, that's where they live."

"You ain't got a life?"

"Thieves took it."

She toiled away from him. The handle of the cart was a burning rod. A hat, I ought to have worn a hat! The pins in her bun scalded her scalp. She panted like a dog in the sun. Even the trees looked exhausted: every leaf face downward under a powder of dust. Summer without end, a mistake!

In the lobby she waited before the elevator. The "guests"—some had been residents for a dozen years—were already milling around, groomed for lunch, the old women in sundresses showing their thick collarbones and the bluish wells above them. Instead of napes they had rolls of wide fat. They wore no stockings. Brazen blue-marbled sinews strangled their squarish calves; in their reveries they were again young women with immortal pillar legs, the white legs of strong goddesses; it was only that they had forgotten about impermanence. In their faces, too, you could see everything they were not noticing about themselves —the red gloss on their drawstring mouths was never meant to restore youth. It was meant only to continue it. Flirts of seventy. Everything had stayed the same for them: intentions, actions, even expectations— they had not advanced. They believed in the seamless continuity of the body. The men were more inward, running their lives in front of their eyes like secret movies.

A syrup of cologne clogged the air. Rosa heard the tearing of envelopes, the wing-shudders of paper sheets. Letters from children: the guests laughed and wept, but without seriousness, without belief. Report-card marks, separations, divorces, a new coffee table to match the gilt mirror over the piano, Stuie at sixteen learning to drive, Millie's mother-in-law's second stroke, rumors of the cataracts of half-remembered acquaintances, a cousin's kidney, the rabbi's ulcer, a daughter's indigestion, burglary, perplexing news of East Hampton parties, psychoanalysis . . . the children were rich, how was this possible from such poor parents? It was real and it was not real. Shadows on a wall; the shadows stirred, but you could not penetrate the wall. The guests were detached; they had detached themselves. Little by little they were forgetting their grandchildren, their aging children. More and more they were growing significant to themselves. Every wall of the lobby a miror. Every mirror hanging thirty years. Every table surface a mirror. In these mirrors the guests appeared to themselves as they used to be, powerful women of thirty, striving fathers of thirty-five, mothers and fathers of dim children who had migrated long ago, to other continents, inaccessible landscapes, incomprehensible vocabularies. Rosa made herself brave; the elevator gate opened, but she let the empty car ascend without her and pushed the cart through to where the black Cuban receptionist sat, maneuvering clayey sweat balls up from the naked place between her breasts with two fingers.

"Mail for Lublin, Rosa," Rosa said.

"Lublin, you lucky today. Two letters."

"Take a look where you keep packages also."

"You a lucky dog, Lublin," the Cuban girl said, and tossed an object into the pile of wash.

Rosa knew what was in that package. She had asked Stella to send it; Stella did not easily do what Rosa asked. She saw immediately that the package was not registered. This angered her: Stella the Angel of Death! Instantly she plucked the package out of the cart and tore the wrapping off and crumpled it into a standing ashtray. Magda's shawl! Suppose, God forbid, it got lost in the mail, what then? She squashed the box into her breasts. It felt hard, heavy; Stella had encased it in some terrible untender rind; Stella had turned it to stone. She wanted to kiss it, but the maelstrom was all around her, pressing toward the dining room. The food was monotonous and sparse and often stale; still, to eat there increased the rent. Stella was all the time writing that she was not a millionaire; Rosa never ate in the dining room. She kept the package tight against her bosom and picked through the crowd, a sluggish bird on ragged toes, dragging the cart.

In her room she breathed noisily, almost a gasp, almost a squeal, left the laundry askew in the tiny parody of a vestibule, and carried the box and the two letters to the bed. It was still unmade, fish-smelling, the covers knotted together like an umbilical cord. A shipwreck. She let herself down into it and knocked off her shoes—oh, they were scarred; that Persky must have seen her shame, first the missing button, afterward the used-up shoes. She turned the box round and round—a rectangular box. Magda's shawl! Magda's swaddling cloth. Magda's shroud. The memory of Magda's smell, the holy fragrance of the lost babe. Murdered. Thrown against the fence, barbed, thorned, electrified; grid and griddle; a furnace; the child on fire! Rosa put the shawl to her nose, to her lips. Stella did not want her to have Magda's shawl all the time, she had such funny names for having it—trauma, fetish, God knows what: Stella took psychology courses at the New School at night, looking for marriage among the flatulent bachelors in her classes.

One letter was from Stella and the other was one of those university letters, still another one, another sample of the disease. But in the box, Magda's shawl! The box would be last, Stella's fat letter first (fat meant trouble), the university letter did not matter. A disease. Better to put away the laundry than to open the university letter.

> DEAR ROSA [Stella wrote]:
> All right, I've done it. Been to the post office and mailed it. Your idol is on its way, separate cover. Go on your knees to it if you want. You make yourself crazy, everyone thinks you're a crazy woman. Whoever goes by your old store still gets glass in their soles. You're the older one, I'm the niece, I shouldn't lecture, but my God! It's thirty years, forty, who knows, give it a rest. It isn't as if I don't know just exactly how you do it, what it's like. What a scene, disgusting! You'll open the box and take it out and cry, and you'll kiss it like a crazy person. Making holes in it with kisses. You're like those people in the Middle Ages who worshipped a piece of the True Cross, a splinter from some old outhouse as far as anybody knew, or else they fell down in front of a single hair supposed to be some saint's. You'll kiss, you'll pee tears down your face, and so what? Rosa, by now, believe me, it's time, you have to have a life.

Out loud Rosa said, "Thieves took it."
And she said, "And you, Stella, *you* have a life?"

> If I were a millionaire I'd tell you the same thing: get a job. Or else, come back and move in here. I'm away the whole day, it will be like living alone if that's what you want. It's too hot to look around down there, people get like vegetables. With everything you did for me I don't mind keeping up this way maybe another year or so, you'll think I'm stingy for saying it like that, but after all I'm not on the biggest salary in the world.

Rosa said, "Stella! Would you be alive if I didn't take you out from there? Dead. You'd be dead! So don't talk to me how much an old woman costs! I didn't give you from my store? The big gold mirror, you look in it at your bitter face—I don't care how pretty, even so it's bitter —and you forget who gave you presents!"

And as far as Florida is concerned, well, it doesn't solve anything. I don't mind telling you now that they would have locked you up if I didn't agree to get you out of the city then and there. One more public outburst puts you in the bughouse. No more public scandals! For God's sake, don't be a crazy person! Live your life!

Rosa said again, "Thieves took it," and went, scrupulously, meticulously, as if possessed, to count the laundry in the cart.

A pair of underpants was missing. Once more Rosa counted everything: four blouses, three cotton skirts, three brassieres, one half-slip and one regular, two towels, eight pairs of underpants . . . nine went into the washing machine, the exact number. Degrading. Lost bloomers—dropped God knows where. In the elevator, in the lobby, in the street even. Rosa tugged, and the dress with the blue stripes slid like a coarse colored worm out of twisted bedsheets. The hole in the armpit was bigger now. Stripes, never again anything on her body with stripes! She swore it, but this, fancy and with a low collar, was Stella's birthday present, Stella bought it. As if innocent, as if ignorant, as if *not there*. Stella, an ordinary American, indistinguishable! No one could guess what hell she had crawled out of until she opened her mouth and up coiled the smoke of accent.

Again Rosa counted. A fact, one pair of pants lost. An old woman who couldn't even hang on to her own underwear.

She decided to sew up the hole in the stripes. Instead she put water on to boil for tea and made the bed with the clean sheets from the cart. The box with the shawl would be the last thing. Stella's letter she pushed under the bed next to the telephone. She tidied all around. Everything had to be nice when the box was opened. She spread jelly on three crackers and deposited a Lipton's tea bag on the Welch's lid. It was grape jelly, with a picture of Bugs Bunny elevating an officious finger. In spite of Persky's Danish, empty insides. Always Stella said: Rosa eats little by little, like a tapeworm in the world's belly.

Then it came to her that Persky had her underpants in his pocket.

Oh, degrading. The same. Pain in the loins. Burning. Bending in the cafeteria to pick up her pants, all the while tinkering with his teeth. Why didn't he give them back? He was embarrassed. He had thought a handkerchief. How can a man hand a woman, a stranger, a piece of her own underwear? He could have shoved it right back into the cart, how would that look? A sensitive man, he wanted to spare her. When he came home with her underpants, what then? What could a man, half a widower, do with a pair of female bloomers? Nylon-plus-cotton, the long-thighed kind. Maybe he had filched them on purpose, a sex maniac, a wife among the insane, his parts starved. According to Stella, Rosa also belonged among the insane, Stella had the power to put her there. Very good, they would become neighbors, confidantes, she and Persky's wife, best friends. The wife would confess all of Persky's sexual habits. She would explain how it is that a man of this age comes to steal a lady's personal underwear. Whatever stains in the crotch are nobody's business. And not only that: a woman with children, Persky's wife would speak of her son and her married lucky daughters. And Rosa too, never mind how Stella was sour over it, she would tell about Magda, a beautiful young woman of thirty, thirty-one: a doctor married to a doctor; large house in Mamaroneck, New York; two medical offices, one on the first floor, one in the finished basement. Stella was alive, why not Magda? Who was Stella, coarse Stella, to insist that Magda was not alive? Stella the Angel of Death. Magda alive, the pure eyes, the bright hair. Stella, never a mother, who was Stella to mock the kisses Rosa put in Magda's shawl? She meant to crush it into her mouth. Rosa, a mother the same as anyone, no different from Persky's wife in the crazy house.

This disease! The university letter, like all of them—five, six postmarks on the envelope. Rosa imagined its pilgrimage: first to the *News*, the *Post*, maybe even the *Times*, then to Rosa's old store, then to the store's landlord's lawyers, then to Stella's apartment, then to Miami, Florida. A Sherlock Holmes of a letter. It had struggled to find its victim, and for what? More eating alive.

DEPARTMENT OF CLINICAL
SOCIAL PATHOLOGY
UNIVERSITY OF KANSAS-IOWA

April 17, 1977

DEAR MS. LUBLIN:

Though I am not myself a physician, I have lately begun to amass survivor data as rather a considerable specialty. To be concrete: I am presently working on a study, funded by the Minew Foundation of the Kansas-Iowa Institute for Humanitarian Context, designed to research the theory developed by Dr. Arthur R. Hidgeson and known generally as Repressed Animation. Without at this stage going into detail, it may be of some preliminary use to you to know that investigations so far reveal an astonishing generalized minimalization during any extended period of stress resulting from incarceration, exposure, and malnutrition. We have turned up a wide range of neurological residues (including, in some cases, acute cerebral damage, derangement, disorientation, premature senility, etc.), as well as hormonal changes, parasites, anemia, thready pulse, hyperventilation, etc.; in children especially, temperatures as high as 108°, ascitic fluid, retardation, bleeding sores on the skin and in the mouth, etc. What is remarkable is that these are all *current conditions* in survivors and their families.

Disease, disease! Humanitarian Context, what did it mean? An excitement over other people's suffering. They let their mouths water up. Stories about children running blood in America from sores, what muck. Consider also the special word they used: *survivor*. Something new. As long as they didn't have to say *human being*. It used to be *refugee*, but by now there was no such creature, no more refugees, only survivors. A name like a number—counted apart from the ordinary swarm. Blue digits on the arm, what difference? They don't call you a woman anyhow. *Survivor*. Even when your bones get melted into the grains of the earth, still they'll forget *human being*. Survivor and survivor and survivor; always and always. Who made up these words, parasites on the throat of suffering!

For some months teams of medical paraphrasers have been conducting interviews with survivors, to contrast current medical paraphrase with conditions found more than three decades ago, at the opening of the camps. This, I confess, is neither my field nor my interest. My own concern, both as a scholar of social pathology and as a human being . . .

Ha! For himself it was good enough, for himself he didn't forget this word *human being!*

. . . is not with medical nor even with psychological aspects of survivor data.

Data. Drop in a hole!

What particularly engages me for purposes of my own participation in the study (which, by the way, is intended to be definitive, to close the books, so to speak, on this lamentable subject) is what I can only term the "metaphysical" side of Repressed Animation (R.A.). It begins to be evident that prisoners gradually came to Buddhist positions. They gave up craving and began to function in terms of nonfunctioning, i.e., non-attachment. The Four Noble Truths in Bud-

dhist thought, if I may remind you, yield a penetrating summary of
the fruit of craving: pain. "Pain" in this view is defined as ugliness,
age, sorrow, sickness, despair, and, finally, birth. Non-attachment is
attained through the Eightfold Path, the highest stage of which is
the cessation of all human craving, the loftiest rapture, one might
say, of consummated indifference.

It is my hope that these speculations are not displeasing to you.
Indeed, I further hope that they may even attract you, and that you
would not object to joining our study by means of an in-depth interview to be conducted by me at, if it is not inconvenient, your home. I
should like to observe survivor syndroming within the natural setting.

Home! Where, where?

As you may not realize, the national convention of the American
Association of Clinical Social Pathology has this year, for reasons of
fairness to our East Coast members, been moved from Las Vegas to
Miami Beach. The convention will take place at a hotel in your
vicinity about the middle of next May, and I would be deeply grateful if you could receive me during that period. I have noted via a New
York City newspaper (we are not so provincial out here as some may
think!) your recent removal to Florida; consequently you are ideally
circumstanced to make a contribution to our R.A. study. I look forward to your consent at your earliest opportunity.

> Very sincerely yours,
> JAMES W. TREE, PH.D.

Drop in a hole! Disease! It comes from Stella, everything! Stella saw
what this letter was, she could see from the envelope—Dr. Stella! Kansas-Iowa Clinical Social Pathology, a fancy hotel, this is the cure for the
taking of a life! Angel of Death!

With these university letters Rosa had a routine: she carried the
scissors over the toilet bowl and snipped little bits of paper and flushed.
In the bowl going down, the paper squares whirled like wedding rice.

But this one: drop in a hole with your Four Truths and your Eight
Paths together! Non-attachment! She threw the letter into the sink;
also its crowded envelope ("Please forward," Stella's handwriting in-
structed, pretending to be American, leaving out the little stroke that
goes across the 7); she lit a match and enjoyed the thick fire. Burn, Dr.
Tree, burn up with your Repressed Animation! The world is full of
Trees! The world is full of fire! Everything, everything is on fire! Florida is burning!

Big flakes of cinder lay in the sink: black foliage, Stella's black will. Rosa turned on the faucet, and the cinders spiralled down and away. Then she went to the round oak table and wrote the first letter of the day to her daughter, her healthy daughter, her daughter who suffered neither from thready pulse nor anemia, her daughter who was a professor of Greek philosophy at Columbia University in New York City, a stone's throw—the philosophers' stone that prolongs life and transmutes iron to gold—from Stella in Queens!

MAGDA, MY SOUL'S BLESSING [Rosa wrote],

Forgive me, my yellow lioness. Too long a time since the last writing. Strangers scratch at my life; they pursue, they break down the bloodstream's sentries. Always there is Stella. And so half a day passes without my taking up my pen to speak to you. A pleasure, the deepest pleasure, home bliss, to speak in our own language. Only to you. I am always having to write to Stella now, like a dog paying respects to its mistress. It's my obligation. She sends me money. She, whom I plucked out of the claws of all those Societies that came to us with bread and chocolate after the liberation! Despite everything, they were selling sectarian ideas; collecting troops for their armies. If not for me they would have shipped Stella with a boatload of orphans to Palestine, to become God knows what, to live God knows how. A field worker jabbering Hebrew. It would serve her right. Americanized airs. My father was never a Zionist. He used to call himself a "Pole by right." The Jews, he said, didn't put a thousand years of brains and blood into Polish soil in order to have to prove themselves to anyone. He was the wrong sort of idealist, maybe, but he had the instincts of a natural nobleman. I could laugh at that now—the whole business—but I don't, because I feel too vividly what he was, how substantial, how not given over to any light-mindedness whatever. He had Zionist friends in his youth. Some left Poland early and lived. One is a bookseller in Tel Aviv. He specializes in foreign texts and periodicals. My poor little father. It's only history—an ad hoc instance of it, you might say—that made the Zionist solution. My father's ideas were more logical. He was a Polish patriot on a temporary basis, he said, until the time when nation should lie down beside nation like the lily and the lotus. He was at bottom a prophetic creature. My mother, you know, published poetry. To you all these accounts must have the ring of pure legend.

Even Stella, who *can* remember, refuses. She calls me a parable-maker. She was always jealous of you. She has a strain of dementia, and resists you and all other reality. Every vestige of former existence is an insult to her. Because she fears the past she distrusts the future

—it, too, will turn into the past. As a result she has nothing. She sits and watches the present roll itself up into the past more quickly than she can bear. That's why she never found the one thing she wanted more than anything, an American husband. I'm immune to these pains and panics. Motherhood—I've always known this—is a profound distraction from philosophy, and all philosophy is rooted in suffering over the passage of time. I mean the *fact* of motherhood, the physiological fact. To have the power to create another human being, to be the instrument of such a mystery. To pass on a whole genetic system. I don't believe in God, but I believe, like the Catholics, in mystery. My mother wanted so much to convert; my father laughed at her. But she was attracted. She let the maid keep a statue of the Virgin and Child in the corner of the kitchen. Sometimes she used to go in and look at it. I can even remember the words of a poem she wrote about the heat coming up from the stove, from the Sunday pancakes—

> Mother of God, how you shiver
> in these heat-ribbons!
> Our cakes rise to you
> and in the trance of His birthing
> you hide.

Something like that. Better than that, more remarkable. Her Polish was very dense. You had to open it out like a fan to get at all the meanings. She was exceptionally modest, but she was not afraid to call herself a symbolist.

I know you won't blame me for going astray with such tales. After all, you're always prodding me for these old memories. If not for you, I would have buried them all, to satisfy Stella. Stella Columbus! She thinks there's such a thing as the New World. Finally—at last, at last —she surrenders this precious vestige of your sacred babyhood. Here it is in a box right next to me as I write. She didn't take the trouble to send it by registered mail! Even though I told her and told her. I've thrown out the wrapping paper, and the lid is plastered down with lots of Scotch Tape. I'm not hurrying to open it. At first my hunger was unrestrained and I couldn't wait, but nothing is nice now. I'm saving you; I want to be serene. In a state of agitation one doesn't split open a diamond. Stella says I make a relic of you. She has no heart. It would shock you if I told you even one of the horrible games I'm made to play with her. To soothe her dementia, to keep her quiet, I pretend you died. Yes! It's true! There's nothing, however crazy, I wouldn't say to her to tie up her tongue. She slanders. Every-

where there are slanders, and sometimes—my bright lips, my darling!
—the slanders touch even you. My purity, my snow queen!

I'm ashamed to give an example. Pornography. What Stella, that
pornographer, has made of your father. She thieves all the truth, she
robs it, she steals it, the robbery goes unpunished. She lies, and it's
the lying that's rewarded. The New World! That's why I smashed up
my store! Because here they make up lying theories. Even the professors—they take human beings for specimens. In Poland there used to
be justice; here they have social theories. Their system inherits almost
nothing from the Romans, that's why. Is it a wonder that the lawyers
are no better than scavengers who feed on the droppings of thieves
and liars? Thank God you followed your grandfather's bent and studied philosophy and not law.

Take my word for it, Magda, your father and I had the most
ordinary lives—by "ordinary" I mean respectable, gentle, cultivated.
Reliable people of refined reputation. His name was Andrzej. Our
families had status. Your father was the son of my mother's closest
friend. She was a converted Jew married to a Gentile: you can be a
Jew if you like, or a Gentile, it's up to you. You have a legacy of
choice, and they say choice is the only true freedom. We were engaged to be married. We would have been married. Stella's accusations are all Stella's own excretion. Your father was not a German. I
was forced by a German, it's true, and more than once, but I was too
sick to conceive. Stella has a naturally pornographic mind, she can't
resist dreaming up a dirty sire for you, an S.S. man! Stella was with
me the whole time, she knows just what I know. They never put me
in their brothel either. Never believe this, my lioness, my snow
queen! No lies come out of me to you. You are pure. A mother is the
source of consciousness, of conscience, the ground of being, as philosophers say. I have no falsehoods for you. Otherwise I don't deny
some few tricks: the necessary handful. To those who don't deserve
the truth, don't give it. I tell Stella what it pleases her to hear. My
child, perished. Perished. She always wanted it. She was always jealous of you. She has no heart. Even now she believes in my loss of you:
and you a stone's throw from her door in New York! Let her think
whatever she thinks; her mind is awry, poor thing; in me the strength
of your being consumes my joy. Yellow blossom! Cup of the sun!

What a curiosity it was to hold a pen—nothing but a small pointed
stick, after all, oozing its hieroglyphic puddles: a pen that speaks, miraculously, Polish. A lock removed from the tongue. Otherwise the tongue
is chained to the teeth and the palate. An immersion into the living

language: all at once this cleanliness, this capacity, this power to make a history, to tell, to explain. To retrieve, to reprieve!

To lie.

The box with Magda's shawl was still on the table. Rosa left it there. She put on her good shoes, a nice dress (polyester, "wrinkle-free" on the inside label); she arranged her hair, brushed her teeth, poured mouthwash on the brush, sucked it up through the nylon bristles, gargled rapidly. As an afterthought she changed her bra and slip; it meant getting out of her dress and into it again. Her mouth she reddened very slightly—a smudge of lipstick rubbed on with a finger.

Perfect, she mounted the bed on her knees and fell into folds. A puppet, dreaming. Darkened cities, tombstones, colorless garlands, a black fire in a gray field, brutes forcing the innocent, women with their mouths stretched and their arms wild, her mother's voice calling. After hours of these pitiless tableaux, it was late afternoon; by then she was certain that whoever put her underpants in his pocket was a criminal capable of every base act. Humiliation. Degradation. Stella's pornography!

To retrieve, to reprieve. Nothing in the elevator; in the lobby, nothing. She kept her head down. Nothing white glimmered up.

In the street a neon dusk was already blinking. Gritty mixture of heat and toiling dust. Cars shot by the large bees. It was too early for headlights: in the lower sky two strange competing lamps—a scarlet sun, round and brilliant as a blooded egg yolk; a silk-white moon, gray-veined with mountain ranges. These hung simultaneously at either end of the long road. The whole day's burning struck upward like a moving weight from the sidewalk. Rosa's nostrils and lungs were cautious: burning molasses air. Her underpants were not in the road.

In Miami at night no one stays indoors. The streets are clogged with wanderers and watchers; everyone in search, bedouins with no fixed paths. The foolish Florida rains spray down—so light, so brief and fickle, no one pays attention. Neon alphabets, designs, pictures, flashing undiminished right through the sudden small rain. A quick lick of lightning above one of the balconied hotels. Rosa walked. Much Yiddish. Caravans of slow old couples, linked at the elbows, winding down to the cool of the beaches. The sand never at rest, always churning, always inhabited; copulation under blankets at night, beneath neon-radiant low horizons.

She had never been near the beach; why should her underpants be lost in the sand?

On the sidewalk in front of the KOLLINS KOSHER KAMEO, nothing. Shining hungry smell of boiled potatoes in sour cream. The pants were not necessarily in Persky's pocket. Dented garbage barrels, empty near the curb. Pants already smoldering in an ash heap, among blackened tomato cans, kitchen scrapings, conflagrations of old magazines. Or: a simple omission, an accident, never transferred from the washing machine to the dryer. Or, if transferred, never removed. Overlooked. Persky unblemished. The laundromat was locked up for the night, with a metal accordion gate stretched across the door and windows. What marauders would seek out caldrons, giant washtubs? Property misleads, brings false perspectives. The power to smash her own. A kind of suicide. She had murdered her store with her own hands. She cared more for a missing pair of underpants, lost laundry, than for business. She was ashamed; she felt exposed. What was her store? A cave of junk.

On the corner across the street from the laundromat a narrow newspaper store, no larger than a stall. Persky might have bought his paper there. Suppose later in the day he had come down for an afternoon paper, her pants in his pocket, and dropped them?

Mob of New York accents. It was a little place, not air-conditioned. "Lady? You're looking for something?"

A newspaper? Rosa had enough of the world.

"Look, it's like sardines in here. Buy something or go out."

"My store used to be six times the size of this place," Rosa said.

"So go to your store."

"I don't have a store." She reconsidered. If someone wanted to hide —to hide, not destroy—a pair of underpants, where would he put them? Under the sand. Rolled up and buried. She thought what a weight of sand would feel like in the crotch of her pants, wet heavy sand, still hot from the day. In her room it was hot, hot all night. No air. In Florida there was no air, only this syrup seeping into the esophagus. Rosa walked; she saw everything, but as if out of invention, out of imagination; she was unconnected to anything. She came to a gate; a mottled beach spread behind it. It belonged to one of the big hotels. The latch opened. At the edge of the waves you could look back and see black crenellated forms stretching all along the shore. In the dark, in silhouette, the towered hotel roofs held up their merciless teeth. Impossible that any architect pleasurably dreamed these teeth. The sand was only now beginning to cool. Across the water the sky breathed a starless black; behind her, where the hotels bit down on the city, a dusty glow of brownish red lowered. Mud clouds. The sand was littered with bodies. Photograph of Pompeii: prone in the volcanic ash. Her pants were under the sand; or else packed hard with sand, like a piece of torso, a broken statue, the human groin detached, the whole soul gone, only the loins left for kicking by strangers. She took off her good shoes to save them and nearly stepped on the sweated faces of two lovers plugged into a kiss. A pair of water animals in suction. The same everywhere, along the rim of every continent, this gurling, foaming, trickling. A true smasher, a woman whose underpants have been stolen, a woman who has murdered her business with her own hands, would know how to step cleanly into the sea. A horizontal tunnel. You can fall into its pull just by entering it upright. How simple the night sea; only the sand is unpredictable, with its hundred burrowings, its thousand buryings.

When she came back to the gate, the latch would not budge. A cunning design, it trapped the trespasser.

She gazed up, and thought of climbing; but there was barbed wire on top.

So many double mounds in the sand. It was a question of choosing a likely sentinel: someone who would let her out. She went back down onto the beach again and tapped a body with the tip of her dangling shoe. The body jerked as if shot: it scrambled up.

"Mister? You know how to get out?"

"Room key does it," said the second body, still flat in the sand. It was a man. They were both men, slim and coated with sand; naked. The one lying flat—she could see what part of him was swollen.

"I'm not from this hotel," Rosa said.

"Then you're not allowed here. This is a private beach."

"Can't you let me out?"

"Lady, please. Just buzz off," the man in the sand said.

"I can't get out," Rosa pleaded.

The man who was standing laughed.

Rosa persisted, "If you have a key—"

"Believe me, lady, not for you"—muffled from below.

She understood. Sexual mockery. "Sodom!" she hissed, and stumbled away. Behind her their laughter. They hated women. Or else they saw she was a Jew; they hated Jews; but no, she had noticed the circumcision, like a jonquil, in the dim sand. Her wrists were trembling.

To be locked behind barbed wire! No one knew who she was; what had happened to her; where she came from. Their gates, the terrible ruse of their keys, wire brambles, men lying with men . . . She was afraid to approach any of the other mounds. No one to help. Persecutors. In the morning they would arrest her.

She put on her shoes again, and walked along the cement path that followed the fence. It led her to light; voices of black men. A window. Vast deep odors: kitchen exhaust, fans stirring soup smells out into the weeds. A door wedged open by a milk-can lid. Acres of counters, stoves, steamers, refrigerators, percolators, bins, basins. The kitchen of a castle. She fled past the black cooks in their meat-blooded aprons, through a short corridor; a dead end facing an elevator. She pushed the button and waited. The kitchen people had seen her; would they pursue? She heard their yells, but it was nothing to do with her—they were calling Thursday, Thursday. On Thursday no more new potatoes. A kind of emergency maybe. The elevator took her to the main floor, to the lobby; she emerged, free.

This lobby was the hall of a palace. In the middle a real fountain. Water springing out of the mouths of emerald-green dolphins. Skirted cherubs, gilded. A winged mermaid spilling gold flowers out of a gold pitcher. Lofty plants—a forest—palms sprayed dark blue and silver and gold, leafing out of masses of green marble vessels at the lip of the fountain. The water flowed into a marble channel, a little indoor brook. A royal carpet for miles around, woven with crowned birds. Well-dressed men and women sat in lion-clawed gold thrones, smoking. A golden babble. How happy Stella would be, to stroll in a place like this! Rosa kept close to the walls.

She saw a man in a green uniform.

"The manager," she croaked. "I have to tell him something."

"Office is over there." He shrugged toward a mahogany desk behind a glass wall. The manager, wearing a red wig, was making a serious mark on a crested letterhead. Persky, too, had a red wig. Florida was glutted with fake fire, burning false hair! Everyone a piece of impostor. "Ma'am?" the manager said.

"Mister, you got barbed wire by your beach."

"Are you a guest here?"

"I'm someplace else."

"Then it's none of your business, is it?"

"You got barbed wire."

"It keeps out the riffraff."

"In America it's no place for barbed wire on top of fences."

The manager left off making his serious marks. "Will you leave?" he said. "Will you please just leave?"

"Only Nazis catch innocent people behind barbed wire," Rosa said. The red wig dipped. "My name is Finkelstein."

"Then you should know better!"

"Listen, walk out of here if you know what's good for you."

"Where were you when we was there?"

"Get out. So far I'm asking nicely. Please get out."

"Dancing in the pool in the lobby, that's where. Eat your barbed wire, Mr. Finkelstein, chew it and choke on it!"

"Go home," Finkelstein said.

"You got Sodom and Gomorrah in your back yard! You got gays and you got barbed wire!"

"You were trespassing on our beach," the manager said. "You want me to call the police? Better leave before. Some important guests have come in, we can't tolerate the noise and I can't spare the time for this."

"They write me letters all the time, your important guests. Conventions," Rosa scoffed. "Clinical Social Pathology, right? You got a Dr. Tree staying?"

"Please go," Finkelstein said.

"Come on, you got a Dr. Tree? No? I'll tell you, if not today you'll get him later on, he's on the way. He's coming to investigate specimens. I'm the important one! It's me he's interviewing, Finkelstein, not you! I'm the study!"

The red wig dipped again.

"Aha!" Rosa cried. "I see you got Tree! You got a whole bunch of Trees!"

"We protect the privacy of our guests."

"With barbed wire you protect. It's Tree, yes? I can see I'm right! It's Tree! You got Tree staying here, right? Admit you got Tree! Finkelstein, you S.S., admit it!"

The manager stood up. "Out," he said. "Get out now. Immediately."

"Don't worry, it's all right. It's my business to keep away. Tree I don't need. With Trees I had enough, you don't have to concern yourself—"

"*Leave,*" said the red wig.

"A shame," Rosa said, "a Finkelstein like you." Irradiated, triumphant, cleansed, Rosa marched through the emerald glitter, toward the illuminated marquee in front. HOTEL MARIE LOUISE, in green neon. A doorman like a British admiral, gold braid cascading from his shoulders. They had trapped her, nearly caught her; but she knew how to escape. Speak up, yell. The same way she saved Stella, when they were pressing to take her on the boat to Palestine. She had no fear of Jews; sometimes she had—it came from her mother, her father—a certain contempt. The Warsaw swarm, shut off from the grandeur of the true world. Neighborhoods of a particular kind. Persky and Finkelstein. "Their" synagogues—balconies for the women. Primitive. Her own home, her own upbringing—how she had fallen. A loathsome tale of folk sorcery: nobility turned into a small dun rodent. Cracking her teeth on the poison of English. Here they were shallow, they knew nothing. Light-minded. Stella looking, on principle, to be light-minded. Blue stripes, barbed wire, men embracing men . . . whatever was dangerous and repugnant they made prevalent, frivolous.

Lost. Lost. Nowhere. All of Miami Beach, empty; the sand, empty. The whole wild hot neon night city: an empty search. In someone's pocket.

Persky was waiting for her. He sat in the torn brown plastic wing chair near the reception desk, one leg over the side, reading a newspaper.

He saw her come in and jumped up. He wore only a shirt and pants; no tie, no jacket. Informal.

"Lublin, Rosa!"

Rosa said, "How come you're here?"

"Where you been the whole night? I'm sitting hours."

"I didn't tell you where I stay," Rosa accused.

"I looked in the telephone book."

"My phone's disconnected, I don't know nobody. My niece, she writes, she saves on long-distance."

"All right. You want the truth? This morning I followed you, that's all. A simple walk from my place. I sneaked in the streets behind you. I found out where you stay, here I am."

"Very nice," Rosa said.

"You don't like it?"

She wanted to tell him he was under suspicion; he owed her a look in his jacket pocket. A self-confessed sneak who follows women. If not his jacket, his pants. But it wasn't possible to say a thing like this. Her pants in his pants. Instead she said, "What do you want?"

He flashed his teeth. "A date."

"You're a married man."

"A married man what ain't got a wife."

"You got one."

"In a manner of speaking. She's crazy."

Rosa said, "I'm crazy, too."

"Who says so?"

"My niece."

"What does a stranger know?"

"A niece isn't a stranger."

"My own son is a stranger. A niece definitely. Come on, I got my car nearby. Air-conditioned, we'll take a spin."

"You're not a kid, I'm not a kid," Rosa said.

"You can't prove it by me," Persky said.

"I'm a serious person," Rosa said. "It isn't my kind of life, to run around noplace."

"Who said noplace? I got a place in mind." He reflected. "My Senior Citizens. Very nice pinochle."

"Not interested," Rosa said. "I don't need new people."

"Then a movie. You don't like new ones, we'll find dead ones. Clark Gable. Jean Harlow."

"Not interested."

"A ride to the beach. A walk on the shore, how about it?"

"I already did it," Rosa said.

"When?"

"Tonight. Just now."

"Alone?"

Rosa said, "I was looking for something I lost."

"Poor Lublin, what did you lose?"

"My life."

She was all at once not ashamed to say this outright. Because of the missing underwear she had no dignity before him. She considered Persky's life: how trivial it must always have been: buttons, himself no more significant than a button. It was plain he took her to be another button like himself, battered now and out of fashion, rolled into Florida. All of Miami Beach, a box for useless buttons!

"This means you're tired. Tell you what," Persky said. "Invite me upstairs. A cup of tea. We'll make a conversation. You'll see, I got other ideas up my sleeve—tomorrow we'll go someplace and you'll like it."

Her room was miraculously ready: tidy, clarified. It was sorted out: you could see where the bed ended and the table commenced. Sometimes it was all one jumble, a highway of confusion. Destiny had clarified her room just in time for a visitor. She started the tea. Persky put his newspaper down on the table, and on top of it an oily paper bag. "Crullers!" he announced. "I bought them to eat in the car, but this is very nice, cozy. You got a cozy place, Lublin."

"Cramped," Rosa said.

"I work from a different theory. For everything there's a bad way of describing, also a good way. You pick the good way, you get along better."

"I don't like to give myself lies," Rosa said.

"Life is short, we all got to lie. Tell me, you got paper napkins? Never mind, who needs them. Three cups! That's a lucky thing, usually when a person lives alone they don't keep so many. Look, vanilla icing, chocolate icing. Two plain also. You prefer with icing or plain? Such fine tea bags, they got style. Now, you see, Lublin? Everything's nice!"

He had set the table. To Rosa this made the corner of the room look new, as if she had never seen it before.

"Don't let the tea cool off. Remember what I told you this morning, the hotter the better," Persky said; he clanged his spoon happily. "Here, let's make more elbowroom—"

His hand, greasy from the crullers, was on Magda's box.

"Don't touch!"

"What's the matter? It's something alive in there? A bomb? A rabbit? It's squashable? No, I got it—a lady's hat!"

Rosa hugged the box; she was feeling foolish, trivial. Everything was frivolous here, even the deepest property of being. It seemed to her someone had cut out her life organs and given them to her to hold. She walked the little distance to the bed—three steps—and set the box down against the pillow. When she turned around, Persky's teeth were persisting in their independent bliss.

"The fact is," he said, "I didn't expect nothing from you tonight. You got to work things through, I can see that. You remind me of my son. Even to get a cup of tea from you is worth something, I could do worse. Tomorrow we'll have a real appointment. I'm not inquiring, I'm not requesting. I'll be the boss, what do you say?"

Rosa sat. "I'm thinking, I should get out and go back to New York to my niece—"

"Not tomorrow. Day after tomorrow you'll change your life, and tomorrow you'll come with me. We got six meetings to pick from."

Rosa said doubtfully, "Meetings?"

"Speakers. Lectures for fancy people like yourself. Something higher than pinochle."

"I don't play," Rosa acknowledged.

Persky looked around. "I don't see no books neither. You want me to drive you to the library?"

A thread of gratitude pulled in her throat. He almost understood what she was: no ordinary button. "I read only Polish," she told him. "I don't like to read in English. For literature you need a mother tongue."

"*Lit*erature, my my. Polish ain't a dime a dozen. It don't grow on trees neither. Lublin, you should adjust. Get used to it!"

She was wary: "I'm used to everything."

"Not to being a regular person."

"My niece Stella," Rosa slowly gave out, "says that in America cats have nine lives, but we—we're less than cats, so we got three. The life before, the life during, the life after." She saw that Persky did not follow. She said, "The life after is now. The life before is our *real* life, at home, where we was born."

"And during?"

"This was Hitler."

"Poor Lublin," Persky said.

"You wasn't there. From the movies you know it." She recognized that she had shamed him; she had long ago discovered this power to shame. "After, after, that's all Stella cares. For me there's one time only, there's no after."

Persky speculated. "You want everything the way it was before."

"No, no, no," Rosa said. "It can't be. I don't believe in Stella's cats. Before is a dream. After is a joke. Only during stays. And to call it a life is a lie."

"But it's over," Persky said. "You went through it, now you owe yourself something."

"This is how Stella talks. Stella—" Rosa halted; then she came on the word. "Stella is self-indulgent. She wants to wipe out memory."

"Sometimes a little forgetting is necessary," Persky said, "if you want to get something out of life."

"Get something! Get *what?*"

"You ain't in a camp. It's finished. Long ago it's finished. Look around, you'll see human beings."

"What I see," Rosa said, "is bloodsuckers."

Persky hesitated. "Over there, they took your family?"

Rosa held up all the fingers of her two hands. Then she said, "I'm left. Stella's left." She wondered if she dared to tell him more. The box on the bed. "Out of so many, three."

Persky asked, "Three?"

"Evidence," Rosa said briskly. "I can show you."

She raised the box. She felt like a climber on the margin of a precipice. "Wipe your hands."

Persky obeyed. He rubbed the last of the cruller crumbs on his shirt front.

"Unpack and look in. Go ahead, lift up what's inside."

She did not falter. What her own hands longed to do she was yielding to a stranger, a man with pockets; she knew why. To prove herself pure: a Madonna. Supposing he had vile old man's thoughts: let him see her with the eye of truth. A mother.

But Persky said, "How do you count three—"

"Look for yourself."

He took the cover off and reached into the box and drew out a sheet of paper and began to skim it.

"That has to be from Stella. Throw it out, never mind. More scolding, how I'm a freak—"

"Lublin, you're a regular member of the intelligentsia! This is quite some reading matter. It ain't in Polish neither." His teeth danced. "On such a sad subject, allow me a little joke. Who came to America was one, your niece Stella; Lublin, Rosa, this makes two; and Lublin's brain —three!"

Rosa stared. "I'm a mother, Mr. Persky," she said, "the same as your wife, no different." She received the paper between burning palms. "Have some respect," she commanded the bewildered glitter of his plastic grin. And read:

DEAR MS. LUBLIN:

I am taking the liberty of sending you, as a token of my good faith, this valuable study by Hidgeson (whom, you may recall, I mentioned in passing in my initial explanatory letter), which more or less lays the ethological groundwork for our current structures. I feel certain that —in preparation for our talks—you will want to take a look at it. A great deal of our work has been built on these phylogenetic insights. You may find some of the language a bit too technical; nevertheless I believe that simply having this volume in your possession will go far

toward reassuring you concerning the professionalism of our endeav-
ors, and of your potential contribution toward them.

Of special interest, perhaps, is Chapter Six, entitled "Defensive
Group Formation: The Way of the Baboons."

Gratefully in advance,
JAMES W. TREE, PH.D.

Persky said, "Believe me, I could smell with only one glance it wasn't
from Stella."

She saw that he was holding the thing he had taken out of the box.
"Give me that," she ordered.

He recited, "By A. R. Hidgeson. And listen to the title, something
fancy—'Repressed Animation: A Theory of the Biological Ground of
Survival.' I told you fancy! This isn't what you wanted?"

"Give it to me."

"You didn't want? Stella sent you what you didn't want?"

"Stella sent!" She tore the book from him—it was heavier than she
had guessed—and hurled it at the ceiling. It slammed down into Persky's half-filled teacup. Shards and droplets flew. "The way I smashed
up my store, that's how I'll smash Tree!"

Persky was watching the tea drip to the floor.

"Tree?"

"Dr. Tree! Tree the bloodsucker!"

"I can see I'm involved in a mistake," Persky said. "I'll tell you what,
you eat up the crullers. You'll feel better and I'll come tomorrow when
the mistake is finished."

"I'm not your button, Persky! I'm nobody's button, not even if they
got barbed wire everywhere!"

"Speaking of buttons, I'll go and push the elevator button. Tomorrow I'll come back."

"Barbed wire! You took my laundry, you think I don't know that?
Look in your dirty pockets, you thief Persky!"

In the morning, washing her face—it was swollen, nightmares like
weeds, the bulb of her nose pale—Rosa found, curled inside a towel,
the missing underwear.

She went downstairs to the desk; she talked over having her phone
reconnected. Naturally they would charge more, and Stella would
squawk. All the same, she wanted it.

At the desk they handed her a package; this time she examined the
wrapping. It had come by registered mail and it was from Stella. It was

not possible to be hoodwinked again, but Rosa was shocked, depleted, almost as if yesterday's conflagration hadn't been Tree but really the box with Magda's shawl.

She lifted the lid of the box and looked down at the shawl; she was indifferent. Persky too would have been indifferent. The colorless cloth lay like an old bandage; a discarded sling. For some reason it did not instantly restore Magda, as usually happened, a vivid thwack of restoration, like an electric jolt. She was willing to wait for the sensation to surge up whenever it would. The shawl had a faint saliva smell, but it was more nearly imagined than smelled.

Under the bed the telephone vibrated: first a sort of buzz, then a real ring. Rosa pulled it out.

The Cuban's voice said, "Missus Lublin, you connected now."

Rosa wondered why it was taking so long for Magda to come alive. Sometimes Magda came alive with a brilliant swoop, almost too quickly, so that Rosa's ribs were knocked on their insides by copper hammers, clanging and gonging.

The instrument, still in her grip, drilled again. Rosa started: it was as if she had squeezed a rubber toy. How quickly a dead thing can come to life! Very tentatively, whispering into a frond, Rosa said, "Hello?" It was a lady selling frying pans.

"No," Rosa said, and dialled Stella. She could hear that Stella had been asleep. Her throat was softened by a veil. "Stella," Rosa said, "I'm calling from my own room."

"Who is this?"

"Stella, you don't recognize me?"

"Rosa! Did anything happen?"

"Should I come back?"

"My God," Stella said, "is it an emergency? We could discuss this by mail."

"You wrote me I should come back."

"I'm not a millionaire," Stella said. "What's the point of this call?"

"Tree's here."

"Tree? What's that?"

"*Doctor* Tree. You sent me his letter, he's after me. By accident I found out where he stays."

"No one's after you," Stella said grimly.

Rosa said, "Maybe I should come back and open up again."

"You're talking nonsense. You *can't.* The store's finished. If you come back it has to be a new attitude absolutely, recuperated. The end of morbidness."

"A very fancy hotel," Rosa said. "They spend like kings."

"It's none of your business."

"A Tree is none of my business? He gets rich on our blood! Prestige! People respect him! A professor with specimens! He wrote me baboons!"

"You're supposed to be recuperating," Stella said; she was wide awake. "Walk around. Keep out of trouble. Put on your bathing suit. Mingle. How's the weather?"

"In that case you come here," Rosa said.

"Oh my God, I can't afford it. You talk like I'm a millionaire. What would I do down there?"

"I don't like it alone. A man stole my underwear."

"Your *what?*" Stella squealed.

"My panties. There's plenty perverts in the streets. Yesterday in the sand I saw two naked men."

"Rosa," Stella said, "if you want to come back, come back. I wrote you that, that's all I said. But you could get interested in something down there for a change. If not a job, a club. If it doesn't cost too much, I wouldn't mind paying for a club. You could join some kind of group, you could walk, you could swim—"

"I already walked."

"Make friends." Stella's voice tightened. "Rosa, this is long-*dis*-tance."

On that very phrase, "long-*dis*-tance," Magda sprang to life. Rosa took the shawl and put it over the knob of the receiver: it was like a little doll's head then. She kissed it, right over Stella's admonitions. "Goodbye," she told Stella, and didn't care what it had cost. The whole room was full of Magda: she was like a butterfly, in this corner and in that corner, all at once. Rosa waited to see what age Magda was going to be: how nice, a girl of sixteen, girls in their bloom move so swiftly that their blouses and skirts balloon, they are always butterflies at sixteen. There was Magda, all in flower. She was wearing one of Rosa's dresses from high school. Rosa was glad: it was the sky-colored dress, a middling blue with black buttons seemingly made of round chips of coal, like the unlit shards of stars. Persky could never have been acquainted with buttons like that, they were so black and so sparkling; original, with irregular facets like bits of true coal from a vein in the earth or some other planet. Madga's hair was still as yellow as buttercups, and so slippery and fine that her two barrettes, in the shape of cornets, kept sliding down toward the sides of her chin—that chin which was the marvel of her face; with a different kind of chin it would have been a much less explicit face. The jaw was ever so slightly too long, a deepened oval, so that her mouth, especially the lower lip, was not crowded but rather made a definite mark in the middle of spaciousness. Consequently the mouth seemed as significant as a body arrested in orbit, and Magda's sky-filled eyes, nearly rectangular at the corners, were like two obeisant satellites. Magda could be seen with great clarity. She had begun to resemble Rosa's father, who had also had a long oval face anchored by a positive mouth. Rosa was enraptured by Magda's healthy forearms. She would have given everything to set her before an easel, to see whether she could paint in watercolors; or to have her seize a violin, or a chess queen; she knew little about Magda's mind at this age, or whether she had any talents; even what her intelligence tended toward. And also she was always a little suspicious of Magda, because of the other strain, whatever it was, that ran in her. Rosa herself was not truly suspicious, but Stella was, and that induced perplexity in Rosa. The other strain was ghostly, even dangerous. It was as if the peril hummed out from the filaments of Magda's hair, those narrow bright wires.

My Gold, my Wealth, my Treasure, my Hidden Sesame, my Paradise, my Yellow Flower, my Magda! Queen of Bloom and Blossom!

When I had my store I used to "meet the public," and I wanted to tell everybody—not only our story but other stories as well. Nobody knew anything. This amazed me, that nobody remembered what happened only a little while ago. They didn't remember because they didn't know. I'm referring to certain definite facts. The tramcar in the Ghetto, for instance. You know they took the worst section, a terrible slum, and they built a wall around it. It was a regular city neighborhood, with rotting old tenements. They pushed in half a million people, more than double the number there used to be in that place. Three families, including all their children and old folks, into one apartment. Can you imagine a family like us—my father who had been the director-general of the Bank of Warsaw, my sheltered mother, almost Japanese in her shyness and refinement, my two young brothers, my older brother, and me—all of us, who had lived in a tall house with four floors and a glorious attic (you could touch the top of the house by sticking your arm far out its window; it was like pulling the whole green ribbon of summer indoors)—imagine confining *us* with teeming Mockowiczes and Rabinowiczes and Perskys and Finkelsteins, with all their bad-smelling grandfathers and their hordes of feeble children! The children were half dead, always sitting on boxes in tatters with such sick eyes, pus on the lids and the pupils too wildly lit up. All these families used up their energies with walking up and down, and bowing, and shaking and quaking over old rags of prayer books, and their children sat on the boxes and yelled prayers, too. We thought they didn't know how to organize themselves in adversity, and, besides that, we were furious: because the same sort of adversity was happening to *us*—my father was a person of real importance, and my tall mother had so much delicacy and dignity that people would bow automatically, even before they knew who she was. So we were furious in every direction, but most immediately we were furious because we had to be billeted with such a class, with these old Jew peasants worn out from their rituals and superstitions, phylacteries on their foreheads sticking up so stupidly, like unicorn horns, every morning. And in the most repulsive slum, deep in slops and vermin and a toilet not fit for the lowest criminal. We were not of a background to show our fury, of course, but my father told my brothers and me that my mother would not be able to live through it, and he was right.

In my store I didn't tell this to everyone; who would have the patience to hear it all out? So I used to pick out one little thing here, one little thing there, for each customer. And if I saw they were in a hurry—most of them were, after I began—I would tell just about the tramcar. When I told about the tramcar, no one ever understood that it ran on tracks! Everybody always thought of buses. Well, they couldn't tear up the tracks, they couldn't get rid of the overhead electric wire, could they? The point is they couldn't reroute the whole tram system; so, you know, they didn't. The tramcar came right through the middle of the Ghetto. What they did was build a sort of overhanging pedestrian bridge for the Jews—they couldn't get near the tramcar to escape on it into the other part of Warsaw. The other side of the wall.

The most astounding thing was that the most ordinary streetcar, bumping along on the most ordinary trolley tracks, and carrying the most ordinary citizens going from one section of Warsaw to another, ran straight into the place of our misery. Every day, and several times a day, we had these witnesses. Every day they saw us—women with shopping sacks, and once I noticed a head of lettuce sticking up out of the top of a sack. Green lettuce! I thought my salivary glands would split with aching for that leafy greenness. And girls wearing hats. They were all the sort of plain people of the working class with slovenly speech who ride tramcars, but they were considered better than we, because no one regarded us as Poles anymore. And we, my father, my mother—we had so many pretty jugs on the piano and shining little tables, replicas of Greek vases, and one an actual archeological find that my father had dug up on a school vacation in his teens, on a trip to Crete—it was all pieced together, and the missing parts, which broke up the design of a warrior with a javelin, filled in with reddish clay. And on the walls, up and down the corridors and along the stairs, we had wonderful ink drawings, the black so black and miraculous, how it measured out a hand and then the shadow of the hand. And with all this—especially our Polish, the way my parents enunciated Polish in soft calm voices with the most precise articulation, so that every syllable struck its target—the people in the tramcar were regarded as Poles—well, they *were*, I don't take it away from them, though they took it away from us—and we were not! They, who couldn't read one line of Tuwim, never mind Vergil, and my father, who knew nearly the whole first half of the Aeneid by heart. And in this place now I am like the woman who held the lettuce in the tramcar. I said all this in my store, talking to the deaf. How I became like the woman with the lettuce.

Rosa wanted to explain to Magda still more about the jugs and the drawings on the walls, and the old things in the store, things that nobody cared about, broken chairs with carved birds, long strings of glass beads, gloves and wormy muffs abandoned in drawers. But she was tired from writing so much, even though this time she was not using her regular pen, she was writing inside a blazing flying current, a terrible beak of light bleeding out a kind of cuneiform on the underside of her brain. The drudgery of reminiscence brought fatigue, she felt glazed, lethargic. And Magda! Already she was turning away. Away. The blue of her dress was now only a speck in Rosa's eye. Magda did not even stay to claim her letter: there it flickered, unfinished, like an ember, and all because of the ringing from the floor near the bed. Voices, sounds, echoes, noise—Magda collapsed at any stir, fearful as a phantom. She behaved at these moments as if she were ashamed, and hid herself. Magda, my beloved, don't be ashamed! Butterfly, I am not ashamed of your presence: only come to me, come to me again, if no longer now, then later, always come. These were Rosa's private words; but she was stoic, tamed; she did not say them aloud to Magda. Pure Magda, head as bright as a lantern.

The shawled telephone, little grimy silent god, so long comatose— now, like Magda, animated at will, ardent with its cry. Rosa let it clamor once or twice and then heard the Cuban girl announce—oh, "announce"!—Mr. Persky: should he come up or would she come down? A parody of a real hotel!—of, in fact, the MARIE LOUISE, with its fountains, its golden thrones, its thorned wire, its burning Tree!

"He's used to crazy women, so let him come up," Rosa told the Cuban. She took the shawl off the phone.

Magda was not there. Shy, she ran from Persky. Magda was away.

wife and whatever else has kept tongues from going out of use since the year before.

We couldn't remember when we'd seen so many pickups and cars parked around the Alcoma Baptist Church. It's an old white frame building sinking on its cement blocks, the walls leaning in like they might fall any minute. We climbed the rickety steps from the dark and came to the double open doors and saw the church was just bursting with people and hot lights. The little children had to sit sweating on their mamas' laps, and every pew was filled and spilling people onto folding chairs in the aisles. A Baptist crowd, ladies with home-permanent hair and men that would never look at home in a white shirt, even without a tie. They were all fanning with Revell fans, but all the faces were glistening under the bare ceiling lights. Five-hundred-watt bulbs the fools had up there, no shade a-tall, moths circling around them. Brother used to say they have revivals in the hottest time of year to put people in mind of what Hell will be like. And the Baptists go one better by putting those hot bare lights on so you think you've got a toe in there for trial.

Well, I told myself, I guess the worse that can happen is you'll have a heat stroke and they'll have to carry you out.

Then I got a look at the visiting preacher.

He was sitting up front of the choir platform behind the altar, his face turned up to the ceiling and his eyes squeezed closed. Meditating. He was just a short, bald, fat little man, with a fringe of gray hair around his shiny scalp and little white hands and little feet in high-cut shiny black shoes. Little low-set eyes, and his cheeks sagged down and ran into a dewlap. But deep lines sunk down each side of his mouth and made him look like he meant business. Just as we stood there, a snatch of laughing came from the choir room behind, and he snapped open his eyes and frowned back mean at them. He meant business, all right.

Of course there weren't three seats together, so Irma sent Lamar up front to sit in a little space by Harvey Giles, the next-to-richest man in Alcoma. Harvey was in the same grade with me at school and used to be Methodist, but he couldn't get along at our church with Mr. Fallbriar, who is the richest man in Alcoma, so Harvey moved over to the Baptist church, got himself immersed, and runs things on the strength of his tithe. He's Mr. Big Baptist.

Irma and I squeezed into two folding chairs at the far right, and we all sat there sweating like Trojans, feeling that preacher warming up, while all through the quiet crowd an uneasiness was running through the heat and babies' squalls. Like lambs penned up while the slaughter fires are lit.

Because we all knew that little fat preacher could wind up the biggest man in the place and run him around like he was nothing but a child's hoop. How? By knowing how to stir him up. And to tell the truth, that's what they had come for. Hardworking people that are God-fearing and keep their self-respect by living by the Commandments and caring for themselves and tending their own sick and old folks. That doesn't leave much room for stirring up of other kinds but coming to church and hearing some visiting preacher scare you about Hell.

But I'm against that. What is it when you get all wrought up and come down crying to the preacher and let him fall on your neck shouting "Bless you, bless you, you've made the right decision"? It sure dudn't look like religion to me. It looks like people losing their heads. And if the Lord gave us one unmixed blessing, it's our heads, and losing your head, I say, is just throwing away the best thing you got. So seeing that fat preacher getting set to make everybody do just that, I got a headache right off.

Well, be durn if Irma didn't hit me with something else. She jabbed me in the side. "See who just walked in? I *told* you. Bet this is the first time he's darkened the door of a church in forty years. They say the doctor's told him his liver can't last more than six months."

Who should be standing uncertain at the open doors but Gene Paul Prescott! He'd got so old and dried up, I had to look twice to know him. Gone plumb white-headed and wearing gold-rimmed glasses like I'd never imagined on him. Everybody else was craning around at him too—he ducking his head to one side from all that staring. Then he saw a little space in the middle of a pew halfway down and squeezed in and stuck his face in a hymnbook without saying a word to a soul.

Well, sure didn't make any difference to *me* if he wanted to show up at the Baptist church. But he was the last person I'd expect—a drunk but besides that he's from one of the oldest families in town and raised rich and Presbyterian. Not that his coming was the slightest concern of mine. I'd rather not ever set eyes on him again. I've got my pride.

The choir came in from behind the altar, singing self-conscious in a single marching line and looking like they'd just been anointed in the choir room by Jesus personally. The young preacher followed them—he *was* better looking than the visiting preacher—and announced the first hymn. It was a loud old foot-thumping song, and naturally the singing was loud enough to wake the dead out back.

> Revive us again!
> Fill each heart with Thy love
> Let each soul be rekindled
> With fire from above . . .

Windy Diker's big horse-face grinned from the choir while he thundered the bass in the chorus.

Hallalujah! sang the sopranos.

THINE THE GLORA, sang Windy loud as all them put together.

> Hallalujah!
> ARMEN
> Halla*lu*jah!
> THINE THE GLORA

and all together . . .

> REVIVE US AGAIN!

We kept on sweating and got through the scripture and the hymns and offertory until the nice-looking preacher sat down and the fat one —Brother Benson was his name—got up and came to the altar, walking surprisingly light for a fat man in those high-cut shiny black shoes. He looked out over us a minute, narrowing his eyes, until the little coughs and stirring stopped right quick. With everybody quiet and watching, he took out his pocket watch and laid it to the side of the altar.

"*Brethern and sistern,*" he said in a loud, carrying voice. "I understand some of the membership don't like the way I been preaching."

Some of the ladies squirmed around. Harvey Giles sat up real straight.

The preacher smiled at the rest of us and started in telling that old joke about the negro preacher that gets up and says "Everybody ought to quit cussing," and the little old negro woman on the front row says "Amen," and the preacher says "Everybody ought to quit drinking," and she says "Amen" again. That goes on till he gets down to "Everybody ought to quit dipping snuff." And the little old negro woman, with her lip full of snuff, says "*Now he's quit preachin' and gone to meddlin'.*"

A big wave of laughing rose up when he said the last, like everybody hadn't heard it at every revival since time began.

As the last laughing died, Brother Benson raised a hand like he was calming a flood. "Call me a meddler if you want to. But let me tell you, if you had seen some of the sad sights I have, you'd be on your knees up here beside me, begging, pleading with all the poor sinners to repent . . .

"Just last week I was holding a meeting up in Tennessee, and I went out to see a farming man who'd broke away from God. I talked with him and I prayed with him and finally I thought he was about to make a commitment. But the Devil got aholt of his heart again, and he says not today, Brother, I got too much to think about today, I got my crops to think about today, maybe next week, not today. But my dear friends, the *Lord* don't wait till *you* say you're ready. Next week was too late for that man. That very night he took a pain in his side and was *dead* by morning. Oh, brother! oh, sister! how my heart bleeds for that sinner, cast out into eternal darkness, into the *ee*-ternal fires of Hell!"

His voice broke off high and loud, and he was quiet while he walked around to the front of the pulpit, his head hanging down like he couldn't stand the thought of that poor man burning in Hell.

You could have heard a pin drop. A lot of folks drew their arms down tight over their sides like they'd just remembered having a pain there like that Tennessee man.

When Brother Benson started talking again, his eyes looked out over us through the open doors at the dark sky, his hands folded together like a undertaker's. His voice went quiet but threatening too.

"*Revive us again* . . . while I was sitting there," he jerked his head backward toward the choir, "meditating on that wonderful old hymn, I heard God talking to me. He said: 'Son, there's somebody here that needs to get right with Me tonight, somebody that had better make it right with Me 'cause he don't have much time left.' *No!*"—he was back to shouting and shaking his finger so you felt God's wrath—"he don't have much time left! Now, brothers, I don't know who that man or that woman is, and I don't know what your sin is, friend; but I do know you better make it right with God this very night. You better accept Jesus Christ tonight!"

He walked back behind the pulpit letting that sink in, and everybody hung there like just when the doctor looks down and away from you before giving you the bad news, suddenly you're scared sick and all alone with the bad news hanging over you about to fall. We all hung onto that preacher's eyes, wondering Does he know something I've done that I don't? Oh, you start thinking of lots of little things you shouldn't of done, but which one is my big sin? Does he know something that is keeping me from God? And what if I should be taken right now tonight—nobody knows when his hour will come. Is there something that will keep me from going to His home when I die, cast me back into that awful black *nothing*ness that we come out of and so quick go back to forever unless someone has the mercy and the power to save us? It's what you push out of your mind every day, that last minute when you're facing eternity and the end of yourself, lying weak and helpless with your family already so far away, no way for them to help you, it's you dying, not them. You know you will be terrified, falling helpless into that dark nothingness. It's that realizing at revivals that that time *will be* for you, and you know you've been oh! so careless, that moment is so awful you must live every minute in your life preparing for it.

That devilish preacher had me going right along with the rest, what with his eyes boring right into me and his voice sliding from loud to soft. But when he got back behind the pulpit he changed again so quick I saw through him. He wasn't really worrying about that Tennessee man burning in Hell or about the person here about to die. He was cool as ice inside while he was stirring us up.

I trembled inside before I got control. There's enough fools I meet every day, I said, that I don't need to be made one of by you. If the world was made just like everybody thinks it should be—to go *his* way —then you could allow yourself to get stirred up. You could just be soft, like women especially want to be, and let yourself ride along where your feelings lead you and you'd come to no harm. But you come to find out that the world isn't made anywhere like it should be. The only way you can stand up to it is to steel yourself and hold on and hold on some more, more than you ever thought you could.

It's what I been doing all these years. One weary day after another at school and thinking plenty of days I can't make myself get up and do it one single more day. And knowing, oh, since way back there was no need to let myself dream about anything but putting up with children's runny noses and jealous mamas and grumpy principals, all just to live alone in the rented back apartment of some old widow. Oh, if you want to get married, I'll give you some free advice: Don't be a Mississippi schoolteacher. Whether you're pretty or not pretty, like me, the men shy away. Like they'll be put in the shade just because you know some algebra and where Cape Horn is! And then when I'd accepted that, Mama and Papa and Brother all taken within two years . . . until I wondered who was ruling in Heaven. So steeling yourself is the only way to get through, and even then—and this I threw back to that fat preacher—it gets so hard you stop being afraid of dying. When every year you lose something else, and you don't see anything ahead . . . It was Brother's death finally made me realize that one by one things will go and the only thing left is steeling yourself.

So I told that fat preacher that had everybody else sweating and leaning toward him out of their pews while he waved his little hands and opened them up to Heaven like he was talking to God, if I have lived through all that without breaking, I don't have to worry about somebody who has no particular business with me stirring me up so *he* can feel righteous and claim God sends messages down direct to him about who is saved and who isn't. If he has got messages from God, I've talked to Ulysses S. Grant.

But that Benson could read my mind as plain as those lighted headlines that run flickering at night around the Sterick building in Memphis. That devil fired back, "Brethern, God told me there was one here tonight I might be privileged to save, one who wasn't going to have another chance. And I *aim* to find that man tonight!" He was looking straight at Gene Paul.

I had forgot all about him. I peeped over and the sight could break your heart. His head was popped out in big drops of sweat; his pinched-in old-man's lips were pulled up scared, like a rabbit trapped by the dogs and knowing it's caught and is afraid even to squirm this way or that. He looked at me and I said to him, looking right back at him so he could read my eyes: "Are you going to let this fat preacher take you in?" And then I thought, well, it would be just like you. And it was like watching a fire blazing at your house with everything you have in the world inside and praying it will stop, and then you see the roof go up.

Because Gene Paul hadn't ever done anything in his life like you would have expected him to, just looking at him. Who would ever have thought when we were young he would turn into what he is—a drunk that even little children make jokes about. Living in the Prescotts' old cookhouse while his big two-story house in front sits closed-up, and seeing nothing except rough hill-men, the scrapings of the earth, and drinking rotgut with them at a still in the woods, a wonder he hadn't gotten himself killed by their likes, and most days for the past thirty years getting so liquored up he can't walk straight.

But that isn't enough to shame you, I said. And shame me that was once fool enough to care about you. Now you want to go down to the altar for this Benson to gloat over, tears coming down your old cheeks for everybody to gape at, and within three weeks you'll be back to drinking with that much more reason to be shamed. Can't you see for once what *is* and act accordingly?

No, he never did anything like a mother would hope for him. When we were growing up he was always doing things nobody else had the nerve to. Went over the waterfall once in a barrel and come over it, the Lord only knows how, without killing himself. All through high school, he never had one particular girl, although he dated them all. Oh, all the girls chased him, and fell in love with him, fine-looking and devil-may-care as he was. He was polite to all, even me the bookworm, but never got serious about anyone. To me none of the other boys came up to his level with their roughness and no brains. But when Mr. Prescott sent him off to Ole Miss (he was the only one of the Alcoma boys that got to go back then with so little money around in the town), Gene Paul dropped out after the first semester. I can still see Irma's letter to me— I was going to Normal in Moorehead then: "Guess who you were sweet on once has quit Ole Miss and is off traveling in Texas. Hint: Mrs. P. is fit to be tied."

It was 1916, my second year of teaching, that Irma wrote me Gene Paul had come home and brought a wife with him. Some woman with dyed blonde hair and bad grammar. Poor Mrs. Prescott. He got a house on the corner below his mother's and went into Mr. Prescott's drugstore, driving two nights a week the thirty miles over to Ole Miss to get his pharmacy degree.

Well, it came as a blow. I was working in this little poor Delta town, hardly making enough to stay alive and nobody there my age, day in and out the same thing with my pupils. I was impatient then. Well, one night Gene Paul comes home early from Oxford and finds his wife is entertaining an old boyfriend in the house *(where* in it, I'm not prepared to say).

Harvey Giles next door heard the ruckus and came running over. As he told it, Gene Paul had gone for his shotgun but the other man got it away from him and knocked Gene Paul on the floor and was holding the gun on him. Gene Paul was sitting helpless with the blood coming out of his mouth, looking up at the man that took his wife and now was holding a gun on him. Harvey shouted for them to break it up, and Gene Paul got up real slow, wiping his mouth with the back of his hand. And then, looking shamed as a man could, he just walked out, turning once at the door to look back at his wife. Harvey followed him, afraid he'd be back with another gun. But all Gene Paul did was walk up the street to his mother's. The wife and the boyfriend ran off that night, although maybe you couldn't call it running off since nobody tried to stop them.

A few days later Mrs. Prescott closed down the empty house and had her negro move the new furniture to her storehouse, and Gene Paul moved out to the Prescotts' old cookhouse where he's lived ever since.

Oh, why does a man throw his life away when any fool could tell him not to! Like you didn't have any *reason* to start drinking. He kept on at the drugstore, and one morning Mr. Prescott didn't wake up, so Gene Paul took over the business complete. When I was home that summer, I went in every day and he wouldn't look me straight in the eye, him a fine-looking young man that had been so devil-may-care, and now he just kept his eyes down on his hands when he gave me whatever I asked for. I thought he'd be able to tell by the way I spoke to him he wasn't shamed as a man just because of that one no-good woman. That was a summer, well, it seemed to me—I was still young—that something *had* to happen to me in the years going by.

Something *did* happen. We got so I could tease him a little when I'd be looking around the drugstore and nobody else was in there. It was cool and smelled from where he stood behind the counter of iodine and tinctures and camphor and things I couldn't recognize but that he must know like the palms of his hands, able to mix and heal folks with. That was the way I saw him, able to be strong and heal others if he would.

"I guess you're making a lot of money, getting rich, Gene Paul," I would tease him when he rang up that cash register, while somebody shut the front door that tinkled.

He would shoot a look over going by me, but grinning one-sided, handsome as could be. "Looks to me like you're buying an awful lot of headache powders, BC's and all. Maybe you got schoolteacher's headaches and need to change your line of work? Maybe you ought to go to pharmacy school; you were always smart."

Didn't sound like that dead voice he talked to everybody else with, but more like the boy I'd known. I got to feeling he looked for me every morning.

One July morning I went in, not really anything I needed to buy, and I looked over the boxes of candy up front while he waited on this one and that one. I knew he was busy, and I didn't even notice when everybody went out.

"Buying some candy for your sweetie?" he said sudden behind me, and I jumped ten feet. He'd never stood without the counter between us.

I guess I blushed blood-red. Then I caught myself and teased, "I just might. But I need a mighty big box, he's a mighty big man."

And he looked like I slapped him.

"I'm just joking, Gene Paul. You know that," I blurted out. I couldn't stand to see him hurt if that was what he was.

He looked at me like he never had, like he needed something but couldn't say what it was.

"Is it something you want to say, tell me?" I said after the time ticked by, him looking at me naked with whatever it was. Nothing like this had happened to me, I didn't know men's hearts, what he could be thinking. I didn't know how not to be a lady, wait for a man to say what he wanted. And he said it, grinned with one side of his mouth going up higher than the other, so my heart jumped just to see that grin.

"You be home tonight, because I'm coming over to see you." I was as excited as I've ever been. I took my time getting dressed and then about dark I went out and sat on the front porch. I waited thinking about that one-sided grin, and trying not to imagine what would happen. Daddy told Irma to quit meddling, but she couldn't keep from sticking her head out every half-hour. And then every fifteen minutes until I asked her to please refrain. It got later and I began to strain at every noise in the yard. Well, that was a long night. Inside they all went to bed. But it wasn't until about midnight, when I saw the last of the moon slide off the other side of the porch, that I let myself cry.

Next morning, when I went for the mail, everybody downtown was just buzzing over how Gene Paul was wild drunk in the streets last night and the sheriff had to take him home.

I kept hope for a few days, but I never heard one word from him. I had to face the truth. Either he'd already been drunk out of his mind when he said he was visiting me, or else he was having a good joke on the old maid. Take your pick, either way I was a fool.

After that everybody could notice him smelling of whiskey every day, getting worse all the time, until one day he shut up the drugstore and gave himself over to full-time drinking. He stopped caring a-tall what people thought, and some said it was that that killed Mrs. Prescott, although goodness knows she was eighty-eight when she finally died, so it took a while. But after a spell, one spring led to one cotton-ginning time and that to one more spring until time got by and nobody ever thought about how Gene Paul had wasted himself—it just didn't bear remarking on, like a lot of things about yourself that you put away from your mind and can't grieve about if you are to keep going, and you don't remark on any more, except once in a blue moon when something brings it back fresh.

And now we're not so far from the end of our road, and the only thing to be proud of is that you have looked at things straight as you could and called them what they were, hard as they were to admit, and now that you're old you at least don't act like a fool any more and you can walk along to your end with dignity.

That fat preacher was marching back and forth behind the pulpit on his little feet. Yelling that we were all sinners, all guilty of original sin. Oh, he could just taste that Presbyterian drunkard-convert in his mouth, like a cat with a canary.

Suddenly Gene Paul stirred in his seat. My Lord, he was ready to jump up and go down, not even wait for the invitation! I glared right at him, and he looked right back. *Please don't make a fool of yourself*, my eyes begged him.

And he leaned back, his pinched old-man's lips fallen apart. But the preacher was closing in, shouting "Won't you accept Him, friend? It's so easy to believe on Him. The Bible says 'Believe on the Lord Jesus Christ and *thou shalt be saved.*' Won't you trust Him? As the choir sings the invitational, won't you come up here to the altar and say *Yes*, I accept, *yes*, I'm through with sinning, *yes Jeezus* is my Savior . . ."

The choir started the slow begging first verse of *Just As I Am Without One Plea*, and the preacher said "Won't you come, brother? Just put your hand in His as the choir sings. Won't you come? Not only you lost, but those that need to rededicate their lives, all you church members come too to rededicate. Won't you come?" He held out his hands over us like he was Jesus Christ and if I was going to die of a stroke, I would have then . . .

You would have thought he was giving away money down at the altar. Harvey Giles started down and the whole church nearbout followed. The noise was loud from all over the church of people coming, even a loud *bang* once. Somebody hurrying so fast he knocked a hymnbook down, I figured. All I could do was look at the floor and not let anybody see my face. The choir went on singing *Just As I Am* and

Benson was gloating. "Welcome, brother, praise the Lord, welcome, sister . . ."

Down front the crush of people were crying and confessing things and hugging in that heat that was about to take us all over into a faint, and I looked away, not able to bear seeing him in that Benson's hands. I told Irma, who was dabbing her eyes, I'd meet her at the car. I walked out into the dark down the gravel road.

I heard somebody coming behind me on the gravel, and being in no mood to exchange remarks, I stepped out of sight between two pickups. It was a man walking brisk. He stopped, his face in shadows but not so much I couldn't see who it was.

Gene Paul held his suit jacket out like it was wet. Threw some broken pieces of glass on the gravel. A strong raw smell hit my nose— the *nerve* of him, bringing a pint of whiskey right into church in his jacket pocket! And then it came clear—that loud bang I heard was Gene Paul breaking his whiskey bottle on the pew when he hurried to get to that Benson. To think *that* had brought him to his senses!

Gene Paul said something to himself in an unsteady old drunk's voice like "Safe until next year." Well, that will be all right with me, buddy, I thought—join the Baptists when they got somebody besides Benson that thinks he is God's messenger. And Gene Paul walked off whistling *Revive Us Again*, all jazzed up, like he never heard of liver trouble.

I stepped along that gravel road and a little breeze blew my headache away good as a BC powder. I sat in the car, enjoying the little breeze and smelling sweet honeysuckle. When Irma and Lamar came up, she picked up her fan and said "Sister, what did you think of the revival?" and I said, feeling that breeze and smiling to myself out the window, "Oh, it was just fine. Guess we're all good and revived for this year."

Lamar, cranking the car, sings out "Amen."

RISK

CHARLES DICKINSON

Charles Dickinson was born in Detroit, Michigan, in 1951. He is a graduate of the University of Kentucky. His stories have appeared in *The New Yorker*, *Esquire*, *The Atlantic Monthly*, *Grand Street*, and *The Pikestaff Forum*. His first novel, *Waltz in Marathon*, was published in October 1983 by Alfred A. Knopf. He lives with his wife and son in Palatine, Illinois.

Owen is the host tonight. Washing glasses, he flips them in the air until they are just winks in the light. Catching them again takes his breath away.

Frank is the first to arrive. Then Nolan. Frank wore dirty clothes that afternoon when he took his laundry down to the big machines in the basement of his apartment building; with the load in the washer, soap measured, and coins slotted, he added the clothes he was wearing and made the long walk back upstairs to his apartment naked. He paused to read the fine print on the fire extinguisher. Noises in the building set birds loose in his heart. Frank takes the red armies when they gather to play the game of world conquest.

They hear Alice arrive in a storm of gravel. She has moved herself stoned across twenty-two miles of back roads in just under twenty minutes. She lives with a man she has known for seven months, in a rented farmhouse on a hundred acres of land. The man is good with a garden and with his hands, a warm-hearted, full-bearded man who plays the banjo professionally, an amicable host when the game is at their house. He loves Alice, but still she meets another man on the sly. Half her appointments and reasons for being away from home are fabrications. This other man treats her like a child, making fun of her gaps of knowledge, hurting her feelings, which she perversely enjoys. It is a counterpoint to the sweet man at home. Alice plays black.

The world is arranged on Owen's kitchen table. A strong yellow light

Copyright © 1982 by the Atlantic Monthly Company, Boston, Mass. First appeared in *The Atlantic Monthly*. Reprinted by permission.

shines down through the night's first gauzy sheets of smoke. The game's six continents—North and South America, Africa, Asia, Europe, and Australia—are not entirely faithful to the earth's geography. Each continent is formed from territories, and between these territories war will soon be waged with armies and dice.

Owen pours Frank a beer. Owen hosts as often as possible; he would play three or four times a week if he could. The gathering of his friends soothes him and fills dark spaces in the house. The smoke softens edges. He tries to get Eileen, his wife, to play, but she refuses. She remains in the other rooms. None of the players press on this point of awkwardness.

Owen shuffles through the game cards, a glass of beer at his elbow, a cigarette in an ashtray. Alice comes into the kitchen and shades her glassy eyes. "Hi," she says.

"Speak for yourself," Frank says.

Nolan, who has arrived in a sour mood, says, "The nation's motorists are safe for a few hours."

Alice hangs her coat on the tree by the door. She takes her makings out of her purse and carefully arranges them by her place at the board.

"Wine in the fridge," Owen says. "I'll get it for you in a second." He shakes the white dice and throws them across the face of the world. A pair of fives and a six.

"Oo," Alice says. "Hot."

"I'll take that all night."

Frank asks, "Who's late again?"

Les is late again; he makes a point of it. He never offers to host, nor does he ever bring beer or food. He feels that his presence is sufficient. Les always rolls good dice. It is something he demands of himself. He wins more often than the other players. From early March to early December, he drives a 1,000-cc motorcycle without a helmet. The others allow him to continue to play despite his cheap habits because he is so good; to bar him would be cowardly. But Frank has dreamed of Les hitting ice on his cycle, his unprotected head bouncing sweetly on the highway.

Les and Pam arrive at the same time, though not together. Les's hair is swept back like Mercury's wings. Where Les is allowed to play because he is the best player, Pam, the worst, is invited back because she is so generous and so good-looking. She has large green eyes, long, curly, pale-red hair, and heavy breasts tucked into a loose sweater. She is usually the last to arrive and the first to lose all her armies and be

IMC HORIZON CAMPUS
ZION-BENTON TWNSHP

eliminated. She has been playing for a year and still does not have a
handle on the game. She tries to have a sense of humor about this. She
always brings a large bag of pretzels and two six-packs of Dutch beer.
She is always welcome. She plays pink.

Pam is in love with Nolan. She tries to catch his eye from across the
room as she hands Owen her sack of food and beer. She has been with
Nolan just that afternoon. It is stitched in her memory in dim light.
The run through stinging branches to his basement, their time there,
their almost being caught by his wife. They met at one of these gather-
ings and have known each other a year; Nolan's presence kept her
coming back after she learned that she was not very good at the game
and probably never would be. She liked his lean frame and dark blue
eyes and the clever look his glasses gave him. But he is married, to a
woman named Beth. Pam has met her once, a shy, tall woman with a
plain face—she played the game a half-dozen times, even winning
once.

Pam knew from the first she appealed to Nolan. She learned long ago
that she appeals to most men. They had a cup of coffee out in the
open, later a lunch in the shadows, then a drink that afternoon and a
sly sneaking into his house from the rear basement door. She takes her
seat at the table. Nolan won't look at her. Her head swims in dates and
half-remembered cycles. She had thought she was between lovers and
was using no contraception. Her calculations told her she was safe but
she is not absolutely sure.

Getting settled, Owen shakes the dice, sips his beer, smokes, observes. Frank has his twenty red armies in five neat rows of four. Alice
has rolled a joint thick as her little finger and touched a match lovingly
to one twisted end. Blue smoke flows upward. A seed explodes and Pam
jumps, laughs. Nolan grimaces.

Les counts out his twenty green armies. He is serene. The night, so
clean and cold out on the highway, has purpose. He has won the
previous two times they played. He smiles idly around at those soon to
fall. He asks Owen, "Did you buy that stock I told you about?"

"I don't have the money, Les."

"Get it. I went in at 3½, and it's 7 already." He pauses to decline
the joint Alice offers. "It's a great place for your money."

"I like banks," Frank says.

Les proclaims, "Banks are for suckers."

"They're insured," Frank says.

"So? You've got to go for the big return in this economy. Most people aren't chickenshit like you, Frank."

Owen, who as host strives for player equanimity, says mildly, "I still don't have the money."

Les shrugs. He can do only so much. He says, "Let's get this carnage under way."

Two red dice go around the table, each player rolling to see who goes first. With six players, the world's forty-two territories will be divided evenly. But the player who starts will be the first to have three cards (a card earned each turn if a territory is conquered), which he or she might be able to cash for extra armies. Nolan's throw of ten is tops. Owen smiles and deals out the cards. They diverge from the rules in allotting territories. Each card represents a territory that a player will soon occupy with armies. Luck is involved, and time is saved. The players bring the cards up off the table, fan them in their hands, try to plot.

Les has been dealt New Guinea, and that is toehold enough for him on the continent of Australia. He deposits every available army there.

"A clear signal from down under," Nolan says. "Les is going for his continent early."

Les smiles beatifically.

Alice's seven territories are spread all over the world. She smokes her joint and studies her options. She knows that with six players, one or two will be eliminated early. A player without a firm base will be picked off a little at a time. Four of her territories are in Asia, which is much too large to try to hold as a continent. As she thinks, she feels herself float out of her seat, she feels her heels tap the chair seat as she rises clear. When she is on the ceiling, she lets out a laugh that is like taking on weight and drifts back down. Nobody witnessed her brief ascension. They are too engrossed in the coming war. She sips wine and comes to a decision. She doesn't like Les very much when they play, and she owns Siam. It is the doorway to Asia from Australia, which Les will inevitably control. She puts all her armies in Siam.

Les looks over at her. She loves it when she makes his eyes go mean and flat. Les has green eyes, not as green as the color he plays, but green like dirty dollar bills. His eyes are always so cool and rich and calculating. He expects to win; this attitude rankles Alice no end. He may win tonight, but first he will have to fight through her.

Nolan has been splitting his armies between Central America and

Greenland, preparatory to a run at North America. Seeing Alice's troop placement, he announces, "A bloodbath on the horizon in Siam."

Alice says, "I'm ready." Les drinks his wine.

"Les may want to invest in body bags," Frank says.

"I'm ready," Alice repeats.

Through all this, the only thing Owen hears is his wife moving in the room next to the kitchen. She has gone in there to get a book or the night's paper. She makes soft flutterings like a bird caught in the wall. He wishes she would come in, watch the game, have a glass of wine or a beer. An hour before the players arrived, they talked about having another baby. More than a year had passed, they were both in their early thirties, a better time would not arrive. But she could not give him an answer. Her willingness and her sadness remained locked together inside her.

Through the crack beneath the door he sees the light in the next room go out. He hears Eileen move deeper into the house, away from him; he thinks he hears her moving away long after the sounds have been hidden by the war around him.

Owen has Egypt, North Africa, and Madagascar, and he is delighted. He will soon control the continent of Africa. He won't be one of the first players eliminated, the host forced to sit and top off drinks and think.

Frank says cheerfully, "It's a gas to have the Middle East," and loads it full of his armies. He has nowhere else to go. His other armies are scattered in every continent, and worthless. He says, "The Middle East is the territory around which the world revolves."

"Frank's trying to sell himself a bill of goods," Les says.

"The poor jerk has nothing *but* the Middle East," Alice says.

Frank replies, "It's oily yet."

Pam owns Brazil and Venezuela, the doors in and out of the continent of South America. She divides her armies between the two territories.

"A bold move," Nolan announces. She looks to see if he is making fun of her, but his eyes trip away from hers.

The world is full of colored armies soon to contend. Nolan begins. After placing his three free armies, he attacks Les's lone army in the Northwest Territory, loses an army before advancing, then loses another getting Owen out of Alaska.

"It's never easy," Nolan says. But he now controls the three routes in and out of North America. He takes his card. The game moves to Frank.

"Am I in danger?" Owen asks.

"Possibly," Frank says. He puts his three free armies in the Middle East.

"Because I want to go to the john."

"I just want to go for a card," Frank replies.

Owen leaves the kitchen. Let them wait for him if he can't get a straight answer. Eileen is in their bedroom. She sits against the head-board reading; she looks up almost warily when her husband appears.

"Who's winning?" she asks.

"Just started. Why don't you come out and say hello? Have a little wine."

His wife shakes her head. Her hair is a thick caramel wave that runs in and out of the light like surf. Her face is delicate and oval-shaped. He reads in her eyes that she expects the worst possible news at any moment. "I'd have to get dressed all over again," she explains. She is ready for sleep, in a flannel nightgown buttoned up the front and tied with a ribbon at the base of her throat. He kisses this spot, then uses the bathroom before returning to the game. Making his way down the shadowed hall, he glances into his house's second bedroom, but forces himself to think about getting hold of Africa instead.

Frank has darted into Southern Europe, taken his card, regrouped back in the Middle East, and stopped. Les has taken Australia. His armies wait in a clot in Indonesia, across a strait of blue-green water from Alice's Siamese force.

"The world is taking shape," Owen notes.

"Les suggests everyone invest in philatelic devices," Frank says.

"They're illegal in this state," Alice says.

Owen says nothing. He won't sit down just yet; not until it is his turn. He is unable to lose himself in the game. This has never been a problem. Tonight, though, he is itchy.

While he gets wine and beer and opens Pam's pretzels and pours them into a bowl, hosting the event in all earnestness, Pam takes South America. She and Les have continents, though they are the two conti-nents easiest to win and hold, and hence worth only two bonus armies per turn. Still, they are continents. Les and Pam won't drift rootless over the world.

Alice's three free armies go into Siam. She looks at Les, her left eyebrow cocked, a question asked. He meets her look blankly. She sees that he has pushed his anger down. His cash-green eyes have reclaimed their arrogance.

Not yet, she decides. She attacks Nolan in India for her card, then pulls back into Siam.

"Buy body bags," Frank urges one and all. "Buy stock in the Red Cross."

Now Owen takes his seat. "Who has hot dice?" he asks.

"Nobody, really," Nolan reports. "Still too early. I think Alice should go after Les before his heat up."

"Les suggests we invest in numismatic tools," Frank says.

Owen rolls the dice against Pam and takes the Congo. His armies advance down through South Africa and up into East Africa. Just like that, Africa is his. He is spread too thin to hold it, he supposes, but he has a continent.

Nolan's turn again, and he can't remember what he wants to do next. Beth's face swims up to him, fitted on Pam's lush body. He stirs in his seat and tries to concentrate. He must fortify North America. One minute he was having a beer with Pam and the next he had come to this dangerous decision and they were parking her car a block over from his house. Cutting through the lawns, the darkening spaces between the houses, he could think only of the lack of cover. All the leaves were fallen; this was an affair meant for summer. He pulled the girl along by the hand. They went into the basement by the back door and undressed in the failing light. She tasted of flat beer when he kissed her for the first time. Chimes went off upstairs; he counted with them to five as he kissed her belly—an hour before Beth was due.

"Whose turn is it?" Les asks pointedly. Nolan's attention jerks back to the game. The world spreads before him. The girl keeps looking at him; she will give him away if she isn't careful. He is playing blue. Her sexual presence hit him the first time he saw her: a chemical lust. She never had to open her mouth. In fact, he preferred that she didn't. The peeling back of layers of existence that was life with Beth was never a factor with Pam. She was not very good at the game, and he knew nothing about her life otherwise. At their early meetings he filled the silent spaces talking about himself. He never thought about Beth at those times; she existed on a different plane. He found it remarkably easy to ask Pam to make that run to the basement with him. It would be the extent of what he wanted to know about her. Only when they were out in the open and on the run did it strike him what a wild chance he was taking.

And after they had been in the basement only twenty minutes, as they were finished and sitting in an awkward envelope of silence, a door opened above them and Beth's heels cracked smartly on the floor over their heads.

"Nolan," Les snarls, "it's too early in the game for such long thoughts."

Frank says, "It will be the rumination of your soul."

Nolan looks at Pam, then his eyes fly past. She waited with him in his basement like a canny burglar. Her ripe body had become an unwieldy burden he must transfer out of there for his own safety. His wife moved about upstairs, and the sky outside darkened. Then they slipped out the basement door and back to her car. She drove him to where he had left his car. They did not say a word, moving on those dark streets, as though his wife might yet hear. He took deep breaths to calm himself. Leaving, he had looked back up at the house, and in the rectangle of light of the upstairs bedroom window he had thought he saw a woman looking out. But he had lost his glasses in the rush of adultery. He was flying blind. He had to be careful driving. At home he put on a spare pair and made a quick, surreptitious inspection of the basement. Nothing. No glasses. They were buried somewhere like a land mine. He might step on them at any moment and blow himself up. Beth, happy to see him, undressed and pulled him into bed with her. He said he didn't have time but she insisted; he noted no strangeness in her behavior, no knowledge of what he had done, of what he had become.

Owen gravely says, "As host, I'll have to rule you either move immediately, Nolan, or forfeit your turn."

Nolan slaps his three free armies down in Alaska. He conquers Les in Quebec from Greenland, then takes his card and sits back. Pam is a little disappointed. After such long consideration, she had expected something grand from Nolan.

"Bold," Les sneers.

"Jam it."

Frank drops more armies into the Middle East. Les says, "You can't let Owen keep Africa."

"Always fomenting trouble," Owen says good-naturedly. The possibility of attack hurries his blood, though. Frank moving on Egypt or East Africa is strategically sound. By the next turn, Owen will be better fortified. If he survives here, Africa will be his, probably for the entire game, with its three bonus armies per turn. Frank has the manpower at the moment and Owen's dice are rarely better than fair.

Frank attacks Owen in East Africa. Africa falls in six rolls of the dice. Les says, stirring more trouble, "You're poised to cut across North Africa and take South America away from Pam."

"No thanks," Frank says. Too many armies wait in North Africa and Brazil. There is nothing in it for him. "I am content, not contentious," he says, and moves half his force back into the Middle East.

Les shakes Alice's shoulder, pretending she has fallen asleep. "You with us?" he asks in a loud voice. "Enough brain cells still alive to finish the game?"

She purses her lips as if to kiss and blows blue smoke in his face.

"I am ready," she says carefully, from the ceiling. These three words falling down to Les pull her after them like anchors. She wraps her leg around a leg of the table for balance and the table leg convulses. Les shrieks theatrically, "God! She's trying to get me sexually aroused so I'll go easy on her in Siam. But it won't work!"

He untangles his leg from Alice's. She grabs the table edge lest she float away again. A balloon of nausea rises in her. She puts her hand to her mouth and concentrates.

"Looking pale," Les says to the others, pointing at Alice.

"No fair throwing up on the world," Frank warns. "If you don't like your situation, be a man and live with it."

Les puts three armies in Indonesia, two in the Ukraine. He decides he is in no hurry. Let things build. He rolls the dice and there is a six. He gets a card from another point on the globe.

"Uh-oh," Frank says.

"Very efficient use of that six."

"Thank you," Les says modestly.

Alice smiles at them all. "It's early yet."

The world comes to Owen and it goes away. He is a fine host, and breaks out corn chips and roast beef sandwiches, empties ashtrays, opens beers, pours wine. He spills liquids into the oceans and across the plains of Asia. The players groan and protest. A whale dives in the Mid-Atlantic. To the south, a tall ship moves under sail. He excuses himself. The light is out in their bedroom. It is 1 A.M., and Eileen sleeps in blankets wrapped tight as a premium cigar.

He passes the second bedroom going back and decides to go in. The crib had been dismantled right away. Even a year later the four indentations remain in the carpet where the casters pressed, stake holes for a precise parcel of ground. The baby had been so weightless, and home for such a short time; he is always amazed that she could mark the room so indelibly.

A night-light remains in the wall socket. His wife might have overlooked it when she was clearing out the room. She might have been afraid to look down. He kneels by it and snaps it on. A mouse's head, a glowing white face, round black ears, cartoon rodent eyes; it's kind of unnerving. The head of a tiny ghost floating above the floor. Not the sort of thing for a baby girl. Had she been scared to death?

Owen returns to the game. Without Africa he is nothing, and the game has become a chore. He will be eliminated soon. Frank is gone already. Les took him out with the force he built in the Ukraine, using this secondary force to win cards and let some of the steam out of the situation brewing between Siam and Indonesia. Frank waited too long to take this Ukraine army seriously, and now he has gone outside; nobody knows what has happened to him.

Pam is pinned in South America. Owen's last armies block her in North Africa. Nolan has a major force in Central America. He will march on her in Venezuela.

The bloodbath between Alice and Les approaches. "You've got to come through me pretty soon," Alice taunts. "Nolan's getting too strong."

"This is a fact," Owen says. He desires resolution of this conflict so he can send his guests away.

The door opens and Frank is back.

"Where you been?"

"Standing naked in the dark," Frank replies.

No one pays any attention. Nolan is attacking Pam. He goes after her in Venezuela because it is the sound move at that point in the game, and also because he wants her gone. She usually leaves after she has been eliminated. Nights past, he was sorry to see her go. Now she embarrasses him. He expects her to slip up or start crying. She keeps looking at him.

Nolan rolls the dice and Pam waits. If he would look at her they might reach some understanding, but his eyes are fixed to that spot on the board where her dice will fall.

"Come on, come on," he says impatiently.

She rolls and loses two armies. Alice says, "Don't let him badger you."

"It's okay," Pam says softly. She thinks she will cry. Everything is wrong.

"Would you roll the dice?" he asks sharply.

She flings the dice across the board. She keeps them in sight through filmed eyes and sees sixes come up, which on closer inspection are really fours. Her tears make the pits shiver and drift. But fours are enough to win a pair of armies from Nolan, who rolls nothing higher than a three.

"Get him," Alice cheers.

But they are only dice; only Les has learned to tap their souls. Nolan's superior forces pick implacably away at Pam. Her armies fall like threads in a garment until they are all gone and she feels naked and stupid. Out of the game again. She turns her cards over to Nolan. He cashes them for extra armies and moves without a word against Owen in North Africa. Pam watches this action blankly. She could open her mouth and tell everyone of the time she spent with Nolan in the recent past. She wields this knowledge like an ax on her tongue and is larger within herself for not using it.

She takes her empty glass and washes it out in the sink. At her back, Nolan eliminates Owen.

"You'll pardon me if I don't stay for the end," she says.

Owen stands, wipes his palms on his trousers. "I don't blame you for leaving," he says. "I'm bored myself."

"The pitiable whine of the previously conquered," Les observes dryly.

Owen smiles and takes Pam's coat off the tree and helps her into it. He walks her out to her car.

"Thanks for coming," he says. He likes being outside, away from the smoke and the bloodlust. The white gravel of his driveway gleams. The air feels like it wants to snow. He takes Pam's keys gallantly, and after she shows him the one, he unlocks her car door. Owen leans in and kisses her good-night. She hands him a pair of glasses.

"They belong to the guy playing blue," she says. "I saw him downtown today and we had coffee together and he left them with me by mistake."

These words break over Owen in a rush; he can only say, "Okay."

He stays outside after Pam is gone. Nolan's car is unlocked; he puts the glasses on the dash. He has no interest in the truth of their coming into Pam's possession. He returns to his house through the front door. He hears the voices of the players in the kitchen, the labored buzz of an old digital clock turning a minute over. Through the dark passages of the house, moving with a freedom bestowed by his guests' believing he is still outside, Owen glides into the bedroom. His wife lies wrapped and asleep. He understands now why the night's game offered him nothing; it was an event out of order of importance. Eileen comes half awake at the way he pulls the covers and makes a space for himself in this loose, warm cylinder. He gets her nightgown unbuttoned and untied and fights through the clumsy hands she throws in his path. He plants a long kiss on her sour mouth. She utters a word into his own mouth that he ignores. She will kill his desire if he lets her.

"Where are your friends?" she whispered, warm in his ear.

"In the kitchen. The world will fall soon."

"You aren't being a good host." He is stirred unimaginably to hear teasing in her voice. Her hands have opened against his back.

"They think I'm outside," he whispers. "This way, I can be two places at once."

She kisses him on the neck. They move on together, Owen careful of dark chasms of memory he must transport his wife over. She proceeds along a fine edge that her husband slowly widens.

Les says, "Siam from China."

"Hand me the bones, please," Alice says. Frank gives her the white dice. "Like skulls," she says, "with twenty-one lance holes."

"Siam from China," Les repeats.

"Pincer movement," Nolan announces.

"Pinch her movement and she'll follow you anywhere," says Frank.

Les has moved his second force into China so he can attack Alice's Siamese armies from both north and south. He rolls dice the same way from first to last: three shakes of his left fist, then a gentle, coddling, tipping of the dice out onto the board, as though they might bruise. It is his secret that he treats the dice well so they will reciprocate. He once revealed this secret while drunk and voluble, and seven straight games of cold dice followed as punishment.

He beats on Alice from China: a softening action. Alice is poised for defeat. He can see in her slack face that she has had enough: enough grass, enough of their company, enough of this game. She is tired and anxious to go home.

"Where's Owen?" Nolan asks.

"He walked Pam to her car," Frank says.

"That was a half-hour ago."

"So?" Les asks, impatient at this break in his concentration. "Go look for him if you're so concerned. But shut up."

"Gee, Les, you're such a charming guy," Frank says.

"Eat it."

"Come on, Les," Alice complains. "Roll the dice. I wanna go home."

"The night is breaking up in a sea of bad juices," Frank says. "Why does it always have to be this way? Like love."

"Shut up, Frank."

Nolan is at the window, cupping hands around his eyes to see through the light reflected on the glass. Chrome winks from the handlebars of Les's motorcycle. He can see Alice's car, his car, Frank's car. Not Pam's car, though.

"They left together," he says.

"Who did?" Frank asks.

"Pam and Owen."

"No way," Alice says.

"Intriguing, though," Les admits.

"Her car is gone. So is Owen. You put it together."

"He's married," Frank says.

"Frank, you're such an innocent," Alice says.

Frank says, "And his wife's in the other room. Who'd have the nerve to go off with another woman under those conditions?"

Nolan says, "Maybe she's asleep. Maybe he figures she figures he's still out here. She never checks on him. Maybe he figured it was worth the gamble."

"Are we still playing?" Alice asks Les. He is startled; he has been thinking about Pam. The dice feel funny in his hand, as though the corners have been shaved fractionally, or the pits rearranged. They feel cool at being ignored in the midst of their performance for him. He is afraid to roll, and when he does it's all ones and twos. He rolls cold for the next five minutes, losing armies, losing confidence. In time his China force is wiped out, and Alice still exists firmly in Siam. Outnumbered, she nonetheless has the hot dice that ordinarily are his province, as though they have taken another lover. Fives and sixes roll languorously from her hand. Alice licks her lips, wide awake now. Hot dice get everyone's attention. Les awaits her exclamation of disbelief in her good fortune, which will drive the dice spitefully back to him. But it does not come. He loses armies in pairs. By and by, they are evenly matched, Siam and Indonesia, and Les stalls to count armies, trying to cool her dice this way.

Nolan says, "I feel uncomfortable without a host." He opens himself a fresh beer. He begins to look through bills that Owen keeps stacked on the counter next to the telephone.

"Jesus, Owen has $1,108 on his Visa," he informs the others.

"Stop that," Alice scolds.

Les likes this unexpected turn; Nolan's rude exploration has taken Alice's mind off the game.

"Many people are faced with serious and potentially catastrophic debt," Les says.

Nolan goes on. "A phone bill for $79.21."

"What if Owen comes back and finds you doing that?" Alice asks. When her head is turned away from Les, he blows gently toward the dice in her hand to cool them.

"He's with Pam," Nolan says. Saying this makes it a fact; makes him feel released.

"Roll the dice," Les orders. "I want to get out of here before daylight." He is certain that the dice have come back to him. Alice has lingered too long between throws. She has lost favor by ignoring the good fortune that the dice were eager to bestow. He reminds her, "I'm still attacking."

Alice rolls, thinking of Owen. He had telephoned her when the baby died, the phone seeming to explode with compressed tragedy in the middle of the night. To this day, she can't talk to Eileen without seeing grief encasing her like an invisible jar. Only lately has Alice seen her smile. Would Owen go off with Pam at just such a time?

Les wins two armies. Then two more.

Nolan says, "A bill for $177.44 from People's Gas."

Alice wishes Owen would return and discover Nolan and banish him forever. But the house is silent except for the click of dice. Maybe Owen *has* left with Pam; maybe it is the only response to this time in history. The man she meets on the sly is married to a sweet woman who he claims has nothing of interest to say. And Alice has never considered herself fascinating. The man she shares the farmhouse with had a marriage end years ago when he was caught in a hammock with another woman. She thinks this might make her safe, that he might understand if he ever catches her.

Les rolls and Alice falls. He was right; the dice have come back. When he clears her out of Siam, he still has ten armies in Indonesia. He takes the four cards Alice holds, and with the cards already in his hand cashes twice for forty-five armies, a huge green force he places with care to battle Nolan while his dice are running hot. It takes another hour to finish the game. The dice are at home in Les's loosely cupped fist and at two minutes to four o'clock in the morning he is the winner for the third consecutive time. Alice and Frank sit quietly and watch.

"Dear Les," Alice says, standing and stretching. "You do go on."

"And on . . . and on," Frank says. "Like a fungus." He shakes Les's hand. He folds Owen's board, puts the cards away, puts the armies in their containers.

Nolan asks, "Did Owen take his key?"

"I couldn't tell you," Les says.

"If we lock the door," Frank says, "and he has to knock to get in, we could be inadvertently exposing him to exposure. Or exposure. A guy like Owen could die of exposure."

"He should've thought of that," Nolan says.

"He can just say he forgot it," Les says. "He could say he went to breakfast after the game and forgot it."

Alice puts the wine in the refrigerator and washes out the glasses. They leave a small light on over the stove.

Birds stir outside, though it is still dark. The four of them stand, corners of a square, in the driveway.

"Somebody mentioned breakfast," Nolan says.

Frank pats his pockets. "I'm broke."

"I'll buy," Nolan says. "The vanquished will buy with the reparations they receive from the victors."

"Ha! You'll get nothing from me," Les says.

"I'll still buy."

"I think I'll pass," Alice says.

"You'll pass on a free meal?" Nolan asks.

"I don't feel so hot."

"Suit yourself," Frank says.

The other three turn from her and make their plans. She does not want to be alone just then, though a sleeping man who loves her awaits at the end of the drive home. Nolan and Frank start their cars and drive off and she is left standing there with Les. He sits astride his motorcycle, pulling on his gloves and watching her.

"Come with us," he urges.

She moves to his side. "I'm tired of Nolan and Frank." She kisses Les. "Can't we go somewhere?"

He laughs. "That might be difficult to explain. I've been coming and going at awfully odd hours. She thinks I play this game at all hours of the day and night."

"Coward."

Owen is awakened by Les's motorcycle starting. Unwinding himself from Eileen, he feels her stir. She loops an arm around his waist when he sits up on the edge of the bed. His friends will be going for breakfast at this early hour. It is a tradition of the game. The night's war will be replayed. Stories will be told, rumors will be spread. Owen would love to go with them, but he doesn't dare.

COUNTING MONTHS

DAVID LEAVITT

David Leavitt was born in 1961 in Pittsburgh, Pennsylvania, grew up
in Palo Alto, California, and attended Yale University. His fiction has
appeared in *The New Yorker* and *Harper's*. This story will be included
in a collection of his work to be published by Knopf. He lives in New
York City.

Mrs. Harrington was sitting in the oncology department waiting room
and thinking about chicken when the realization came over her. It was
like a fist knocking the wind out of her, making her need to gasp and
whoop air. Suddenly the waiting room was sucking up and churning;
the nurses, the magazine racks, the other patients turning over and
over again like laundry in a washer. Faces grew huge, then shrank back
away from her until they were unrecognizable. Dimly she felt the magazine she had been reading slip out of her hand and onto the floor.

Then it was over.

"Ma'am?" the woman next to her was asking. "Ma'am, are you all
right?" she was asking, holding up the magazine Mrs. Harrington had
dropped. It was *Family Circle*. "You dropped this," the woman said.

"Thank you," said Mrs. Harrington. She took the magazine. She
walked over to the fish tank and dropped herself onto a soft bench. The
fish tank was built into a wall that separated two waiting rooms and
could be looked into from either side. Pregnant guppies, their egg sacs
visible through translucent skin, were swimming in circles against the
silhouette of a face, vastly distorted, that peered in from the other
waiting room. One angelfish remained still, near the bottom, near the
plastic diver in the corner.

Mrs. Harrington's breath was fogging the fish tank.

Copyright © 1983 by David Leavitt. First appeared in *Harper's*. Reprinted by permission.

The thought had come to her the way the carrier of a plague comes to an innocent town. She was reading a Shake 'n' Bake ad, thinking about the chicken waiting to be cooked in the refrigerator at home, and whether she would broil it; she was tense. She began to consider the date, December 17: who was born on December 17? Did anything historic happen on December 17?

Then, through some untraceable process, that date—December 17 —infected her with all the horror of memory and death. For today was the day she was supposed to be dead by.

"Mrs. Harrington?" she heard the head nurse call.

"Yes," she said. She got up and moved toward the long hallway along which the doctors kept their secret offices, their examination rooms. She moved with a new fear of the instruments she could glimpse through slightly open doors.

It was an intern who had told her, "Six months."

Then Dr. Sanchez had stood in front of her with his greater experience and said, "That's youthful hubris, bravado. Of course, we can't date these things. We're going to do everything we can for you, Anna. We're going to do everything humanly possible. You can live a long time, a full life."

But she had marked the date on a mental calendar: six months. December 17 would be six months. And so it was. And here she was, still alive, having almost forgotten she was to die.

She undressed quickly, put on the white paper examination gown, lay down on the cold table. Everything is the same, she told herself. Broil the chicken. Chicken for dinner. The Lauranses' party tonight. Everything is the same.

The the horror swept through her again. Six months ago she had been planning to be dead by this day. Her children on their way to a new home. But it had been a long time.

Things dragged on. Radiation therapy, soon chemotherapy, all legitimate means of postponement. She lost quite a bit of hair, but a helpful lady at the radiation therapy center directed her to a hairdresser who specialized in such cases as hers, could cut around the loss and make it imperceptible. Things dragged on. She made dinner for her children.

She went to one meeting of a therapy group, and they told her to scream out her aggression and to beat a pillow with a hammer. She didn't go back.

"Hello, Anna," Dr. Sanchez said, coming in, sitting at the opposite end of the table. He smelled of crushed cigars, leather. "How're things?"

He obviously didn't remember. December 17.

"Fine," she said.

As if she didn't notice, he began to feel around her thighs for lumps.

"The kids?" he said.

"Fine," she said.

"You've been feeling all right, I hear," he said.

"Fine," she said.

"And you aren't finding the results of the radiation too trying?"

"No, not bad."

"Well, I've got to be honest with you, when you start the chemotherapy in January, you're not going to feel so hot. You'll probably lose quite a bit of weight, and more hair. Feel like you have a bad flu for a while."

"I could stand to lose a few pounds," Mrs. Harrington said.

"Well, what's this?" said Dr. Sanchez, his hand closing around a new lump.

"You know, they come and go," said Mrs. Harrington, turning over. "That one on my back is pretty much gone now."

"Um hum," said Dr. Sanchez, pressing between her buttocks. "And have you had any pain from the one that was pressing on the kidney?"

"No."

"That's good, very good."

He went on, thank God, in silence. Every now and then he gave grunts of approval, but Mrs. Harrington had long since realized that rather than indicating some improvement in her condition, these noises simply signified that the disease was following the course he had mapped out for it. She lay there.

It no longer embarrassed her, because he knew every inch of her body. Though there were certain things she had to be sure of before she went. She always made sure she was clean everywhere.

"Well," Dr. Sanchez said, pulling off his plastic gloves and throwing them into a repository, "you seem to be doing fine, Anna."

Fine. What did that mean? That the disease was fine, or her?

"I guess I just keep on, don't I?" she said.

"Seriously, Anna, I think it's marvelous the way you're handling this thing. I've had patients who've just given up to depression. A lot of them end up in hospitals. But you keep up an active life. Still on the PTA? Still entering cooking contests? I'll never forget those terrific brownies you brought. The nurses were talking about them for a week."

"Thank you, Doctor," she said. He didn't know. No more than the woman hitting the pillow with the hammer. All these months she had been so "active," she suddenly knew for a lie. You had to lie to live through death, or else you die through what's left of your life.

As she got dressed she wondered if she'd ever be able to sleep again, or if it would be as it was at the beginning, when she would go to sleep in fear of never waking up, and wake up unsure if she were really alive.

Lying there, terrified, in her flannel nightgown, the mouthpiece firmly in place (to prevent teeth-grinding), her eyes searching the ceiling for familiar cracks, her hands pinching what flesh they could find, as if pain could prove life.

It had taken her many months to learn to fall asleep easily again.

She was one with the people in the lobby now. She had been aloof from them before. One she knew, Libby, a phone operator. She waved from across the waiting room. Then there was the man with the bandage around his head. A younger woman, probably a daughter, always had to bring him. She noticed an older man with a goiter on his neck, or something that looked like a goiter, in the corner, looking at a fish.

"Good night," she said to the nurses, tying her scarf around her head. Paper Santa Clauses were pasted to the walls; a tiny tree gleamed dully in a corner. Outside the waiting room, the hospital corridors extended dim and yellow all the way to the revolving door. Mrs. Harrington pushed at the glass, and the first gusts of wind rose up, seeping in from outside. She pushed the glass away, emerging, thankfully, outside, and the cold, heavy wind seemed to bruise her alive again, brushing away the coat of exhaustion that had gathered on her eyelids while she was inside. It was cold, very cold. Her small heels crushed frozen puddles underfoot, so that they fragmented into tiny crystal mirrors. Rain drizzled down. California winter. She smoothed her scarf under her chin and walked briskly toward her car, a tall, thick woman, a genteel yacht in a harbor.

The car was cold. She turned on the heat and the radio. The familiar voice of the local newscaster droned into the upholstered interior, permeated it like the thick, unnatural heat. Rain clicked against the roof. Slowly she was escaping the hospital, merging into regular traffic. She saw the stores lit up, late-afternoon shoppers rushing home to dinner.

She wanted to be one of them, to push a cart down the aisles of a supermarket again. She pulled into the Lucky parking lot.

In the supermarket the air was cool and fresh, smelled of peat and wet sod and lettuce. Small, high voices chirped through the public address system:

> It's a world of laughter, a world of tears,
> It's a world of hopes, and a world of fears . . .

Mrs. Harrington was amazed by the variety of brightly colored foods and packages, as if she had never noticed them before. She felt among the apples until she found one hard enough to indicate freshness; she examined lettuce heads. She bought Spaghetti-Os for her youngest son, gravy mix, Sugar Pops. A young family pushed a cart past her, exuberant, the baby propped happily in the little seat at the top of the shopping cart, his bottom on red plastic and his tiny legs extending through the metal slats. She was forgetting.

An old woman stood ahead of her in the nine-items-or-less line. She was wearing a man's torn peacoat. She bought a bag of hard candy with seventy-eight cents in pennies, then moved out the electric doors. "We get some weird ones," the checkout boy told Mrs. Harrington. He had red hair and bad acne and reminded her of her oldest son.

Back in the car, she told herself, "Try to forget. Things aren't any different than they were yesterday. You were happy yesterday. You weren't thinking about it yesterday. You're not any different." But she was. The difference was growing inside her, through the lymph nodes, exploring her body.

It was all inside. At the group therapy session a woman had said, "I think of the cancer as being too alive. The body just keeps multiplying until it can't control itself. So instead of some dark interior alien growth that's killing me, it's that I'm dying of being too alive, of having lived too much. Isn't that better?" the woman had said, and everyone had nodded.

Or is it, Mrs. Harrington was thinking, the body killing itself, from within?

She was at a red light. "If the light changes by the time I count to five," she said, "I will become normal again. One. Two. Three. Four. Five."

It changed.

And maybe if I had asked for six, Mrs. Harrington was thinking, that would have meant another ten years. Ten years!

As soon as Mrs. Harrington got home, she hurried into the kitchen. Her son Roy was watching "Speed Racer" on television. He was fourteen. She heard loud music in the background: Jennifer; Blondie: "Dreaming, dreaming is free." And then the sounds of her youngest child, Ernest, imitating an airplane. She was grateful for the noise, for the chance to quiet them with her arrival.

"What's for dinner?" Roy asked.

"Nothing," Mrs. Harrington answered, "unless Jennifer cleans up like she promised. Jennifer!"

"Ma," Ernest said, flying into the kitchen, "the party's tonight, right? Timmy's gonna be there, right?"

"Right," she said. He was her youngest child. His nose was plugged with cotton because it had been bleeding.

Her daughter came in, sucking a Starburst. She had on a pink blouse Mrs. Harrington didn't much care for. "How was it?" she asked, beginning to scrub the pots.

"Fine," said Mrs. Harrington.

"What's for dinner?" Roy asked again.

"Chicken. Broiled chicken."

"Again?"

"Yes," Mrs. Harrington said, remembering the days before when chicken hadn't mattered. Those days took on a new luxury, a warmth to match Christmas, in this light—the four of them, eating, innocent.

"Can I make some noodles?" Roy asked.

"Noodles!" Ernest shouted.

"As long as *you* make them," Jennifer said.

Roy stuck out his chest in a mimicking gesture.

"I'll make them, I'll make them. In a few minutes," he said.

The boys left the room.

"Dad called," Jennifer said.

"Was he at home?"

"He and Sandy are in Missoula, Montana."

"Ha," said Mrs. Harrington. "One minute in Trinidad, the next in Missoula, Montana."

"He asked how you were."

"And what did you tell him?"

"The truth," said Jennifer.

"And what might that be?" asked Mrs. Harrington.

"Fine."

"Oh." Mrs. Harrington melted butter in a saucepan, for basting.

"Are you looking forward to the party tonight?" Mrs. Harrington asked.

"Yes," Jennifer said. "As long as there are some kids my age."

Occasional moments it came back to her, and she had to hold on to keep from fainting. Such as when she was sitting on the toilet, in her green bathrobe, among the plants, her pantyhose and underpants around her knees. Suddenly, the horror swept through her again, because in the last six months the simple act of defecation had been so severely obstructed by the disease—something pushing against the intestine.

She held the edges of the toilet with her hands. Pushed. She tried to imagine she was caught in ice, frozen, surrounded by glacial cold, and inside, only numb.

But then, looking at the bathroom cabinet—the rows of pills, the box with the enema, the mouthpiece to keep her from grinding her teeth (fit into her mouth like a handkerchief stuffed in there by a rapist)—it came back to her, all of it.

Roy tossed the noodles with butter and cheese; Jennifer sliced the chicken. A smell of things roasting, rich with herbs, warmed the kitchen.

"Niffer, is there more cheese?"

"Check the pantry."

"I'd get it if I could reach," Ernest said.

Their mother came in. "Looks like you've got everything under control," she said.

"I put paprika on the chicken," Jennifer said.

"I helped with dessert," Ernest said.

"It's true, he helped me operate the blender."

Mrs. Harrington set the table, laid out familiar pieces of stainless steel. One plate was chipped.

"Rat tart!" Roy was shrieking in a high imitation of a feminine voice. He was recounting something he had seen on television to his sister. She was laughing as she tossed salad. Ernest rolled on the floor, gasping, as if he was being tickled. Mrs. Harrington smiled.

They sat down to dinner.

Food made its way around the table—the bowl of noodles, the chicken, the salad. Everyone ate silently for a few minutes, in huge mouthfuls. "Eat more slowly," Mrs. Harrington said.

She wondered where they'd be today if, indeed, she had died. After all, in those frantic first weeks, she had planned for that possibility. Jennifer and Roy, she knew, were old enough to take care of themselves. But her heart went out to Ernest, who had stayed at her breast the longest, born late in life, born after the divorce had come through. Little Ernest—he had lots of colds, and few friends; crybaby, tattletale, once, a teacher told her, even a thief. He sat there across from her, innocent, a noodle hanging from his mouth.

"I wonder if Greg Laurans will be at the party," Jennifer said.

"Why, do you like him?" asked Roy, leering.

"Screw you. He's very involved." Jennifer reached to put a chicken liver she had accidentally taken back on the platter. "He runs a singing group at the state hospital through Young Life."

"Watch out for him, Jennifer," Mrs. Harrington said. "This is just another phase for him. Last year he was stealing cars."

"But he's been born again!" Ernest said loudly. He said everything loudly.

"Talk softer."

"He's reformed," Jennifer said. "But anyway, he won't be there. His parents aren't speaking to him, Gail told me."

Mrs. Harrington didn't blame the Lauranses. They were good Jews —gave a sizable chunk of their income to the UJA. Jennifer played loud music and got low grades; Roy had bad acne, didn't wash enough, smoked a lot of marijuana; but compared to Greg Laurans, they were solid, loving kids, who knew what they wanted and weren't blinded by the insanity of the world.

Jennifer and Roy both knew about the illness—though of course she couldn't tell them "six months," and they never talked about time. She guessed, however, that they guessed what she guessed. Dr. Sanchez had told her, "If you're alive in two years, it won't be a miracle, but if you're not, we can't say it would be unexpected."

Ernest, however, knew nothing. He wasn't old enough. He wouldn't be able to understand. It would be hard enough for him, she had reasoned, after she was gone; at least let him live while he could under the pleasant delusion that she would be there for him forever.

But now, Mrs. Harrington stared across the table at her son, and the reasoning that had kept her going for six months seemed warped, perverse. The way it stood, she would die, for him, as a complete surprise. It might ruin him. He might turn into Greg Laurans. And already she saw signs that worried her.

She knew she would have to tell him soon. In a way that his seven-year-old mind could understand, she would have to explain to him the facts of death.

For in light of new knowledge, she was questioning everything. In those dim months when the doctors themselves, as well as Mrs. Harrington, had stopped thinking about the fact that she was to die, she had become too complacent, she had not made enough plans for what would be left after her. Die. The word struck, and bounced off her skull. Soon, she knew, she would start to get thinner—when the chemotherapy began—and her hair would fall out in greater quantities. She envisioned herself, then, months, or perhaps only weeks from now, so different—bones jutting out of skin, hair in clumps like patches of weeds on a desert. She anticipated great weariness, for she would be lucid, fiercely lucid, and though she would look like death, she would live for the day when once again she would feel well. Her friends would come to see her, frightened, needing reassurance. "You look so tired, Anna," they'd say. Then she would have to explain, it's the radiation, the drugs, it's all to make me better. And when they marauded her, begging that she complete that tantalizing hint of hopefulness so that they could leave her without worry or fear for themselves, she would have to temper their desire for anything in only the middle ranges of despair by pointing out that though she was getting better, she would probably be dead by next Christmas.

Dead by Christmas; she wondered if her children suspected that this would be her last Christmas. Then Jennifer would go to college, Roy and Ernest to her sister in Washington (though her ex-husband would probably fight for a custody she had made sure he would never get; she had at least covered that base).

Now she looked at her children. They ate, they gossiped between bites. Dear God, she thought, how will they get along without me? For if she had died today, they would probably be eating in a friend's kitchen—the Lauranses' or the Lewistons'—in shock, as yet not really believing she was gone. There would be the unfamiliar smell of someone else's cooking, someone else's dinner, another way of making spaghetti sauce. And at home, the unmade bed, her clothes, her *smell* still in the closet, in the bed, lingering a few days, then disappearing from the world forever. Soon Ernest would start to cry for her, and alien arms would take him up. There would be nothing she could do. She would be gone.

They didn't notice anything different. Happily eating, arguing, in the cramped kitchen full of steam and the smell of butter.

"Pass the noodles," Mrs. Harrington said.

"Mom, you never eat noodles."

She dressed in a big, dark gown with an Indian design stitched into it —a birthday present from Jennifer. A life of objects spread out before her—the bed, the television, so many cans of Spaghetti-Os for Ernest. New products in the grocery store. The ads for reducer-suits in *TV Guide*.

"Mom, let's go, we're gonna be late!" Ernest shouted.

"Ern, let's watch 'The Flintstones,' " Jennifer said. To help her mother. She tried to help.

"Is Ernie dressed?" Mrs. Harrington asked.

"Yes, he is."

But when she emerged, perfumed, soft, Ernest didn't want to leave. "Dino's run away," he said.

"We have to go, Ern," Jennifer said. "Don't you want to go to the Lauranses'? Don't you want to see Timmy?"

Ernest started to cry. "I want to watch," he said in a tiny voice.

"All your friends will be at the party," Mrs. Harrington consoled.

"Oh shit," said Roy, "why do you treat him like such a baby when he mopes like this? You're a baby," he said to his brother.

"I am not a baby," Ernest said.

"Babies cry 'cause they can't watch TV 'cause they're going to a party instead. You're a baby."

Ernest's crying got suddenly louder.

"You've done it," Jennifer said.

Thirty minutes later, Dino was safely home, and the Harringtons were on their way. Dry-eyed. "Happy now?" Mrs. Harrington asked.

Jennifer and Ernest climbed into the back. "I hope Timmy's there," Ernest said.

"Can I drive?" Roy asked.

"Not tonight, I'd be scared," Mrs. Harrington said.

"Then can we at least listen to KFRC?" Roy asked.

"Yeah! Maybe they'll have the Police!" Ernest shouted gleefully.

"Okay, sure," said Mrs. Harrington.

"You're in a good mood," said Roy, switching one of the preset buttons to the station he wanted.

They pulled out of the driveway. The dark, warm car filled up with a loud, sad song:

> Why did you have to be a heartbreaker,
> When I was be-ing what you want me to be . . .

Roy beat his hand against the dashboard. He looked funny in his orange shirt and green tie—long hair spilling over corduroy jacket—as if he had never been meant to dress that way and had adjusted the standard male uniform to his particular way of life.

Oh, Mrs. Harrington relished that moment: her children all around her. What amazed her was that she had made them—they wouldn't be who they were, they wouldn't be at all, if it hadn't been for her. Aside from a few sweaters and a large macrame wall hanging, they were her life's artwork. She was proud of them, and fearful.

They turned onto a dark road that twisted up into the hills. From the Lauranses' high window, Mrs. Harrington's house was one of a thousand staggered lights spreading like a sequined dress to the spill of the bay.

The Lauranses had introduced her to a woman who was involved with holistic healing. "Meditate on your cancer," the woman had said. "Imagine it. Visualize it inside of you. Then, imagine it's getting very cold. Imagine the tumors freezing, dying from freezing. Then, a wind chips at them until they disappear."

"Oh," Mrs. Harrington said, overcome again. "Oh."

"Mom, what's wrong?" Roy asked her. In the dark car, concern seemed to light up his face. She could only look at him for a second because the road was curving up to meet her stare.

"Nothing," she said. "I'm sorry. Just a little pensive tonight, that's all."

But in her mind she could see Dr. Sanchez's hairy hands.

The party was already in full swing when they arrived. All over the Lauranses' carpeted living room the clink of drinks sounded, a slow, steady murmur of conversation. Ernest held Mrs. Harrington's hand.

She lost Jennifer and Roy instantly, lost them to the crowd, to their friends. Suddenly. They were on their own, moving in among the guests, who said hello, asked them what their plans were. They smiled. They were good kids, eager to find their friends.

"Hey, Harrington!" she heard a gravelly adolescent voice call, and Roy was gone. Jennifer lost as well, to the collegiate generation—a boy just back from Princeton.

Mrs. Harrington's friends the Lewistons were the first to greet her. Mr. Lewiston had taught in the law school with Mrs. Harrington's ex-husband, and they had remained friends.

"How are you feeling, Anna?"

"How're the kids?"

"You know, anything we can do to help."

She motioned toward Ernest with her eyes, don't talk about it. Ernest, who had not been listening, asked, "Where's Timmy?"

"Timmy and Kevin and Danielle are in the family room playing," Mrs. Lewiston said. "Would you like to join them?"

"Kevin!" Ernest turned to his mother, his eyes and mouth breaking. There was a red sore on his chin from drool.

He started to cry.

"Ernie, baby, what's wrong?" Mrs. Harrington said, picking him up, hugging him fiercely.

"I don't like Kevin," Ernest sobbed. "He's mean to me."

Kevin was the Lewistons' son. As a baby, he had been on commercials.

And the Lewistons looked at Mrs. Harrington in vague horror.

"When was he mean to you?" Mrs. Harrington asked.

"The other day on the bus. He threw—um, he threw—he took my lunch and he threw it at me and it got broken. My thermos."

Mrs. Harrington looked at the Lewistons, for a brief moment accusingly, but she quickly changed her look to one of bewilderment.

"He did come home the other day with his thermos broken. Ernest, you told me you dropped it."

"Kevin told me not to tell. He—he said he'd beat me up."

"Look, Anna, how can you—how can you think . . ." Mrs. Lewiston couldn't complete her sentence. "I'll get Kevin," she said. "Your son's accused him of something he'd never do."

She ran off toward the family room.

"Anna, are you sure Ernest's not making all this up?" Mr. Lewiston asked.

"Are you accusing him of lying?" Mrs. Harrington said.

"Look, we're adults. Let's keep cool. I'm sure there's an explanation to all of this." Mr. Lewiston took out a handkerchief and swatted at his face.

Ernest was still crying when Mrs. Lewiston came back, dragging Kevin by the arm.

Ernest wailed. Mrs. Laurans, the hostess, came over to find out what was causing such a commotion. She ushered the families into the master bedroom to have it out.

"Kevin," Mr. Lewiston said, seating his son on top of forty or fifty coats piled on the bed, "Ernest has accused you of doing something very bad—of taking his lunch and hitting him with it. Is this true? Don't lie to me."

"Bill, how can you talk to him that way?" Mrs. Lewiston cried. "You're never that way with him."

Kevin, a handsome, well-dressed child, began to cry. The adults stood among their sobbing children.

"Oh dear," Mrs. Harrington said. Then she laughed just a little.

Mrs. Lewiston took her lead, and laughed too. The tension broke.

But Mr. Lewiston, overcome by guilt for treating his son badly, was holding Kevin, and begging his forgiveness.

Mrs. Harrington knew what that was like. She also knew that Ernest had lied before. She led him over to the corner.

"Did you make that story up, Ernest?" she asked him.

"No."

"Tell the truth."

"I didn't," Ernest said.

"Kevin says you did," Mrs. Harrington said with infinite gentleness.

"He's lying."

"You can't pretend with me, young man." Her voice grew stern. "Look, I want the truth."

Sternly, she lifted up his chin so that his eyes met hers; she was on her knees. For a moment, he looked as if he might once again break out in full-fledged sobs. But Ernest changed his mind.

"All right," he said. "He didn't throw it at me. But he took it."

"I gave it back!" Kevin yelled. "I threw it to you, and you dropped it and the thermos broke!"

"Ah!" all the parents said at once.

"Two parties misinterpret the same incident. Happens all the time in the courts. I teach about it in my class," Mr. Lewiston said. Everyone laughed.

"Now, Mrs. Harrington, I think both these young men owe each other an apology, don't you? Kevin for taking Ernest's lunch, and Ernest for saying he threw it at him."

"Boys," Mrs. Harrington said, "will you shake hands and make up?"
The children eyed each other suspiciously.

"Come on," Mr. Lewiston said to Kevin. "Be a good cowboy, pard-
ner."

Kevin, like a good cowboy, reached out a swaggering arm. Sheep-
ishly, Ernest accepted it. They shook.

"All right, all right," Mrs. Lewiston said. "Now why don't you two
go play with Timmy and Danielle?"

"Okay," Kevin said. The two ran off.

"And we'll all get a drink," Mr. Lewiston said.

The adults emerged from the bedroom and made their way through
the crowd. All of them were relieved not to have to face the possibility
that one of their children had done something consciously malicious.
But Mrs. Harrington had to admit that, of the two, Ernest had come
off the more childish, the less spirited. Kevin Lewiston was energetic,
attractive. He had spirit—took lunch boxes but gave them back, would
go far in life. Ernest cried all the time, made more enemies than
friends, kept grudges.

Small children, dressed in their best, darted between and among
adult legs. Mrs. Harrington, separated from the Lewistons by a dashing
three-year-old girl, found herself in front of a half-empty bowl of
chopped liver.

A trio of women whose names she didn't remember greeted her, but
they didn't remember her name either, so it was all right. They were
talking about their children. One turned out to be the mother of the
boy from Princeton. "Charlie spent the past summer working in a
senator's office," she told the other women, who were impressed.

"What's your daughter doing next summer?" the woman asked Mrs.
Harrington.

"Oh, probably doing what she did last summer, working at Kentucky
Fried Chicken." Or, perhaps, living in another town.

The ladies made noises of approval. Then, looking over their heads
to the crowd to see if her children were within earshot, Mrs. Harrington saw someone she had no desire to talk to.

"Excuse me," she hurriedly told the women. But it was too late.

"Anna!"

Joan Lensky had seen her; now she was done for. The old woman,
her black hair tied tightly behind her head, dressed (as always) in black,
was coming to greet her.

"Anna, darling," she said, grasping Mrs. Harrington's hand between sharp fingers, "I'm so glad to see you could come out."

"Yes, well, I'm feeling quite well, Joan," Mrs. Harrington said.

"It's been so long. Are you really well? Let's chat. There's a room over there we can go to and talk privately."

Regretfully, Mrs. Harrington was pulled away from the crowd into an empty room. She did not enjoy talking to Joan Lensky; the details of their histories, at least on the surface, bore too much resemblance to each other. Up until his death, Joan's husband had been famous for making advances to his female graduate students—so often, and so clumsily, that his lechery had become a joke at the faculty wives' teas. Mrs. Harrington's husband was more serious; he left her suddenly and flatly for a law student, quit his job, and moved with her to Italy. After that Mrs. Harrington stopped going to the faculty wives' teas, though most of the wives remained steadfastly loyal—none more so than Joan, who seized on the wronged Mrs. Harrington as a confidante. It made Mrs. Harrington nervous to realize how much she knew about Joan's life that Joan herself didn't know—Joan, with her black poodles, her immaculate kitchen. Nevertheless, she put up with this demanding friendship for many years, chiefly because she felt sorry for the old woman, who seemed to need so badly to feel sorry for her. When she got sick she changed her priorities. Now she only saw Joan when she had to.

"Tell me, then, how are you?" Mrs. Lensky asked her gravely. They were sitting on an Ultrasuede sofa in a small sitting room, close together. Mrs. Harrington could feel Mrs. Lensky's breath blowing on her face.

"I'm all right. I feel well. The kids are doing fine."

"No, no, Anna," Mrs. Lensky said, shaking her head emphatically. "How *are* you?"

She couldn't put off the inevitable any longer.

"All right. I'm on the tail end of radiation therapy. It's having a fifty percent effectiveness rate."

"Oh, you poor, poor dear," Mrs. Lensky said. "Is there much pain?"

"No."

"And your hair? Is that a wig?"

"No, I have it specially cut."

Mrs. Lensky looked toward the ceiling and closed her eyes rapturously.

"You are so lucky, my dear Anna, you don't know," she said. "My sister has a friend who is going through terrible ordeals with the radiation. All her hair. She weighs seventy pounds. Terrible. Don't let them increase your dose! Or that awful chemotherapy!"

"All right," Mrs. Harrington said.

"You must avoid chemotherapy. I know a woman who died from it. They said it was the treatment that killed her, because it was worse than the disease. Another woman I know was so sick she had to stay in bed for three months. She's still so pale. Also, during surgery make sure they don't leave any of their sponges inside your stomach . . ."

Mrs. Harrington counted her breaths, thought, it's all she has to live for, other people's sorrows to compare with her own.

"Have you heard from Roy? Is he still married to that child?"

"Yes," Mrs. Harrington said. "He is. She's actually very nice. They're quite happy."

Mrs. Lensky nodded. Then she moved even closer to Mrs. Harrington, to deliver some even greater confidence.

"I heard of an organization I thought you would want to know about," she said. "It arranges for . . . things . . . before you go. So that your children won't have to worry about it. I'm a member. The dues aren't heavy, and they take care of everything . . . just everything."

She handed Mrs. Harrington a small slip of paper that she had produced from her purse. "That's all you need to know," she said.

At that moment, thank heavens, the door opened.

Jennifer had come to rescue her mother. To help her out.

"Mom, I need to talk to you," she said.

"I'm sorry, Joan," Mrs. Harrington said, standing. "We'll talk."

"Thank you for rescuing me," Mrs. Harrington whispered to her daughter.

"Mom, you're not going to believe it," Jennifer said. "Greg Laurans is here. And he brought . . . those people with him."

"You mean from Young Life?"

"Them . . . and some others."

In the dining room, the mass of guests had separated into small clumps, all engaged in *not* looking at the sunken bowl of the living room, *not* listening to the music rising up from it.

Mrs. Harrington glanced down curiously. Seated around the fireplace, by the Christmas tree, were Greg and a group of cherubic young people, all clean-cut, wearing little gold glasses and down vests. One had a guitar, and they were singing:

> *And she draws dragons*
> *And dreams become real*
> *And she draws dragons*
> *To show how she feels*

Mrs. Harrington looked behind her. Mrs. Laurans was dropping an olive into a martini; *this,* she thought, is cruel and unusual punishment.

Then she noticed the others. There were three of them. Two boys, dressed neatly in sweaters. One had dark blond hair and round eyes. Occasionally the girl next to him had to take his chin between her thumb and forefinger and wipe it with a Kleenex. The other boy was darker, squatter, and could not seem to keep his head up. Every few minutes, the girl with the Kleenex would lift up his chin and he would look around himself curiously, like a child held before an aquarium. Near them was a dwarf girl with a deformed head, too large, the shape of an ostrich egg, and half of it forehead, so that the big eyes seemed to be set unnaturally low. Yet they were alert eyes, more focused than those of the boys. From the corner where they were gathered, the three sang along:

> *An se dwaw daguhs*
> *And de becuh ree*
> *An se dwaw daguhs*
> *Ta so ha se fee*

"They're from the state hospital," Jennifer told her mother. "They'll probably live there all their lives. It was really amazing that they let them go to come here. It's incredibly nice, really, even though it's pretty horrifying for us."

"And for Greg's mother," Mrs. Harrington said, distantly.

She stared down at the circle of singers. Now some of them were shoving pieces of paper and crayons into the invalids' hands.

> *And she draws unicorns*
> *And makes us all free*
> *(An se dwaw oonicaws)*

"Come on," the pretty young people were saying. "Draw a daguh. Draw an oonicaw."

And after this, how would it be for them, to return to the wards?

"This is the cruelest thing of all," Mrs. Harrington said to her daughter.

She turned around again, but Mrs. Laurans had disappeared. Quickly she walked toward the bedroom. She rapped on the door, opened it. Ursula Laurans lay on her bed, on top of fifty or sixty coats, crying.

Mrs. Harrington sat down next to her, rubbed her back.

"I'm sorry, Ursie. I'm sorry," she said.

"Why does he do this to me?" Mrs. Laurans asked. "He was getting so much better, he went to synagogue. For Christ's sake, he was a physics major, a goddamn physics major. Then one day he comes home and he tells me he's found Jesus. He tries to convert *us*, his parents. You don't know how it upset Ted. He tried to argue with him. He wouldn't even accept the theory of evolution. A physics major! He thinks everything in the Bible is true! And now this."

"I'm sorry, Ursie," Mrs. Harrington said.

Ted Laurans entered the room. "Oh God," he said to his wife. "Oh God. I'll kill him. How can he do this?"

"Shut up," Ursula said. "It's futile. You gave him all this bullshit already, about questioning. He's beyond reason."

Why were they telling her this? Mrs. Harrington tried to be comforting. "Oh, Ursie," she said.

Then, very suddenly, Ursula Laurans launched up and landed against Mrs. Harrington. She fell against her, dead weight, cold and heavy. Mrs. Harrington's arms went around her instinctively.

Ted Laurans was crying too. Standing and crying, softly, his hand over his face, the way men usually do.

"Maybe this is his way of trying to re-establish a relationship," Mrs. Harrington offered. "It's very kind, bringing them here. No other person would have done it."

"It's all aggression," Ursula said. "We've been seeing a family therapist. It's all too clear. I wasn't enough of a mother to him, so he took the first maternal substitute he came across."

Mrs. Harrington chose not to say anything more. Soon Ted Laurans ran into the bathroom, leaving the two women alone with the coats.

Eventually, Mrs. Harrington emerged. Many of the guests were leaving; in the kitchen she bumped into the dwarf girl, who was washing a glass in the sink with remarkable expertise despite the fact that her chin barely reached the counter.

"Excuse me," she said quite clearly. "I get under people's feet a lot."

They both laughed. The dwarf girl smiled pleasantly at her, and Mrs. Harrington was glad to see that she had the capacity to smile. The dwarf girl wore a houndstooth dress specially tailored for her squat body, and fake pearls. She had large breasts, which surprised Mrs. Harrington; she wore a gold necklace and a little ring on one of her fingers. Obviously she wasn't as retarded as the two boys.

Mrs. Harrington turned around to look for her children. Then Ernest ran into the kitchen. He was crying again. He held his arms out, and she lifted him up. "Oh, Ernie, you'll get sick from so much crying," she said.

"I want to go home," Ernest said.

"What's wrong? Didn't you have fun?"

"They ditched me."

"Oh, Ernie."

Three little children, two boys and a girl, ran into the kitchen, laughing, stumbling. As if she were a red light, they screeched to a halt at Mrs. Harrington's feet. "Ernie, you don't want to play anymore?" Kevin Lewiston asked. All the children's faces stared up, vaguely disturbed.

"Go away!" Ernest screamed, turning in to his mother's shoulder.

"All right, that's enough," Mrs. Harrington said. "I think you kids better find your parents."

"Yes, ma'am," they said in unison. Then all three ran out of the room.

Mrs. Harrington was left in the kitchen, holding her child like a bag of wet laundry. He would probably want to sleep in her bed tonight, as he did all those nights he had to wear the eye patch, to deflect lazy left eye syndrome. "We'll go home, Ernie," she said to him. Then she noticed the dwarf girl. She was still standing by the sink, staring up at her.

"Roy's in the bedroom with some boys and they're smoking pot," Ernie mumbled to Mrs. Harrington's shoulder, which was now soaked through with tears and drool.

"Don't be a tattletale," Mrs. Harrington whispered.

She looked down at the dwarf girl, who looked up at her. The dwarf girl held a glass of water in her tiny fat hand; the owl eyes in the huge head seemed gentle, almost pretty; in the bright light of the kitchen, she wore an expression that could have indicated extreme stupidity, or great knowledge.

Unmoving, the dwarf girl stared at Mrs. Harrington, as if the big woman were a curiosity, or a comrade in sorrow.

CONVENIENCES

EDITH PEARLMAN

Edith Pearlman's stories have been published in *Ascent, The Massachusetts Review, Redbook, Seventeen,* and other magazines. Her essays and opinion pieces have been published in *Ms,* the *Boston Globe,* the *Boston Herald,* and elsewhere. She appears occasionally on public TV. An earlier story, "Hanging Fire," received an O. Henry award in 1978. She lives in Brookline, Massachusetts, with her husband and children.

Amanda Jenkins was having a little trouble with her article, *Connubis.*

"*Not* cannabis," she explained to Frieda, the girl from downstairs. "Heavens, child, do you think anybody would read yet another dissertation on grass? Be your age."

"I'd rather be yours," said Frieda, who was fifteen to Amanda's twenty. "What's *connubis?*"

Amanda hesitated. Ben Stewart, eavesdropping from the bedroom, could hear for a few moments only the sound of crockery being stacked. He and Amanda had agreed that dishes would be her task, laundry his. Now, at five-thirty in the afternoon, she and her young friend were washing last night's plates, which had lain odorously in the sink all day.

"Connubis," Amanda resumed, "a coined word, refers to being married. Or being as if married."

"Like you and Ben," said Frieda.

"More or less."

Ben wondered why she was so wary. They were indeed living together as if married, a conventional enough arrangement these days. Only the difference between their ages was exceptional. But that difference was a mere ten years . . .

"Actually," Amanda was saying, "I am not Benjamin's lover but his daughter . . ."

Copyright © 1982 by Ascent Corporation. First appeared in *Ascent.* Reprinted by permission.

"Stop it," sighed Frieda.

"His niece," Amanda smoothly corrected. "By marriage," she further invented. "His relationship with my aunt soured considerably when he fell in love with me. We eloped. Now we live in fear of detection. If a large weeping gray-haired woman should one day appear —Ben's wife, my aunt, is a great deal older than he—please tell her . . ."

She paused. Frieda waited. Ben waited, too.

"Tell her what?" said Frieda at last.

"To peddle her vapors," said Amanda triumphantly.

"Mandy!" shouted Ben.

She appeared in the bedroom doorway, curly-haired and ardent. Her tee shirt said: AUTEUR.

"Please stop feeding nonsense to poor Frieda," said Ben. "What will she think?"

Amanda moved closer to the bed. "She'll discount the nonsense and think what she already thinks. That we're libertines."

"Ah. And are we that?"

"I don't know. What are we, Benjy?"

Ben considered the question. He himself—dark, thickset, Brooklyn-born—was a respectful sort of person. Particularly did he respect Amanda, whose upright Maine family he also respected. Once, years ago, he had loved her older sister, presently married. Now he loved Amanda, but in a cousinly way.

And impudent Amanda—what was she? At the least, an excellent student of literature. He wished that the college kids he taught were as clever.

"I am a conformist," he said, illustrating his words by curving his hand around her breast. She giggled. He muzzled the Auteur, then put his chin into her curls. He noticed that her double stood in the doorway. Frieda's tee shirt read GODOLPHIN HIGH.

"But, Frieda, you don't even live in Godolphin," Ben remarked across Amanda's head.

"The shirt belongs to my cousin," Frieda said with her usual blush.

Godolphin was the town—really a wedge of Boston—in which Ben, who worked in New York, and Amanda, who went to school in Pennsylvania, had elected to spend the summer. They had sublet a snug apartment at the top of a three-decker house. On the first floor lived an old couple, and on the second lived Frieda's aunt, a divorcee with a son at camp. This aunt exhausted herself day and night in her antique store. Frieda herself was a child of Manhattan. Her parents, both art historians, were spending their summer in Italy, and Frieda had chosen Godolphin over *I Tatti.*

Now Ben said gravely to Frieda, "Your cousin would not recognize his garment."

Amanda was on her feet again, "Come into the kitchen with us, Ben," she said agreeably. "Have you been asleep all afternoon?"

Ben got out of bed. "I'll be with you in a minute."

He used the bathroom, then paused in the dining room. He and Amanda were in the habit of eating at the round table in the kitchen and reserving the heavy oak table in the dining room for work. Their two typewriters, one at either end, looked like combatants. Each machine was surrounded by papers and books, Ben's piles orderly, Amanda's in disarray. Though he had no intention of working at this hour, Ben sat down in front of his typewriter in order to groan.

Frieda had an affinity for jambs. Now she stood aslant between kitchen and dining room. "What are *you* writing about?"

"Hawthorne," he said. "The first novel," he expanded. "Name of *Fanshawe,*" he summed up.

She waited for a while. "Oh," she said. "I haven't read any Hawthorne."

"Do so soon."

"*Fanshawe.* A book of Gothic posturing," Amanda called from the kitchen. "But the setting is excellent. And there are a couple of more or less comic characters. I find Hawthorne a not-bad writer."

"Hawthorne is grateful," muttered Ben.

"What are you going to say about *Fanshawe?*" asked Frieda.

Ben wished he knew. "I wish I could tell you," he said. "But reticence is essential to the scholar. Ideas have to be nurtured in the dark silence of the mind before they can live in the bright light of discourse. When they can bear your intelligent scrutiny I will reveal them." He went on in this vein for some time, unable to stop. Finally Amanda called him in to dinner.

"Will you stay, Frieda?" she said with her beautiful smile. "Your aunt's at the store tonight."

Frieda did not have to be asked twice.

In the kitchen hung some plants that had been in beautiful condition a few weeks ago. The framed squares of needlepoint on the walls were the work of Mrs. Cunningham, from whom, through the proxy of Frieda's aunt, Ben and Amanda had subrented the apartment. Mr. and

Mrs. Cunningham, both school teachers, had gone to Iowa for the summer.

"What are the Cunninghams like?" Amanda asked as she served the tuna fish salad.

"I arrived only a week before they left," said Frieda cautiously.

"Tell us your impressions."

Frieda cleared her throat. "Clean and tidy and traditional."

"All those china cats in the living room," agreed Ben. He helped himself to a carrot. "Couldn't you have scraped this, Amanda? When it's my turn to do dinner I always scrape the carrots."

"I forgot."

"I never forget."

"But you often forget to flush the toilet," she reminded him sweetly.

Ben addressed Frieda. "The Cunninghams, I am persuaded, never argue . . ."

"I don't know."

". . . for she has her needlepoint, and he has his *Time*. Such mutuality. Theirs is a marriage of two minds. Did you remember to pick up some strawberries, Amanda?"

"Have a pickle," said Amanda. "Mutuality is exactly the point I was trying to clarify last night. Mutuality isn't the least bit important in marriage, Ben. It counts only in romance. Marriage has no truck with the smarmy mutual gratification that you have just attempted to extol by sarcastic, by sarcastic . . ."

"Implication?"

"Implication. The idea in my article, *Connubis*, is that . . ."

"Will the idea bear scrutiny?" asked Frieda. "Will it live in the light of day?"

"Of course. I'm beginning to realize that conventional wisdom about the reasons for marriage is out-of-date. Like most conventional wisdom. People do not marry for security any more. Security is provided by the welfare state."

"But we live under capitalism," said Frieda.

"Maybe you do at the Brearley School for Girls. The rest of the country is on welfare. In some form. Where was I? Oh yes, security. Security is out. And people don't marry for status, either, because marriage no longer confers it. Nor do they marry for sexual satisfaction, because anybody can attain that at any time . . ."

"I hadn't noticed," said Ben, looking hard at her.

". . . as easily single as wed," she blandly went on.

"So why should a person get married?" asked Frieda.

Amanda considered the question. Ben meanwhile thought of Hawthorne's wedded contentment. Finally Amanda answered, "There are two creditable reasons to get married. Financial and dynastic."

Frieda said, "Financial? You told me we were already secure."

"Secure isn't prosperous."

"Dynastic?" wondered Ben.

Amanda turned on him one of her shining gazes. "Think of it! To raise a family a couple need not be passionate. They need not even be compatible."

"Need they be of different sexes?"

She waved an impatient hand. "They *must* be, as a pair, complete. Whatever they want for themselves and their progeny has to be provided by one or the other. If my family has influence, yours had better have cash. If I am worldly wise, you had better be empathetic . . ."

"Empathic."

". . . and so on. We choose each other on the basis of the needs of the future family rather than our personal desires. Those we satisfy elsewhere . . . The *mariage de convenance!* That's it, in a word."

"In a phrase," corrected Ben. "The old *mariage de convenance* had nothing to do with love."

"Neither will the new."

Ben gave his pretty paramour a long look. Did she believe this stuff? Or were she and her sidekick playing some deep, female game?

He knew he would not marry her. He was proud of her, and he enjoyed her company, but she was not what he had in mind as lifetime partner. For her part, Amanda claimed loftily that she was employing him to guide her through earthly delights. They would emerge from the summer as warm friends, nothing more. After college she intended to embark on an adventurous career. She would live amid palaces, and also dung.

" 'Life is made up of marble and mud,' " he had quoted softly.

"Hawthorne?"

"Hawthorne."

"Hawthorne was right."

She was in some ways as green as Frieda. Now he looked across the table at the two sweet faces, Frieda's still vague under a cloud of hair, Mandy's excited. Her dancing eyes showed that she considered her new theory to be revealed truth. He knew she would not rest until she had revealed it to others. It had been base of him to suspect her of clever

falseness. Oh, her Yankee honesty! And, oh, his Brooklyn suspicious-
ness. Such a misalliance. And what on earth were the two of them
doing here, messing up the Cunninghams' place and overstimulating
the worshipful Frieda? His stomach rumbled, as if in protest.

"What have we for dessert?" he formally inquired.

"For dessert," Amanda told him, "we have nothing."

The summer wore on. Amanda went every day to her typist's job at
the offices of the Godolphin Weekly *Gazette.* Then she came home to
work on her article, which was going better. Ben taught his two courses
at the University, and then came home to work on *his* article. Frieda
continued to hang around their doorways.

Connubis got retitled *Mariage de Convenance.* Amanda had con-
ceived of it as an intelligent young woman's guide to marriage customs
past and present. But it was now a manifesto, a call to common sense.

"If marriage does not confer an advantage," she declared one night,
"it should not be undertaken. The new woman must not wed for sentimental reasons."

"I think the dinner is burning," said Frieda.

Mandy took the pot off the stove and served the baked beans. When
they were all eating she continued.

"The Roman custom of *concubinitas* might have demeaned the in-
stitution of marriage, but it didn't demean the participants. However,
dignitas, despite its name, was exploitative. The woman was expected
to bear children, and she and the children were under the *potestas* of
the male. As for the trustee marriage in the Dark Ages, it is being
revived today in the much-touted 'extended family.' But the eager
beavers who want to restore and strengthen the extended family don't
realize that the trustee system involved blood vengeance, bride purchase, and sometimes bride theft."

Silence from her companions. Finally Ben said, "Take out 'eager
beavers.' "

"What? I was just making conversation."

"You were quoting non-stop."

A hand fluttered to her curls. "Oh, was I?"

"These beans are awful," said Frieda.

United for once, her hosts glared at her.

"I was just making conversation," protested Frieda. "Listen, tomorrow night I'll do the cooking."

Soon she was making their breakfasts as well as their dinners, running up early in the morning to start coffee. Amanda and Ben enjoyed sleeping late. Frieda cleaned up, too. Ben liked coming home to a well-kept apartment. Each afternoon he sat down at his dusted typewriter with a vigorous feeling. Worthy pages began to pile up on the table beside the machine. He felt more and more benevolent towards Hawthorne's first novel. The great author himself had repudiated *Fanshawe* —had even cast all available copies into the flames—but he, Dr. B. Stewart, would rescue the work, would reveal it as the precursor, however flawed, of the later masterpieces.

It was a help on these afternoons to know that there was a bowl of strawberries in the refrigerator, and a pound cake on the counter. Frieda herself was never in the way.

"All daughters should be like you," said Ben one night.

Frieda flushed. Amanda frowned at Ben.

"All younger sisters, I mean," he said, getting the same response. "Silent partners? What do you consider yourself, toots?"

"A helpmeet," she said.

"Like Phoebe in *Seven Gables?*"

"Yes." She had been doing her homework.

Every Friday the three of them went out for pizza and a movie. Every Tuesday Frieda went off with her aunt to visit another aunt, and Amanda and Ben were left to amuse themselves. They took the girl's absence with the same good nature as they took her presence. Sometimes they talked about her devotion to them.

"She adores you," said Amanda.

"She adores you," returned Ben politely.

"She adores us both. My exuberance. Your scholarly wit. It's wonderful, being adored. But whatever will Frieda do back on West End Avenue with those two esthetes her parents?"

"I'll call her every so often," said Ben. "I'll come up from the Village and treat her to a concert. I'll buy her tea afterwards, like an uncle."

"Where?" asked Amanda.

"At the Palm Court," said the expansive Ben.

"Will you really do that for Frieda?" asked Amanda unjealously.

It was midnight. They had just made love. Mandy in a long nightshirt sat on the porch glider looking at the moonlit streetscape of three-decker houses, each with its maple tree. Ben kissed her, then stood up with his back to the scene and leaned against the railing. "I don't know if I'll really do anything for Frieda." He yawned. "I can't look past this moment."

But that was untrue. He was looking past this moment at this moment. Gazing at the tumbled young woman before him he could see clearly another version of that young woman, wearing a cap and blazer as befitted a college girl. The maples were yellowing. Amanda waved good-bye. He saw himself, also purposefully clad, headed back to New York and the intense, exophthalmic psychiatric social worker whom destiny no doubt had in store for him. He groaned.

"We'll always be friends," Amanda soulfully promised.

It became Ben's turn to do the dinner table lectures.

"Hawthorne had a surprisingly gloomy view of life, considering how conventionally domiciled he was. That supportive wife, those devoted children. Yet his point of view remains tragic. Especially in *The Marble Faun*, with its plot of murder and paganism, its theme of sin and suffering, does he . . ."

"Supportive wife?" Amanda sniffed. "Sophia Hawthorne was a milksop, if you ask me. Letting him wallow in free love at Brook Farm while she waited celibately in Salem."

"There is no indication of sexual irregularity in the Brook Farm documents."

"I can read between the lines."

"Nathaniel considered himself saved by his marriage."

"Sophia knew herself ruined."

"They went off to Italy, didn't they?" Frieda said. "What a pair of nitwits. Please have some more bouillabaisse."

Ben considered arguing further but chose the bouillabaisse instead. Mandy's sassy comments did serve to illuminate the novels, in which placid arrangements within the house were threatened by the turbulence without. Only away from the hearth could the moral order be upset. This seemed particularly true of *Fanshawe*, which was now revealed to him as a morality tale: domestic continuity triumphing over unregulated passion. Afternoons, sitting in the Cunninghams' dining room, Ben felt the rightness of his position. In their comfortable place it was possible for him to gaze long and hard at Hawthorne's devils. Frieda's lemonade helped, too.

The summer was drawing to a close. Late one hot August night Ben and Amanda sat on the porch drinking wine and watching the stars over the three-deckers. Amanda was on the glider, Ben on a canvas chair.

For a while they were silent. Then: "We've been happy here," Amanda began.

"Of late we have not been miserable," Ben allowed.

"So happy," she said again.

He refrained from further comment.

"But would you mind terribly if I left a bit earlier than we'd planned? Say just before Labor Day Weekend? Because I have an invitation."

He examined his heart. Certainly there was a twinge. "An invitation? From that self-centered jackass you see at school, I suppose. He's back from abroad?"

"His family has the loveliest house at the Vineyard. Would you mind, Ben?"

Well, would he? Her eyes glittered at him. Oh the darling. "I'll mind a little," Ben said truthfully. "But I myself have an invitation to Fire Island," he lied. "So go, sweetheart."

"Come sit beside me," came her soft voice.

He found his way to the glider. He slipped an arm around her shoulders. " 'What we did had a consecration of its own,' " he whispered.

"Poor Hester."

"We *have* been happy here," he said.

"Like an old married couple," she said.

"Or a brother and sister."

"It's the same thing. The best marriages have a strong incestuous component."

"Is that so?" he murmured into the side of her neck.

"That's so. The best marriages have complementarity rather than similarity. The best marriages have a sense of the past as well as a sense of the future. The best marriages . . ."

"The best marriages," said Ben, suddenly enlightened, "have a maid."

Frieda hated to cry. Instead she was baking a Queen of Sheba cake.

"I thought you'd get married," she loudly complained, "and here you are splitting. You've ruined my summer."

"Shh," said Amanda. "Ben is trying to work."

Ben, in the living room, set up a corroborating clatter on the keys. Then he resumed his eavesdropping.

". . . madwomen in the family, and certain inherited disorders in Ben's," Amanda was explaining. "Gingivitis, that sort of thing. No, no, it would have been impossible. Not to mention illegal, Ben being already married to my aunt."

"Shove it," said Frieda.

"The place looks wonderful," Amanda went on. "I hope the Cunninghams are grateful. We certainly are. We'll miss you."

"Won't you miss each other?"

"Oh, excessively!" said Amanda, forcing Ben the didact to shout "Exceedingly!", after which he rushed into the kitchen and with promiscuous joy embraced both his girls.

ALASKA

ALICE ADAMS

Alice Adams grew up in Chapel Hill, North Carolina, and graduated from Radcliffe; since then she has lived mostly in San Francisco. Her fourth novel, *Rich Rewards*, was published by Knopf in 1980, and a collection of short stories, *To See You Again*, was published in the spring of 1982. She has a new novel, *Superior Women*, coming out this fall.

Although Mrs. Lawson does not drink any more, not a drop since New Year's Day, 1961, in Juneau, Alaska, she sometimes feels a confusion in her mind about which husband she will meet, at the end of the day. She has been married five times, and she has lived, it seems to her, almost everywhere. Now she is a cleaning lady, in San Francisco, although some might say that she is too old for that kind of work. Her hair, for so many years dyed red, is now streaky gray, and her eyes are a paler blue than they once were. Her skin is a dark bronze color, but she thinks of herself as Negro—Black, these days. From New Orleans, originally.

If someone came up and asked her, Who are you married to now, Lucille Lawson? of course she would answer, Charles, and we live in the Western Addition in San Francisco, two busses to get there from here.

But, not asked, she feels the presences of those other husbands— nameless, shadowy, lurking near the edges of her mind. And menacing, most of them, especially the one who tromped her in Juneau, that New Year's Day. He was the worst, by far, but none of them was worth a whole lot, come to think of it. And she was always working at one place or another, and always tired, at the end of her days, and then there were those husbands to come home to, and more work to do for them. Some husbands come honking for you in their cars, she remembers, but

Copyright © 1983 by Washington and Lee University. First appeared in *Shenandoah: The Washington and Lee University Review*. Reprinted by permission.

usually you have to travel a long way, busses and street cars, to get to where they are, to where you and them live.

These days Mrs. Lawson just cleans for Miss Goldstein, a rich white lady older than Mrs. Lawson is, who lives alone in a big house on Divisadero Street, near Union. She has lots of visitors, some coming to stay, all funny looking folk. Many foreign, but not fancy. Miss Goldstein still travels a lot herself, to peculiar places like China and Cuba and Africa.

What Mrs. Lawson is best at is polishing silver, and that is what she mostly does, the tea service, coffee service, and all the flatware, although more than once Miss Goldstein has sighed and said that maybe it should all be put away, or melted down to help the poor people in some of the places she visits; all that silver around looks boastful, Miss Goldstein thinks. But it is something for Mrs. Lawson to do every day (Miss Goldstein does not come right out and say this; they both just know).

Along with the silver polishing she dusts, and sometimes she irons a little, some silk or linen shirts; Miss Goldstein does not get dressed up a lot, usually favoring sweaters and old pants. She gets the most dressed up when she is going off to march somewhere, which she does fairly often. Then she gets all gussied up in a black suit and her real pearls, and she has these posters to carry, NO NUKES IS GOOD NUKES, GRAY PANTHERS FOR PEACE. She would be a sight to behold, Mrs. Lawson thinks: she can hardly imagine Miss Goldstein with all the kinds of folks that are usually in those lines, the beards and raggedy blue jeans, the dirty old sweat shirts, big women wearing no bras. Thin, white-haired Miss Goldstein in her pearls.

To help with the heavy housework, the kitchen floor and the stove, bathtubs and all like that, Miss Goldstein has hired a young white girl, Gloria. At first Mrs. Lawson was mistrustful that a girl like that could clean anything, a blonde-haired small little girl with these doll blue eyes in some kind of a white pants work outfit, but Gloria moves through that big house like a little bolt of white lightning, and she leaves everything behind her *clean*. Even with her eyesight not as good as it was Mrs. Lawson can see how clean the kitchen floor and the stove are, and the bathtubs. And she has *looked*.

Gloria comes at eight every morning, and she does all that in just two hours. Mrs. Lawson usually gets in sometime after nine, depending on how the busses run. And so there is some time when they are both working along, Mrs. Lawson at the sink with the silver, probably, or dusting off Miss Goldstein's bureau, dusting her books—and Gloria down on her knees on the bathroom floor (Gloria is right; the only way to clean a floor is on your knees, although not too many folks seem to know that, these days). Of course they don't talk much, both working, but Gloria has about twenty minutes before her next job, in that same neighborhood. Sometimes, then, Mrs. Lawson will take a break from her polishing, dusting, and heat up some coffee for the both of them, and they will talk a little. Gloria has a lot of worries, a lot on her mind, Mrs. Lawson can tell, although Gloria never actually says, beyond everyone's usual troubles, money and rent and groceries, and in Gloria's case car repairs, an old VW.

The two women are not friends, really, but all things considered they get along okay. Some days they don't either of them feel like talking, and they both just skim over sections of the newspaper, making comments on this and that, in the news. Other times they talk a little.

Gloria likes to hear about New Orleans, in the old days, when Mrs. Lawson's father had a drugstore and did a lot of doctoring there, and how later they all moved to Texas, and the Klan came after them, and they hid and moved again, to another town. And Gloria tells Mrs. Lawson how her sister is ashamed that she cleans houses for a living. The sister, Sharon, lives up in Alaska, but not in Juneau, where Mrs. Lawson lived. Gloria's sister lives in Fairbanks, where her husband is in forestry school.

However, despite her and Gloria getting along okay, in the late afternoons Mrs. Lawson begins to worry that Gloria will find something wrong there, when she comes first thing in the morning. Something that she, Mrs. Lawson, did wrong. She even imagines Gloria saying to Miss Goldstein, Honestly, how come you keep on that old Mrs. Lawson? She can't see to clean very good, she's too old to work.

She does not really think that Gloria would say a thing like that, and even if she did Miss Goldstein wouldn't listen, probably. Still, the idea is very worrying to her, and in an anxious way she sweeps up the kitchen floor, and dustmops the long front hall. And at the same time her mind is plagued with those images of husbands, dark ghosts, in Juneau and Oakland and Kansas City, husbands that she has to get home to, somehow. Long bus rides with cold winds at the places where you change, or else you have to wait a long time for the choked-up sound of them honking, until you get in their creaky old cars and drive, drive home, in the dark.

Mrs. Lawson is absolutely right about Gloria having serious troubles on her mind—more serious in fact than Mrs. Lawson could have thought of: Gloria's hideous, obsessive problem is a small lump on her leg, her right leg, mid-calf. A tiny knot. She keeps reaching to touch it, no matter what she is doing, and it is always there. She cannot make herself not touch it. She thinks constantly of that lump, its implications and probable consequences. Driving to work in her jumpy old VW, she reaches down to her leg, to check the lump. A couple of times she almost has accidents, as she concentrates on her fingers, reaching, what they feel as they touch her leg.

To make things even worse, the same week that she first noticed the lump Gloria met a really nice man, about her age: Dugald, neither married nor gay (a miracle, these days, in San Francisco). He is a bartender in a place where she sometimes goes with girlfriends, after a movie or something. In a way she has known Dugald for a long time, but in another way not—not known him until she happened to go into the place alone, thinking, Well, why not? I'm tired (it was late one afternoon), a beer would be nice. And there was Dugald, and they talked, and he asked her out, on his next night off. And the next day she discovered the lump.

She went with Dugald anyway, of course, and she almost had a very good time—except that whenever she thought about what was probably wrong with her she went cold and quiet. She thinks that Dugald may not ever ask her out again, and even if he did, she can't get at all involved with anyone, not now.

Also, Gloria's sister, Sharon, in Fairbanks, Alaska, has invited her to come up and stay for a week, while Sharon's forestry-student husband is back in Kansas, visiting his folks; Sharon does not much like her husband's family. Gloria thinks she will go for ten days in June, while Miss Goldstein is in China, again. Gloria is on the whole pleased at the prospect of this visit; as she Ajaxes and Lysols Miss Goldstein's upstairs bathroom, she thinks, *Alaska,* and she imagines gigantic glaciers, huge wild animals, fantastic snow-capped mountains. (She will send a friendly postcard to Dugald, she thinks, and maybe one to old Lawson.) Smiling, for an instant she makes a small bet with herself, which is that at some point Sharon will ask her not to mention to anyone, *please,* what she, Gloria, does for a living. Well, Gloria doesn't care. Lord knows her work is not much to talk about; it is simply the most money she can get an hour, and not pay taxes (she is always afraid, when not preoccupied with her other, more terrible worries, that the IRS will somehow get to her). On the other hand, it is fun to embarrass Sharon.

At home though, lying awake at night, of course the lump is all that Gloria thinks about. And hospitals: when she was sixteen she had her tonsils out, and she decided then on no more operations, no matter what. If she ever has a baby she will do it at home. The hospital was so frightening, everyone was horrible to her, all the doctors and nurses (except for a couple of black aides who were sweet, really nice, she remembers). They all made her feel like something much less than a person. And a hospital would take all her money, and more, all her careful savings (someday she plans to buy a little cabin, up near Tahoe, and raise big dogs). She thinks about something being cut off. Her leg. Herself made so ugly, everyone trying not to look. No more men, no dates, not Dugald or anyone. No love or sex again, not ever.

In the daytime her terror is slightly more manageable, but it is still so powerful that the very idea of calling a doctor, showing him the lump, asking him what to do—chills her blood, almost stops her heart.

And she can feel the lump there, all the time. Probably growing.

Mrs. Lawson has told Gloria that she never goes to doctors; she can doctor herself, Mrs. Lawson says. She always has. Gloria has even thought of showing the lump to Mrs. Lawson.

But she tries to think in a positive way about Alaska. They have a cute little apartment right on the university campus, Sharon has written. Fairbanks is on a river; they will take an afternoon trip on a paddleboat. And they will spend one night at Mount McKinley, and go on a wild life tour.

"Fairbanks, now. I never did get up that way," says Mrs. Lawson, told of Sharon's invitation, Gloria's projected trip. "But I always heard it was real nice up there."

Actually she does not remember anything at all about Fairbanks, but for Gloria's sake she hopes that it is nice, and she reasons that any place would be better than Juneau, scrunched in between mountains so steep they look to fall down on you.

"I hope it's nice," says Gloria. "I just hope I don't get mauled by some bear, on that wild life tour."

Aside from not drinking and never going to doctors (she has read all her father's old doctor books, and remembers most of what she read) Mrs. Lawson believes that she gets her good health and her strength—considerable, for a person of her years—from her daily naps. Not a real sleep, just sitting down for a while in some place really comfortable, and closing her eyes.

She does that now, in a small room off Miss Goldstein's main library room (Miss Goldstein has already gone off to China, but even if she were home she wouldn't mind about a little nap). Mrs. Lawson settles back into a big old fat leather chair, and she slips her shoes off. And, very likely because of talking about Alaska that morning, Gloria's trip, her mind drifts off, in and out of Juneau. She remembers the bitter cold, cold rains of that winter up there, the winds, fogs thicker than cotton, and dark. Snow that sometimes kept them in the little hillside cabin for days, even weeks. Her and Charles: that husband had the same name as the one she now has, she just remembered—funny to forget a thing like that. They always used to drink a lot, her and the Charles in Alaska; you had to, to get through the winter. And pretty often they would fight, ugly drunk quarrels that she couldn't quite remember the words to, in the mornings. But that New Year's Eve they were having a real nice time; he was being real nice, laughing and all, and then all of a sudden it was like he turned into some other person, and he struck her. He grabbed up her hair, all of it red, at that time, and he called her a witch and he knocked her down to the floor, and he tromped her. Later of course he was sorry, and he said he had been feeling mean about not enough work, but still, he had tromped her.

Pulling herself out of that half dream, half terrible memory, Mrs. Lawson repeats, as though someone had asked her, that now she is married to Charles, in San Francisco. They live in the Western Addition; they don't drink, and this Charles is a nice man, most of the time.

She tries then to think about the other three husbands, one in Oakland, in Chicago, in Kansas City, but nothing much comes to mind, of them. No faces or words, just shadows, and no true pictures of any of those cities. The only thing she is perfectly clear about is that not one of those other men was named Charles.

On the airplane to Alaska, something terrible, horrible, entirely frightening happens to Gloria, which is: a girl comes and sits in the seat next to hers, and that girl has—the lower part of her right leg missing. Cut off. A pretty dark-haired girl, about the same size as Gloria, wearing a nice blazer, and a kind of long skirt. One boot. Metal crutches.

Gloria is so frightened—she knows that this is an omen, a sign meant for her—that she is dizzy, sick; she leans back and closes her eyes, as the plane bumps upward, zooming through clouds, and she stays that way for the rest of the trip. She tries not to think; she repeats numbers and meaningless words to herself.

At some point she feels someone touching her arm. Flinching, she opens her eyes to see the next-seat girl, who is asking, "Are you okay? Can I get you anything?"

"I'm all right. Just getting the flu, I think." Gloria smiles in a deliberately non-friendly way. The last thing in the world that she wants is a conversation with that girl: the girl at last getting around to her leg, telling Gloria, "It started with this lump I had, right here."

Doctors don't usually feel your legs, during physical examinations, Gloria thinks; she is standing beside Sharon on the deck of the big paddleboat that is slowly ploughing up the Natoma River. It would be possible to hide a lump for a long time, unless it grew a lot, she thinks, as the boat's captain announces over the bullhorn that they are passing what was once an Indian settlement.

Alaska is much flatter than Gloria had imagined its being, at least around Fairbanks—and although she had of course heard the words, midnight sun, she had not known they were a literal description; waking at three or four in the morning from bad dreams, her nighttime panics (her legs drawn up under her, one hand touching her calf, the lump) she sees brilliant sunshine, coming in through the tattered aluminum foil that Sharon has messily pasted to the window. It is all wrong—unsettling. Much worse than the thick dark fogs that come into San Francisco in the summer; she is used to them.

In fact sleeplessness and panic (what she felt at the sight of that girl with the missing leg has persisted; she knows it was a sign) have combined to produce in Gloria an almost trancelike state. She is so quiet, so passive that she can feel Sharon wondering about her, what is wrong. Gloria does not, for a change, say anything critical of Sharon's housekeeping, which is as sloppy as usual. She does not tell anyone that she, Gloria, is a cleaning person.

A hot wind comes up off the water, and Gloria remembers that tomorrow they go to Mt. McKinley, and the wild life tour.

Somewhat to her disappointment, Mrs. Lawson does not get any postcards from Gloria in Alaska, although Gloria had mentioned that she would send one, with a picture.

What she does get is a strange phone call from Gloria on the day that she was supposed to come back. What is *strange* is that Gloria sounds like some entirely other person, someone younger even than

Gloria actually is, younger and perfectly happy. It is Gloria's voice, all right, but lighter and quicker than it was, a voice without any shadows.

"I'm back!" Gloria bursts out, "but I just don't think I want to work today. I was out sort of late—" She laughs, in a bright new way, and then she asks, "She's not back yet, is she?"

Meaning Miss Goldstein. "No, not for another week," Mrs. Lawson tells her. "You had a good trip?"

"Fabulous! a miracle, really. I'll tell you all about it tomorrow."

Hanging up, Mrs. Lawson has an uneasy sense that some impersonator will come to work in Gloria's place.

But of course it is Gloria who is already down on her knees, cleaning the kitchen floor, when Mrs. Lawson gets there the following day.

And almost right away she begins to tell Mrs. Lawson about the wild life tour, from Mt. McKinley, seemingly the focal point of her trip.

"It was really weird," says Gloria. "It looked like the moon, in that funny light." She has a lot to say, and she is annoyed that Mrs. Lawson seems to be paying more attention to her newspaper—is barely listening. Also, Lawson seems to have aged, while Gloria was away, or maybe Gloria just forgot how old she looks, since in a way she doesn't act very old; she moves around and works a lot harder than Sharon ever does, for one example. But it seems to Gloria today that Mrs. Lawson's skin is grayer than it was, ashy looking, and her eyes, which are always strange, have got much paler.

Nevertheless, wanting more attention (her story has an important point to it) Gloria raises her voice, as she continues, "And every time someone spotted one of those animals he'd yell out, and the man would stop the bus. We saw caribou, and these funny white sheep, high up on the rocks, and a lot of moose, and some foxes. Not any bears. Anyway, every time we stopped I got real scared. We were on the side of a really steep mountain, part of Mt. McKinley, I think, and the bus was so wide, like a school bus." She does not tell Mrs. Lawson that in a weird way she liked being so scared. What she thought was, If I'm killed on this bus I'll never even get to a doctor. Which was sort of funny, really, now that she can see the humor in it—now that the lump is mysteriously, magically gone!

However, she has reached the dramatic disclosure toward which this story of her outing has been heading. "Anyway, we got back all right," she says, "and two days after that, back in Fairbanks, do you know what the headlines were, in the local paper?" She has asked this (of course rhetorical) question in a slow, deepened voice, and now she pauses, her china-blue eyes gazing into Mrs. Lawson's paler, stranger blue.

"Well, I don't know," Lawson obliges.

"They said, BUS TOPPLES FROM MOUNTAIN, EIGHT KILLED, 42 INJURED. Can you imagine? Our same bus, the very next day. What do you think that means?" This question too has been rhetorical; voicing it, Gloria smiles in a satisfied, knowing way.

A very polite woman, Mrs. Lawson smiles gently too. "It means you spared. You like to live fifty, sixty years more."

Eagerly Gloria bursts out, "Exactly! That's just the way I figured it, right away." She pauses, smiling widely, showing her little white teeth. "And then, that very same afternoon of the day we saw the paper," she goes on, "I was changing my clothes and I felt of the calf of my leg where there'd been this lump that I was sort of worried about—and the lump was gone. I couldn't believe it. So I guess it was just a muscle, not anything bad."

"Them leg muscles can knot up that way, could of told you that myself," Mrs. Lawson mutters. "Heavy housework can do that to a person." But Gloria looks so happy, so bright-faced and shiny-eyed, that Mrs. Lawson does not want to bring her down, in any way, and so she adds, "But you sure are right about that bus accident. It's a sure sign you been spared."

"Oh, that's what I think too! And later we saw these really neat big dogs, in Fairbanks. I'm really thinking about getting a dog. This man I know really likes dogs too, last night we were talking." Her voice trails off in a happy reminiscence.

Later in the day, though, thinking about Gloria and her story, what she and Gloria said to each other, Mrs. Lawson is not really convinced about anything. The truth is, Gloria could perfectly well get killed by a bus in San Francisco, this very afternoon, or shot by some sniper; it's been saying in the paper about snipers, all over town, shooting folks. Or Gloria could find another lump, some place else, somewhere dangerous. Missing one bus accident is no sure sign that a person's life will always come up rosy, because nobody's does, not for long. Even Miss Gold-stein, in China, could fall off of some Chinese mountain.

In a weary, discouraged way Mrs. Lawson moved through the rest of her day. It is true; she is too old and tired for the work she does. Through the big street-floor windows she watches the cold June fog rolling in from the bay, and she thinks how the weather in California has never seemed right to her. She thinks about Charles, and it comes to her that one Charles could change into the other, the same way that first Charles in such a sudden way turned violent, and wild.

That thought is enough to make her dread the end of her work, and the day, when although it is summer she will walk out into streets that are as dark and cold as streets are in Alaska.

THE OLD LEFT

DANIEL MENAKER

Daniel Menaker was born in New York City in 1941. He has worked at *The New Yorker* magazine for fifteen years, the last eight as an editor, and has contributed stories and humor to *The New Yorker* and many other publications. He lives in Manhattan with his wife, the writer Katherine Bouton, and their son, Willy.

Uncle Will is supposed to leave for Mexico next Sunday, escorted by the Blooms, a couple of retired-schoolteacher friends who are younger than he is but still of the Very Old Left. They own a house in San Miguel. They have been in my uncle's thrall ever since they did volunteer work for the settlement house he ran in Brooklyn until he retired, fifteen years ago. But today, which is *this* Sunday, Uncle Will is having his doubts. He is eighty-six now, which is old, no getting around it. He still puts in some unpaid time writing captions for the *Daily World*, and he still calls me "boy," but he doesn't make any more jokes about being middle-aged, and he has stopped saying things like, "I'd like to visit Russia when I grow up." All his doctors have been warning him that to stay in the Northeast for the rest of January and February and March would be dangerous for him. There are a lot of them—a heart specialist for his heart failure, a joint man for the arthritis in his neck and back, an ear-nose-and-throat man for his chronically inflamed sinuses, and an eye man for his aged, tearless eyes. And there are a lot of other people who from a safe distance (usually over the telephone) give advice to Uncle Will—a few old pals in the city from the Spanish Civil War, ancient progressives and their children and grandchildren, and locals and summer people up in the Berkshires, where Uncle Will lives from May through September in his big, red farmhouse. Everyone has been urging him to get out for the winter.

Still, when he called me earlier this morning, an hour or so ago, to

Copyright © 1982 by Grand Street Publications, Inc. First appeared in *Grand Street*. Reprinted by permission.

maneuver me into offering him a ride to the dentist tomorrow, to have a bad tooth looked at, he seemed to be taking a strange pleasure in describing the swelling of his face and the pain he'd been suffering for the last couple of days. The affliction sounded like an unexpected but welcome guest whom Uncle Will would have to entertain for some time. "I don't know, Nicky," he said feebly on the phone. "If this keeps up, I'll have wings of my own by the end of the week. I won't need to take a plane anywhere."

He didn't ask me to drive him to the dentist. (He never asks me directly to do any of the small favors I do for him when he's in the city, like picking up a prescription for him on a nasty day, helping him balance his checkbook, or spending a couple of hours at his place on a Saturday afternoon while he inveighs against the evils of our system and the lies of the press—this last he pokes at me like a prospector looking for pay dirt, since I was once a reporter at City Hall for the *Times* and now teach at Columbia Journalism School.) He simply asked me to remind him which number bus would take him from Chelsea, where he has an apartment in a city housing project, to Central Park West, where his dentist's office is. When I first said I'd take him, he said, "Don't be ridiculous." But I kept at it until, finally, he found the generousness of spirit to accommodate my stubborn and foolish insistence.

When I hung up, I found my wife, Patricia—not Pat, mind you, or Patty or Patsy or Trish, but Patricia—standing behind me. She's got to know what's going on.

"Why can't he get someone who lives nearer to help?" Patricia said. She walked back into the bedroom, where she collapsed on the bed. "I guess nobody else has a car."

"Oh, it's O.K.," I said. "I've got a whole week of semester break left with no papers to grade."

"But you were going to start on course plans for the fall tomorrow," Patricia said. She shivered and pulled her brown bathrobe—which is actually *my* brown bathrobe—around her. It turned lethally cold in New York New Year's Day—the worst cold of the century, the papers and television have been calling it, as if it were a circus attraction—and only the bedroom in our apartment has been halfway habitable, because the living room, study, and kitchen all face the Hudson River and the keen, cold winds that rush across it and detonate on Morningside Heights.

"All that can wait," I said. "Listen, if he doesn't get away now, I'm going to have to be running down to his place for the next two or three months. Besides, the Blooms think he's the cat's pajamas, and they have a separate little suite for him down there, and a doctor lives next door. And it's warm. I'd rather take him to the dentist than—"

"The cat's pajamas?" Patricia said.

Patricia is eight years younger than I am—thirty-two. We got married two years ago, when I was thirty-eight. Late. She had come to New York to be assistant curator of the Museum of Natural History's Hall of Marsupials after working at the Endicott Museum in Boston for four years, and after six years of a bad marriage to a fellow-biology graduate student, who to this day is working on his thesis at Boston University. Actually, the last I heard, he hadn't even finished the outline. Patricia introduced herself to me at the museum, in front of a sort of variety-pack diorama of extinct pouched creatures, and got me to take her out to lunch. Patricia's mother and father, who still live in Sharon, Connecticut, where she was born, are in their mid-fifties. *My* parents are in their mid-seventies, having had me, their only child, in their mid-thirties. Late again, especially for that day and age. Soon I'll have to be running up to Palisades to attend to them, just as I go downtown now for Uncle Will. And when that sadness is over, Patricia's parents will need looking after. And then it will be my turn. And then Patricia's. Before all that happens, we want to have a child or two, to balance the future with a little youth and hope.

Anyway, I have a repertoire of antique expressions, like "spooning" and "bub" and "the cat's pajamas" that I learned from Uncle Will or my parents, and that Patricia finds quite hilarious. When I use one of them, or idly sing some vintage popular tune, like "The Band Played On," or "Sleepy Time Gal," Patricia raises her eyebrows and looks at me as though one of her fossils had suddenly come to life and turned up in her apartment. It's all very funny, but often at those moments I get the feeling that Patricia doesn't really know me and never will—the kind of feeling that until she came along and put me in her pocket had been strong enough to give me a secret excuse for not settling down with anyone. You don't stay unmarried until you're thirty-eight unless you think you've got secrets.

It's Sunday night, and Patricia and I are eating dinner in front of the television set in the bedroom, wishing we could join the little English girl who with her family is trying to make a go of it in Kenya. It looks very warm in Kenya. The temperature in New York today never got above ten, and now it's five, and the windows in all the other rooms are covered with ice, especially the kitchen, where the water that boiled off while I made spaghetti, under Patricia's watchful eye, reappeared quickly as a thick rime on the frigid glass. While the spaghetti was cooking, I went into the living room and with a table knife scraped out a peephole on one of the windows there. On the river, five freighters had dropped anchor during the day; we assumed it was because the ice farther north was impassable. When I peered out, the freighters all had their deck lights on, and they looked like a line of stores in a shopping mall. It must be frustrating for the men on board, who most likely became sailors because they wanted to stay on the move, to sit paralyzed in the middle of what they probably thought was nowhere. Each ship was surrounded by a flange of ice, like a ballerina's tutu, and just before sunset they all pivoted in a cumbersome half pirouette as the tide turned.

Now the little girl is going to get an old Dutch trekker to help her family and their neighbors kill a leopard that has been skulking around their homesteads. "I think it's rather important," she says to the grizzled hunter as she gives him the note from her father. She is handling him as if he were the child and she the adult.

The phone rings in the hall. I go out and answer it and reclose the door, to keep the warmth in.

"Well, where are you, boy?" Uncle Will says, in a weak voice.

"I'm here at home—what do you mean?" I say.

"Well, it's nine-thirty. Aren't you supposed to pick me up for the dentist now?"

"But that's tomorrow morning, Uncle Will." The door opens behind me. Patricia, *semper vigilis.*

"Is it morning or night?" Uncle Will asks.

"Night."

"Oh, God, I'm all balled up. I took a sleeping pill. I think I did. But that was at night. It's crazy."

"It's nighttime now, Uncle Will. You probably took the pill and woke up, and now you're confused."

"Well, this is a fine fettle of kish. O.K., boy, see you tomorrow. If you'd just quit calling me at all hours, maybe I could get some rest."

"Didn't take enough to finish the job, huh?" Patricia says after I hang up. "I didn't mean it, I didn't mean it."

"Why aren't you in there keeping an eye on the leopard?" I say.

"I brought you this blanket in case you had to stand out here for a long time," she says.

Uncle Will and I are waiting for the elevator outside his apartment, on the twenty-third floor. His black overcoat hangs on his small frame like a hand-me-down, and his big bald head looks too heavy for the rest of him. He's wearing his jaunty brown beret. Only artists and Communists wear brown berets. His jaw is badly swollen, I must admit, and he seems weak and still confused, and I can understand a little better how he might fear the prospect of a long trip. He took forever to get ready to leave for the dentist, as I expected he would. In his apartment, he picked up a set of keys, looked at it as though it were a Martian artifact, put it down again, and picked up another. He put on and then took off two pairs of gloves before settling on a third. He gave me a letter he wanted to mail and a little later spent five minutes looking for it, before I figured out what was going on. He's forgetful, of course, but I'd never before seen him so baffled by ordinary tasks. And his place seemed unutterably lonely, with its north view of the tall slabs of Midtown skyscrapers, the desolate West Side, and, farther to the west, the river. It is clear and stunningly cold outside, and far up the river I could make out my five freighters, motionless amid the rubble of ice washing down from somewhere north of the Tappan Zee Bridge, north of my parents' house. And inside, every object—the small upright piano, the television set, the pots and pans in the kitchen, the furniture, the desk top with its windfall of little reminder notes—seemed brushed with the dust of a lonely old age.

The elevator arrives, but instead of getting on, Uncle Will turns around and walks back to his door.

"Where are you going now?" I say.

"Timbuktoo—where do you think?" he says.

He lets himself in and reappears almost immediately with a small black leather bag.

"You look like you're about to make a house call," I say. "What have you got in there?"

"Wait-and-see pudding," he says.

Finally we get down to the street. Just before we reach the car, a terrific gust of wind comes along and nearly sends Uncle Will sprawling into a dirty, icy snowbank. I reach out to steady him, and am surprised at the raptor-like strength with which he grasps my arm. "Aren't you ashamed of yourself—pushing an old man," he says, shading his eyes against the sun. I open the door for him, and he eases himself into the front seat as if he were dangerous cargo, I go around to the driver's side, and we're off at last.

Traffic is slow. Pedestrians, bundled up as round as onions, are crossing against the lights because they can't bear to stand still in the raw, blustery weather. For no particular reason that I can see, Uncle Will starts a story about my mother and father's wedding. We stop at a red light, and I look over at him and see that he is nearly enveloped by the bucket seat. His eyes are far away. I think I know this story—these twelve stories, I should say. "Well, your father did get nervous after all," Uncle Will says. "He couldn't seem to forget that Emily's father didn't approve of the marriage. I'd gotten to know the old man—we had become good friends—and I can assure you it wasn't because our family was Jewish or radical or anything like that. No, it was because your father was so handsome and charming that he was kinda spoiled, and the old boy wasn't sure how responsible he would be as a husband." I was right. I do know this complicated tale, almost by heart. It used to be that Uncle Will's stories enchanted me, even after I learned that they involved considerable embroidery. He had a way of making me and himself and the rest of my family seem colorful and funny and sometimes heroic, of endowing our lives with a kind of shape and meaning. That bright gift has become tarnished by the garrulousness of age, and I often find myself daydreaming like this instead of listening. "Oh, Emily was a knockout herself," Uncle Will says. "But she was bright and serious besides—a most remarkable gal, as she still is. So, as I was saying, your father was so nervous that he took a flask with him when I drove him to the church, and"

My mother's parents will watch in shock as my father takes a swig from a flask while Uncle Will drives him past the church. Later, Uncle Will's role as peacemaker will loom larger and larger, until he has become the principal figure in the marriage. It is as if he had married the marriage. The enchantment has given way to a kind of desperate self-reassurance. Maybe it was that all along, only better disguised.

We stop for another light at Fifty-seventh Street. Uncle Will has come to the end of a chapter, and, in case I think he has finished, he utters a drawn-out "So," as if he were beginning a new verse of the kind of old-time ballad that would cause Patricia's eyebrows to rise.

"There's no reason why this should keep you from going away," the dentist tells Uncle Will as we're about to leave his office. "Barring

complications, of course," he adds, peering over his eyeglasses for ad-
monitory effect. The catch is that Uncle Will will have to have three
more appointments during the week.

We are standing at the elevator, when Uncle Will turns to me and
says, "Are you in a hurry?" I say no. "Of course you are," he says. "But
you're just going to have to hold your horses. I have some private
business to attend to. Wait here." He takes from me the little black bag
that he had almost forgotten to bring along this morning and totters
back down the hall toward the dentist's receptionist. I follow him. He
puts the bag down on the receptionist's desk, opens it, and takes out a
clear plastic bag containing four or five potatoes. "Something for you
from the country," he says to the receptionist, a West Indian woman
with an extremely reserved manner. She breaks into a delighted smile,
as if she'd just been named Queen of the Bahamas and were being
presented with the crown jewels, and thanks Uncle Will profusely.
What is private about this? Is it that he has no potatoes for me? Or did
he trick me into following him? When he turns around and sees me
standing there, he says, "Well, if it isn't Mr. Nosy Parker."

I returned from Uncle Will's after four. I did some shopping, went
home, and in the face of three more such dental odysseys fell asleep.
When Patricia came home from work, she woke me from a dream in
which I was trying to drive a Galapagos tortoise to Mexico in a truck
that wouldn't start moving because vines and tendrils, anchored to
huge rocks under the surface of the soil, were growing out of its sides
and tires. I got up, and Patricia and I huddled together in the kitchen
for warmth while I made some salad and some saffron rice and cleaned
and sautéed the shrimp I'd bought on the way back from putting the
car in the garage. Patricia coached me on the rice and the shrimp.

Once again, we are eating in the bedroom. The outdoor-indoor ther-
mometer in the living room says four and fifty-two, and the blanket
that Patricia hung over the door to the living room is stirring in the
draft like a ghost's robe. The freighters are still moored there, in the
middle of the river, pointing upstream after another imperceptibly slow
tidal sweep.

"Nosy Parker?" Patricia says quizzically, after I describe the potato
episode for her. "Is that some kind of Australian slang?"

"And on the way back to his place," I go on, like a witness warming
to his own testimony, "he took a half an hour to explain to me how he

had managed to persuade someone to participate in the sixties antiwar demonstrations."

"It's going to be a rough week," Patricia says.

"He told me how he had made this person read the *Daily World* and practically dragged him to the Moratorium marches."

"How extremely annoying that must have been for the person," Patricia says.

"The trouble is, this whole conversion story was a complete fabrication, because it was me he was talking about."

"Oh, no!"

"He just sat there and bald-facedly said, 'And then, Nicky, don't you remember, I made the train reservations for both of us, because I knew you'd end up doing the right thing.' "

"And did you correct him?"

"I said, 'Look, Uncle Will, oddly enough I happened to be inhabiting my own body at the time, and I can tell you that I didn't read the *Daily World* and I took a bus to Washington all by myself.' "

"And what did he say?"

"He said, 'I'm surprised at you, boy. I didn't know you had such a bad temper. To say nothing of your memory.' "

"Yes, it's a wonder he can put up with you," Patricia says.

Patricia was right. It has been a rough week. A rough six days, I should say, since today is Sunday. Uncle Will takes off for Mexico in a few hours. I mean, he's supposed to. Every day he has told me that he doesn't think he's going to make it, even though the swelling in his jaw has gone way down and he has complained about his pain only when he remembered to. I'm lying here in bed trying to figure out why he's dragging his heels up to the last minute like this, especially since many past winters have seen him depart, with no louder complaint than "I don't really want to go but they're begging me," for a stay with one of his old Progressive friends who long ago gave up New York's ideological and climatic extremes for Arizona, California, and Mexico. The only thing I can come up with is that for the first time in his life, he really believes that he's not too far away from death, and that he wants to die at home. I think of New York as his Kremlin, and that if he dies somewhere outside its walls he will have been caught out in some kind of geographical revisionism.

He has also been warning his escorts for the trip, the patient Blooms, that he might decide to stay behind. Every night he has called them and every night they have called me, to ask me what I think the chances are. My father has been calling me, too, to ask the same question and to apologize for being too old to be his brother's keeper, and so have some of Uncle Will's other friends. I've been urging the trip on him—quietly and subtly, I thought, until Friday, after his last dentist appointment. When I dropped him off and promised to go back down this morning and help him pack if he decided to go, he said, with an edge of bitterness, "You can't wait to see the last of me, can you?"

That was merely the most direct evidence that Uncle Will had put me on trial. During the week I've been told that the CIA is solely responsible for the unrest in Poland, that my interest in food is probably a sign of moral degeneracy, that members of the Moral Majority shouldn't even be allowed to speak, and that it's a crime to let people have private cars in the city—this last just after we'd driven past a subway station with a token line that for some subterranean reason extended up the stairs and halfway down the block.

We were on our way to pick up some Percodan that the dentist had prescribed for Uncle Will. I'd bet it was that Percodan, in combination with a Seconal, or one of the other narcotics that Uncle Will has on hand and on occasion dips into at the wrong time of day, that caused Thursday's frightening Unscheduled Appearance. It was the coldest day so far, and the only one that held any promise of being uncle-free. Even the bedroom was cold, and to be able to sit still and read I'd not only put on many layers of clothing but wrapped myself in Patricia's voluminous Icelandic-wool shawl. At about four-thirty, having stuffed myself into an armchair and feeling like somebody's granny, I got a call from Uncle Will's dentist. He said that Uncle Will had just shown up, looking woozy and pale, for a nonexistent appointment. Had he left again? Yes.

Oh, terrific! Uncle Will, who shunned taxis as if they were as retrograde as royal litters, was out there somewhere, stunned by drugs, staggering through the frozen twilight to catch a bus that would probably land him in front of a gutted tenement in the South Bronx. Even if he got the right one, he had a tough two-block crosstown walk at the other end against the cutting Arctic winds to get to his place.

Patricia got home a little after five, her nose and ears as red as stoplights. When I told her what was going on, she looked utterly stricken. "That poor old man," she said.

"Poor old man my ass," I said. "He's doing it so that he'll get sick and won't be able to leave. He's doing it to make us worry about him. God forbid I should go one day without him at the center of my attention." But in my mind I saw him fighting his way through the deepening gloom of Chelsea, going slower and slower, as if in a dream, and finally freezing in his tracks in the midst of his abstractly beloved poor, his hand up to hold his thin and pitifully rakish brown beret against the wind. I only hoped that his eyes were filled with euphoric visions of a world without taxis or tuxedos, that his ears were ringing with the "Internationale," and his soul was brimming with joy as Marx and Engels, their beards even more magnificent than they had been in life, gathered him from the dark streets and into the bosom of a state-less, profitless, Godless paradise.

Together, Patricia and I, fat with clothes, paced the bedroom wait-ing till it made sense to start calling him at home. Then I dialed him every five minutes for half an hour, and just before I was going to hang up and call in the police to start looking for a petrified Communist with the *World* folded into the pocket of his overcoat, he picked up the phone. He was all right.

I get to Uncle Will's place at about nine. The limousine that the Blooms have hired to pick him up and then them for the trip out to LaGuardia is due at ten. I knock on Uncle Will's door and let myself in with the set of keys he gave me a long time ago, "so that the under-taker won't have to break the door down," as he put it. He is sitting in his living room reading the Sunday *Times*, which his neighbor, a Puerto Rican woman he has been trying to indoctrinate for ten years, bought for him on her way back from early Mass. He hasn't done any packing.

"What are you doing here, bub?" he says to me, looking over his glasses. "You were supposed to call first."

"I decided to take matters into my own hands," I say.

"You're just going to ship me off, huh? Well, I'm sorry, Nicky, but I think I may not be up to it. I was just about to call the Blooms."

"Where's your suitcase?"

"Listen to him," Uncle Will says.

"You're going; I've decided for you," I say. I find a large leather suitcase in a closet off the hall between the living room and the bed-room. I take it into the bedroom and open it on the bed, which is made, and neat as a pin. "I'm starting with your delicate underthings," I call to Uncle Will. "If there's anything you think you're going to have particular need of in Siberia, you better let me know."

I hear Uncle Will shuffling in the hall. He stands in the doorway to his bedroom and watches me as I open one of the drawers in his dresser, a handsome old thing, mahogany, and almost as tall as its proprietor.

"So the Cossacks have finally arrived," Uncle Will says. "Look on the top of the dresser. I found it in my desk the other day."

I do, and there is a silver-framed picture of me from my college graduation, looking as though I had nothing more to learn.

"Too bad you've regressed so badly since then," Uncle Will says.

"I'm not the only one," I say, beginning to pack.

"O.K., this has gone far enough," he says.

I straighten up and face him. "Listen, if you can take four hours in no degrees traipsing all over the city and waiting for buses and giving your relatives heart attacks, you can sit on a plane for five hours to Mexico."

"You know what's best for me, do you?" he says.

"That's right."

"You don't."

"Oh, all right, I give up," I say. I start to unpack the few things I've put in the suitcase.

"Don't sulk," Uncle Will says.

"Well, it's ridiculous."

"Everyone is just trying to get rid of me," Uncle Will says, with not quite enough irony.

"I'm not," I say, and slam the drawer closed. "I'm trying to keep you."

Uncle Will scrutinizes me as if he were trying to read some complicated meteorological instrument. "Well, then," he says, "the least you could do is use the right suitcase. It's in the closet behind you."

"Someday you will drive me as crazy as you already are," I say, wheeling around and snatching the other suitcase from the closet.

"When you're finished in here," Uncle Will says, "you can go into the kitchen and pack the potatoes."

It's Sunday night, and Patricia and I are having dinner in front of the TV again, watching the apparently endless series about the masterful little English girl. We turned it on a bit late, and I'm having trouble distinguishing one young frontiersman with a mustache from another. Actually, there is a dark one with a mustache, a blond one with a mustache, and a blond one without a mustache. Patricia flattered me into watching the show by telling me that the dark one looked like me. Anyway, the wife of one of these men is having an affair with another of them, probably because she can't tell them apart, either. It's all too much for me, and to keep from eating too fast in the presence of narrative confusion and the absence of conversation, I get up and walk out to the living room. It became habitable again this afternoon, with the day's rising temperatures and falling winds. In fact, when I got home from Uncle Will's, at about one, after Uncle Will was picked up by the Tel Aviv limousine service (which he grumbled about, because of the Zionism implicit in its name), I found Patricia in the process of reclaiming the front part of our apartment. Sun was streaming in the living-room windows, and Patricia, having dusted and swept and watered all the plants, which seem to have flourished in the chilliness, was playing hymns on the piano.

"Did he get away all right?" she asked.

"Yes—barely," I said.

"What a relief. Well, he's probably over Missouri right now, making them earn their wings."

"I had to convince him that I wasn't just trying to get him out of my hair. I told him it was only because I cared about him. The thing is, I'm not sure it's true."

"Of course it's true," Patricia said. She turned back to the piano and started picking out "After the Ball."

"When did you learn that?" I said.

"I heard you humming it when you were making the marinade last night," she said. "It's pretty. What's it called?"

Now I'm standing in the dark at the window. Patricia comes and stands beside me. She kisses me on the cheek. "It's nothing but shots of water buffalo right now," she says. "Look—there's another freighter way down at the end of the line. Can you see it?"

"So there is," I say.

"If this thaw keeps up, they'll probably leave soon."

"I hope so," I say. "They're beginning to get on my nerves."

LIVING ALONE IN IOTA

LEE K. ABBOTT, JR.

Though raised in the desert of southern New Mexico, Mr. Abbott is an associate professor of English at Case Western Reserve University in Cleveland. His first book, *The Heart Never Fits Its Wanting,* a collection of stories, won the St. Lawrence Award for Fiction in 1981. He has a second book, *Love Is the Crooked Thing,* with stories that have appeared in the *Ohio Review,* the *Georgia Review,* the *Missouri Review,* and the *Southern Review,* ready for publication.

Ten months after she left (he told the boys), he got the letter. "I am calling myself Ida now." Her penmanship was barely inside the margins of human communication. "For a time, I was a Louise, a T. Mama, and in Cisco a Velva." She was Harmonized, a Changed Lady, the Foul and Lackluster set aside for the satisfying Tinkle of Beauty (her caps). "I have seen Despair and licked it," she wrote. "Ill Humor, also. Plus, I am uplifted spiritually by my new man. His name is Chuck, but I call him King Daddy on account of his smile and many muscles."

Reese felt he'd been whanged with a tire iron. "Shit," he moaned, "why now?" When he'd known her, she was Billy Jean La Took—deep-socketed, complex, skin as smooth as quote the far-flung impossible unquote, foolish, bewildered, and astray, a body like stolen money. "She makes my ears bleed," he'd told the boys at the well-site. "I mean, when she starts kissing my neck, I go off into a dark land. It's like death, only welcome."

Then she vamoosed.

"I don't believe it," he said, stumbling through the trailer, calling her name. All her stuff was gone—toothbrush, clothes, even a pair of mysterious, unlovely and flesh-like plants that looked like imports from Mars. "It was like waking up in a grave," he confided to the boys the next day. "You should've seen me crying. It was a humiliating spectacle, what it was. Severe and eternal."

Copyright © 1980 by Lee K. Abbott. First appeared in *Fiction International,* No. 14. Reprinted by permission.

The weekend passed before he found the note. It was in the refrigerator, but he hadn't been eating, just sitting in that gloomy living room, feeling the panhandle winds rock the trailer, dust swirling mercilessly, thinking about dew-fairies, the Boogey-man, the whole terrible sad history of hurtful facts. TV wasn't a help—nor fantasy, nor memory. "I'll drink," he said, a path out of the pain coming clear to him.

The note was propped against a six-pack of Buckhorn: "Reese, honey," it read, "I am truly sorry for the evil way I have sneaked off. By now I am well gone, almost vanished. You could look for me in Goree. Even Olney. But I have fled Texas. I have talents and numerous dreams of glamour. You never saw me dance. Plus, I have improved my mind."

He read the whole letter to the boys. It was full of grimness addressed to a narrow-minded, slack, fearsome, idle and raunchy man. It mentioned Faith and Shared Duties, and, moving easily between the Hard and the Terrible, it drew freely from Science and the Modern Life, the last paragraph a touching mangle of tiny truths. Reese was dumbstruck.

"I will write you again," she'd scribbled, "when I re-enter the world. For now, think of me as a pleasant memory and something soft you knew. Bye-bye."

Reese was love-sawed; and the drunk he sought that night was positively medieval. There was slop in his thoughts—as well as self-pity, sorrow, and wicked lessons in heartcraft. "I am without solace or affection in this world," he hollered. "You're looking at a man who *aches!*" He made all the bars around Iota—El Corral, Miss Lilly's Silver Slipper, E's Joint, etc.—marching into each, his shirttail flapping behind, his tearful eyes flashing with woeful and frenzied lights, shouting that he was a left man and full of doom. "Somebody hit me!" he cried. "I want to leave this vulgar planet!" Nobody obliged, of course, until he stormed into the Mile 39 outside of Tatum. Pale and rancid with some kind of consumptive sweat, he was drunk-clobbered then, the world swirling without comfort, calm, or knowable center. "You're looking at a feeble and pained hombre," he said to the bartender. "I want black booze and a straw. Then loan me an axe so I can cut off your nose." The dude kept an Al Kaline Louisville Slugger behind the bar for hard cases like Reese. "I know your wife," Reese declared, swinging his attention to a pair of slick-dressed cowpokes at the bumper-pool table. "She's a lapdog. I know men who'd eat her hair. I know some fellas who'd—" Whacking the bar with his hand, steadying himself against a stool, he was just coming—"I am familiar with everything!"—to the smelly and splendid notions of Betrayal and Sin when the fellow clipped him, Reese spinning down with a smile and a shiver.

"I am laying aside trouble," he told the boys at work the next day, a lump the size of a tomato behind his ear. "I am reaching out for sense and duty. I have opened myself up to the fortunate future."

First thing, he fixed up the Airstream, bought new furniture, laid carpet (a gold thing with the fine texture of cat fur), got himself a self-warming and restful waterbed. "May my dreams be colorful and baby-like," he said. "If not, may I then forget them." He started taking guitar lessons. "Music lessens the tensions of the spirit," he told the boys. He was learning tunes quickly, his favorites melodious with melancholy: "You don't miss your water," he crooned, "till your well runs dry."

At the Junior College, he went purposefully into a wrathful and morbid kung fu, working private and paranoid embellishments on the ancient art with queer bellywork, some toecraft of uncertain origin, and special desert words. "Chop-chop!" he'd howl, his face a snarl of desire and grue, taking patient aim on a cinderblock—"Evil and Wrong!"—and he'd cut loose as if forsaking everything humanoid; his face said, *Listen up, I am into mortification and the promise of a new life; without reason, I have been abandoned; I am twenty-eight, raised by ordinary mortals and profitably employed in the oil business; folks, you are looking at a sore and confused man.*

Then he started dating again.

The first lady answered the door in an eccentric, flamenco ensemble, her shining and blank face a machine to crush hearts. Her name was Tucker. Tarvez Tucker.

"Reese," she began, "I am an adult, a Leo, and so cannot be hoodwinked. I do not respond to normal wooing."

"Nor do I," he said. "I appreciate hand-holding and gifts."

"You will like me," she said. "Even my interiors are irresistible."

They went to the Rocket Drive-In and, sitting in the back seat of her Fairlane, they went round and round—"Speak to me, Sweetness," she kept barking. "Tell me I'm grand!"—ending in an athletic tangle of ears, hips and necks. The courtship was modern—loopy and subtle as chain. "You're wonderful," Reese insisted, going for her throat. "You remind me of a pearl." She was squatting on his stomach, her face breath-taking, pit-free and strange as heaven.

"You got any dope?" she said. "I like to be numb when I kiss."

The next one was Dorene, a Texas Tech Zeta in town for the summer. Her face a blaze of idealism, she talked about Ruin and Intrigue; and the heart went right out of Reese. He was for Goodness, he said. He was against dwelling in the grief-plagued regions of the human condition.

"I am for Light," he declared, "and Air and Friendship. You won't catch me being naughty."

"Shoot," Dorene said.

The next day he received the letter that said that Billy Jean La Took had re-entered the world. "Jesus," he bawled. He stayed in bed, sleeping raggedly, thrashing, his toilsome and cheerless dreams a feast of sadness and regret. Hungry and unshaved, he once got up to watch TV, but the themes of the daytime shows were too familiar: Dread and Disappointment. Everyone—harridan, coquette, shopgirl, and wealthy patron of the arts—reminded him of Billy Jean La Took. On that one he'd note her long, finely boned and lickable neck, on another her youthful legs. Here was a something anatomical—a pore, say, or loose coil of hair—and there a gesture or sympathetic word. She was the pretty ones and the ugly, both. The ignorant, the poor, the infirm, the fit, the stay-at-home, the innocent—she was them all. She was stomped love, expectation, reward and fulfillment.

Shaking and fevered, he searched the trailer all Sunday, hunting for something—a hairpin, shower thong—she might have forgotten. He could almost smell her—something between ripe and medical, somewhere between soap and the outdoors. Under the bathroom sink, he found a knot of her hairs—so red and fine that speech left him and he found himself standing stiff-backed and trembling in front of the mirror, sputtering, "Uh-uh-uh-uh." In a dresser drawer, he found lipstick. It was the shade, Peach Lustre, that did it, nearly smashed him.

On Monday, he merely walked through work, practically blind. You could have been talking to a wrench. It must've been an instinct for caution which got him through without injury, fitting pipe, doing the mud just so. "Boys," he said, "I am being sandbagged by memory."

He could see her sitting across from him at the kitchen table, lacquering her sharp and now worshipped fingernails or studying a romance that turned her good face dark in the contemplation of villainous but handsome heroes. "Reese," she'd murmur, "tell me again about your vandal days and petty crimes." And he'd travel the whole route of his average, reckless youth—from shoplifting at Woolworth's to shooting out streetlights with fence staples. He'd touch everything: adolescence, maturity, his minor achievements. "Tell me, too," she'd continue, "about your stern Daddy and always fretful Mama."

Then the idea hit him. "I will see her," he said. He got out the letter and looked at the address: Deming, New Mexico.

That night he settled into a profound sleep. It was a brave and simple picture he made, supine and stiff and snoring, his long fingers steepled over his stubborn heart, his face alive yet frozen in wholesome mirth—as if he'd touched, by accident or by design, a wild and evil beauty.

Before sunup, he hit the road, racing out to meet those two hundred miles between hither and yon with an expression lit by derelict joy. It was the hair and grit of life, what it was. He was singing—"Come back and try me again, Mama!"—his voice scaling all but the high and sissy notes; he was beating time on the steering wheel—sunlight orange, streaming and glorious—the desert shimmering and speaking to him of Triumph and Virtue. You could tell that the Contrary, Curious and Puzzling were gone, and he was high-balling in the realm of the Superb and Jaunty, his three-dollar Feed hat squashed low on his forehead, his eyes twinkling with vim and understanding.

"I am happy and elevated by knowledge," he told the dude who filled the pickup at the Standard station near Mescalero. The man was hangdog—grave, thoughtful and tragic—the very picture of failure. "My name's Meat," he said. "I gave up a long time ago. I'm into mongrelism now."

"You got to buck up," Reese told him. "You got to practice vigilance and patience. Trust me, you'll get what you need."

Outside Alamogordo, Reese picked up two six-packs and, eighty miles later, liquored and popeyed and vanquished, he plugged into a surly interior dialogue with his subconscious. It was turmoil, what it was—doubt and the threat of failure. "Holy Jesus!" he hollered to himself, "I am hearing uproar and harangue." He'd grab hold of a thought, hang on for a frenzied instant, then see another. "She loves me, I know it!" He sang the Wang-Wang blues and, bouncing viciously down the highway, went eyeball-to-eyeball with his life story. "Billy Jean," he shouted, "I am going to fetch you away."

Near Las Cruces, his truck rattling and banging, the engine screeching, the cab a furnace of dust and heat and madness, he took a deep bite of some first-rate doodley-squat philosophy: "Son," he yelled at a Mercury with Arizona plates as it passed, "they should've never put the idea of love in the mind of a man!" So, by the time he blasted into Deming, his face yellow with hope, he was in a state as pure and unbecoming as loneliness, his heart thumping furiously, his well-folded brain crimped and throbbing.

"I am standing in a phone booth across the street," he said, "and I can tell you are sad and angry. Come out of your house."

She appeared in a flash, and Reese went manfully to the curb of Iron Street, his internal juices running hot, and told her that she'd gone to seed, was in a dire funk, couldn't live without his heedful care. "You're depressed and idle," he shouted. "Look at your hands, you're nervous. Jealous, too. You're living in a mansion of pain."

"I'm pretty," she yelled back. "You ought to see my skin."

She showed him her hard and well-remembered tummy, and Reese felt all intelligence drain right out of him.

"I am missing you," he said.

"I'm strong now," she answered. "Useful, also. You ought to practice toughness. King Daddy recommends crafts and daily exercise."

"You miss me," he said. "I can tell. I can see it in your hair." It was a magnificent and complicated pile, the product of timely tending.

"How's the trailer?"

He made up a story about selling it to the Dead. He was just renting it, he said, from the raggedy-ass spirits of Hamlet and the Count of Monte Cristo. Those boys, too, were butchered by love. "Why don't you come back with me?"

"Can't," she said. "King Daddy would disapprove. He might break my arms. Plus, I love him."

"Could we kiss?"

She said yes, and he lurched across the street, weak-kneed and stiff-armed, zeal tugging him this way, dread the other. "My life is dandy," he said, "except you're not in it." It was a moment of supreme expectancy. "No tongue," she warned. "I'm keeping my eyes open, too." You could tell that kiss really ripped the spine out of him. She stood as still and icy and unyielding as a glacier.

"Say bye-bye to me, Reese."

"I'm melting inside," he groaned.

"Don't," she said. She gave him some advice: Stand up straight. Be forthright. Avoid fat and salt. Choose yourself in all things. Never drink alone. Look on the bright side. "King Daddy told me those and now I am gorgeous and content. Adios."

All the way back to Iota, he kept going over it in his mind. Be cool, he told himself. You're a handsome creature. And tall. You got a whole inventory of good points and few low habits. You are a helpful co-worker, pay debts regular, and know how to eat with a fork. The only thing you lack is the woman you love. By Las Cruces, he was limp and weepy, his truck whipping all over the road. He was drenched with weakness. "Okay," he said to himself, "I will be strong. Watch my smoke."

Immediately, he surged into a new program—suave haircut, close-fitting shirts and new trousers. "I am an emporium of pride," he told the boys. "I am reading books about almost unexplainable concepts—space and such. I'm learning dance, too. You should see my routines." He went out with Tarvez Tucker.

"Sweet thing," he told her, "before I was swamped with loneliness. I now want to swallow you whole."

Next night he called Dorene, the Texas Tech Zeta.

"You're talking to a new hombre," he said. "Look outside your window."

"Why?"

"In five minutes, I will be there. You will see by my gleaming face that I mean business."

But the gloom only deepened.

Everything reminded him of Billy Jean La Took. Instead of disappearing or shrinking from memory, she got bigger, tastier, more moral, stronger, slimmer, lovelier, smoother, more substantial. She was his heartbone and his tendons, all the grit that made him yelp and swell with fondness. She was nighttime, lovers' sunset, refreshing winds and soothing rainstorms. Everywhere he went, he kept seeing her: in the Safeway, her khaki shorts riding up her cheeks; at the A&W, her voice husky and permanent; at the wheel of his truck, her arms golden and fragile. And when he lay on his waterbed, listening to nightsounds, the past atop him like a fat man, the nightsweats hot and slick, he often imagined her standing on the edge of his memory, sweet and moist and without rival on this worthy earth.

"Dorene," he said one night, "I have stopped sniveling. I am upright in all things. I am courteous and control my temper. But you, honey, are still a cruel disappointment to my heart."

Another month passed before he told the boys what he planned. "I will see her once more," he said. "I been thinking about it the whole while. She is gone, true. But I am not convinced."

He didn't write, phone, nothing. Just one morning, flush-faced and tense with righteousness, he roared up the Chevy, closed the window to concentrate, and stomped on the gas pedal with a force that rippled the chassis and had the engine smoking and clanking and knocking by Ruidoso. "You remember me," Reese said to the guy who put in the oil. It was Meat, the same sour gent Reese'd seen before. "I came through months ago. I was talking knowledge and wisdom. My thoughts were fragrant."

Meat's face was pinched with suspicion.

"Well, forget that crap," Reese was saying. "You're looking at a man in awful condition. If I weren't healthy, I'd be dead."

This time he didn't buy beer in Alamogordo—just zipped through, headers banging, something greasy throwing off a shower of sparks— yelling out the window that his name was Reese Joe Newell and the words that applied to him were *hard-bitten, driven, perilous, wasted, crazed, fitful, heartsore* and *within an eyelash of beautiful.* Not to mention *sad* and *well-intentioned.*

"I am desperate," he yelled at the D.J., Fast Eddie Morris. Bouncing, the seat springs going "Boing-Boing!", he hammered on the dash, several plastic pieces popping loose, one nicking him on the cheek. "Play me music that speaks to heartbreak!"

He clattered into Deming in a purblind state, mouth-breathing and jumpy like an abused animal. "Gimme green lights and wary drivers," he yowled, his head pounding. Twice he leaned on the horn, truly frightening the unobservant, before he slammed to a stop outside Billy Jean La Took's house. It was afternoon, and he peeked in her window.

"Jesus," he groaned, pounding himself on the breastbone. She was wearing a sporty and virtually illegal nightie—one so sheer and frilly that he felt crippled by despair. It was then that he felt her falling away from him. For keeps. The effect was swift, primary and consummate. "Who is that woman?" he wanted to say. "Is it true that she loved me once?"

"Hey," she said when she saw him, "I thought I was done with you. You're lunatic, Reese."

"I am here to put you out of my mind," he said. "I want to get on to the next phase of my life."

Her face was earnest and sexy. "You should come back later. Meet King Daddy. He'd inspire you too."

"Open the door," Reese said. "I want to see your living room. Kitchen, too. Think of me as a guest."

"You've seen enough already." She was pulling on a robe, in the process exposing generous and well-defined thigh muscles.

He couldn't believe it. She was as distant from him as he from his ancestral fishes.

"I am dismayed," she was saying. "You're an exasperating person, Reese."

"Did you love me?"

"You're a mistake, Reese honey." Nervously, she hustled around that bedroom, straightening knick-knacks—Teddy bears, glass doodads, even touching those two horrible plants—and fluffing the bedspread. "Yes, I loved you once," she said. "I love you no more. Now, go home."

He saw himself as she must have seen him: sullen and lame-headed, grim and stupid.

"I am at the peak of my powers," she was saying, "I bowl, think well of myself and my neighbors, am charitable and take according to my needs. My love is elsewhere, sweetness. Now, split. King Daddy is due in a jiffy."

"I will think of you always," Reese said, moving from the window.

All the way back to Iota, he was in a state of genuine peace, abstract and solemn, waving good-naturedly to truckers, humming a pleasant tune of his own creation, and, every third mile or so, smacking himself in the head. "You can never tell about love," he told Meat. "It's a nice thing for many." His smile was as stiff as a clown's. "She wanted me back," he told the boys the following day. "From now on, I'm putting up a whole series of promises: be smart and go willingly to the end of a thing." It was a lie, of course, but the boys accepted it as being as important to him as the memory of his first fight, and they hung with him until one day, three months later, when a look of real insight filled his eyes and he said:

"Boys, I'm a fool."

A PRIVATE LANDSCAPE

MELISSA BROWN PRITCHARD

Melissa Brown Pritchard was born in 1948 in San Mateo, California, graduated in 1970 from the University of California, Santa Barbara, and now lives in Evanston, Illinois, with her husband and two daughters. Her fiction has appeared in *Ascent, Prairie Schooner, The Kenyon Review, Story Quarterly* and other magazines. She has received three Illinois Arts Council Awards and is now at work on a novel.

Slouched in the window seat, Deirdre dutifully reads a novel for her schoolwork. Her young face is remote, attending to more complex characters than mine.

"Tea?" I ask again.

She hesitates. "No. What are you making?"

I smack two eggs one-handedly against the bowl, a trick Mother insisted I inherit.

"Carrot cake. These carrots from last year's garden are crying to be done away with."

Deirdre's slight smile indicates that I am simple, overly concerned with food and trivialities; she goes back to her reading, her education.

I shall wind up swallowing this cake myself. Deirdre is on a health kick this week, claiming that yoghurt and grapefruit juice are all she needs. Martin, in an uncharacteristically vain humor, has also gone off his feed.

Last night, he commented on my weight problem. Undressing with no eye toward pleasing anybody, dropping my frayed nightgown over my head, I was unaware, until I heard his soft but disapproving words, that I was being observed from our bed, my flesh critically measured. Martin's aesthetics, I tell myself, were always sadly predictable. He wistfully watches Deirdre these days, hugs her waist tightly, strokes her long black hair while I scrape dishes and carry up laundry from the basement. Perhaps I'll move back into the guest room whenever I

Copyright © 1982 by The Kenyon Review. First appeared in *The Kenyon Review*, Vol. IV, No. 4. Reprinted by permission.

undress, fetch back the humble privacy I had trustingly set aside upon my marriage.

"Deirdre? Kindly remember to keep your legs together when you wear a dress."

She sighs over my prudery and with intense exaggeration rearranges herself in the window seat. Yesterday I requested that she not loll about the house in her bikini underwear when her father was expected home. "You're nearly fourteen years old," I said by way of justification. She had shrugged and brushed wearily past me; her skin, I thought, smelled strongly of my best perfume.

After driving alongside miles of immaculate white fencing, I turn into the graveled driveway of the horse-farm and pull up near the house. I walk over to the fence, rest my arms upon the top railing, and watch the horses, their necks languidly dropped, mouths tearing the grass in small arcs. That bowing curve of a horse's neck suggests the prehistoric, an era comfortingly free of human conflict. I wonder how such powerful animals could be content, moving listlessly behind expensive but brittle fencing.

The owner steps out from her house, and we walk across to the green and white stables. Inside it is dim and smells strongly of hay and salt. Crossing bands of sunlight are flecked, like coarse tweed, with bits of hay and dust. Most of the stalls are vacant but a few horses turn their heads toward us as we approach, their eyes white-rimmed, shining past us toward the open doors.

We stop in front of one stall where a dark red horse holds his head suspiciously high and tight, his ears laid back. Only tentatively proffered, I withdraw my hand as his square lip curls back. Foul-tempered, I think, succumbing to a private notion about red horses, red anything. His eyes pitch back defiantly and I shake my head, no, not this one.

The stable phone rings, the woman excuses herself, and shielding my eyes from the cutting sunlight, I walk outside again. The pasture is sprinkled with the yellow blurs of dandelion and the mild blue wheels of chicory. Sparrows skim and cry out over the glistening backs of grazing horses. I climb a white railing and watch as a stocky black mare trots over to another horse and gives it a sly, aggressive nip in the rear. The bitten horse mildly moves aside and continues grazing. Over by the highway, reduced to a fine porcelainlike figure, stands a white horse, head lifted as though reading the fertile spring wind. He crosses the pasture and stops within a few yards of me. His expression is peculiarly intelligent. I notice that his underbelly is a soft gray.

"I would like to purchase this white horse," I say as soon as the owner finds me. We agree on a price, more than I had intended to spend, but I know better than to bargain with fate. We discuss terms of payment, veterinarians, places to buy tack and feed. She promises to deliver the horse to me on the day before my daughter's fourteenth birthday.

On the drive back home, I consider how Deirdre will look, sitting upon the back of a pale, galloping horse, her dark hair lifting and falling. I imagine them set against the black and green tracery of the woods behind our property.

The box with the monogrammed blouse lies unwrapped beside Deirdre's dinner plate. In the bathroom, the faucets are switched on, absorbing her disappointed sobs.

Martin is looking worried, so I finally whisper, "Go in and comfort her, tell her next year we promise her a horse, we couldn't afford one this year, and I'll go up to the barn and get him."

From running the slight uphill to the barn, I am breathless, sliding back the wooden bar and stepping into the darkness. The barn is old, with loose tongues of air between the sagging plankings; it has been empty for the two years we've owned it. We are not farmers or husbandmen, our possessions fit neatly into the house. My garden tools stand upright in a small metal shed. Nothing overlaps.

I pick out the gleam of the white horse before the electric light abruptly haloes him; his neck curved around, his eyes fixed on me. Unhitching the rope, I lead him out of the barn and down the soft, grassy path into the corral. I stroke his back, comparing its milky tint to that of the moon overhead, neither of them purely white. Against his flesh, my hand feels heavy, forgetful, and with a small, bitter feeling in me, I go back to the house.

Deirdre sits at the kitchen table, Martin holds one of his hands over hers, grateful for any contact she allows him. Eye shadow is smudged on the lids of her lowered eyes. Martin's hand is covering hers. She smiles thinly, her face blotched.

"Sorry, Mom. Still a baby about some things I guess." She looks ready to cry again, but brave girl, crunches up another flowered Kleenex, adds it to the pile in front of her, and thanks me for the blouse.

"That's all right, darling." I bend down, kiss the top of her head. Martin says, "Come on down to the creek with us. I'll get the flashlights and afterwards we can drive into town for some ice cream."

She winces, but still subdued from her own outburst, answers, "Sure, Dad."

The moon shines upon our property, exposing our small family. I tell Deirdre that she must shut her eyes for a minute or two. She stumbles between us and when Martin opens the corral gate, I think she has guessed, but her eyes remain shut. We place her a few feet from the white horse.

"Open your eyes, darling." I am crying now. "And Happy Birthday!"

My original feeling for the horse had minimized; he became, for a time, an oversized pet I watched from a distance as I worked in the garden or as I backed the car down the driveway. I paid a number of expensive vet bills. My daughter persuaded me into one disastrous riding lesson under her instruction, with Martin looking on. I contrasted her vital buoyant manner with my own clayish, clumsy ability and did not ride again.

At some moment during summer's peak, the garden overreaches its own ripeness; vegetation hangs exhausted, overcome by its own lush growth. This is my least favorite time of year, when the harvest is forgotten; unpicked tomatoes split open on trailing, imperfect vines. This is also my least favorite wedge of the afternoon, between noon and four o'clock, an empty, glaring period for me. I can, with some accuracy, match my own age and season to this month and this hour. From the porch where I sit, pinned to my chair by a humidity more potent than gravity, I see the white horse, standing inert and passive. I always envisioned horses as magnificent, dreamlike creatures, rearing heavenward, manes swirling like seagrass. It is not so. A horse passes its time like most anything else, placid, concerned only with whatever passes before its eyes. The horse, sapped by domesticity, confined by fences, has disillusioned me. I expected more from it.

Deirdre and Martin quarreled again last night. Instinctively, I stayed clear of their conflict, scenting its primitive, disturbing theme. The omnipotent, adored father, supplanted in the child's affections by a young stranger, in this case, our neighbor's pleasant-mannered, nice-looking son.

They argued over the horse, over Deirdre's neglect of him. She goes out with her young friend, forgets to groom the horse. She rides him less and less. Martin says he is upset with her for so casually abandoning a creature who depends on her for care and affection. Of course, he has a point.

I have gone out myself to groom the horse, tugging at his mane with the metal comb, plucking out burrs from his tail, and with the curved pick, prying rocks from the greenish, mossy trenches of his hooves. I brush along the supple hills of his hips, following the direction, the grain. I remind myself that the horse was a gift to my daughter, and that I should not long for a thing which lies beyond my personal, private landscape.

I prattle on about a letter from an old school friend, about a greedy crow I chased from the garden. Deirdre licks yoghurt off the tip of her spoon, then excuses herself to go and dress for her date. Martin eats in order to be done with eating, then says he is going out for a walk. I praise myself for not feeling hurt that I am not invited and dump dishes in the sink, wipe down counters, and feel vexed that no one thought to help me. But I never ask for help, or even demand it; I wish to appear self-sufficient before my family because I suspect I am not. Damn. I turn off the water, leave the kitchen undone, and go after my husband in the summer twilight.

In the middle of the creek, we sit on rocks as bleached and flattened as the horse's flank I brushed this morning. Martin snaps a dry stick into pieces, letting each bit drop into the swirling water and take its course. He flicks the last chip of wood; it lodges between our two stones, resisting the current of water.

Martin looks tired. The loss of weight from his recent diet has not improved him; it has left him slack, gaunt.

Plunging my arm into the softly buckling water, I am shocked by its coldness.

"I asked Deirdre to stop going about the house in her underwear when you're home."

I remember Martin's criticisms as I undressed in our bedroom that night, and holding my wet, reddened hand up to the sky, hear my voice admit, "Sometimes I almost hate her."

I climb awkwardly over to my husband and crouch down. He puts an arm around me, draws me close. We sit, needing comfort, upon a large, flat stone until we become cramped and stiff from sitting so motionless, surrounded by water.

Walking home in the dark, without a flashlight, I trip across a fallen cottonwood tree, bruising my shin on its upreaching, tangled root. Martin is concerned and helps me up.

Back home, relieved that our house is emptied of her, we make oddly exuberant love. Afterward, we are reserved toward one another, sitting up late, drinking brandies, and reading fiction, the light steady between our two chairs, waiting for Deirdre.

One-thirty and she has not come home. Martin, furious with me for not knowing the address of the party she has gone to, is in the kitchen, watching television and thinking about calling the police. In the living room, I am trying to understand the jealousy and resentment I feel toward my only child. When the telephone rings, Martin answers, comes into the doorway.

"She wants you. She wants to talk to you."

In a crisis, she has always reached for me.

I wave a signal to Martin that she is all right. He frowns, so, muffling the phone, I explain that it's a problem with her new boyfriend.

"Deirdre, please, stop it. Stop crying now. It's all right."

Martin sets down a pencil, a pad of paper, and I write down the address she gives me.

"OK, honey, hang on, we'll be there in about twenty minutes. Yes, Daddy's fine. He's right here and he's just fine."

Martin is gone. Looking through the house, I discover him in Deirdre's room, a place he has seldom entered, respectful of his child's privacy. Now he is bent over her dressing table, holding open a grocery sack, and all of it, cosmetics, mirrors, ribbons, hair rollers, all the paraphernalia of a young female, is tumbling into the bag. When the dressing table is bare, he goes to the bulletin board above her bed and tears down pictures of rock stars and movie stars. They float, without a change of expression, into the grocery bag. Martin takes the bag outside, sets it inside the garbage can, and we drive into town to find Deirdre. She sits in the back seat on the way home, and none of us says anything.

Sitting on the edge of her bed, I apologize and try to explain for Martin, and I am the one who smooths her dark hair. She has lately denied me this power to comfort her and, hungrily, I draw her back into myself. She relates a small, scattered story of betrayal and jealousy at a friend's party. I am proud that she defended the values we taught her, but with apprehension I read her expression, which tells me that one day she will risk a different choice, hurting us in the process. But now Deirdre says she loves me, and believing her, I leave her sleeping and safe again, a recovered part of my own self.

In the dark living room, Martin, at a loss in his own house, is staring out of a window.

"She's fine," I say lightly. "You'd be proud of her." I feel myself the center of the family once again, though this is temporary power, splinted and artificial. He answers only that he is exhausted and is going to bed.

The late-summer moon, like a veined marble bowl, spills out an abundance of light. I walk up the hill to the barn, take down the saddle, the bridle, and go back down to the corral. Here, come here, hey, and the white horse, splashed with shadow, moves over to me. Calmly, I slip the bit and the bridle over him and cinch up the saddle. I have watched Deirdre do this many times. He absorbs my clumsiness as I climb up upon his broad back.

Passing out of the corral gate, I see the house where my daughter and my husband sleep in rooms broken off from each other. I turn away from them and ride unburdened through damp grasses, straying from those boundaries set by daylight, by marriage, by family, by the erosion of time upon my private life.

With an urge to swiftness, the horse gallops forward and forward into the humid and calling darkness. A wildness begins to rise up in me, when I glimpse the uprooted cottonwood, the tree I had fallen across earlier this evening.

In steady, lulling rhythm, the white horse goes straight for it, his breath drawing in and out of the moist swell of his lungs. We rise dreamlike, above the tree, both of us soaring up, freed from the heavy, clinging earth.

Not far away, glittering like falseness, runs the silver and black cord of creek water, which, even in this particular season, is considered pure, quite excellent for our family to drink.

THE MODEL

BERNARD MALAMUD

Mr. Malamud teaches at Bennington College and lives in New York
City and Vermont. His *Collected Stories* was published in October
1983.

Early one morning, Ephraim Elihu rang up the Art Students League
and asked the woman who answered the phone how he could locate an
experienced female model he could paint nude. He told the woman
that he wanted someone of about thirty. "Could you possibly help
me?"

"I don't recognize your name," said the woman on the telephone.
"Have you ever dealt with us before? Some of our students will work as
models, but usually only for painters we know." Mr. Elihu said he
hadn't. He wanted it understood he was an amateur painter who had
once studied at the League.

"Do you have a studio?"

"It's a large living room with lots of light. I'm no youngster," he said,
"but after many years I've begun painting again and I'd like to do some
nude studies to get back my feeling for form. I'm not a professional
painter, but I'm serious about painting. If you want any references as to
my character, I can supply them."

He asked her what the going rate for models was, and the woman,
after a pause, said, "Six dollars the hour."

Mr. Elihu said that was satisfactory to him. He wanted to talk
longer, but she did not encourage him to. She wrote down his name
and address and said she thought she could have someone for him the
day after tomorrow. He thanked her for her consideration.

That was on Wednesday. The model appeared on Friday morning.
She had telephoned the night before, and they had settled on a time
for her to come. She rang his bell shortly after nine, and Mr. Elihu

Copyright © 1983 by Bernard Malamud. First appeared in *The Atlantic Monthly*.
Reprinted by permission of Farrar, Straus & Giroux, Inc.

went at once to the door. He was a gray-haired man of seventy who lived in a brownstone house near Ninth Avenue, and he was excited by the prospect of painting this young woman.

The model was a plain-looking woman of twenty-seven or so, and the old painter decided her best features were her eyes. She was wearing a blue raincoat, though it was a clear spring day. The old painter liked her but kept that to himself. She barely glanced at him as she walked firmly into the room.

"Good day," he said, and she answered, "Good day."

"It's like spring," said the old man. "The foliage is starting up again."

"Where do you want me to change?" asked the model.

Mr. Elihu asked her her name, and she responded, "Ms. Perry."

"You can change in the bathroom, I would say, Miss Perry, or if you like, my own room—down the hall—is empty, and you can change there also. It's warmer than the bathroom."

The model said it made no difference to her but she thought she would rather change in the bathroom.

"That is as you wish," said the elderly man.

"Is your wife around?" she then asked, glancing into the room.

"No, I happen to be a widower."

He said he had had a daughter once, but she had died in an accident. The model said she was sorry. "I'll change and be out in a few fast minutes."

"No hurry at all," said Mr. Elihu, glad he was about to paint her.

Ms. Perry entered the bathroom, undressed there, and returned quickly. She slipped off her terry-cloth robe. Her head and shoulders were slender and well formed. She asked the old man how he would like her to pose. He was standing by an enamel-top kitchen table near a large window. On the tabletop he had squeezed out, and was mixing together, the contents of two small tubes of paint. There were three other tubes, which he did not touch. The model, taking a last drag of a cigarette, pressed it out against a coffee-can lid on the kitchen table.

"I hope you don't mind if I take a puff once in a while?"

"I don't mind, if you do it when we take a break."

"That's all I meant."

She was watching him as he slowly mixed his colors.

Mr. Elihu did not immediately look at her nude body but said he would like her to sit in the chair by the window. They were facing a back yard with an ailanthus tree whose leaves had just come out.

"How would you like me to sit, legs crossed or not crossed?"

"However you prefer that. Crossed or uncrossed doesn't make much of a difference to me. Whatever makes you feel comfortable."

The model seemed surprised at that, but she sat down in the yellow chair by the window and crossed one leg over the other. Her figure was good.

"Is this okay for you?"

Mr. Elihu nodded. "Fine," he said. "Very fine."

He dipped his brush into the paint he had mixed on the tabletop, and after glancing at the model's nude body, began to paint. He would look at her, then look quickly away, as if he were afraid of affronting her. But his expression was objective. He painted apparently casually, from time to time gazing up at the model. He did not often look at her. She seemed not to be aware of him. Once she turned to observe the ailanthus tree, and he studied her momentarily to see what she might have seen in it.

Then she began to watch the painter with interest. She watched his eyes and she watched his hands. He wondered if he was doing something wrong. At the end of about an hour she rose impatiently from the yellow chair.

"Tired?" he asked.

"It isn't that," she said, "but I would like to know what in the name of Christ you think you are doing? I frankly don't think you know the first thing about painting."

She had astonished him. He quickly covered the canvas with a towel.

After a long moment, Mr. Elihu, breathing shallowly, wet his dry lips and said he was making no claims for himself as a painter. He said he had tried to make that absolutely clear to the woman he had talked to at the art school when he called.

Then he said, "I might have made a mistake in asking you to come to this house today. I think I should have tested myself a while longer, just so I wouldn't be wasting anybody's time. I guess I am not ready to do what I would like to do."

"I don't care how long you have tested yourself," said Ms. Perry. "I honestly don't think you have painted me at all. In fact, I felt you weren't interested in painting me. I think you're interested in letting your eyes go over my naked body for certain reasons of your own. I don't know what your personal needs are, but I'm damn well sure that most of them have nothing to do with painting."

"I guess I have made a mistake."

"I guess you have," said the model. She had her robe on now, the belt pulled tight.

"I'm a painter," she said, "and I model because I am broke, but I know a fake when I see one."

"I wouldn't feel so bad," said Mr. Elihu, "if I hadn't gone out of my way to explain the situation to that lady at the Art Students League."

"I'm sorry this happened," Mr. Elihu said hoarsely. "I should have thought it through more than I did. I'm seventy years of age. I have always loved women and felt a sad loss that I have no particular women friends at this time of my life. That's one of the reasons I wanted to paint again, though I make no claims that I was ever greatly talented. Also, I guess I didn't realize how much about painting I have forgotten. Not only about that, but also about the female body. I didn't realize I would be so moved by yours, and, on reflection, about the way my life has gone. I hoped painting again would refresh my feeling for life. I regret that I have inconvenienced and disturbed you."

"I'll be paid for my inconvenience," Ms. Perry said, "but what you can't pay me for is the insult of coming here and submitting myself to your eyes crawling on my body."

"I didn't mean it as an insult."

"That's what it feels like to me."

She then asked Mr. Elihu to disrobe.

"I?" he said, surprised. "What for?"

"I want to sketch you. Take your pants and shirt off."

He said he had barely got rid of his winter underwear, but she did not smile.

Mr. Elihu disrobed, ashamed of how he must look to her.

With quick strokes she sketched his form. He was not a bad-looking man, but felt bad. When she had the sketch, she dipped his brush into a blob of black pigment she had squeezed out of a tube and smeared his features, leaving a black mess.

He watched her hating him, but said nothing.

Ms. Perry tossed the brush into a wastebasket and returned to the bathroom for her clothing.

The old man wrote out a check for her for the sum they had agreed on. He was ashamed to sign his name, but he signed it and handed it to her. Ms. Perry slipped the check into her large purse and left.

He thought that in her way she was not a bad-looking woman, though she lacked grace. The old man then asked himself, "Is there nothing more to my life than it is now? Is this all that is left to me?"

The answer seemed to be yes, and he wept at how old he had so quickly become.

Afterward he removed the towel over his canvas and tried to fill in her face, but he had already forgotten it.

THE THIRD COUNT

ANDREW FETLER

Andrew Fetler is the author of *The Travelers*, a novel, and *To Byzantium*, stories. He teaches at the University of Massachusetts, Amherst. This is his second appearance in the O. Henry collection.

I am waiting for my sister Nina to drive up from Boston for our Saturday lunch in my house on Bay Road, an old country road near Dudleyville. For a bachelor of fifty-nine, I make good lunches, she says. I have covered the salad with Saran Wrap and put it in the fridge. She wants her lettuce crisp, with a tomato from my garden and a sliced boiled egg. Besides the salad, we will have chicken rice soup (we had chicken noodle last week), cold cuts, and toast with Diet Mazola. For dessert, fresh peaches and cottage cheese. She is dieting again.

For thirty years my sister Nina has been seeing psychiatrists and feeling better about herself. "It's a *process!*" She has discovered health foods, but won't refuse an offer of Bavarian cream pie. She has tried *est*, folk dances of many cultures (Roumanian dances are fantastic), protein powders for clearing her blood, sweetened calcium tablets for her puffy eyelids, and human potential encounters for raising her consciousness. But not until Jesus saved her, a year ago, could she forgive our father for having been a Christian.

Our father, Hamilton Crail, was a successful businessman and a founding father of the Full Gospel Church in Boston. As an elder of that church he practiced a mixture of Scottish Calvinism and American fundamentalism. He struggled continually against sins of the flesh. When my sister Nina was fourteen, for example, he marched her off to his study one night for bringing the devil into our home. I don't know how she could have provoked our father. Did he catch her fondling herself, or wearing a pretty dress, or smiling while wearing a pretty

Copyright © 1983 by TriQuarterly. First appeared in *TriQuarterly*. Reprinted by permission.

dress? Shamed and bewildered in his study, she sobbed and on command croaked the Repentance Song: "Just as I am, without one plea." Apparently not satisfied, he took her to his study again the following night, for closer questioning behind his locked door.

And then, two months after these curious interrogations in Nina's fourteenth year, she fell sick and had to be taken to the hospital. She was brought home looking pale and wilted, cured of an "infection." Our father praised the Lord, and in church, as if inspired by Nina's recovery, he stirred up the congregation against our pastor for false preaching, and had him fired. God, our father cried from the pulpit, holding up the Bible for his authority, could not use a modernist who doubted Creation Science and tolerated immoral books in public schools. Our false pastor, moreover, had done nothing to rescue from a mental hospital a young widow, a firecracker for the Lord, who had branded the foreheads of her two children with the emblem of the cross, to protect them from demons. The widow ought not to have used a heated knife, our father allowed, but her love and faith were great.

We were happy, Nina and I and our three brothers, when we could tiptoe through the day without attracting our father's attention. We scattered when we heard him coming, or froze in guilty attitudes when his figure loomed in the doorway. We could not live up to his standards. But we were not to despair. Our sins were God's opportunities. Hamilton Crail never hugged his children, flesh revolted him, but he worried about our souls. He believed in spiritual diagrams and drew pictures of our souls—a rectangle, say, containing circles and arrows going in and out.

Silent and withdrawn since her visit to the hospital, Nina found music harder to ignore than diagrams. Sometimes, when the church choir sang "Perfect submission, perfect delight," she was touched by the love of Jesus and wept. "Filled with His goodness, lost in His love."

But when the call to repent thundered from the pulpit, she did not go forward to prostrate herself before the elders, among whom Hamilton Crail stood waiting darkly.

My sister Nina is fifty-five years old now and very fat, and she has spent her life worrying about her weight. A year ago, at a meeting in Boston of charismatic youngsters who call themselves The Disciples, she found happiness, she tells me, that cannot be expressed in words. She gave herself to Jesus completely, without reservations—Nina insists upon her surrender by tapping her chest with her chubby fist—and in return Jesus has taken her burdens upon Himself. "The only word for it is bliss!" she says, chattering without stop—she who used to hesitate before speaking—and smiles at my wonder. She feels omnipotent, she could do anything, she declares, and looks around my living room for a mountain to move.

Nina has backslidden twice since her conversion a year ago. During these dark spells that test her faith, lasting two or three weeks, she looks miserable and mutters about our father. "He must have hated me," she says. Would I say she had been hateful as a little girl? She says he never forgave her for the "unspeakable secret" between them, which Nina has never revealed to me beyond its being her unspeakable secret. "I hope you never guess," she stammers, her intelligence lapsing strangely, and tears fill her eyes.

Poor fat Nina takes her backslidings to her overworked psychiatrist, who gives her two Valiums and sends her to The Disciples for another fix. The Disciples rally round her. Lovely youngsters with effulgent eyes. They chant and clap to the accompaniment of electric guitars and drums, and raise their hands, palms up, when the Spirit begins to move, drums beating, until Nina shudders and jiggles with hiccups, and the storefront resounds with jubilation. "I'm a Jesus junkie, there's no way without Him," she says happily, between backslidings, and has taken to quoting chapter and verse and using evangelical language not heard in our family since our father died in the Lord thirty-five years ago.

She is an honest soul, my sister, and frankly expresses doubts about The Disciples and their Apostle, who has spoken face to face with Gautama Buddha, Moses, and Jesus, and who will be translated bodily into heaven. Their Apostle sends pamphlets, tape cassettes, and instructions to his flocks from headquarters in Los Angeles. Her doubts are received with love and understanding by the joyful youngsters. They don't say much about Father, as they call their Apostle, to new converts. Her doubting is beautiful, they tell her. Her every opinion is beautiful. And after the meeting they have coffee and cake, and the elders (ages eighteen to twenty-six) organize the week's Outreach activities. Think of all the people who will be left behind, any day now. Next week, the Boston flock will divide for missionary forays into Worcester and Amherst, scheduled for the same Monday, a college holiday, and Nina has offered to transport a load of them in her Plymouth Volaré.

The minister is a twenty-six-year-old sweetie from Salt Lake City, Utah, for whom the Apostle picked a darling girl from Dallas, Texas. Nina has never seen such a happy couple, so in love with each other. The girl's parents tried to have the marriage annulled, spending more money on lawyers than they ever spent on their daughter. The Apostle limits the happy couple to spiritual intercourse for two years and may separate them in different missions far from home, to deepen their God-centered commitments to each other. His missions are nursing and foster homes in thirty-eight states—God's plan is to cover all fifty —into which are funneled federal and state moneys, only the Apostle knows how much and the Lord's work cannot have enough. The god- less parents of that darling girl, Nina tells me with a mildly crazy look in her eyes, have not seen these kids at work, in prayer and praise.

At the meeting in their temple, a Boston storefront, Nina sits with the young minister, paper plate on her lap, Styrofoam cup in her hand, and tells him how she relapsed from her slimming diet. Does her re- lapse signal another backsliding? "That's beautiful," says the attentive young man, and places his hand lovingly on her fat arm. "You're a beautiful person, Nina."

All this Nina relates with a full heart, her eyes shining. Her eyes are too old for clone-like effulgence and cloud over when she gives a scared smile of hope for me as well. We should be in this thing together, she says. Our three brothers rejected Jesus, she reminds me, and look at what happened to them. All dead. "You're all I have left, Jim," she says. Jesus takes pity on her backsliding and turns His face to her again, and pulls her to His forgiving bosom, and even lets her eat if she wants to. Eat or don't eat, but don't make such a big deal of it. "Look at the flowers of the field!" she cries. What am I going to do about Jesus? she wants to know. After all His suffering for us, will I accept Him or reject Him? If I accept Him He will accept me, and if I reject Him He will reject me.

The child's garden in her soul has had a long time to grow into a jungle. Lost in those senseless mazes, Nina is at last finding a way out, or believes that a way out is being found. I am glad for her and am almost grateful to The Disciples. Better than Valium, maybe. We were five once, four boys and one girl. Now Nina and I alone are left and our Saturday lunches are the last gasps of our family.

She forgoes some of our Saturdays for The Disciples. She lends them her car and gets it returned with a bashed fender. One Saturday she

joined them in a street demonstration against Moonies, followers of a
false prophet who claims that Jesus was hot to get married when He
was killed, a doctrine the true Apostle in Los Angeles has pronounced
unbiblical, inspired by Satan, leading to such Communist godlessness
as the mass suicide-murder in Jonestown, Guyana. Full proof available
on request, without cost or obligation.

Nina called last Monday to say that she would be free—*free?*—to
visit me this Saturday, and suggested chicken rice soup for lunch. "Father says we should eat more rice, less potatoes." So the Apostle of The
Disciples is her new father. She would arrive at noon, she said, and
added that she had committed ten percent of her stock portfolio to
The Disciples. The principal, not the income. That would come to
$30,000, roughly. She sounded pleased with herself.

"The *principal?*"

"I knew you'd gasp. It's the tithe I owe them. I'm ashamed I didn't
promise more. I owe them *everything!*"

Imagine owing anybody everything. Since her religious conversion,
she has begun to talk like a fourteen-year-old. "Nina, you can't do
that."

"I knew you wouldn't understand," she said with harrowing patience. "Just trust me, O.K.? I know what you think of The Disciples,
but you're dead wrong. You're still blinded, like I was. Please don't
bring it up again when I see you."

If it made me feel better, she said, the young minister talked her out
of giving more than ten percent. She had to grow stronger in the Lord
before her new father in Los Angeles would consider accepting her
total commitment: Caesar could contest large donations in court if
they were not done right. I felt a weakness in my knees and sat down
by the telephone, at my kitchen table. "I'm sorry I mentioned it," she
babbled. "Just fix the salad and I'll be there by noon. You know what
it's like, Jim? Coming to Jesus is like coming home again!"

Right.

Ten percent to that fellow in Los Angeles—for a start. "A tithe," I
said, "is a tenth of your *income*, not your *principal*, for Christ's sake!"

"I won't have you taking the Lord's name in vain!" But she allowed
herself a pause, perhaps for the shadow of a doubt to cross her mind. "I
don't care what a tithe is. I'd rather be dead than live without Jesus.
It's called faith, if that still means anything to you. For all his faults,
Father had *faith*. Now I'm sorry for every bad thought I ever had about

him. I beg his forgiveness!" she began to yell. "I repent in dust and ashes! I *was* hateful! Yes, I love him! Do you hear me, Jim? I just can't hate him any more, don't you understand? I'm *tired!* I've made peace, and you're still ranting after all these years. Except now you are ranting at *me* instead of at Father."

Before The Disciples got to Nina we talked about lawn fertilizers and stock options, and walked in the woods, and came in for coffee and an oldie showing Fred Astaire and Ginger Rogers. Now Nina talks about Jesus. I had rather we talked about fertilizers and stock options again, and about a little elephant in our county.

I want to talk about a local inbred, Sloan Mudge, a spawn of incest who keeps a female dwarf elephant in his zoo. Sloan Mudge is physically and mentally deformed, and his elephant, recently acquired, resembles Nina in her obesity. I hold them in view when she talks about Jesus.

Last summer I took her out to Teewaddle Road for a look at Sloan Mudge and his dwarf elephant. Nina did not want to go, she loathes Mudge and his slithery ways. but she had not seen his elephant and came along.

Mudge sat askew on his crate, clutching a roll of zoo tickets, and greeted us with his professional " 'Joy yourself, now!"

She ignored him, and she hated his dirty elephant standing in its own muck, regarding her with little eyes. Raising its trunk, it worked its prehensile lips an inch from her face. Nina would not stay another minute in that damned zoo. "Is *that* what you brought me out here for?"

On the telephone, Nina's voice quavered, suddenly plaintive. "Are you there, Jim?"

"Look," I said. "I don't mind your Disciples. They give me an idea to buy Sloan Mudge's elephant."

"What are you talking about?"

"If you can spend ten percent on Jesus, I can spend a few dollars on an elephant."

Her intake of breath was followed by a threatening silence.

"We could trade," I said. "You give me Jesus, I'll give you the elephant."

"Is that all you can feel about me now? Ridicule?"

She was crying. Kids in a Boston storefront, gone from pot to pushing an Apostle in Los Angeles, taking their guitars with them, attract a sad fat woman who has never married and loves children. They give her a Jesus-fix and she feels bright, a beautiful person with beautiful opinions. But there is a side to Nina that is not primitive: her backslidings will grow longer, darker.

"I'm sorry," she said, sniffling, when she'd had her cry. "I didn't mean that about you. But listen. Are you listening?"

"I'm listening."

What she said next chilled me, as if she were offering lemonade and cyanide in Jonestown, Guyana. "Jim, you mustn't be afraid. I'm not afraid any more. I'll be with you, we'll go together. I *know* God will reclaim you, even if He has to break you first—remember? Father *was* right, after all."

He was right. All our brothers suffered diseases or accidents or bad marriages. The eldest was broken by all three, the second by suicide, the third by madness. Two to go, Nina and me. Hamilton Crail's ghost has been stalking his children and now has Nina cornered, a lonely woman too weary to keep running, a broken and a contrite heart. In a year she will be ready to give her last stitch to The Disciples, mop floors in a barracks in Beulah, and write, when permitted contact with the doomed world, of her fears for me, and send unbelievers to hell, and pray for my salvation. It would be too awful for Nina to go alone, as the Bible threatens: sister taken, brother left behind.

In parting, Nina said on the telephone, "I'll pray for you, Jim, and I won't stop praying for you. That's all Father could ever do for us."

"Thank you very much."

"Don't *trifle* with God! I can't ever, *ever*, allow you to use that tone again—praise the Lord!"

That did not sound like Nina but like the old Full Gospel Church.

Salad, cold cuts, peaches and cottage cheese—all is ready for Nina's arrival at noon. The table in my dining room is set with our father's silverware, his monogram engraved indelibly. In the kitchen I find a squat vase with narrow neck, for my glass flowers. I bought them yesterday at the Crafts Fair from two scrubbed members of a commune, a man and a woman—bare feet, Levis, plaid shirt, mop of hair, torpor common to both. These two were working out their salvation by selling handmade clay pipes, ceramic medallions on thongs, glass flowers with long metal stems, and home-sewn cotton tunics piled rumpled in a dirty cardboard box. Their eyes drifted and they gave me slack-jawed smiles.

At my kitchen window I can keep an eye out for Nina's car to appear on Bay Road, while I arrange the glass flowers in the vase. Blue, green, red, and yellow—two of each. I got them for my crystal collection, glass flowers for my crystal dancer. They are supposed to sway and tinkle.

In the living room the grandfather clock Nina picked up at an auction chimes the eleventh hour, a ghostly sonority recalling the ordered days and years of a family long gone. It occurs to me, with a spasm, that I need some disorder in my house, something alive and warmer than my crystal dancer. Nina's religious estrangement is cooling the weekly warmth she used to bring. Her voice has a hard edge when she talks about Jesus. Her face looks tight. She'll end up a missionary, if I know the signs. How keep myself warm? My incontinent old Airedale had to be put away last year. How about Sloan Mudge's dwarf elephant? A little madness would be nothing new in our family.

The owner of the elephant is of a race of New England inbreds still to be seen in our parts, a stunted little man with matted hair, low forehead, yellow eyes. At today's prices he could make a good living cutting firewood, but he can't stick to any one task. He sets up a stand of blackberries for the sparse traffic on his road, hires himself out to pick cucumbers at child-labor rates, patches car tires at the Mobil station in Dudleyville. Sometimes, he disappears for a month, nobody knows where. Life has taught Sloan Mudge to be secretive. Once, an alarming rumor compelled a Congregational minister to bear a gift of groceries to his shack, and ask the recluse if he kept a grown daughter chained to his bed. "Nope," said Mudge, and took the groceries. The minister did notice a fall of chain in the rubbish on the rickety porch, but no daughter in the shack or near it. "He *had* a daughter by his sister," Nina said when we gossiped, her belief unshaken. Nobody had ever seen a woman in his vicinity, and all other Mudges, young and old, were safely tucked away in Mildwood Cemetery.

Sloan Mudge put up signs for a quarter of a mile along his road, boards nailed to trees, reading "CAMPING $2" in whitewash and an arrow pointing to the sky. He had run a water pipe from his well to the camp, and clapped together an outhouse with boards from his collapsed barn. A few out-of-state explorers pulled in with their campers and were driven out by mosquitoes from Mudge's swamp. His camp fared no better the second summer, though an agent from a state agency in Boston, studying water resources, offered to drain the swamp and kill the mosquitoes. Government interference did not sit well with Mudge, but the threat may have fired his ingenuity to come up with a better idea for pulling in campers. His dream of the good life would not die, and, in the third summer of his camp's existence, below his amended "CAMPING $4" appeared a second sign: "ZOO." I did not drive out to Teewaddle Road for a look at his zoo until two college students stopped by my house soliciting signatures for a petition to free the animals. The Society for the Prevention of Cruelty to Animals had been alerted, and legal machinery had been set in motion to close Sloan Mudge's private enterprise.

Driving out on a hot summer Saturday, when Nina was serving The Disciples, I was touched to see that in his "ZOO" signs along Teewaddle Road Sloan Mudge had not availed himself of the adman's exclamation mark. His "ZOO" stated a fact, take it or leave it. I felt instinctive sympathy for Mudge, and rejoiced at the sight of cars pulled up by the zoo entrance, a classic example of Mudge architecture: gravel dumped over a culvert.

Here, Sloan Mudge himself sat on a crate, sweating and scratching himself, wearing a new T-shirt over stained pants, and guarded the entrance with a board reading "25" propped up beside him. He looked a happy man, his aches forgotten. Without raising his yellow eyes to mine, he snatched the coin from my hand before I could give it, and, turning to spy who else might be coming up the road, said, " 'Joy yourself, now!"

Seven campers and two tents showed in the trees on the swampside, striped awnings unfurled. In the foreground, a dozen locals converged around a snack wagon featuring popcorn, Fritos, hot dogs, Table Talk pies, and sodas in the drifting dust.

Setting forth on my tour, I came upon a fox in a chicken wire enclosure, lying dusty beside a dusty tin plate. The fox was being urged to move—"Move it!"—by a malt-nourished son of the people who had taken his denim shirt off in the heat, his paunch hanging over his belt. "Bet this critter's dead," he guffawed, jabbing me with his elbow, and tossed his crushed beer can at the fox, just missing the tail.

The next attraction was a coughing mongrel tied by a rope to a post. Atop the post was fastened a five-inch cage made of window screening, containing a spider watching flies trying to get in. Then the path forked, offering choices. The left path took me to the birds: a pintail duck sitting in the dust, a turkey in a swarm of flies, a ring-necked pheasant with a broken tail, and two chickens and transient sparrows, all in one enclosure. Chicken wire, strung between two pines and a young elm, housed a screech owl asleep on a truncated branch. Beneath this triangular cage, small bones and droppings littered the ground, and from the hexagonal mesh of the cage floor hung bits of rodent skins.

Returning to the spider's post, I took the more traveled path to the most impressive structure in Sloan Mudge's Zoo, a massive cage of four-by-fours, spacious enough for tiger or lion, but as yet vacant. Fortified with hot dogs and sodas, the locals had preceded me to a dwarf elephant beyond.

This captive, a spiritless female and the only animal in the zoo foreign to our parts, was no larger than a donkey. She was chained by a hind leg to an iron stake driven into the ground. Behind her lay the predictable dry bucket in the dust, overturned. Children reached out to slap her lethargic trunk—"Don't get too close!"—and the man with the beer paunch stood pelting her dusty hide with popcorn, expressing the general disapproval, for in her prolonged exposure to the hot sun the little elephant ignored her visitors. In the minutes I watched, she did not rest from her comatose swaying, back and forth, each forward motion forcing her chained hind leg off the ground as she pulled the chain taut. Her trunk hung unresponsive amid flying popcorn and candy wrappers.

When I left the zoo, Mudge called from his crate, "Come again, now!"

Three months later—I had taken Nina to the zoo in the interval— the SPCA succeeded in having Sloan Mudge's zoo closed and his animals impounded, including a knock-kneed pony I had missed seeing, an emaciated pony that had been kept in a narrow stall for such a long time (four years, the Dudleyville *Gazette* said) that its hooves had curled up like Turkish slippers. Mudge's domestic animals, except his coughing mongrel and spider, were taken to the university's Agricultural Station for documentation.

But for some legal reason the authorities could not impound his dwarf elephant, for which he was able to produce a dubious bill of sale. The elephant had to await separate legal action.

Yes, I am dwelling on Sloan Mudge. Arranging the glass flowers in the vase and keeping an eye out for Nina's car to appear on Bay Road, I sit at my kitchen table and dwell on Mudge. Consider. In town Mudge has been showing acquaintances his picture in the *Gazette*. How, I wonder, given his material and mental resources, did he achieve so much in so little time? A zoo, no less, with an elephant and a screech

owl and other birds and beasts, and maybe a lion or tiger on the way. A
good idea builds. He had actually pulled it off, his greatest idea. He had
looked happy that day, snatching the coin from my hand and wishing
me joy in his paradise. He and his generations of inbred artists have
always run afoul of the law; it is not his fault that the law wrecked his
great zoo. Tenacious, ingenious Mudge has tried. He can rest now and
feel in his weary bones the tug of millennia and the deliverance that
lies in extinction.

In my mind I have christened Mudge's elephant Baby. What if I
offered him $2,500 for her? Would he hold out for $3,000? I foresee
problems with Baby, not the least of them local publicity. But the
publicity will pass and Mudge inspires. Of course Baby would be better
off in the Boston Children's Zoo—or would she? I could give her my
love and a good home. Her bucket would never run dry. Hell, I'd give
her a whole pool to play in, in a fine expansive paddock of upright
railroad ties, even if I had to dip into my stock portfolio to do it.

Apparently Mudge does have title to Baby, though how he acquired
her, with what money, where, remains nobody's business but Mudge's.
His bill of sale for her, an incomprehensible German *"Rechnung"* on
which Mudge's name is superscribed, was pictured on page 20 of *The
Boston Globe: "Sie erhalten auf Grund Ihrer Bestellung als Postpaket: 1
Elephas africanus pumilio."* Signed by one "G. Hagenbeck, Hamburg,"
the bill is originally addressed to *"Herrn, Frau, Frl., Firma* Nelly Billiard, Philadelphia, Pa., U.S.A." Did G. Hagenbeck ship the elephant
to Nelly Billiard by parcel post? Beyond the *"Elephas africanus,"* this
bill of sale, in its every aspect and unimaginable connection with
Mudge, or indeed with Nelly Billiard, is as unintelligible to me as my
own life—those aspects and connections of my life that occupy my
thoughts.

My main difficulty would be providing for Baby's comfort so late in
the season. Fall is upon us, the leaves are turning, you can smell arctic
regions in breezes from Canada. Winter is coming. Whoever has no
house will not build one now. If I kept Baby in the garage I would need
a shed for my tractor mower and workbench. I'd have to lay a drainpipe
for hosing the garage floor, and run the pipe out to the septic tank. The
garage would need enough insulation and heating to be warm as the
Congo during snowstorms. All this needs planning, contracting, time.
For this winter, I see, I would have to take Baby into my house. Needless to say . . .

Is it really impossible?

Who would consent to having a child if he foresaw in a flash all the expense and terrors which the rearing of his child would visit upon him? My sister Nina and I are vulnerable in this regard, our father's religion having tinted our souls with expectations of catastrophes. I worry, for example, that Baby's progress through my house would punch holes in the floor, like tracks in snow. But stop and think. Look at her. This specimen of a pigmy Congo race is no larger than a donkey, which some Sicilians keep in their houses. She is no heavier than my Yamaha upright piano, which I have rolled about the house for a good acoustical spot, without cracking the floor. Baby could safely mount the two steps from garage to kitchen and find her own way to the running water, down the hall to the right.

Oh, I can see my little elephant sitting in the tub, filling her trunk with water and spraying it around the walls. I'll have the walls and doorway hung with plastic curtains, and the floor tiled toward a drain-pipe, a simple job in the bathroom with its wealth of plumbing. Baby could easily climb in and out of the tub, for it is a modern tub, only twelve and one-quarter inches deep, designed for space calculated by efficiency engineers. She would not want to get out of the water, I would have to scold her through the plastic curtain, mop in hand, my view blurred by drops and rivulets on the curtain: "You've had all morning. Nina is coming. You don't want Nina catching you here, do you?"

Waiting for Nina to arrive for our Saturday lunch, I sit at the kitchen table turning the vase of prismatic glass flowers. The ceiling glitters with refracted sunlight. Outside, the wind has risen. The forecaster promised a calm day. I know a meteorologist who does not forecast; he marks the sweeping picture of the years. The prodigious elm tree on my lawn flutters in a frenzy of yellows and browns, seemingly on fire in a blizzard of elm seeds. In the light of this conflagration, Nina's car, sporting the fender bashed by The Disciples, turns into my drive at last.

"If I thought you were serious," Nina says when we have eaten the peaches and cottage cheese, "I'd commit you to a mental hospital."

She is taking my elephant fantasy more seriously than I expected. "Baby would be in the house only this winter," I say, testing Nina's credulity. "By spring I'd have the garage ready for her. The paddock would take no time at all. The big job would be the pool, but she could wait for that."

"Baby will certainly want to express her gratitude. She'll corner you one day, right there by the TV, and crush you to death."

Nina has gained weight again. She has exchanged her tweed suit for a loose batiste in penitent gray, resembling a maternity dress, too light for the season. Over her shoulders she has thrown a girlishly pink sweater, pink on gray like fall leaves awaiting winter.

A horrible thing happened when we sat down to lunch. She could not fit herself between the arms of her chair. Too fat. I hastened to substitute an armless guest chair. Seating herself precariously, she composed her face and said: "Disgusting, ain't I. Well, it's true. Why pretend?" It was a bad moment for me to go on spinning my elephant fantasy for my elephantine sister. But I would have done worse to drop the subject abruptly, after introducing it with such a toot for something a bit messy in my life.

We take our coffee to the couch in the bay window. I see the elm burning in the sun, positively on fire. Every fall Nina remarks on the turning colors, but for once I don't call her attention to my elm. A trick of light does something unpleasant to it, something other than pretty. I stand transfixed.

"Why don't you get a dog?" she says, impressing the couch enormously with her buttocks. Her body seems to be inflating before my eyes.

I sit beside her. "No dog," I say. "After Emmy"—my Airedale gone to glory—"there is no other."

"Get a cat," says Nina.

"Emmy was afraid of cats."

"You're beginning to irritate me. You're doing it on purpose, aren't you. To get back at me?"

"For what?"

"For Jesus," she says.

"I don't know Jesus. I know some people who know Jesus."

"Your joke is wearing thin. Why do you keep hammering away at it?"

"What makes you think I'm joking?"

"Because an elephant is unthinkable, even to you."

"The unthinkable can become thinkable. Jesus, for example."

"Jesus *unthinkable?*"

"Of course Jesus is unthinkable. Born of a virgin? Passing understanding. Why else would you need faith? If you can think about Jesus, why can't I think about an elephant?"

"Where in *hell*," Nina explodes, "do you propose to keep your damned elephant! In the guest room?"

"The guest room is too small. So is the sewing room."

"You considered the sewing room?" she wails. "With all my things in the sewing room?"

"I wouldn't touch your things. You can come live here any time you want."

"Bay Road," she says with a moan. "I can't live on Bay Road. I need people. How can you live on Bay Road? You must have ice in your veins, like that crystal dancer of yours. Why don't you move to Boston?"

"I'd go crazy in Boston."

"You're going crazy on Bay Road, talking about elephants."

In the bay window the wind is subsiding, the elm stands burning like an iceberg.

"I couldn't keep Baby in this room, either," I say, pushing my fantasy. "I'd have to move the couch to your bedroom and the TV to the kitchen. But where would I put the piano? The kitchen isn't big enough for the piano."

Nina rolls her eyes, an expression she reserves for my inanities.

"The dining room," I say, "is long enough, but too narrow. The den is my library. I'm not giving that up, not even for Baby. The only room left is your bedroom, Nina. It's large enough for Baby, private bath and all. Just for this winter, remember. You could have my bedroom when you stay over. I'll sleep in my den."

She is stunned.

She says, "Why do you hate me?"

"I don't hate you."

"I have nobody."

I ought to hug her now, divert her with something light, affecting, a confection on Channel 3 or a home-fried gospel song to make her clap her hands with all the people, and let her have her cry, and sniffle, and smile again. But I shall not divert her from my fantasy. She will divert herself in a moment. I am thinking of the children of Hamilton Crail, no less than of a little elephant whose keeper shows doubters a mysterious bill of sale for his authority to chain her to an iron stake. Seeing God-appropriators pelting Nina with religious popcorn, I am brightening the corner where I am. "Stand thou on that side, for on this am I!"

the Full Gospel Choir used to sing in transports of self-confidence. Here is my own song, about a little elephant.

Nina recovers, going from tearful to tough in twenty seconds. "You're not hurting me, James. What I can't understand is why you should want to hurt Jesus. Because that's what you are doing. After all He has done for us! Never mind me, but Jesus *does* matter." And she quotes John 3:16 to prove that Jesus matters. "Come with me to the temple," she says, referring to the Boston storefront of The Disciples. "Just once. Your eyes will be opened."

The elm on my lawn burns icily. Shall I ask her to look? She would not see the terrible tree. She would see God's glory in the fall colors. Nina is moved by nature. "That's the glory of God," she will say. She is learning or recovering pretty ideas about God. She knows as much about God as TV evangelists and Job's comforters. She knows how loving God is, for God is Love, and, though just, He is merciful, her loving Father.

Silent, we sit on the couch, and then she is crying.

"I want to pray," she says. "Will you pray with me?"

"You go ahead."

"It's something we can do together, Jimmy."

"I'm not stopping you. Go ahead and pray."

"I want to *help* you!"

I feel a double-take. She wants to help me. I live in perpetual astonishment, in a kind of low dread that does not respond to sing-alongs sung ardently off key. Nina must have happiness, warmed and passed through many hands.

Hurt by my resistance, she sits rocking back and forth like my little comatose elephant chained to the stake. With great effort she pulls herself up from the couch, her effort so great that her eyeballs show their whites as if she's gone blind. She lumbers out between couch and coffee table and turns uncertainly, casting about for a way to kneel on the rug.

Somehow, she lands softly and stands on hands and knees, on all fours like Baby, her huge bulk breathing, her loose dress flowing in gray folds from her buttocks, revealing a blotched, liver-spotted, awesome circumference of thigh one might glimpse in the jungle.

Her pink sweater has fallen from her shoulders and lies hooked on the coffee table. She rights herself from all fours to her knees and raises her hands for praying, her body cantilevered like that of a circus elephant.

And then, horribly, our old Repentance Song breaks from her throat in her sweet little-girl voice; and I see her bewildered at fourteen, locked up with our father in his study, humiliated at his feet: "Just as I am, without one plea . . ."

But I have always *loved Jesus, even as a little girl,* Nina has told me since Jesus saved her, as if she were eager to please Jesus even in her memories.

"Jesus, my Lord and Savior," she says, swallowing a catch in her throat, and prays in whispers inaudible to me.

I sit on the couch studying her desolation. Thus have I known her since her fourteenth year. I can still see a vestige of that little girl in poor Nina, an outlined innocence in elbows and hands clasped in prayer. She is backsliding again and hanging on for dear life. Now and then my name rises from her slurred whispers, so she is praying for me too. Maybe I could help her by drawing the curtains: the light in which the tree stands is too harsh—too harsh altogether. I could play my stereo record of Mendelssohn's *Elijah:* "If with all your hearts ye truly seek me, ye shall ever surely find me." I'd like that myself, make no mistake. I'd need a hanky, hearing Elijah, and Nina would weep torrents and feel better, much better.

As Nina prays in her loneliness, I turn to look at the tree. The wind has fallen, the leaves are stilled. The great tree stands motionless like a crystal arrangement. It is a muted incandescence suffused with cold blue. I once sailed in a luxury liner dwarfed by a radiant iceberg that inclined my voyage, I know today, to this tree on my own lawn.

Yesterday, I happened to see the ruins of Sloan Mudge's Zoo. Stopping by his culvert, I got out of the car and scanned the blighted field for relics. A rank odor, sweetly putrescent, infected the air. A stark post stood where his zoo once stood. Rotting boards lay strewn about. A bit of window screening had curled and, with grass grown through, disguised itself as tumbleweed. The massive cage of four-by-fours, once intended for a miraculous lion or tiger, had vanished without a trace.

May not such a miracle live in the pilgrim's reverence, on evidence not seen?

Pilgrims not lacking. Three distinct truck tracks, made by vehicles heavy enough to churn up mud, snaked across the field to Mudge's swamp. There, where campers once camped in clouds of mosquitoes, I now discerned a scattering of industrial drums, indifferently concealed from the road. The drums led the eye beside the still waters of the swamp proper, a glimmering darkness streaked with silver and foam, such as may be painted by chemical wastes.

When Mudge gets caught he will be fined $50 for polluting his own drinking water, and admonished. "Yes, sir," he will say.

I drove on but slowed down and stopped again as Mudge's shack came in view on high ground, etched against the sky. He had prospered. In his weedy yard stood a new pickup and a horse trailer. A junked car lay on its back. Within the dark proscenium of his porch, a naked light bulb shone in an uncurtained window. Beside the shack stood the wreck of a barn, somehow keeping its feet, whole sections of walls missing, the roof caved in as if smashed by a fist. In a gaping hole in the barn I saw what I had not consciously come to see, the dwarf elephant.

I got out of the car for a better look. From the road I could not make out Baby's trunk or judge which way she faced. She stood under the caved-in roof, a shadow.

A shadow, polluted waters, a stark post in a blighted field, relics—Sloan Mudge never disappointed. True to his generations of inbred artists, he continued to provide. The westering sun played its light on his old sign, a board nailed to a tree by the side of the road. The sign was weathered now, hung askew, the whitewash faded but still legible: "CAMPING $4" and an arrow pointing to the sky. And below, in witness of a bygone marvel: "ZOO."

He will never knock down these joyful tidings. If a traveler should ask, Sloan Mudge will steal a look at the out-of-state license plate, shift his yellow eyes to the swamp, and in time, with hindsight and foresight, spin a myth.

I felt tired approaching my sixtieth year and was struck by the similarity between Mudge's road and mine. Too far from shopping malls, schools, and churches, both roads were shunned by home builders. Abandoned farms on Bay Road had been reclaimed by woods, while Teewaddle Road favored swamps and thickets. At twilight in October, roads more solitary than Mudge's and mine may not be seen in our parts, nor vistas more withdrawn from the human concourse. Such roads are sometimes pictured in tabloids. I could not loiter. A parked car on these desolate stretches suggested something less definable than lovers or bird watchers.

Nina's prayer smolders and goes out. It is hard to pray with an unbeliever in the room. I steady her as she reaches for the coffee table and maneuvers herself up from her knees. Having regained her feet, she pulls away from my supporting hand, recovers her pink sweater, and looks about for her overcoat.

"You're leaving?" I ask.

She is. She is going back to her friends in Boston. "I really must. We have an early meeting today."

My silly elephant fantasy has ruined our lunch. We'll not be walking in the fall colors and tart air promising winter. How pleasant it would have been, then, to come in for coffee and an oldie on TV, Basil Rathbone and Nigel Bruce this afternoon. *Great Heavens, Holmes!*

"What about *our* day?" I remonstrate. "There's a Sherlock Holmes movie today. Basil Rathbone."

"Really." She smiles in token that she has passed beyond such pabulum.

Besides losing our family hour with Sherlock Holmes, I have forfeited the moment for moderating Nina's caprice to squander $30,000 on The Disciples—her promised "tithe." Had I been sensible I might have nudged her to reconsider the sum for The Disciples. What possessed me to offer her bedroom to an elephant? I cannot reach her now, as she stands poking in her shoulder bag for the car keys.

"The chicken soup was great," she says. "Thanks for reminding me of my nothingness."

"That's not what I meant."

"That's exactly what you meant." She clasps her hands in mock gratitude. "Isn't that what you always meant—*all* of you? Didn't I get to wash the dishes while you played the piano? Nina the moron?" And she stings herself three times with our childhood singsong: " 'Nina the moron!' "

Is that what her prayer tossed up? As I move to mollify her, she wards me off and whimpers the old incantation through gritted dentures. I can't get near her. She is spitting hellfire.

I follow Nina out to her Plymouth Volaré.

Bay Road passes through woods here and my clearing is surrounded by woods. Summer and winter, my garden (now bedded in straw) stands in shadows well after sunrise and well before sunset. From the road my house, fieldstone and wood painted white, looks neatly tucked away in the woods. When the leaves turn, an occasional tourist car slows and sometimes the driver points at my house for his passengers to see. The sky is bright now but darkness abides in the underbrush.

As I hold the car door for Nina, she falls in expertly backwards. Then she pulls her thick legs in after her, one at a time. I wonder how she avoids collisions: she drives reclining at an angle of forty-five degrees. The seat belt is not long enough for her girth. I close the car door. She fumbles with the keys and rolls down the window. Her cheek does not respond to my kiss.

"Are you really going to a meeting?" I ask.

She sits touching up her hair before the rearview.

"You treat me like a stranger," she says, adjusting a curl. Satisfied, she turns to give me a parting shot. "I wanted to talk about something important to me, and you talk about keeping an elephant in my bedroom. You think that's funny? You think it's funny telling me to trade Jesus for your damned elephant?"

"I'm sorry. It was a stupid joke. You came to talk, let's talk. Come on, get out. It's time for our walk. Then we'll have coffee and Sherlock Holmes. Won't that be fun?"

"I've had quite enough, frankly," she says. The car engine sparks to life.

Reclining now in her fearful driving position, she shifts her automatic into Reverse but keeps her foot on the brake pedal, hesitantly. "Giving money to The Disciples doesn't really do it, does it?" she says.

"I couldn't agree more."

"Money is not enough," she says, resolutely, and shifts back into Park. "I want to go to a Bible College. I've been thinking about Okeko in San Diego. But my friends say Okeko discriminates against fatsos. They say fatsos are cursed by God. Do you know anything about it? Is it true?"

Is this what Nina came to talk about, and I talked about an elephant?

Is it true that Okeko Bible College discriminates against fatsos, or that God has cursed fatsos, or cursed the lot of them?

"If Okeko says so," I say, "it must be in the Book."

"But that's only a human *interpretation!* Why can't they read the Bible like it's written!"

I stand looking at her. She is close to tears again. Unaccountably, Nina wears her hair short, effectively lowering her forehead to simian proportions, capped by stiff ringlets of thinning hair blasted by beauty parlors. Her hair is graying. The ringlets do not altogether conceal the curvature of her skull, when viewed against light.

"It's great your wanting to go to college," I say. "I wish you'd told me sooner. I'll find a perfect little college for you. Just don't do anything in the meantime—all right?"

"I know all about your perfect little colleges. No thanks. But find out about Okeko. If I can't go to Okeko, I'll try Father. It's just that I'm not worthy of him yet."

"Worthy of Father?"

"Our Apostle," she says curtly, and seems to regret having blurted that much to an outsider. A guarded expression veils her eyes.

"Does that mean you will leave The Disciples, if you go to Okeko?"

"Why do you pretend interest? You're not interested. You haven't the faintest idea what it takes to be worthy of Father. What can you know on this deserted island of yours?"

"Are you coming next Saturday?"

"Are you inviting me?"

"Of course. Always."

"Not next Saturday," she says. "We're doing Outreach. I'll call you when I can."

So she leaves. Her car passes my roadside mailbox and glides out of my clearing into the woods.

Will she pay $30,000 to be found worthy of Father, and boil her brains into the bargain, in some Bible College that teaches Creation Science in the name of truth, *avoiding profane and vain babblings, and oppositions of science falsely so called: which some professing have erred concerning the faith?* . . . Nina would have made a good horticulturist, or a pastry chef. She has a green thumb, can talk to plants, and her pleasure in sweets would impress an effendi in Istanbul.

Silence flows back. Bay Road is a quiet old country road, traffic having abandoned it for a better one. From the lawn bench under my elm I contemplate the empty road and hear the wind in the trees and the raucous slang of a blue jay, a bird whose insolence is bred by violent dislike of predators. A hawk is about, or a roosting owl. Inhaling the cool air, I return to myself on this deserted island of mine.

I have never known a man whose agonies about the sins of his children matched my father's intensity. His after-dinner Bible Hour brought the Full Gospel Church into our home every day between Sundays, and when he judged we needed more he summoned us to the living room at bedtime, or later. On such occasions, while waiting for him to appear, we sat without speaking, as ordered, and scowled accusations at each other. Who among us had transgressed?

Hamilton Crail did not account himself the most blameless man in Boston, only the most God-loving. Shortly after Nina's "infection" in her fourteenth year, his rage for glory tortured him to confess himself the Chief of Sinners.

I do not recall what else he said that night. Our family meetings were all alike, indistinguishable from church services and the Radio Gospel Hour, without the latter's pitch for a Free Grace-Faith ("golden metal") Prosperity Cross prayed over according to God's promises in Deuteronomy and Matthew. My father had indeed prospered, he could not love God enough, and he used to conclude our family meetings with a swing of the evangelical cudgel: "Pray with me!"

What I remember lucidly is my falling into a troubled sleep after one of those meetings, a sleep that conjured up the meeting in the form of a dream. It is my dream of the event, rather than the event itself, that has stuck in my memory through the years. From time to time I dream that dream again.

In my dream, the five of us have been summoned and sit waiting in the living room for our father to appear. My two younger brothers grow restive and pull at me to climb up on a ladder-back chair. They want to sled me around the room. I mount the chair, our eldest brother watches to see if we dare, and just then the door opens and a gigantic stranger enters, instead of our father.

Our summons is explained by the stranger's cropped hair and uniform of a prison guard from a 1930s melodrama. Massive neck and shoulders, blunt nose, stump of chin. He surveys the room with an air of authority. Much has happened behind the scenes last night while we slept, his manner tells us. We have all broken the law, and our father has had to go to the authorities and do his duty. The guard advances heavily into the room, an immoderate hulk suggesting restrained force, and speaks without raising his voice: "You all get ready to move, now."

He will brook no disobedience, it is clear. All except Nina rise to their feet. She slumps on the floor by the bookshelf, a dropped puppet in a pretty dress, her face that of an old woman, oddly darkened.

The guard seats himself in a Windsor chair and looks us over. His eyes rest on Nina and move on, unconcerned. Oblivious of my elevated position on the ladder-back chair, I remain standing on it, guessing that we will be marched out to a wagon and taken to our destination. I face the guard with confidence in my alacrity to obey. Hypocritical obedience is my strong suit. I will hop on one leg when ordered, fling myself to the ground when ordered. What can't I do, when ordered? I shall be a model prisoner, I shall win over the guard and get a commendation for good behavior, and maybe privileges.

"Now," says the guard, after he has scrutinized us. "When I count to three, you all start running out that door."

He will see what a good boy I am. Standing on my chair, I brace myself as for the start of a race. I want to be the first in the wagon.

"One . . . two . . ."

As the guard holds off the third count, I become aware of his watching me narrowly to see if I jump the gun. I will not jump the gun, never never. I will make for the door on the third count precisely, not a split second before or after.

I keep this promise to myself, inspired by fear of the unknown and by my need to survive. I don't jump the gun. And the third count never comes.

The guard sits scanning the room. All stand frozen like dummies.

We wait for the third count, and the guard's silence persists. My forward knee begins to tremble with the effort of holding still. I can't abandon my feeling that he is only doing his job, an elementary humanity behind the functionary must respond to my good will. I read in his eyes, as he returns my look, that he understands my sentiment. But he appraises me with an animal's vacant regard, and then I see that his skull is empty but for an implacable, unqualified, impersonal hatred, hatred without sense, directed not at transgression or transgressor but simply there like a reptile.

The third count never comes. But for a moment the pain of its not coming is transcended. My two younger brothers, ages nine and eleven, below the age of reason, one could plead, suddenly give the chair I stand on a shove, and, as I catch my balance, sled me around the room. In an eruption of play they push me in a delightful circle over the carpet, to the far end of the room and back. I feel securely fixed on the careering chair, and with the momentum gained I steer myself as on skis to the guard and come to a stop with a happy flourish.

He leans sideways and holds me in his reptilian gaze. He can't punish me, I'm sure. Technically, I did not disobey him, I did not leave the chair, I remained standing on it, waiting for his third count, I was shoved and the chair slid about by itself.

"Having fun?" he says, and turns to the room at large. "You all accept Jesus, now. There's no other way. By the time I count three it will be too late."

Who could have invented such an instrument?

LOST SONS

JAMES SALTER

James Salter has appeared in the O. Henry Collection three times
before this. North Point Press will publish his collected stories in the
fall of 1984.

All afternoon the cars, many with out-of-state plates, had been coming
along the road. The long row of lofty brick quarters appeared above.
The grey walls began. By the corner of the library a military policeman,
his arm moving with fierce precision, directed traffic past a sign for the
reunion of 1960, a class on which Viet Nam had fallen as stars fell on
1915 and 1931.

West Point was majestic in the early evening. Its dignified foliage lay
still. June with its heat was at hand. Beneath, the river was silent,
mysterious islands floating in the dusk. Darkened generals stood posed
about the Plain. Far out on Trophy Point a few couples strolled past the
rows of ancient guns.

In the reception area a welcoming party was going on. There were
faces that hadn't changed and others less familiar, like Reemstma's
whose name tag was read more than once. Someone with a camera and
flash attachment was running around in a cadet bathrobe. Over in
barracks a number of those who had come without their wives were
staying. Doors were open. Voices spilled loudly out.

"Hooknose will be here," Dunning insisted. There was a bottle of
Jack Daniel's on the desk near his feet. "He'll show, don't worry. I had
a letter from him."

"A letter? He's never written a letter."

"His secretary wrote it," Dunning said. He looked like a judge, large
and well fed. His glasses lent a dainty touch. "He's teaching her to
write," he said.

"Where's he living now?"

Copyright © 1982 by Grand Street Publications, Inc. First appeared in *Grand Street*.
Reprinted by permission.

"Florida."

"Remember the time we were sneaking back to Buckner at two in the morning and all of a sudden a car came down the road?"

Dunning was trying to arrange a serious expression.

"We dove in the bushes. It turned out it was a taxi. It slammed on the brakes and backed up. The door opens and there's Klingbeil in the back seat, drunk as a lord. Get in, boys, he says."

Dunning roared. His blouse with its rows of colored ribbons was unbuttoned, gluteal power hinted by the width of his lap.

"Remember," he said, "when we threw Devereaux's Spanish book with all his notes in it out the window? Into the snow. He never found it. He went bananas. You bastards, I'll kill you!"

"He'd have been a star man if he wasn't living with you."

"We tried to broaden him," Dunning explained.

They used to do the sinking of the *Bismarck* while he was studying. Klingbeil was the captain. They would jump on the desks. *Der Schiff ist kaputt!* they shouted. They were firing the guns. The rudder was jammed, they were turning in circles. Devereaux sat head down with his hands pressed over his ears. Will you bastards shut up, he screamed.

Bush, Buford, Jap Andrus, Doane, and George Hilmo were sitting on the beds and windowsill. An uncertain face in the doorway looked in.

"Who's that?"

It was Reemstma whom no one had seen for years. His hair had turned grey and was thin. He smiled awkwardly.

"What's going on?"

They looked at him.

"Come in and have a drink," someone finally said.

He found himself next to Hilmo, who reached across to shake hands with an iron grip. "How are you?" he said. The others went on talking. "You look great."

"You do, too."

Hilmo seemed not to hear. "Where are you living?"

"Rosemont. Rosemont, New Jersey. It's where my wife's family's from," Reemstma said. He spoke with a strange intensity. He had always been odd. Everyone wondered how he had ever made it through. He did all right in class but the image that persisted was of someone bewildered by close order drill which he seemed to master only after two full years and then with the stiffness of a cat trying to swim. He had red lips which were the source of one unpleasant nickname. He was also known as To The Rear March because of the disasters he caused at the command.

He'd been given a used paper cup. "Whose bottle is this?" he asked.

"I don't know," Hilmo said. "Here."

"Are a lot of people coming?"

"Boy, you're full of questions," Hilmo said.

Reemstma fell silent. For half an hour they told stories. He sat by the window, sometimes looking in his cup. Outside, the clock with its black numerals began to brighten. From the distance came the faint sound of a train. Lighted coaches were strung along the river. There were cries of occasional greeting from below, people talking, voices. Feet were leisurely descending the stairs.

"Hey," someone said abruptly, "what the hell is that thing you're wearing?"

Reemstma looked down. It was a necktie of red, flowered cloth. His wife had made it. He changed it before going to dinner.

"Hello, there."

Walking calmly alone was a white-haired figure with an armband that read, 1930.

"What class are you?"

"Nineteen-sixty," Reemstma said.

"I was just thinking as I walked along, I was wondering what finally happened to everybody. It's hard to believe but when I was here we had men who simply packed up after a few weeks and went home without a word to anyone. Ever hear of anything like that? Nineteen-sixty, you say?"

"Yes, sir."

"You ever hear of Frank Kissner? I was his chief of staff. He was a tough guy. Regimental commander in Italy. One day Mark Clark showed up and said, Frank, come here a minute, I want to talk to you. Haven't got time, I'm too busy, Frank said."

"Really?"

"Mark Clark said, Frank, I want to make you a B.G. I've got time, Frank said."

The mess hall, in which the alumni dinner was being held, loomed before them, its doors open. Its scale had always been heroic. It seemed to have doubled in size. It was filled with the white of tablecloths as far as one could see. The bars were crowded, there were lines fifteen and twenty deep of men waiting patiently. Many of the women were in dinner dresses. Above it all was the echoing clamor of conversation.

There were those with the definite look of success, like Hilmo who wore a grey summer suit with a metallic sheen and to whom everyone liked to talk although he was given to abrupt silences, and there were also the unfading heroes, those who had been cadet officers, come to life again. Early form had not always held. Among those now of high rank were men who in their schooldays had been relatively undistinguished. Reemstma, who had been out of touch, was somewhat surprised by this. For him the hierarchy had never been altered.

A terrifying face blotched with red suddenly appeared. It was Cranmer, who had lived down the hall.

"Hey, Eddie, how's it going?"

He was holding two drinks. He had just retired a year ago, Cranmer said. He was working for a law firm in Reading.

"Are you a lawyer?"

"I run the office," Cranmer said. "You married? Is your wife here?"

"No."

"Why not?"

"She couldn't come," Reemstma said.

His wife had met him when he was thirty. Why would she want to go, she had asked? In a way he was glad she hadn't. She knew no one and given the chance she would often turn the conversation to religion. There would be two weird people instead of one. Of course, he did not really think of himself as weird, it was only in their eyes. Perhaps not even. He was being greeted, talked to. The women, especially, unaware of established judgments, were friendly. He found himself talking to the lively wife of a man he vaguely remembered, R. C. Walker, a lean man with a somewhat sardonic smile.

"You're a what?" she said in astonishment. "A painter? You mean an artist?" She had thick, naturally curly blond hair and a pleasant softness to her cheeks. Her chin had a slight double fold. "I think that's fabulous!" She called to a friend, "Nita, you have to meet someone. It's Ed, isn't it?"

"Ed Reemstma."

"He's a painter," Kit Walker said exuberantly.

Reemstma was dazed by the attention. When they learned that he actually sold things they were even more interested.

"Do you make a living at it?"

"Well, I have a waiting list for paintings."

"You do!"

He began to describe the color and light—he painted landscapes—of the countryside near the Delaware, the shape of the earth, its furrows, hedges, how things changed slightly from year to year, little things, how hard it was to do the sky. He described the beautiful, glinting green of a hummingbird his wife had brought to him. She had found it in the garage; it was dead, of course.

"Dead?" Nita said.

"The eyes were closed. Except for that, you wouldn't have known." He had a soft, almost wistful smile. Nita nodded warily.

Later there was dancing. Reemstma would have liked to go on talking but he had gotten sleepy and the tables had broken up after dinner into groups of friends.

"Bye for now," Kit Walker had said.

He saw her talking to Hilmo, who gave him a brief wave. He wandered about for a while. They were playing *Army Blue*. A wave of sadness went through him, memories of parades, the end of dances, Christmas leave. Four years of it, the classes ahead leaving in pride and excitement, unknown faces filling in behind. It was finished, but no one turns his back on it completely. The life he might have led came back to him, almost whole.

Outside barracks, late at night, five or six figures were sitting on the steps, drinking and talking. Reemstma sat near them, not speaking, not wanting to break the spell. He was one of them, as he had been on frantic evenings when they cleaned rifles and polished their shoes to a mirror-like gleam. The haze of June lay over the great expanse that separated him from those endless tasks of years before. How deeply he had immersed himself in them. How ardently he had believed in the image of a soldier. He had known it as a faith. He had clung to it dumbly, as a cripple clings to God.

In the morning Hilmo trotted down the stairs, tennis shorts tight over his muscled legs, and disappeared through one of the salley-ports for an early match. His insouciance was unchanged. They said that before the Penn State game when he had been first-string the coach had told them they were not only going to beat Penn State, they were going to beat them by two touchdowns. Turning to Hilmo, he said,

"And who's going to be the greatest back in the East?"

"I don't know. Who?" Hilmo said.

Empty morning. As usual, except for sports there was little to do. Shortly after ten they formed up to march to a memorial ceremony at the corner of the Plain. Before a statue of Sylvanus Thayer they stood at attention, one tall maverick head in a cowboy hat, while the choir sang *The Corps*. The thrilling voices, the solemn, staggered parts rose through the air. Behind Reemstma someone said quietly, "You know, the best friends I ever had or ever will have are the ones I had here."

Afterward they walked out to take their places on the parade ground. The superintendent, a trim lieutenant general, stood not far off with his staff and the oldest living graduate, who was in a wheelchair.

"Look at him. That's what's wrong with this place," Dunning said. He was referring to the superintendent.

"That's what's wrong with the whole army."

Faint waves of band music beat toward them. It was warm. There were bees in the grass. The first miniature formations of cadets, bayonets glinting, began to move into view. Above, against the sky, a lone distinguished building and that a replica, the chapel, stood. Many Sundays there with their manly sermons on virtue and the glittering choir marching toward the door with graceful, halting tread, gold stripes shining on the sleeves of the leaders. Down below, partly hidden, the gymnasium. The ominous, dark patina on everything within, the floor, the walls, the heavy boxing gloves. There were champions enshrined there who would never be unseated, maxims that would never be erased.

At the picnic the class secretary announced that of the 550 original members, 529 were living and 176 present so far.

"Not counting Klingbeil!"

"One seventy-six plus a possible Klingbeil."

"An *im*possible Klingbeil," someone called out.

There was a cheer.

The tables were in a large, screened pavilion on the edge of the lake. Reemstma looked for Kit Walker. He'd caught sight of her earlier, in the food line, but now he could not find her. The speeches were continuing.

"We got a card from Joe Waltsak. Joe retired this year. He wanted to come but his daughter's graduating from high school. I don't know if you know this story. Joe lives in Palo Alto and there was a bill before the California legislature to change the name of any street an All-American lived on and name it after him. Joe lives on Parkwood Drive. They were going to call it Waltsak Drive, but the bill didn't pass, so instead they're calling him Joe Parkwood."

The elections were next. The class treasurer and the vice-president were not running again. There would have to be nominations for these.

"Let's have somebody different for a change," someone commented in a low voice.

"Somebody we know," Dunning muttered.

"You want to run, Mike?"

"Yeah, sure, that would be great," Dunning said.

"How about Reemstma?" someone asked. It was Cranmer, the blossoms of alcoholism ablaze in his face. The edges of his teeth were uneven as he smiled, as if eaten away.

"Good idea."

"Who, me?" Reemstma said. He was flustered. He looked around in surprise.

"How about it, Eddie?"

He could not tell if they were serious. It was all off-handed—the way Grant had been picked from obscurity one evening when he was sitting on a bench in St. Louis. He murmured something in protest. His face had become red.

Other names were being proposed. Reemstma felt his heart pounding. He had stopped saying, no, no, and sat there, full lips open a bit in bewilderment. He dared not look around him. He shook his head slightly, no. A hand went up.

"I move that the nominations be closed."

Reemstma felt foolish. They had tricked him again. He felt as if he had been betrayed. No one was paying any attention to him. They were counting raised hands.

"Come on, you can't vote," someone told his wife.

"I can't?" she said.

Wandering around as the afternoon ended Reemstma finally caught sight of Kit Walker. She acted a little strange. She didn't seem to recognize him at first. There was a soiled spot on her skirt.

"Oh, hello," she said.

"I was looking for you."

"Would you do me a favor?" she said. "Would you mind getting me a drink? My husband seems to be ignoring me."

Though Reemstma did not notice, someone else was ignoring her, too. It was Hilmo, standing some way off. They had come back to the pavilion separately. The absence of the two of them during much of the afternoon had not been put together yet. Friends who would soon be parting were talking in small groups, their faces shadowy against the water that leapt in light behind them. Reemstma returned with some wine in a plastic glass.

"Here you are. Is anything wrong?"

"Thank you. No, why? You know, you're very nice," she said. She had noticed something over his shoulder. "Oh, dear."

"What?"

"Nothing. It looks like we're going."

"Do you have to?" he managed to say.

"Rick's over by the door. You know him, he hates to be kept waiting."

"I was hoping we could talk."

He turned. Walker was standing outside in the sunlight. He was wearing an aloha shirt and tan slacks. He seemed somewhat aloof. Reemstma was envious of him.

"We have to drive back to Belvoir tonight," she said.

"I guess it's a long way."

"It was very nice meeting you," she said.

She left the drink untouched on the corner of the table. Reemstma watched her white skirt make its way across the floor. She was not like the others, he thought. He saw them walking to their car. Did she have children, he found himself wondering? Did she really find him interesting?

In the hour before twilight, at six in the evening, he heard the shouting and looked out. Crossing the area toward them was the unconquerable schoolboy, long-legged as a crane, the ex-infantry officer now with a small, well-rounded paunch, waving an arm.

Dunning was leaning from a window.

"Hooknose!"

"Look who I've got!" Klingbeil called back.

It was Devereaux, the tormented scholar. Their arms were around each other's shoulders. They were crossing together, grinning, friends since cadet days, friends for life. They started up the stairs.

"Hooknose!" Dunning shouted.

Klingbeil threw open his arms in mocking joy.

He was the son of an army officer. As a boy he had sailed on the Matson Line and gone back and forth across the country. He was irredeemable, he had the common touch, his men adored him. Promoted slowly, he had gotten out and become a land developer. He drove a green Cadillac famous in Tampa. He was a king of poker games, drinking, late nights.

She had probably not meant it, Reemstma was thinking. His experience had taught him that. He was not susceptible to lies.

"Oh," wives would say, "of course. I think I've heard my husband talk about you."

"I don't know your husband," Reemstma would say.

A moment of alarm.

"Of course, you do. Aren't you in the same class?"

He could hear them downstairs.

"Der Schiff ist kaputt!" they were shouting. *"Der Schiff ist kaputt!"*

PRAYER FOR THE DYING

WILLIS JOHNSON

Willis Johnson is a former journalist. He worked for the Norwalk (Connecticut) Hour, the Australian Broadcasting Commission and he covered the Vietnam War for the Associated Press. He wrote a political biography, *The Year of the Longley,* which was published by Penobscot Bay Press in 1978. For the past five years he has been writing fiction. Mr. Johnson lives in Gardiner, Maine, and is working on a book of stories about the people of "Prayer for the Dying."

The day Yakov Kaputin died he managed to make the nurse understand that he wanted to see Father Alexey. Yakov had lived in America for thirty years but he did not speak English. He scribbled a faint, wiggly number on the paper napkin on his lunch tray and pointed a long knobby finger back and forth between the napkin and his bony chest. "You want me to call, do you, dear?" the nurse asked in a loud voice that made Yakov's ears ring. Yakov could not understand what she said but he nodded, *"Da."*

When the telephone rang Father Alexey was just dozing off. It was July. Crickets were chirring in the long dry grass outside his window. The priest was lying in his underwear listening to a record of Broadway show tunes on the new stereo his mother had bought him. His long beard was spread out like a little blanket on his chest. The window shade was down and a fan was softly whirring.

He thought it was the alarm clock that rang and tried to turn it off.

"Mr. Kaputin wants you to come to the hospital," the nurse said with finality, as if announcing some binding decision from above.

He did not know how long he had slept. He felt shaky and unfocused.

"I can't," he said.

"Is this the Russian priest?"

Copyright © 1982 by Willis Johnson. First appeared in *TriQuarterly.* Reprinted by permission.

"This is Father Alexey." His voice seemed to echo far away from him. "I'm busy just now."

"Well, we're all busy, dear," the nurse said. She paused as if waiting for him to see the truth in that and do the right thing.

"What is it this time?" Father Alexey said with a sigh.

"I just came from him," the nurse began to converse chattily. ("That's better now," her tone seemed to say.) "He's a real sweetheart. He wrote your number down. He didn't touch his lunch, or his breakfast. I don't think he feels well. Of course we can't understand a word he says, and he can't understand us. . . ."

"He never feels well," Father Alexey said irritably. "You usually do not feel well when you have cancer."

"Well," the nurse said indignantly. "I've called. I've done *my* duty. If you don't want to come. . ."

Father Alexey sighed another large sigh into the receiver. He hated the hospital. He hated the way it smelled, the way grown men looked in little johnny coats, the way Yakov's bones were all pointed. Besides that, it was very hot out. During the entire morning service not even the hint of a breeze had come in the door of his little church. In the middle of a prayer he thought he might faint. He had had to go into the Holy of Holies and sit down.

"It's not a matter of 'not wanting,' " he said pointedly. "I'll have to adjust my schedule, and that's not always easy. I don't know when I can be there. I have to try to find a ride."

He lay for a while longer with the fan blowing on him, his hands clasped on his soft white stomach. The sheet under him was clean and cool. He looked tragically at the window shade. It was lit up like a paper lantern.

Father Alexey lived next to the church in an old house with a cupola, fancy molding and derelict little balconies. A rusty iron fence tottered around the unmowed yard. Once every seven or eight years one or two sides of the house got a coat of paint. The different shades of paint and balusters missing from the little balconies gave the house a patched, toothless look. On rainy days water dripped down the wall next to Father Alexey's bed. He complained to Mr. Palchinsky, the president of the Union of True Russians, which owned the house. Mr. Palchinsky got the Union to provide each room with a plastic bucket. Father Alexey would have tried to fix the roof himself but he did not know how to do it. Yakov said he knew how to do it but he was too old to climb a ladder and besides they did not have a ladder.

Yakov's room was next to Father Alexey's. Each night after the old man said his prayers he would say good night to the priest through the wall.

Father Alexey did not always answer. Yakov was a nice man but he could be a pain. He was always talking, telling stories about himself. Yakov in the forest, Yakov in the Civil War, Yakov in the labor camp, Yakov tending flower beds for some big shot in White Plains. Father Alexey knew them all. And whenever he made an observation with which Yakov did not agree, Yakov would say, "You're young yet. Wait a while. When you're older, you'll see things more clearly."

The priest knew it was one of the things people in town said about him: he was young. He tried to look older by wearing wire-rimmed glasses. He was balding, and that helped. Not that it was a bad thing to say, that he was young. If people really wanted to be disparaging—as when the Anikanov family got mad at him because he forgot to offer them the cross to kiss at their mother's memorial service—they went around reminding their neighbors that he was not Russian at all but an American from Teaneck; if they knew about his mother being Polish they called him a Pole; they brought up the fact that he once had been a Catholic. If they wanted to truly drag his name through the mud, they called him a liberal, even though he almost always voted Republican.

Yakov had been to the hospital before, once when he had his hernia and once for hemorrhoids. This time, even before they knew it was cancer, he sensed he wouldn't be coming home. He was, after all, almost ninety years old. He carefully packed his worn suit, the photographs of his wife, his Army medal, some old books that looked as if they had been rained on, into cardboard boxes which he labeled and stacked in his room. He left an envelope with some money with Father Alexey and also his watering pail for his geraniums. When the car came he didn't want to go. Suddenly he was afraid. Father Alexey had to sit with him in his room, assuring him it was all right, he was going to get well. He carried Yakov's suitcase out to the car. Yakov was shaking. When Father Alexey waved good-bye the old man started to cry.

The hospital was in the city, fifteen miles away. Once a week the senior citizens' bus took people from the town to the shopping center, which was only a mile from the hospital, and you could get a ride if there was room. But if you did not have a car and it was not Thursday, you had to call Mikhail Krenko, the dissident. He had a little business on the side driving people to the city for their errands.

Krenko worked nights on the trucks that collected flocks from the chicken barns. He had arrived in town one day after jumping off a Soviet trawler. It was said that he offered a traffic policeman two fresh codfish in exchange for political asylum. People suspected he was a spy. They were almost certain he had Jewish blood. Why else, they asked each other, would the Soviets have given him up so easily? Why had he come to live in a godforsaken town that did not even have a shopping center?

Krenko was a short man with limp yellow hair and a round face like a girl. He chewed gum to cover the smell of his liquor, sauntered with his hands in his pockets and did not remove his hat upon entering a house, even with a ikon staring him in the face. In the churchyard one Sunday people overheard him call Mr. Palchinsky *Papashka*—"Pops." Anna Kirillovna Nikulin told of the time she rode to the city with him and he addressed her as Nikulina—not even *Mrs.* "Here you are, Nikulina," he said, "the drugstore."

Some female—an American; young, by the sound of her—answered when Father Alexey dialed his number.

"He's in the can," she said.

"Well, would you call him, please?" he said impatiently.

"Okay, okay, don't have a kitten."

She yelled to Krenko. "I don't know—some guy having a kitten," she said.

When Krenko came on the telephone, the priest said as sarcastically as he could, "This is Father Alexey—the 'guy' from your church."

"Hey, you catch me hell of time, with pants down."

"I called you," Father Alexey replied stiffly, "because one of my parishioners happens to be very ill."

He hung his communion kit around his neck and went to wait for Krenko in the sparse shade of the elm tree in front of the house. Only a few branches on the old tree still had leaves. In some places big pieces of bark had come off. The wood underneath was as dry and white as bone.

Across the street was the town's funeral home. Sprays of water from a sprinkler and a couple of hoses fell over the trim green grass and on the flowers along the walk. Father Alexey held his valise with his holy vestments in one hand and in the other his prayer book, a black ribbon at the prayers for the sick. He could feel the sweat already running down his sides.

He thought how it would be to strip off his long hot clothes and run under the spray, back and forth. He saw himself jumping over the flowers. He could feel the wet grass between his toes. Setting down his valise, he took off his hat and wiped his face and bald head with his handkerchief. He fluttered the handkerchief in the air. In a minute it was dry.

Then from behind him a window opened and he heard Mrs. Florenskaya call. He pretended not to hear. He did not turn around until the third time.

"Oh, hello, Lidiya Andreyevna," he said, holding the bright sun behind his hand.

"Somewhere going, *batiushka?*" the old woman asked in her crackly voice.

"Yes," the priest said reluctantly.

"Good," Mrs. Florenskaya said. *"Ich komme."*

The Union of True Russians had bought the house as a retirement home (it had been a fine, sturdy house, the home of a sea captain; the church next door had been the stable for his carriage horses) and at one time all the rooms and flats had been occupied. Everyone was gone now, dead or moved away—mostly dead. The whole parish had grown older all at once, it seemed. Now with Yakov in the hospital, Father Alexey was alone in the old house with Mrs. Florenskaya. Every day she shuffled up and down the empty, echoing hallway in her worn slippers and Father Alexey would hear her crying. In nice weather she cried out on the porch. The first time he heard her—it was shortly after he had arrived to take over the parish a year ago (his predecessor, Father Dmitri, had started to drink and was transferred back to New York)— Father Alexey had run upstairs to see what was wrong. Mrs. Florenskaya listened to his beginner's Russian with a happy expression on her face, as if he were trying to entertain her. Then she had replied in a mixture of English and German, although he didn't know any German, that a bandit was stealing spoons from her drawer.

He no longer asked.

After a minute the front door opened and the little woman came spryly down the stairs carrying a cane which she did not seem to need. A paper shopping bag and an old brown purse hung from one arm. She was wearing a kerchief and a winter coat.

"Where going *Sie*, little father?" She came into the shade and smiled up at him.

When he told her about Yakov, she sighed heavily. "Old people just closing eyes," she said. Her chin started to wobble.

"Aren't you hot in that coat, Lidiya Andreyevna?" he asked.

She pulled a wadded tissue out of her pocket. "*Sie* young man, *Sie* can *arbeiten*. I am old." She wiped her nose, then lifted her chin in the air. "I *arbeiten* in Chicago," she said proudly. "In fine hotel."

Father Alexey looked down the empty street.

"He's late," he said.

"*Ja,*" the old woman said emphatically, as if he had confirmed all she had said. "Many *zimmer* taken care of; wash, clean, making beds."

A short distance from where they stood the road dropped steeply to the river. Father Alexey could see the far bank and the dark pines of the forest beyond. The sky was blue and still. The leaves were motionless on the trees, as if they were resting in the heat. Above the brow of the hill, Father Alexey saw two heads appear then slowly rise like two plants pushing up into the sun. The heads were followed by two bodies, one long, one square. They came up over the hill and came slowly in the heat toward the priest and Mrs. Florenskaya. They were dressed for the city, the woman in a dress with flowers, the man in a suit and tie. The woman was the long one. The man was sheer and square like a block of stone. As they drew near, the man took the woman's arm in his thick hand and stopped her short of the shade. They looked back down the road. The man checked his watch.

Bending around the priest, Mrs. Florenskaya peered at them with curiosity.

"Good heavens," she said at last in Russian, "why are you standing in the sun? Come here, dearies, with us."

The man gave them half a smile. "It's all right," he said as if embarrassed. But the woman came right over.

"Thank you," she said as if the shade belonged to them. "That hill! We had to stop four times. Stepanka, come join these nice people." She took him by the arm. "Now that's much better—no?"

Father Alexey introduced himself and said in Russian that the weather was very hot.

"Fedorenko," the man said but he did not offer his hand. He added in English: "My wife."

"*Ach, Sie sprechen Englisch!*" Mrs. Florenskaya said delightedly. "I, too!"

From time to time Father Alexey ran into them in the market or on the street. The man was Ukrainian, the woman Byelorussian. The woman would always smile. Once in a while the man nodded stiffly. On

Sundays Father Alexey would see them pass by on their way to the Ukrainian church.

"Are you waiting for someone?" the man's wife asked, continuing the English. "We're supposed to meet Mr. Krenko here."

"He was supposed to be here ten minutes ago," the priest said.

"We're going to do a little shopping," the woman informed them. "Stepan's not allowed to drive. It's his eyes. They wouldn't renew his license. We're going to get some glasses for him. He doesn't want them. He thinks they'll make him look old."

"Not old," her husband said sharply. "Don't need it. What for spend money when don't need it?"

"You see?" she said hopelessly.

As they waited the sun grew hotter. They inched closer together under the tree. They could see the heat coming up from the road and from the black shingles of the roofs that showed above the hill. Mrs. Fedorenko fanned her face. Mrs. Florenskaya unbuttoned her coat. They stared longingly at the glistening spray of water across the way. There was a rainbow in the spray and the water glistened on the green grass and on the flowers and on the lawn sign on which the undertakers had painted in gold an Orthodox cross beside the regular Christian one.

Finally they heard an engine straining. Up over the hill through the waves of heat came Krenko's car. It was a big car, several years old, all fenders and chrome. Upon reaching level ground it seemed to sigh. It came up to them panting.

Krenko pushed open the front door.

"You're late," Father Alexey told him. With a look of distaste, he set his valise with his holy vestments on Krenko's zebra-skin seat. Mr. and Mrs. Fedorenko climbed into the back, followed by Mrs. Florenskaya, who nudged Mr. Fedorenko into the middle with her bony hip.

"Where is she going?" Krenko said.

"Ask her," the priest shrugged.

"Where you going, lady?"

"Never mind," Mrs. Florenskaya said.

"Not free, you know. Cost you money."

"Ja. Everything all time is money."

"Ten dollars," Krenko said.

"Ja, ja."

"You have?"

Mrs. Florenskaya took a rag of a bill out of her pocketbook and waved it angrily under Krenko's nose. She put it back and snapped her purse. "Everything is money," she said. Tears suddenly rolled out from under her eyeglasses.

"Crazy old woman," Krenko muttered.

"May we go?" Father Alexey said.

They drove around the block onto the main street of the town. On the street was the market, the bank, the hardware store, the laundromat, the boarding house where old people who did not belong to the Union of True Russians lived, and a variety store where they sold pizzas. Part way down the hill Krenko stopped and blew the horn.

"Another passenger, I presume?" Father Alexey said.

"Make it when sun is shining," Krenko winked.

From a door marked "Private" stepped Marietta Valentinova, the famous ballerina who lived over the hardware store. A white cap with green plastic visor kept the sun from her small severe face. Krenko got out and opened the front door, giving her a mock bow, which she ignored.

She had been at the St. Vladimir's Day service that morning at Father Alexey's church. Several members of the parish were named Vladimir, so there had been a good attendance in spite of the heat, more than a dozen. St. Olga's Day a few days earlier had not been nearly so successful, but then there was only one Olga in town, and she was sick and couldn't come. Marietta Valentinova had stood in her usual place in the center, where she was in range of any idle chatter, which she would silence at once with a scalding look. She also kept an eye on the ikon candles. She did not like to let them burn down more than halfway, and all during the service she was blowing them out and removing them from their holders. People who had lit the candles complained about it to each other but none dared say anything to her. On Sundays or saints' days, it didn't matter, she put a dollar in the basket. No one had ever seen her take back change. But she was very severe.

"Good afternoon, Marietta Valentinova," Father Alexey said. *"Ya yedu v gospital."*

The ballerina glanced at his valise. One corner of her small red mouth lifted slightly. "I thought you have been looking thin," she teased him in English. "That's the trouble with being monk: no wife to feed you."

"It's Yakov Osipovich," he said, reddening.

"Well," she said, "shall you move over or must I stand in sun all day?"

"Maybe you get in first, lady," Krenko said. "With such little legs you fit better in middle."

"I will thank you to pay attention to your own legs. And also your manner. Who do you think you are, blowing that horn?"

"Like joking with her," Krenko winked when the priest got out to let the ballerina in.

"How about the air conditioning?" Father Alexey said when Krenko got back behind the wheel.

"Okay. First got to put up all windows," Krenko said. Then he turned a switch. Air blew out from under the dashboard.

"I think that's the heat," said Father Alexey.

"Is okay," Krenko said. "Got to cool up."

They drove to the bottom of the hill and turned up along the river. The water lay flat and colorless between banks of colorless clay. Soon they were in the woods. The road ran over the tops of hills and down to stream beds filled with rocks. The undergrowth was dense and tangled and they could not see the river. They passed a farmhouse with a barn propped up by poles. In a clearing slashed in the woods a mobile home squatted like a gypsy, its children and its trash strewn round the yard.

The air was blowing out, but the car was stifling. They were squeezed together, Father Alexey with his valise on his lap. Marietta Valentinova smelled Krenko sweating. She moved a fraction closer to the priest, who had pulled out his handkerchief and was wiping his face.

"If I don't get some air, I am going to faint," Marietta Valentinova said.

Krenko moved the switch another notch. The hot air blew out harder.

"Sometimes takes couple minutes," he said.

"In a couple of minutes we will be cooked," the ballerina said. "Can't you see I'm dying?"

"Hold it!" Krenko said. He felt under the dashboard. "Now is coming."

Father Alexey wiggled his small white fingers in the air blowing on his knees. It was still hot.

"*Now* is coming," Krenko said confidently.

"Open a window," the ballerina commanded.

"You going to let air condition out. . ."

"Did you hear me?" she said in a voice so severe that everyone at once rolled down his window.

"Thank God," said the priest as the hot wind blew in on them. They put their hands out into it, groping for a current of coolness.

After a while Mrs. Fedorenko said, "It was very hot in New Jersey, too. That's where we lived."

"Hot like hell," Krenko agreed, although he had never been to New Jersey. "Here is not hot."

"I am very glad to hear that this is not hot," the ballerina said. She held a hanky over her mouth as they passed a chicken barn.

"More hot in California," Mr. Fedorenko said. "I been all over United States. Many Ukrainian people live in California. Many Russian, too," he added for the benefit of the ballerina who had cocked her ear toward him, showing him her profile, the raised eyebrow. "And many Ukrainian. Not same thing."

"Do tell us about it," the ballerina said haughtily. To Marietta Valentinova there was no such thing as a Ukrainian. That was modern nationalist nonsense. What was the Ukraine?—*Malorossiya*, Little Russia. They were all Russians.

"You are from New Jersey, *batiushka?*" Mrs. Fedorenko asked to change the subject.

"Yes. It is very hot in New Jersey. I haven't been to California."

"*I* in Chicago *arbeiten*," Mrs. Florenskaya said.

"You were saying something about the *malorossy*, I believe?" the ballerina said.

"Not Little Russians, lady. Ukrainian."

"All right, Stepanka. Did you hear? *Batiushka* also lived in New Jersey."

Mr. Fedorenko folded his heavy arms. "Don't call us *malorossy*."

"I don't call you anything," the ballerina smiled coldly.

"No?" Mr. Fedorenko pushed forward his big chin. "What are you calling ten million Ukrainians? The ones Russia starved?"

"If you are speaking of the Soviet Union, I'll thank you not to call it Russia," the ballerina said. "I even hate to say the word—*soviet*."

"Okay," Krenko said, "long time ago—okay?"

"I have a question," Father Alexey said.

"You, too," said Mr. Fedorenko accusingly. His face was very red. "Me too, what?"

"Stepanka," Mrs. Fedorenko implored.

"I see you Four July parade. See you turn away when Ukrainian club marching. You don't remember, huh?"

"I didn't turn away."

"I wouldn't blame you if you did," the ballerina said. "I certainly would."

"I didn't."

"That's enough, Stepanka."

"Maybe I just looked somewhere else," the priest said. "There is a big difference between looking somewhere else at a given moment and turning away."

"Of course there is," Mrs. Fedorenko assured him.

"I know how is seeing," her husband said.

"All right, Stepanka. What were you going to ask before, *batiushka?* You had a question."

"I don't know," the priest said dejectedly. After a moment he said, "I guess I was going to ask why everyone is speaking English."

"You're absolutely right," Mrs. Fedorenko said. "You need to learn." And then she said something in Russian, or Ukrainian, or Byelorussian, which Father Alexey did not quite catch. In the conversation that followed, he heard many words he knew but there were many words in between—they spoke so quickly—which he could not understand.

Then there was silence.

He looked around and saw the others looking at him.

"Nu?" the ballerina said.

"Shto?" he asked.

"Shto ti dumayesh?"

"Shto?"

"Heavens, my dear Father Alexey," the ballerina changed to English. "We are talking about poor Mr. Kaputin. Haven't you been listening?"

"Of course I've been listening."

"Well, then?"

"Well, what?"

"Is he getting better? You did say you were going to see him?"

"Yes, of course, Marietta Valentinova. I know. I understand." He had picked out Yakov's name in the wash of words but assumed they were talking about the old man's geraniums. Yakov grew them in his window box. They were big and healthy flowers, all from pinchings from other people's flower pots, and it was the thing people saw when they walked past the house. Father Alexey shifted the valise on his lap. His clothes were stuck to him.

"The nurse said he wasn't feeling well," he said. "Who knows what that means? Last time they said the same thing and I went all the way there and there was nothing wrong with him. He was fine. He just wanted someone to talk to. I walk in and he says, 'I'm glad you came, *batiushka*. Have you paid my electric bill? I think I paid it before I came here, but I can't remember.' I told him everything was taken care of. 'That's good,' he says. 'I was worried. So how are you, *batiushka?* It's hot out, isn't it?' "

"How sweet," the ballerina said.

"Sweet? It cost me—the church—ten dollars."

"Don't blame me," Krenko said. "They don't give the gas away yet."

There were more farms, more rocky fields and unpainted houses that tilted one way and another. Then more woods broken by raw-cut clearings full of stumps and weeds and plastic toys and house trailers on cement blocks.

Of the farms and houses, Father Alexey could almost pick which was Russian, which American. None of the people in them had money, you could see that easily enough, but the American ones almost seemed to be the way they were out of stubbornness. There was something in a savage, defiant way willful about the broken porches, the rusty machinery outside the barns. The Russian yards were unkempt only with weeds and overgrown grass and the woods coming closer and closer. They had little gardens, just tiny patches, with flowers and a few vegetables. Father Alexey started to get depressed.

"Did you ever think," he said, looking out the window, "that you would be here?"

No one said anything.

"Are you speaking to me?" Marietta Valentinova said.

"Yes. To anyone."

"Think I would be here? Of course not. Who would?"

"Then why did you come?"

"We're getting personal, I see." But she wasn't angry.

"I'm sorry. I was just thinking. . ."

"You want to know? All right, I came for my health."

Mr. Fedorenko gave a guffaw. His wife pulled at his sleeve.

"It's true. Why would I leave New Jersey? I had a nice apartment. When I danced I got good write-ups. You should see the people who came to my ballets. You could barely find a seat. And it wasn't a small auditorium in that school, either. Only thing, the air was no good for my health. All that pollution. So where does a Russian go? You've got to have a church. So you go where there are Russians. At least there

there were people with intelligence," she added over her shoulder. "Not like this godforsaken place."

"How many people lived in New Jersey!" Mrs. Fedorenko said before her husband could say anything. "We like it here, though," she said, patting Mr. Fedorenko's thick square hand. "We've had enough big things—the war, DP camp. After the camp we went to Venezuela. On Monday morning you turned on the radio and if there was a revolution you didn't have to go to work. Too many things. Here it's small and quiet. And Stepan always wanted to live near a river. He says that way you will never starve."

"I live in this place eighteen year," declared Mrs. Florenskaya. *"Achtzehn jahr,"* she added for Father Alexey's benefit. "All in this old house."

"Eighteen years," said the ballerina sadly. "I couldn't stand this place so long." But she already had been in the town more than half that.

Father Alexey calculated. Eighteen years ago he was nine years old. It was a whole year in his life, but all he could remember of being nine was being in the fourth grade and Sister Rita St. Agnes being his teacher, a stern little woman with thick black eyebrows who had seemed to take to him after his father died. "The boy with the laughing eyes," she called him affectionately. Sometimes he looked into the mirror to see why she called him that. The eyes belonged to a bald, not very old person who was expected to be full of answers for people far older than he, people who were afraid of getting sick and of nursing homes and hospitals and what was going to happen to them. He dispensed answers like the holy water he flung on heads and shoulders at a feast-day procession. Answers for death and fear and sadness and stolen spoons. And in all his life he had only lived in New Jersey with his mother and in the monastery in New York and now in a little town no one had ever heard of. How could he know?

In another eighteen years he would be forty-five. How much would he know then? Would he see things more clearly, as Yakov said? Krenko, the ballerina might still be around. Krenko probably would be in jail, he thought with some satisfaction, or in the real estate business or some scheme, making money one way or another. The ballerina would be an old woman if she were still alive. The others would surely be dead. Most of the people in the parish would be dead.

He was becoming more and more alone in the world.

The shopping center was on a long broad avenue that ran between the interstate and the city. It once had been a road of fine old houses with wide porches and broad lawns and beds of marigolds and tulips. A few remained. Dentists and lawyers had their offices in them. The rest had been torn down for the fast-food restaurants, gas stations and bargain stores that lined the road like a crowd at a parade. Krenko drove into the shopping center parking lot from the back road that came up from the river and discharged his passengers in front of the K-Mart. He'd be back in two hours, he said.

Father Alexey let the ballerina out and got back in the front seat. His cassock was wet and wrinkled where the valise had been.

"Look like you piss yourself," Krenko said and laughed.

In the hospital Father Alexey carried his valise in front of him to hide the wet place. Two teenaged girls snickered behind him on the elevator. A small boy who got on with his mother gawked up at him all the way to the seventh floor. "Hey, mister—you look like something," the boy said when the elevator stopped.

Father Alexey marched to the nurses' station and set his valise down hard. Then he remembered the wet place and covered it with his prayer book.

"You're here for Mr. Kaputin?" asked the nurse who was there.

"Yes," Father Alexey said curtly. "Are you the one who called?"

"No, Mrs. Dinsmore has gone." She came into the corridor. She was a tall woman with narrow shoulders and a tired face. Even before she said anything, Father Alexey knew that Yakov was going to die.

"The doctor has been in," she said.

He followed her to the room. Yakov was asleep, long and gaunt under the sheet. There was a thick sweet smell in the room. Yakov's bones looked as if they might pop through his face. With each breath his mouth puffed out like a frog's. On the stand beside his bed was an ikon of the Holy Mother of Kazan and a vase with daisies whose petals were falling off.

Father Alexey touched the old man's arm. His eyes blinked open. For a while he stared up at the priest. "It's you," he said.

"How are you feeling, Yakov Osipovich?" the priest asked in Russian.

"I saw my mother." Yakov's voice was hoarse and old. He took a long time between his words.

"Where did you see her?"

"She went away. There are fewer Russians, *batiushka.* . ."

He began to talk incoherently, something about apples in his father's orchard. The words came out in pieces that did not fit, as if something had broken inside of him.

The nurse brought a glass of tea. Father Alexey cooled it with his breath.

"Here, Yakov Osipovich," he said, raising the old man's head. The tea rose halfway up the glass straw, then sank back into the glass.

"Try again, Yakov Osipovich. Pull harder."

"Shall I try?" the nurse asked.

Father Alexey took his communion kit from around his neck. "I don't think it matters," he said.

The nurse went out quietly, leaving the door ajar.

Father Alexey arranged articles from his kit and others from his valise on the stand beside Yakov's bed and put on his holy vestments. He took the ribbon from the place he had marked in his book, then turned through the pages to the prayers for the dying.

He read quietly, occasionally making a cross over the old man's head. Yakov gazed up at him in silence and a kind of wonder, his mouth agape.

The priest softened a piece of bread in a little wine.

"Yakov Osipovich," he said, "are you sorry for your sins?"

The old man looked from the priest's face to the hand with the bread. Then his eyes closed. The priest shook him. "Yakov Osipovich," he said. "Say yes."

He tried to put the bread into Yakov's mouth but the old man's teeth were clenched. He slipped the bread between Yakov's lips, tucking it back into his cheek. Eventually Yakov's mouth began to move. He chewed fast, as if he were hungry.

Yakov opened his eyes just once more. Father Alexey was putting his things away. He heard Yakov's voice behind him. The old man was looking at him calmly.

"How did you come?" he said.

The priest came and sat beside him. "I found a ride. Are you feeling better?"

"Then you have to pay."

"Don't worry about it, Yakov Osipovich."

"Well, I'll straighten it out with you later, *batiushka.*"

Krenko was parked outside the emergency door in a place marked "Doctors Only."

"You make me wait long time," Krenko said. Father Alexey could smell liquor on him.

"I'm sorry."

"Not me, I don't care. But little dancing lady going to be mad like hell."

Marietta Valentinova sputtered at them half the way home. Tiny drops of saliva landed on the dashboard. Father Alexey watched them evaporate, leaving little dots. At last she stopped. They became aware of his silence.

"*Batiushka?*" Mrs. Fedorenko said.

After a while Krenko said, "Well, you got to go everybody sometimes."

"Where going?" Mrs. Florenskaya said.

"Mr. Kaputin," Mrs. Fedorenko told her gently.

"*Ja, alles,*" the old woman said, "*alles kaput. Mein man, meine kinder. Alles* but me."

The sun was gone from the window shade when Father Alexey got back to his room and lay down on his bed. It was still light, it would be light for a while yet. He turned on his fan to move the air and looked at the wall through which Yakov had said good night. He heard Mrs. Florenskaya upstairs in the hallway. She was starting in again.

The priest switched on the stereo with the record from the afternoon. But he could still hear her.

"Christ," he said, and turned up the volume.

THE LIFE AND TIMES OF
MAJOR FICTION

JONATHAN BAUMBACH

Jonathan Baumbach's most recent novel is *My Father More or Less*. "The Life and Times of Major Fiction" is the title story of a recently completed collection of stories. Mr. Baumbach was born in Brooklyn, lives in Brooklyn, and directs the MFA program in Creative Writing at Brooklyn College. He has four children, ranging in age from eight to twenty-six.

1

It wasn't that he was a great reader as a child but that he hardly read anything, hardly even cracked a book until he was in his mid twenties. At least that's the story he told me. He told other people other stories, which is their business and only of peripheral concern in this report. Once he discovered books, he told me in one of his side-of-the-mouth confidences, he couldn't get enough of them. "It was like," Ernie has been quoted as saying, "coming of age in Samoa," though in fact he was stationed in Japan at the time, a supply sergeant in Special Services during the last months of the Korean War. Once he discovered books he wondered where they had been all his life and why no one had ever told him how fantastic they were. It was as if it were some kind of unspoken secret, he said, and those on the inside weren't generous enough to share it with those on the out. Ernie took it on himself to spread the word in a way that would make people pay attention.

2

"He was a real-life Gatsby," my friend Jack said about Ernie, "except that it wasn't a woman that inspired him to reinvent himself but a literary ideal he only partially understood." Ernie read voraciously, read everything that came into his hands, yet we wondered, we couldn't

Copyright © 1983 by Jonathan Baumbach. First appeared in *Antaeus*. Reprinted by permission.

help but wonder—he was always there talking about who to read, who we *had* to read—when he found the time. There was something of the con man about Ernie, but we trusted that it was mostly an act, a facade under which sincerity and sensitivity kept unannounced watch.

3

The first fan letter he wrote, the first time he put his feelings about a book down on paper, he was embarrassed to have the author, whom he admired beyond words, read his "pathetic attempt at appreciation." Despite such misgivings, he posted the letter. "That took real guts," Ernie confided. "I thought, let the guy think I'm some kind of unwashed schmuck. I loved the man's books and I was going to tell him regardless of the impression it made." Jack told me that Ernie sent fan letters to two writers at the same time, commending each as the most important influence in his life. Neither writer answered him, not at first, and the silence on the other end, which was how he experienced no answer, saddened Ernie. He would have answered gratefully, he told us, if someone like himself had written an admiring letter to him.

4

Then there's the story, which only some of us credit, of how Ernie, when in the service, had an extended affair with an English nurse. They were wild about each other, we heard, but various obstacles—the war not the least of them—kept them apart, intensifying the romantic aura of their feelings. Finally, tenacity was rewarded, and they lived together in idyllic circumstances for several months. The woman was pregnant with Ernie's child and Ernie was overjoyed at the prospect of being a father and spending a life with this woman. Then something terrible happened, the kind of thing that warns you against exhilaration. There were unforeseen complications in the delivery. Neither mother nor child survived the birth. The news devastated Ernie, though he made no complaint, walked around in the rain as if he were composed of a thousand fragments held together by lacings of glue.

5

He wrote a second and third time to one of the writers, a recluse who hadn't published a book in eight years, and the third letter elicited a two-line response. It was typed like a ransom note.

IF MY BOOKS PLEASE YOU, FINE
IF THEY DON'T, THAT'S ALSO FINE.

The signature was illegible, or almost illegible, but there was no question whose fine literary hand it was.

Ernie put the letter behind a plastic sheet in a photograph album, though he was unaware at the time that it was the beginning of a collection. Ernie wrote letters of admiration to other writers and began to accumulate over a period of months a handful of answers. When he got a letter from one of his writers—he couldn't help but think of them as his—it brought tears to his eyes. If he admitted it to anyone, he said, admitting it to everyone, he'd become a laughing stock. So please don't tell anyone, he told us all.

6

For a while he lived with a woman who had been a writer, who had in fact published two novels in the distant past, though had written nothing for several years, had reached a point where she could barely get a sentence down on paper she might be willing to acknowledge. "Just think what you're denying the world," Ernie would say to her, closing her in a room with a typewriter for four hours a day. Her name was Zoe. He called her Zo Zo, which occasionally sounded like So So.

Sometimes she would complete a sentence in her four hours of exile, sometimes a half page of x's, an unseen text buried beneath.

Ernie bullied her and shouted at her, but she seemed not to mind, laughed good-naturedly at his excesses.

One day she came out of her prison with a completed story, a vindication of Ernie's regimen for her. He read the story with unqualified admiration, although he had (truth to tell) some minor reservations about the ending. She said she would change a line or two if it would make him happy. "I'm happy with things as they are," he reported himself saying. "It's the opinion of posterity I'm concerned about."

7

Another time Ernie fell in love with a woman whom he used to see every morning on Broadway walking her dog. Ernie tended to walk along with the two of them, paying the dog attention, which ingratiated him with the woman. They had a brief affair, then broke up when it got serious—the woman dependent on her husband in childish ways —then came together again. Their time together was mostly disappointing, informed as it was by regret and the prospect of impending separation. They consoled themselves with the illusion that one day they would live together as an acknowledged couple. It was one of those relationships that never ended, that continued to beguile itself with hope, though Ernie and the woman saw each other less and less. And then not at all. There was a rumor that the woman threw herself under a train or took an overdose of pills, though I suspect it was untrue, had grown out of a wish to give the story a more conclusive ending.

8

It was hard to keep track of the jobs Ernie held before his rise to celebrity. In a sense certainly, they were all the same job. He started out selling aluminum siding at carnivals, then after a brief stint as a radio actor, he emerged as a book traveler for a textbook firm in Boston, which kept him away from home somewhat more than he liked. He worried, from all accounts, that Zoe would leave her room in his absence to talk on the telephone or to smuggle food from the refrigerator, temptations difficult for her to resist. Once seduced from her task, she might never return to it.

What he liked about the job was that it provided occasions to meet some of the writers whose books he admired. Beyond a few obligatory visits to the colleges in his terrain, he could use his time as it pleased him. As a matter of discretion he only looked up those writers who had answered his correspondence. He didn't court rejection, he told us, but on the other hand he didn't let it get him down, never thought of it as personal.

9

After a whirlwind visit to the University of Maine—"I'm in and out," Ernie liked to say—he decided to look up Jason Honeycutt, who lived somewhere on the border between rural Maine and New Hampshire. The reclusive novelist had no phone so Ernie waited for him outside the Deerfield general store where Honeycutt, so said an informer at the university, did his shopping every Friday.

Ernie has told this story differently to different people, but I've pieced together the following account.

Ernie introduced himself to Honeycutt when the man came out of the store, offered to help him carry his groceries, which seemed to overburden the writer. Honeycutt mumbled something unintelligible and walked off to his oversized station wagon.

"I know what your privacy means to you," Ernie shouted after him. "I have no intention of imposing on you."

10

"Your books are very special to me," Ernie said. They were standing in front of Honeycutt's sprawling farmhouse, a box of groceries on the ground between them. "I just want to say that a single line of yours moves me more than the collected works of just about anyone else."

Honeycutt took a deep breath, a sigh of impatience or resignation. "All right, what are you after?" he asked.

Ernie came away from that visit with Honeycutt's avowed friendship and a signed first edition of one of the early novels. Given Honeycutt's reputation for turning away intruders, Ernie's success is all the more mystifying and impressive. The joke was, and Ernie told it on himself, that Honeycutt had bought his departure with that gift. Which didn't explain the literary correspondence that followed and Honeycutt's professed admiration, in several of his letters, for Ernie's understanding of his work.

After Ernie had won over the legendary Honeycutt, the other writers he pursued seemed to fall in line. After a point, it became a symbol of achievement to receive a letter from Ernie Sommer. Almost no writer of any distinction was ignored by him.

"They were very generous to me," Ernie has been quoted as saying. "I might have been the literary equivalent of a mass murderer for all any of them knew."

11

Ernie was extremely attached to his mother, I'm told. His father did some kind of physical labor, which seemed to use him up, shuck him of all vitality and hope. The rare occasions he spent with the family he was often drunk and sometimes violent. Disappointed with her husband, Ernie's mother, who was artistic, turned to Ernie for consolation. Ernie took sustenance from his mother, became dependent on her affection and approval. He showed some talent for painting as a child— it was his mother's idea for him—but then he gave it up. At some point, he realized that he had to get away from his mother to survive. As he got older, he took on something of his father's manner, some of the gruffness and swagger, though he remained, even after her death, essentially his mother's son.

12

When Ernie became a literary editor—eventually he started his own publishing company, Cervantes & Sons—he took his writers with him in surprising numbers. By this time Ernie was almost as well known (his picture on the cover of *People* magazine) as the most celebrated of his writers. Ernie made light of his success, liked to say it was a case of importance by association. "The other guys wrote these books and all I had to do was get the word around." Ernie's authors didn't tour the provinces promoting their books. He saw the practice as demeaning to serious artists, so he went himself, stood in for his authors on talk shows, made public appearances at bookstores, seemed everywhere at once, developed a reputation for saying the most provocative thing that came to mind. That was when he was starting out as a publisher, the first two or three years. In the third year of his publishing venture— things came apart after that—his writers were as dedicated to him as he had been (and maybe still was though it was no longer easy to tell) to them.

13

What went wrong? When a group of Ernie's writers get together at one of the traditional watering spots, that question invariably comes up. The answers tend to be provisional and dogmatic. The favored position is that the culture tends to destroy its heroes to make room for new ones. The rival position, which had almost equal claim, is that Ernie self-destructed. The more celebrated he became, the more outrageous he got. He took to referring to the audience—the first time in a radio interview in Las Vegas—as "those unwashed illiterate peckerheads out there." That didn't ingratiate him a whole lot, I suspect, or maybe it did until his listeners realized the "peckerheads" he was talking about were themselves. According to Jack, Ernie destroyed himself by trying to educate an audience that was wholly content being insulted.

14

Despite the critical success of the books Cervantes & Sons produced, the company, owned in partnership with two traditional types, managed to lose money or make so little, given the favorable attention it attracted, that it seemed like loss. Ernie was advised by his partners to practice greater economy, particularly in regard to his authors. Ernie's answer, he had told us each separately in private unrepeatable confidence, was that he practiced all the time though never seemed to get it right. One of his partners told me that after the first six months or so Ernie lost interest in the running of the firm. "He was more concerned with his own celebrity," the man told me, "than with the nuts and bolts of the business." On the other hand, Ernie had equally harsh things to say about his partners, whom he took to calling Heckyl and Jeckyl. Heckyl, he said, couldn't read and Jeckyl could but didn't.

15

We backtrack a bit here. Ernie is still on the rise, an ascending star in the lit celeb firmament. A collection of his correspondence called *Heroes and Heroines* is about to be published. As soon as he signs the contract for the book, Ernie regrets having made "my private obsession public." He insists that the book is incomplete and initiates new correspondence with a variety of international figures, forestalls publication date, dreams a letter from Tolstoy that he publishes in an obscure literary quarterly. Ernie denies that he is himself a writer. He is a longstanding appreciator of writers, an avaricious reader who is serious about what he reads, and perhaps (evidence the Tolstoy letter) a medium for literary voices. "Do you mean to say," the interviewer asks him, "that you didn't actually write the letter from Tolstoy?" "What can I tell you?" Ernie says. "I've never written anything, have never shown the slightest talent for writing. You could look it up. The 'C' I got in Freshman English at the University of Pennsylvania was a generosity from the instructor. Matter of fact, I don't know how the Tolstoy letter was written. It came to me in a moment of pure light. I think it would be ungracious of me to question the source."

A letter from Sophocles followed, though was never released for publication. Ernie himself questioned its legitimacy. "The man dictated it," he said, "but to tell the truth most of it was Greek to me."

16

Ernie was so self-important, one of his partners complained to me, that he would scotch film deals by abusing the person who wanted to buy the rights to one of his properties. He reputedly asked for a written critique from an independent producer who was after Jack's absurdist novel about Auschwitz. The man said that what interested him most about the novel was its wellspring of humanity. Ernie, according to the partner, told the man not to come back until he read the book word for word and had some idea of what he was buying.

Whether Ernie was subversive of his own business is a moot issue. Ernie said not to believe it, that he only interfered when negotiations became wearisomely protracted. Besides, he added, he thought it immoral to sell the books he loved as if they were underarm deodorants.

Whatever the case, Ernie's partners offered to buy him out by paying him, according to the partner I interviewed, twice what his share in the firm was worth. Eight months after Ernie left, the company, in order to survive, sold itself to a conglomerate, and both surviving partners, in due course, were forced out of the business.

17

Ernie had a friend, a psychologist, who ran an experimental clinic which took on only patients that had been previously diagnosed as incurable. One of the friend's incurable cases was a beautiful schizophrenic seventeen-year-old girl, who had had real or imagined relations with her father when she was twelve. When Ernie visited the friend at his clinic in California, he was moved by the girl's intelligence and courage and spent some time talking to her. Later, they exchanged letters—her letters full of remarkable perceptions—and Ernie found himself longing to see her again. The doctor encouraged the relationship—Ernie's friendship seemed to have a salutary effect on her condition—while warning Ernie not to let himself get too involved. The girl might improve, he told Ernie, but there would be inevitable relapses; she would never be able to lead a wholly normal life. Ernie threw himself headlong into the relationship with the girl, and an odd turnabout took place. As the girl made an astonishing recovery, Ernie began drinking to excess, seemed to come apart. When the girl no longer needed him she rejected Ernie for a man who seemed more confident of himself. After that, Ernie went through a period of bad weather, was drunk more often than not and got into a succession of pointless brawls. Eventually, the experience toughened him, made him more attentive to the demands of self.

18

Women. That's another story, though also inextricably connected to the story of Ernest Sommer's rise and fall. At a certain point in his life, women became almost as crucial to Ernie as books. Their pursuit, their affection, their approval conferred status on him. He was suddenly important enough to be loved for reasons other than himself.

I remember a lunch we had together when all Ernie wanted to talk about was "this absolutely gorgeous lady" who had come to his office to interview him for some magazine. "I said to her," he told me, "that all she had to do was say the word and I'd run off with her to some edenic spot on the other side of the globe and she says, looking directly at me, and this is a gorgeous lady, What word is that, Mr. Sommer? I told her I was serious and she says, this dazzler, the kind of lady that never would have looked at me twice outside of this book-lined office, I think you're a beautiful man, Mr. Sommer."

"I said to myself she had to be kidding. Smart, I may be. Beautiful I ain't. But she meant it and after the interview was concluded—I mean she was there to do a job—she demonstrated her sincerity. You know what I'm saying?"

How could he continue living with one woman when almost every desirable woman he came in contact with was available to him. "I can't handle it," he said whenever the subject came up. It was more of a boast than a self-deprecation, though the remark was not without some regret.

19

Zoe put up with Ernie's womanizing for a time—he would get over it, she must have thought—but then they had a fight at a party over the attention Ernie paid some starlet or princess and everything that had been kept inside came out.

Ernie professed shock at Zoe's abrupt explosion. "How can someone you lived with for twelve years treat you that way?" was his constant question.

Whatever happened next happened quickly. Zoe moved out, took the child, accused Ernie of promiscuous adultery and sued him for two-thirds of his recorded income.

According to Jack, nothing hurt Ernie more than Zoe's disaffection. After she left him his confidence began to erode.

Ernie is reported to have thrown himself at Zoe's feet in the lobby of her apartment building in an attempt at reconciliation. He apparently begged her to come back to him, using all his powers of persuasion.

20

"He hated more than anything not to get his way," Zoe told us. "He absolutely refused being turned down, though he would say—it was one of his favorite lines—that he never wanted anything for himself, that he could survive on nothing if he had to.

"I told him several times to let go of my ankles, that he had no business keeping me from my appointment. When he released me, I said no hard feelings and walked out on him."

"You didn't kick him as he claims?"

"Kick him?" The question seems to amuse her. "I didn't kick him if that's what he says—he would say that—which is to say it wasn't my intention to kick the son of a bitch. When I saw blood coming from his lip I felt awful, was ready to drop everything and look after him for as long as he needed me. I've always felt that way about Ernie. Let's just say that whatever happens, Ernie and I will always be friends."

"Did she really say that?" Ernie asked me. "That's unbelievable. That lady has class."

21

A former acquaintance of Ernie's, an author who had not written anything in years, showed up one morning at his door to accuse Ernie of having ruined his life. The man was unpleasant but also in need—broke and broken—so Ernie, who was temporarily living alone, let him stay over for a couple of nights. The former acquaintance read the gesture as an admission of Ernie's guilt and became even more demanding and abusive. It was the man's idea that Ernie was part of some kind of Jewish establishment that controlled who got published and who didn't. In his crazed view, Ernie had cut off all avenues of publication to him because he had once made an anti-Semitic remark in Ernie's presence. As a consequence of Ernie's perceived treachery, the man had lost the will to write. Although he despised the intruder, Ernie suffered his extended visit, felt in some inexplicable way obligated to the man. The man became fixated with Ernie, dressed in his clothes, imitated his voice on the phone, wrote letters in which he signed himself Ernie Sommer. One night Ernie woke to see his other self lighting a fire in Ernie's bedroom. The attempted murder released Ernie from any feelings of obligation. He threw the man out of his apartment and then subdued the fire. Ernie was burned, we understand, though nothing serious.

Ernie thinks of himself as rising from that fire like a phoenix.

22

The day after Ernie separated from the publishing house he had imagined into existence, it was as if he had never been there. When I called to speak to him—it was how I had learned he had gone—his former employees seemed unable to remember his name.

I was shunted from receptionist to receptionist, was kept waiting for ten minutes, then found myself holding a dead phone. Ernie will be furious at such incompetence, I thought, or else get a good laugh out of it. Colonel Fiction, as we sometimes called him, tended to complain in a seemingly parodic way at the quality of the help. If the gossip can be believed, he once asked a pompous young editor to sweep out his office and polish his desk. The editor quit (a week after he had both swept and polished) and Ernie is reputed to have said, "If you can't last fifteen rounds, there's no point in fighting for the championship of the world."

The second time I phoned, some assistant told me that Ernie was no longer employed at Cervantes & Sons. I thought of saying that a company doesn't employ its owner, but let it pass. I asked to speak to one of the partners. Both were in conference at the moment and were not expected to be free to come to the phone for an indefinite period of time. I left my name in that void, expecting it to disappear as heartlessly as Ernie had.

I called Ernie at home later that day and got no answer. And then, involved in my own work, I didn't concern myself with Ernie for a few days—maybe it was a few weeks—let the issue of his apparent disappearance slide. The next time I called his apartment, his phone had been disconnected.

A few days after that, Jack told me that Ernie had moved out of his loft and no one, at least no one Jack had talked to, knew where he had gone. Traces of him remained in the atmosphere like the fragments of an exploded meteor.

23

Time passes as we wait for Ernie to surface. Zoe publishes a novel centered around a character that resembles Ernie Sommer. This Ernie, called Howard Swift in the novel, is a heavy drinker and semi-heavy womanizer, a man unable to control the least of his desires. (By the time the book came out, Zoe had married her therapist, from whom, one imagines, she had gotten her license to kill.) There is some sympathy for Howard/Ernie in the book, though it relies for the most part on the heroine's willful generosity, the object of it beyond redemption.

It was not a heroic portrait; it was not a portrait of the man we thought we knew as Colonel (sometimes major, sometimes captain) Fiction. Howard Swift is a night club comedian who becomes a talk show host, becoming more ruthless and exploitative (and sexually bizarre) with each new success.

"Perhaps it's not meant to be Ernie at all," Jack suggested. "The character of Howard Swift may have no prototype in the real world but cliché."

I wrote Zoe a long letter protesting the book's portrait of Ernie, but then misplaced it among my papers or threw it out accidentally.

24

A story circulates—it is one rumor among many—that Ernie cut himself off from his old friends in order to pursue his own writing. I tend to accept rumors that have a poetic rightness about them even if their source is less than authoritative. I imagine Ernie writing in longhand on looseleaf pages, working all day and into the night, drinking bourbon and pacing the room, an obsessive figure capable of the most extreme vices and the most intense virtue.

When will we hear from him again? I sit patiently at my desk and put down words, fragments, sentences, paragraphs in what seems to me a telling order. As I write, I glance over my shoulder from time to time (I'm speaking figuratively of course), looking for Ernie, imagining myself as Ernie, wanting to be greeted by my friends as I emerge from obscurity.

25

I am at my desk trying to imagine the next stage of Ernie's career, trying to create an imaginary history more substantial and valid than the real one. Who is Ernie after all?

There are a number of possible conclusions to his story, none absolutely right, almost all with some claim to verisimilitude. I put them down in longhand on the looseleaf sheet in front of me.

> A pseudonymous manuscript of over 1200 pages shows up (delivered by messenger) in the office of an editor of some power and authority. It is accompanied by a note from the reclusive writer, H, commending it to the editor. The book is published, gets mostly excellent if

uncomprehending reviews, sells modestly, is almost sold to the movies. At some point Ernie lets out in an interview that he is the actual author.

Ernie produces a best seller of little or no literary value, talks in interviews about the importance of reaching a large audience. Established as a public figure, he laments the plight of celebrities, says all he wants is to be left alone to write his books.

Ernie reemerges as the editor-in-chief of a new incarnation of a once prestigious men's magazine which in its bid for trendiness had lost its identity. He calls a press conference to announce that the magazine will publish the best writing in America and the world regardless of mass market appeal, that its only aim is to be first rate. The opening issue sells out; the second issue does almost as well; the third sells half as many as the second. Ernie leaves his post after ten months to write a memoir of the experience.

Unable to write at the level of his aspirations, Ernie gives way to depression, drinks heavily, turns himself into a clinic for rehabilitation, writes the story of his breakdown and recovery.

Ernie writes versions of the books he's admired, publishes them under pseudonyms, lives modestly out of the public eye. Most of us never see him again, though over drinks we share anecdotes about his career, keeping Ernie afloat in the collective imagination like a character in a novel.

THE ARTIFICIAL MOONLIGHT

DONALD JUSTICE

Born and brought up in Miami, Donald Justice has recently returned to his native state to teach at the University of Florida. In 1980 his *Selected Poems*, published by Atheneum, was awarded a Pulitzer Prize.

Coconut Grove, 1958

The Langs, Hal and his wife Julie, were giving a party.

From the screen porch of their apartment you could see, strung out across the bay, the colored lights of the neighborhood sailing club—the Langs did not belong—and, farther out, the bulky shadows of the members' boats riding at anchor. Almost always, with nightfall, there would be a breeze. It came from the bay and across the bayshore road past the shaggy royal palms bordering the driveway, cooling the porch like a large and efficient fan.

But tonight was one of those rare end-of-summer nights without any saving breeze. It was past midnight, and still the apartment felt oppressive and close. The heat was spoiling the party. It was a going-away party for an old friend of the Langs', Jack Felton, whom they saw now only when he came home from graduate school to visit his parents, and in a day or two, with summer over, he would be taking off for Europe on a Fulbright. But it was not only the heat. Some vague melancholy of departure and change seemed to have settled over everyone and everything.

In the back room a record player was turning, unattended. Sounds of the jazz of a dozen years ago, early Sarah Vaughan, drifted out to the porch. The casual guests, the friends of friends, had all departed. The few who remained looked settled in, as though they might stay forever, listless and bored, some on the sagging wicker chair and settee, and some on the floor cushions brought out from the stuffy back rooms.

Copyright © 1983 by Donald Justice. First appeared in *Antaeus*. Reprinted by permission.

They looked as though they might never move again, not even to flip the stack of records when the music ended.

If anyone did, it would probably be Julie herself. Of the Langs, Julie was the dependable one. Five afternoons a week she worked as a legal stenographer, while her husband kept up appearances by giving occasional painting lessons to the daughters of tourists. Yet except for a shortage of money from time to time they lived with as much freedom from care and nearly as much leisure as the well-to-do. Approaching their thirties, they seemed as perpetually youthful as movie stars.

The odd hours they kept could be hard on Julie, and occasionally she retired early. She would be so wound up that she could not sleep and would have to read for a long time before her eyes closed. It was an intense sort of reading, beyond simple pleasure. One wall of their bedroom was filled with books, and sometimes when they made love without turning the lights off she caught herself innocently letting her eyes rove across the titles on the spines of the larger books. Once or twice Hal had complained of this publicly, to her embarrassment, but she seemed unable to change.

Alone in their bedroom, reading or not, she liked the sound of conversation floating back late at night from the porch. It was soothing, like the quiet, washing sound of an ocean. It was hot back there, and there was a little fan she could reach out for and turn on, but she did not often use it. She liked the warm weather; she could not imagine living anywhere but Miami.

Still, there were nights when Julie felt left out of things. Their friends all drank, and, except on the most ceremonial occasions, Julie did not. Of course the feeling went beyond that. She would suspect them of planning something incalculably exciting from which she was to be excluded. Unreasonable, but there was nothing she could do about the feeling. Julie gazed with half-closed eyes across the porch at her husband, where he sat perched on an arm of the old wicker settee, bending down to speak to a tall blond woman in slacks. She wondered if she would ever be able to trace this feeling of hers back to its source. How far back would she have to go? She was an orphan, adopted by a couple old enough to be her grandparents, long ago dead. Could it be as simple as that? She thought, sometimes, that she might have Spanish blood. That would account for her dark coloring, for her thick black eyebrows, her almost blue-black hair, which only a few days before she had cut short, despite Hal's protests.

In the back room now the record stopped and another dropped down from the stack—Duke Ellington, slow and bluesy. Shutting her eyes, Julie took a sip of the plain orange juice in her glass and, leaning back, crossed her legs. One tiny sandaled foot, the nails that afternoon painted a deep blood-red for the party, commenced to swing nervously back and forth, back and forth, to some inner rhythm of her own.

However serious his life elsewhere might have become, Jack had kept his old reputation locally for stirring things up. He wondered if the others were waiting for him to take some initiative now. After all, the party was for him.

But he was not the same person they remembered, not really. Whenever he came back home now it was as if the curtain had risen on a new act, with the same actors, but the playwright had without notice shifted the course of the action. It was impossible to point to a time when everything had been as it should be, but that time must have existed once. They all felt it. And lately, to Jack, every change—the divorce of one couple, the moving away of another—came as an unwelcome change.

As for himself, Jack knew that he seemed quieter than he used to seem. In fact, he was. He had no wish to pretend otherwise, but in a very small way, just as he could imagine his friends doing, he missed his old self. He sat now very quietly, stretched out on his floor cushion, leaning back against the wall, his long legs folded in a lazy tangle before him. He looked half asleep. But behind his glasses his eyes were still open. It might have seemed that he was listening to the music, except that it had stopped.

He had intended to listen. He had stacked the records himself, some of his favorites. Then, just as the unforgotten sounds had begun to bear him back towards his own adolescence, it had struck him suddenly why the girl sitting beside him, to whom he had been talking desultorily for the last twenty minutes or so, was wearing so loose and unbecoming a blouse—tardily, for she was, if not very far along, nevertheless visibly pregnant. To Jack, who had known her all his life, the realization came like a blow. When those very records were being cut, this girl, Susan, who was almost certainly the youngest person in the room, had been listening obediently to the nuns of her grammar school, wearing the blue-and-white uniform Jack still remembered. The summer before, when he had last seen her, Susan had not even been married. And already her husband, Robert or Bob, the sallow, sleepy-looking fellow in the corner who never had much to say, had got her pregnant.

For the time being Jack could concentrate on nothing but this, this fact that to him seemed so irremediably, if obscurely, wrong.

Hal was bending down, whispering into the blond woman's ear. Not that there was anything important to be said, but there was a pleasure in merely leaning towards her in that way, some momentary illusion of intimacy. What he had to say was only that soon they would be out of vodka.

And then he sighed. There was a sort of perfume coming, apparently, from a spot just behind her ear. Green was her married name, Karen Green, and Hal had known her longer than he had known his wife. As far back as high school he had had a hopeless crush on her, but never before had he noticed how peculiarly large and yet shapely her left ear was, from which the hair was drawn back, and how many little whorls it contained, impossible to count. Was she wearing her hair some new way?

Hal leaned closer and whispered, "Of course we could always go out to Fox's for more. More vodka."

It was half a question. It was the tone he always adopted with Karen, the tone of casual flirtation, just as though they were in school together still.

A rustling stirred in the palms outside, the first sign of something like a breeze. For a moment the wind rose, the rolled tarpaulins high up on the screen seemed to catch their breath.

All at once, borne to them on the faint edge of wind, they heard a dance band playing, not very far away, a rhumba band—snarling trumpet, bongo drums, maracas. Had it been playing all this time? Everyone listened. Jack straightened up and peered about the room, somewhat crossly, like a person roused from an interesting dream.

"The Legion dance," someone called out.

The large, good-looking man, who from his cushion beside Julie Lang's chair had also been watching Hal and the blond woman, climbed to his feet. This was Sid Green, Karen's husband. Standing, he loomed larger than anyone else in the group.

Normally unassertive, Sid heard his own voice calling across the porch, "Hey, Hal, you by any chance a member?" To himself his voice sounded unexpectedly loud, as if it contained some challenge he did not wish to issue more directly.

"For Christ's sake, Sid, the *Foreign* Legion maybe, not the American."

"If somebody was a member, we could go to the dance," Sid said. "I mean if anybody wanted to."

"Crash it?" the pregnant girl asked.

"Oh, maybe not," Sid said, looking around, and even his flash of enthusiasm was fading.

"I don't know," Hal said, with a glance at Sid's wife beside him.

"Oh, let's do go!" Julie cried out suddenly from across the porch. "For God's sake, let's do something! Just wait a minute till I change my shoes." And kicking her sandals off, fluffing her short crop of hair out as she went, she hurried back through the dark apartment towards the bedroom.

But when she returned it was apparent that something was wrong. Hal and Karen were missing, and Jack as well. Julie peered into the corner where the other women were sitting—Susan and a girl named Annabelle, who appeared to be sound asleep.

"Aren't you coming?" Julie asked nervously.

"Not me," Susan said, placing one hand on her stomach. "Not in my condition." Her silent husband beamed, as if Susan had said something witty or perhaps flattering to him.

Julie felt more uncomfortable than ever. She had never been a mother, and she was a good deal older than Susan, seven or eight years at least, but she did not think that Susan and her husband would intentionally try to embarrass her. Everyone knew that she had never wanted children, that she preferred her freedom.

Julie turned to Sid; their eyes met. He was quiet, too quiet to be amusing in the way that Hal and even Jack could sometimes be, but really quite good-looking in his athletic fashion, dark and mysterious, withheld. They knew very little about Sid. Was it true that his family had money? If only, Julie thought, he would volunteer himself more, like Hal. But at least Sid could be managed.

"Come on, you," she said, taking him by the hand and pulling. "Let's catch up with the others."

Meekly, Sid allowed himself to be led out the door.

On the dock it was very quiet. Only stray phrases of the Cuban trumpet carried out that far.

As they had walked out onto the dock, which was floated on an arrangement of great, slowly rusting oil drums, it had bobbed and swayed with every step. By now it had settled down. The three of them —Hal and Karen and Jack—sat dangling their legs over the end, looking out at the anchored boats which the water rocked as gently as cradles. Above the water, very bright, as if left over from some festivity, were strung the lights of the sailing club. All of the lights together cast a strange glow on the dark waters of the bay, a thin swath of artificial moonlight which reached out perhaps halfway towards the long, indistinct blur of the nearest island.

Jack wanted to touch the water, see how cold it was. Carefully he set the drink he had brought with him down upon the planking and removed his loafers.

Not that he meant to swim. But as he thrust one leg down, and his toes touched water, which was not as cold as expected, he found himself thinking of a woman they all knew, a woman named Roberta, who had once lived in the apartment above the Langs, and how she sometimes used to swim out to the island, which was no more than a dark, low line on the horizon. There was nothing to do out there; it was a mere piny arm of sand. She would wait just long enough to catch her breath and then swim back. That was all. It would not have been, if you were a swimmer, very dangerous. There were plenty of boats along the way to catch hold of if you tired.

Perhaps they were all thinking of Roberta just then, for when Hal asked, out of the blue, if they knew that Roberta was in San Francisco, Karen said, "Funny, I was just thinking of that time she drove her car into the bay."

"Well, not quite all the way in," Hal said. "It stalled, you know."

Hal was the authority on the stories they told about people they used to know. There was a good-sized collection of them, recounted so often the identities of the participants tended to blur, and the facts themselves were subject to endless small revisions and adjustments.

"I thought it was a palm tree that stopped her," Jack commented, rather sourly. He had never been one of Roberta's admirers. At the time, she had seemed a silly romantic girl, mad for attention. He tried to recall her face but could not. Had it been pretty? He seemed to remember it as pale, rather moon-shaped, but perhaps that was someone else's, someone more elusive still.

"You're right," Hal agreed. "There was a palm tree somewhere, but where?" He began to reconstruct. "The car must have caromed off the palm and gone on into the bay. Yes, part way in. I seem to picture it hanging over the edge sort of."

"I always thought she did it on purpose," Karen said.

"No, it was an accident." On that point Hal was definite.

Gradually a deeper melancholy settled over them. All around, the small dinghies tied up at the dock nosed familiarly against the wood. One was painted a vivid orange and white, the colors of the sailing club. A car passed behind them along the bayshore road, swiftly, heading for Miami proper.

Karen looked out across the bay. "Well, she should have done it on purpose. That would have made sense. It would have been—oh, I don't know . . ."

Off and on all evening Jack had been wondering what, if anything, was on between Hal and Karen. Karen was very beautiful, more beautiful than she had been ten years ago, just out of high school, when everyone, himself and Hal too, as he remembered, was buzzing around her. Experience had only ripened her; she made him think of some night-blooming flower the neighbors call you out to see. Probably just then—at that very minute, Jack would have liked to believe—she was at the absolute peak of her beauty. The next summer, surely by the summer after, she would have crossed the invisible line they were all approaching. On the other side of that line strangers would no longer find her quite so remarkable to look at, only old friends like Hal and himself, who would remember her face as it had been lit momentarily by the driftwood fire of some otherwise forgotten beach picnic, or more likely as it was now, shaped by the glow of the lights strung out from the dock over the water.

He recalled a story of Hal's, a story he did not much like to think of, of how Hal and a girl Jack didn't know had rowed out to the island one night and stayed till dawn. Thinking about the story now, with the island itself so near, Jack began to feel curiously giddy, as if the dock were starting to bob again.

"What about the island?" he asked.

"What about it?" Karen said.

"What about going out to the island?"

"I couldn't swim that far," she said. "Not nearly."

"Not swim. We borrow one of these dinghy things. Ask Hal. He's done it before."

Hal grinned. "Right. The night watchman, he sleeps back in that little shack. Besides, he doesn't really give a damn."

In a moment they were climbing down into the orange-and-white dinghy, a trickier operation than it looked. Whenever one of them put a foot down, exploring, the boat seemed to totter almost to the point of capsizing. Jack could not hold back a snort of laughter.

"Shh," Hal said.

"I thought he didn't give a damn," Karen said, tittering.

"Shh," Jack said. "Shh."

Once they were all seated, Hal took up the oars. They were just casting off, Jack had just managed to slip the rope free, when they heard footsteps coming up the walk. The rope dropped with a thick splash.

"Hey, we see you down there," a voice called, and Karen recognized it as her husband's. Just behind him stood Julie, their shadows bent out over the water.

"Shh," Karen hissed. Already the current was bearing them out, and there was a wide dark patch between boat and dock.

"Come on back."

"Can't. Current's got us."

But Hal was able to plant one oar firmly in the water and with that the boat began to turn in a slow circle.

"How was the dance?" Hal called politely.

For reply Julie stamped her foot on the dock. "Come on back," she called.

"Tell me, Julie, I sincerely want to know how it was."

"Oh, Hal, stop it."

"Actually they were very nice about it," Sid said, "but we felt kind of out of place."

"I feel kind of out of place right here," said Jack, dizzy with the motion of the boat.

"Oh, you're all drunk," Julie said. "Every one of you is hopelessly drunk and besotted."

It ended with Sid and Julie untying another dinghy and climbing into it. Quietly then the two boats glided out with the mild current through the lighted water.

Under the lights Jack felt like an escaping prisoner caught in the beam of a spotlight, and he closed his eyes, distinctly giddy now. When he looked again, they were already emerging from the shadows of the anchored boats into the clear space beyond, where it was dark. The other boat was no longer in sight. Hal feathered the oars, and they drifted with the flow, letting Sid and Julie catch up. It was very still. They could hear Sid grunting over the oars before they saw his dinghy coming up, gaining fast. In the dark his bent-over shape looked like part of the ghostly, gliding boat. Their eyes had become used to the dark by now, and they were near enough to make out ahead the narrow strip of sand edged with stunted pines that marked the shore of the island. A moment later the outline of a landing pier with several large nets spread out to dry on skeletal frames came into sight. Hal pointed the boat that way and resumed rowing.

The pier was rickety but apparently safe. When Hal leaped out, the others followed.

Karen lived with the vaguely troubling impression that someone, some man, had all her life been leaning towards her, about to touch her. It was like a dream. Instinctively she wished to draw back but could not. Moments ago, on the island, lying on the little beach, with Hal leaning towards her, whispering something about exploring the island a little farther down, around the point, she had consented without a thought, without strict attention to the words. Tomorrow, thinking back over it, excusing herself, she might suppose that she had thought Hal meant for the others to come too, but now, with that little moment still round and clear in her mind, she could admit that she had come away under no such illusion. She could not understand why she had come. Karen was not in any way angry with her husband, and she had never felt the least tremor of desire for Hal, who was simply an old friend.

Her earliest recollection of Hal was of a brash, rebellious boy in high school, a loud talker, but solitary, whom she had seen once standing alone after classes at the end of a long corridor puffing away at— strange!—a cigar, much too advanced for his years. Perhaps that was why she had been tempted to come with him now, that fragment of memory. Hal had looked up from the end of the corridor and seen her watching him puff away at the forbidden cigar, though neither had spoken at the time, nor, for that matter, had either brought the incident up since. Karen was not certain that Hal would remember it. Even if he did not, Karen believed that out of that moment, in some not-to-be-explained way, this moment had come, and that it was in some way inevitable that the two of them should be standing together now, around the point from the beach where the others were lying, though not yet so far off as to keep an occasional murmur of voices from drifting their way.

Hal was no longer leaning towards her. He had taken her hand to lead her across one stretch of slippery rocks, but he had not otherwise touched her. He was talking softly and at incredible length about a book he was reading, a novel about some boys marooned on an island. Of all things! Karen thought, slightly indignant. Of all things! She had failed at the outset to catch the novelist's name, and the conversation by now was too far advanced to ask. Hal seemed to have reached the point of criticizing the style of the writer. *Seemed*—she could not really say. Her attention was failing, fading. She was overcome by a feeling of surrender, a sense of division that was almost physical, in which she stood watching herself disappear over the water, which was dark, of a deep gemlike hue, and astonishingly calm.

In the distance she could hear Sid's laughter. She had the most vivid sensation of his anxiety and of Julie's as well. She wished she might do something to alleviate it, but it was as if Hal's voice going on and on endlessly about the novel she would never read were fixing her, or a part of her, to a certain point, pinning her there, draining her of all power, while the rest of her drifted out, out. . . . If only Sid would raise his voice and call her! She remembered the after-supper games of hide-and-seek as a child with her large family of sisters and a brother. One game in particular was among her most persistent memories, one that recurred even in her dreams. She was crouching behind a prickly bush—for years afterwards she could go to that same bush and point it out; she knew exactly where it stood on the lawn of her parents' house. She was the last one of all the sisters not yet found by her brother, who was "It," and she could hear her brother's footsteps coming through the dusk and then his soft voice calling, almost whispering, "Karen? Karen? Karen?" And she ran to him and threw her arms around him, whereupon her brother, who was quite a few years older and much larger than she—he was only playing the game as a favor to his sisters— lifted her from the ground and swung her around and around until they both fell to the grass, overcome with laughter and relief.

How tired she was! She wanted Hal to stop talking. She was ready. She wanted him to touch her; she wanted whatever was going to happen to begin. Love! And yet she could not bring herself to say to him that it would be all right, that whatever he did or did not do scarcely mattered any longer.

Jack woke from a sound sleep feeling cold. He was alone.

He sat up and listened, a little apprehensively, for some sound to indicate where the others might be. Except for the water that was licking up along the sand almost to his feet and out again, the silence was complete. Where had they gone? He took it for granted that they were off exploring the island, two by two probably, but by what pairs and for what purpose he hardly considered. His curiosity, brimming not long before, had gone flat.

Somewhere he had misplaced his glasses. Groping in the sand near where he had been sleeping, failing to find them, he blinked out across the water into the sky. The first faint streaks and patches of light were beginning to show. For a long time he sat, reluctant to get up and start looking for the others. He did not like the idea of stumbling across them in the dark, especially half-blind as he was. For the time being he did not care if he never saw any of them again. His stomach felt a little queasy, but he was not sure if it was from drinking. It might have been from emotion. In any case, he had been through worse.

Only after he had made his way back along the path to the landing pier and seen that the boats were missing did he realize what had happened. They had left him behind; they had abandoned him on the island.

At first he was simply angry. He peered as well as he could towards land. The sailing-club lights were still burning over the water. That he could see, but no farther. It was beginning to get light, and soon, he knew, the night watchman would wake up and turn the lights off. Already the lights were beginning to look superfluous. What a stupid joke this was, he thought. He imagined the story they would make out of it—the night they marooned Jack on the island! For a moment he considered the chance of swimming back, like Roberta. If he could make seventy or eighty yards on his own, there would be plenty of boats to hang on to. But the water looked cold, and his stomach was too unsettled.

Cold after the warmth of the night, he wrapped his arms around his shoulders. He felt as alone as he could ever remember having felt, and in an unfamiliar place, a place he could not even, without his glasses, see clearly, all fuzzy and vague—the last absurd touch. Any minute his teeth would start chattering. Standing there like that, realizing how foolish and pointless it was, for he must have been very nearly sober by then, he began to call their names out as loud as he could, one after the other—a kind of roll call—whether out of annoyance or affection he did not pause to consider. *Hal, Sid, Karen, Julie!* He had no idea how far his voice carried over the water, and in any case there was no answer.

At last he sat down on the little rickety pier and began to wait for someone to come and rescue him. And gradually, sitting there, beginning to shiver with the morning cool, Jack reflected, absurdly enough, that he was to be the hero of whatever story came to be told of the night. A curious form of flattery, but flattery of a sort. He had been singled out. At once he felt better about the evening. The party—it had not been a dead loss, after all. He almost found himself forgiving them for having abandoned him; eventually perhaps he would forgive them, forgive them everything, whatever they had done or not done. Without him, whatever had happened—and he did not want to know yet what that was, afraid that his new and still fragile sense of the uniqueness of the evening might evaporate once he knew—would not have happened. In some way, he was responsible. In any case, he would have forgiven them a great deal—laughter, humiliation, even perhaps betrayal—as they would forgive him practically anything. He saw all that now. Well, it was a sentimental time of night—the very end of it —and he had had a lot to drink, but he was willing to believe that the future would indeed be bleak and awful without such friends, willing to take their chance with you, ready even to abandon you on a chunk of sand at four a.m. for nothing but the sheer hell of it. And he was, for the moment, remarkably contented.

Brighton, 1980

The apartment building the Langs had lived in had been gone since the late sixties. There had been a boom. The fine old house—one of the oldest in the area, one to which Indians just before the turn of the century had come up across the bay in their canoes to trade—had lasted as long as any, but it had succumbed in the end to time and money. In any case, it would have been quickly dwarfed by the new high-rises looming around it. On its site stood one of the poshest of the latest generation of high-rises, expensive and grand, with glass and impractical little tilted balconies painted in three bold colors. Admittedly, it had been and was still a grand site, with a marvelous sweeping view of the bay, the little masted boats thick on the water, like blown leaves.

But it was the people who concerned Jack. And he knew none of the new people. In his own place, when he went there now, he felt uncomfortable and alien.

One day—twenty years and more had passed—sitting in a flat in Brighton, England, looking idly out over the gray, disturbed sea in a direction he thought must be towards home, Jack began making a sort of mental catalogue of all his friends from that period. He had not thought it out in advance. The idea just came to him, and he began. He was trying to remember everyone who was together at a certain time in the old life, at a precise moment even, and the night of his going-away party came back to him.

The list began with Susan's son, the one she had been pregnant with at the time, and Jack was pleased with himself for having thought to include her child-to-be in his recollection. She never had another. The son, he had heard, was a fine, intelligent boy, off at college somewhere, no trouble to anybody. Jack had not seen him since the boy started grammar school. The boy's name slipped his memory, but he did remember, if not very clearly, curls and a sort of general shying away from the presence of grown-ups.

The sallow husband—Robert or Bob—had been some trouble or had some trouble. Drinking? Whatever in the past had caused his silence, he was to sink deeper and deeper into it over the years. Eventually he had found his way back north to Philadelphia, into his father's business, a chain of liquor stores. Just the thing, Jack thought ruefully, just the thing.

Susan herself was another story, though not much of one. She owned a small stucco house in the Grove, almost hidden by shrubs and palms and jacarandas. Her time seemed to go into nothing at all, unless it was a little gardening, but it surely went. She had no time for anything, certainly not for friends, and never or very rarely ventured out. She kept a few cats, quite a few. Their number grew.

The great surprise was Sid, the only one to have become famous. Not exactly famous, Jack acknowledged, but well-known. No one had sensed the power and ambition hidden so quietly in Sid back then, certainly not Karen. From small starts, from short sailing trips down into the Keys, later out to the Bahamas, Sid had taken the great dare of a long solo sail across the Atlantic, kept a journal, and published an account of the voyage. Modestly popular. Later, other adventures, other books. He was married now to a minor movie actress, past her prime but still quite beautiful—a brunette, not at all like Karen in appearance—and they lived most of the year, predictably somehow, in southern France. (It was true—his family had had some money.) Jack had recently had occasion to call on them on the continent and found that he enjoyed his visit immensely. Sid had become voluble, a great smiler—of all of them, the most thoroughly and happily changed.

Karen, on the other hand, had been through three more husbands. Two daughters, one of them married, with a daughter of her own. It seemed incredible to Jack that Karen, of all people, should have become a grandmother. It was like a magic trick, seen but not believed. Sometimes, of an evening, as they sat talking over a drink beside the current husband's pool, the bug light sending out its intermittent little zap, he had caught a sidelong glimpse of the former Karen, a Karen absolute and undiminished, still slender, seemingly remote, cool if not cold, not to be found out. Some secret she had, and it had kept her beautiful. Her present husband was often ill, and there was a bad look around her own eyes. She looked away from you much of the time. She had never done anything of any importance in her life, and everybody had always loved her for herself alone. What happiness!

Julie, as she had wished, never had had any children. Over the years she had gone a little to corpulence, but her foot, surprisingly tiny still, still swung back and forth to some nervous rhythm of her own. She, who had always abhorred and fled from the cold, ran a bookstore now in Boston. She had become an expert on books. The way Jack had of explaining this to himself—he had browsed in her shop once or twice when in the city—was simply that she had liked to read, always. Those nights Hal had been out catting around she had read. She had read and read and she had always loved books and, in the end, it had come to this. She seemed satisfied.

Nor was Hal—the great romantic, Hal—a totally lost cause, even though he had, in his maturity, held down a steady job, the same job now, for ten or eleven years, easily a record for him. He managed a gallery. He was perfect for it, a gallery in the Grove popular with everyone, wealthy tourists especially. It also provided him the contacts with women he seemed to need—wives, daughters, perhaps even a youthful grandmother or two. Women, young and old, some beautiful, some rich, pursuing Hal, who was not getting any younger. He let his colorful shirts hang out usually, over a slight belly, wore dark glasses much of the time, rode out his hangovers with good grace and considerable experience. He still painted, excellent miniatures, obsessively detailed, with the clear jeweled colors of Byzantine work. He sold everything he made and never set too high a price, though it was certain he could demand more if he chose. But no, he was as happy as he deserved, perhaps happier. Not married—it was easier that way. Some nights he liked being alone.

Several of his friends, Jack realized, were actually happy. The shape of their futures must always have been there, somehow, just as eye color is built into the chromosomes before birth. Impossible to read, all the same, except backwards, as with some obscure Eastern language. Or perhaps the night of the party had been a sort of key, and it had been clear, or should have been clear then, that the Langs would never last, not as a couple, and if the Langs went, then the Greens constituted a doubtful case; and something in the way her husband had cast his silent, wary, unfathomable glances at the pregnant Susan might have hinted at some future division between them as well. Now no one was married to the right person. No one, as Jack would have it, would ever be married to the right person again. The time when everything was as it should be was always really some other time, but back then, that summer, it had seemed near.

From the window of the flat he could see only a little corner of the sea, and he wanted, for some reason, to be closer to the water. Dressing warmly, Jack walked down to the parade, braced himself against the baby gale and walked and walked, for forty minutes or so. He found himself down on the shingle, almost alone there. It was too nasty a day for there to be much company. A big boat hung on the horizon. Jack thought back to the beach of the little sandy bay island and he guessed that what had happened that night must be why he had ventured down to the sand now, to which he almost never descended. Here in this foreign place he felt again that he was on a little island, isolated, the last civilized speck, himself against a faceless and unpredictable world —unknowable, really. Jack felt like calling out the names again, the names of his friends, but of course he did not. He could not even remember how he had been rescued that other time, who it was that had come out in a dinghy for him, risking the wrath of the sleepy night watchman. Probably Sid. Julie had cooked a nice breakfast—he remembered that. No one would be coming to rescue him now, not that he needed rescuing or wanted rescuing, even in the sort of half-dreaming state he had fallen into. But the thought did occur to him, in passing.

THE EVOLUTION OF BIRDS
OF PARADISE

ELIZABETH TALLENT

Elizabeth Tallent's work has appeared in *The New Yorker*. Her short stories have been included in the *Best American Short Stories of 1981* and *Pushcart Prize VI*. Her small critical study, *Married Men and Magic Tricks*, appeared from Creative Arts Book Company, and Alfred A. Knopf published her first collection of stories, *In Constant Flight*. She received a National Endowment for the Arts fellowship in fiction for 1983 and now lives in Santa Fe, New Mexico.

The *Ptiloris victoriae* has been stealing kitchen matches. The vanilla-white wood of perhaps a hundred matchsticks is visible within the dark weave of her nest, a knobbed oval wedged between two tilted volumes of Simon's 1954 edition of the Universal Standard Encyclopedia. Simon thinks she has chosen handsomely: the encyclopedia spines, although lean and somewhat frayed, are still upright on the desk. One page—in Volume 15, Idah-Jewe—is marked with a flattened orchid whose mummified pistil furls upward like a lizard's tongue, scholarly and dry. Simon tries to remember what continent he retrieved this flower from; he closes his eyes and sees only an island of reeds and the kinked tip of a crocodile's tail vanishing among them.

The desk itself is teak, and the nest spills forward across it in a prow of splayed twigs. Simon studies the massed papers. Lately, he has tried to shuffle them into a parallel-edged heap, but they falter into disorder, acquire the linked sienna rings of coffee-cup stains, crinkle at the edges. Above him, there is the thudding of bare feet. Ashley, his daughter-in-law, always runs down the stairs, although he has lectured frostily on the danger—the narrow treads, the steep, old-fashioned angle of ascent. Once, she did fall, and hit her forehead against the bannister, her hair fanning against the threadbare carpet. Somehow Simon felt it was

Copyright © 1983 by Elizabeth Tallent. First appeared in *The New Yorker*. Reprinted by permission.

his fault: without him, she was blithe, infallible. She had stayed obediently, still, eyes closed, while he washed the blood away with a wetted handkerchief.

"Your handkerchief, Simon," she protested, when she opened her eyes. "You're ruining it."

"It doesn't matter," he said.

"It does matter," she said. "It's an antique."

Startled, he looked down to see that the yellowing linen still bore the tracery of his name, which Anna had long ago cross-stitched in neat Xs of shining thread. Anna had packed and left him thirty-four years ago, while he was in the field. He had returned to find a house magically bare of all signs of life. In her precise fashion, she had even removed their wedding picture from the wall, and plastered over the hole. He had picked at the patch of fresh plaster with his thumbnail and, when it refused to flake away, driven the blade of a kitchen knife into it. He had needed to reassure himself that the hole existed, that it had held a nail supporting a photograph—Anna, smiling sideways at him, her dark eyes expectant. It was true; she *had* expected something of him, and he had failed her.

"I've looked in the Salvation Army," Ashley said. "You just can't find these anymore." She was examining the crescents of the embroidered capitals.

"Keep it, if you like," he said. She looked at him guiltily; she had already thrust one corner into the pocket of her Levi's.

It is only through a foible of the National Science Foundation that Ashley lives in his house at all: the money came through for his son's research, and not for hers. Their subsequent strategy—nearly a year spent apart, with Michael exchanging the classrooms of the University of Colorado for an Army surplus tent pitched not far from Machu Picchu, while Ashley continued to teach—seems to Simon fraught with risk. For Michael, the tombs and terraces of Incan cities are an overwhelming passion, but Simon has observed evidence of uncertainty in Ashley. She bites her fingernails; her lecture notes for "An Introduction to Early Man in North America" are scribbled at the last moment, on the backs of grocery lists or torn telephone bills; she has put two small dents in the fenders of Michael's Fiat. "Why don't you go live with my father?" Michael had said. "We could use the money you'd save, and he has this huge old house where he rattles around all alone, and it makes him a little crazy. He could keep an eye on you, and you'd be terrific for him. You could keep him in touch with reality." "What

makes you think I have any patent on reality?" Ashley said, but nonetheless she had come, settling her books into the shelves in Michael's
old upstairs bedroom, wiping the dust from the narrow brass headboard
of the bed.

Now Simon lifts a Peruvian flute from among the manuscripts. He
blows experimentally. A feather of dust lifts from the other end, star-
tling the *Ptiloris victoriae*, Queen Victoria Riflebird, which has at that
moment alighted on the crown of his bald head. Her feet are skittish
and cool; he feels the claws as a scattering of hesitant pricks against his
scalp. His fingers awkwardly stopper the holes of the flute. His knuckles
seem far too large for such precise maneuvering. When he was twenty-
two he once fished a fragment of bark from a cannibal's eye: the flat
black disc of the pupil had held the reflection of Simon's hand, perfectly miniaturized, and the inside of the lid was the vulnerable, breathing coral of a trout's gill. In gratitude the cannibal had kissed Simon's
knuckles. When he was thirty-four Simon could hold a curved, blue-
gray fragment of eggshell, flecked with dirty-cinnamon spots, in a shaft
of light filtering through the rain-forest canopy and name the female
bird of paradise that had, until recently, harbored it. At forty Simon
could hear bones forming in the egg of a wren. At eighty-two, when the
Queen Victoria's weight is gone from his head, he feels as if a crown
had been removed. Ashley doesn't see the birds, but this has ceased to
bother Simon, as long as she does not blunder into a courtship display,
or drop one of her muddy running shoes into the gnarled fretwork of
twigs and reeds belonging to a nesting female.

The Queen Victoria jumps to his desk, carrying a twig, this one long
and forked and bearing one coppery leaf. It must be from the aspen
tree to the left of the back door. The aspen lost all of its leaves early
this winter, and is certainly failing. Three times, Simon has considered
cutting the tree down, and each time decided against it, in part because
the straight lower branch still holds the two uneven lengths of rope,
fraying and always damp, that once held the yellow board on which
Michael had spent whole afternoons swinging, his legs lifting and falling loosely. Whenever Simon rests the blade of the axe against the
silver bark, he seems to hear the double creak of the vanished swing—
two notes, one for ascent, one for the downward arc.

The placement of the twig puzzles the Queen Victoria. Simon sees
that the nest is nearly finished; the innermost hollow precisely accords
with the span of her breast. She will be guarded by this structure the
way, in fairy tales, princesses are guarded by walls of thorns. She tucks

the twig into a gap between strands of gray lichen and, dissatisfied, thrusts it in farther. Two eggs, Simon thinks, of a color paler than the interior of a conch shell, and far more frail. He knocks on wood. The Queen Victoria disappears into the steeple-shaped shadow between the two encyclopedias.

"I have a bone to pick with you, Simon," Ashley says from the doorway of his study. She has on a pair of Levi's that Michael long ago abandoned, held at the waist by a beaded belt that says "New Mexico." The belt is buckled at the very last notch. She is wearing a black sweatshirt with the sleeves pushed up above her elbows, and a John Deere cap pulled down to shadow her eyes. The leaping deer on the front of the cap mimics the arch of one eyebrow. Even her name, he sometimes thinks, is simply one more aspect of the androgyny in which young women camouflage themselves nowadays. He has never actually questioned her about her name, preserving, for once, the crafty, patriarchal silence he equates with dignity in a father-in-law.

"Oh?" he says. "What bone would that be?"

"You amaze me, you know," she says. "Two wars, treks into New Guinea when it was still riddled with headhunters, a couple of tropical diseases, and you still think that knocking on wood will ward off dangers."

"Three wars," he says. "I was an adviser in the Korean War."

"An adviser?"

"Someone had the bright idea of reintroducing carrier pigeons."

"Oh."

"Not a handsome bird, exactly." After his years spent in the pursuit of birds of paradise, the pigeons had seemed muddling, quiescent, ashcolored. "But they have made a sort of virtue of self-possession. They can find their way through clouds of smoke, and they're not easily rattled."

"I didn't know you'd been involved in something like that."

"It was years ago," he says. "So you think that an old man ought to relinquish superstition? Ought to be dispassionate?"

"I can't imagine you dispassionate."

"You can't? A growing introspection, a calm renunciation of my failing powers?" He holds his hands, palm upward, for her inspection, and is briefly amused to find the fingers trembling. He has always gotten carried away in proving his own points. "Nothing up my sleeve, Madam." Beneath the bill of the skewed man's cap, her eyes go a shade darker. He likes her eyebrows: feather-shaped, the outer tips seeming faintly smudged.

"I have yet to see you renounce anything," she says. "You, introspective? It's an oxymoron. You've had a finger in every pie for decades—at least every pie that had anything to do with birds."

"Four and twenty blackbirds," Simon says.

"Don't go whimsical on me," she says. "Just last week you nearly sent poor Dr. Cooper into cardiac arrest over the taxonomy of birds of paradise. It's not enough that the two of you have been quarrelling since 1924. You have to go and torment him while he's flat on his back in an oxygen tent."

"I went to see him as a gesture of professional courtesy," he says. "I wouldn't have attempted it five years ago, because there were other people around then who were simply better at that sort of thing than I, people who can sit in those gummy metal hospital chairs and contentedly play gin rummy, or discourse on falling snow—"

"You wouldn't touch a deck of cards to save your life, and if you did play gin rummy, it would be so that you could beat him at it," she says. "You must have provoked him, Simon."

"I merely observed that the ancestral stock of the birds of paradise was undoubtedly starlinglike," Simon says. "What happened after that wasn't my fault."

Cooper had sat up against his crisp pillows, enraged. "How can you stand there and spout that crap to me as if it's gospel?" he had shouted. "Next you'll be questioning the existence of the arboreal monogamous ancestors!"

"I *am* leaning toward polygyny," Simon had confessed. "It will mean redrawing the family tree, but I do find myself disenchanted with the idea of those monogamous pairs of ancestors blown down the East Indian archipelago by various punctual hurricanes."

"They had to get to New Guinea somehow," Cooper roared. "It's an island, for the love of God!"

"Starlings are such interesting birds, though, aren't they? Brainy and, in an evolutionary sense, so willing to try anything once."

"You're too late. You can't rewrite the whole of 'The Evolution of Birds of Paradise.' You're too old."

Simon obligingly spread his knuckly hands. The veins on the backs were the color of slate, and there were various spots and flecks. He is growing dappled. "I am old," he said. Cooper shook his head irritably, as if that were an obvious lie. "I eat Cheerios while I watch the ten-o'clock news, and I get to watch the sun come up. I am of course prepared to take on a substantial amount of observation in the field."

"In the field?" Cooper said.

"In the field."

"But the field is New Guinea," Cooper said.

Simon cleared his throat softly.

"That's utterly impossible," Cooper said. "A man of your age, the frailty of your hands. Isn't there something wrong with your heart as well?"

"No," Simon said. "Not a damn thing wrong with my heart." But Cooper had already subsided into a long, unwavering, absent-minded stare. Simon remembered the cannibal's eye, clearing suddenly, enormous and patient. Cooper, although still looking directly at him, had forgotten he was there.

"It was your fault, and you know it," Ashley says.

"Maybe," he amends, because she is still studying him beneath the tilted visor of her cap. "I was also, in part, motivated by curiosity. I wanted to see how he was doing it."

"Doing what?"

"Dying," he says. If he thinks this will daunt her, he is clearly mistaken.

"So why did you take him milkweed pods? When I telephoned to find out why you weren't home, the nurse said you were carrying a whole armful of rattling weeds that you dropped on the bedside table. You didn't even wait for her to bring a jar."

"I know it seems strange," he says, "but I've always found them so beautiful, like small gray canoes filled with bleached silk." Thoughtfully, he moves a chipped glass paperweight across the dusty teak. Within the encyclopedia-framed gap, a black eye gleams. "Cooper spent more than thirty years in the field. In one of our rare amicable moments, we were comparing horror stories, and he bested me—told me how he had once lived for a week on water stored in an enormous hollowed-out ostrich egg that had been given to him by a friendly aborigine. He said the water at first was bitter, then it started to have a medicinal taste, and the last few swallows went down like wine. Now, what would a man like that want with narcissi?"

"I don't know," she says.

"I can tell you," he says. "Nothing. Nothing at all."

An hour later, Simon is standing on a kitchen chair changing a light bulb, as Ashley answers the telephone in the hallway. Her demurral seems courteous and contrived, perhaps for his benefit, and when she finally acquiesces the person at the other end of the line cannot have been astonished. "Somebody must have broken a leg," she calls to Simon after she hangs up. "Because I just got invited to the Petersons' for the evening."

"It wouldn't require a broken leg, surely?"

"They're snobs," she says. "They like to focus on defectors from Soviet-block countries, escapees from the Moonies, ex-convicts. Not Wasp associate professors of anthropology. I'll have to go and change." She runs—still barefoot, skipping every two steps—up the flight of wooden stairs to her room. When she comes back down, he sees that she has changed into a black dress with a shallow neckline. One strap is twisted clumsily, like that of a child's bathing suit. Yearning rises from the pit of Simon's stomach; the back of his throat tastes coarsely of rust. She is wearing a string of amber, one of his many tentative gifts of rapprochement to Anna, which Anna wore once and then abandoned, because, she told him, it made her neck look "blunt." He had thought it made her look queenly. Ashley appropriated it—another of the child-like confiscations with which she unsettles his house. She sits, careless of the dress, in a straight-backed oak chair at the kitchen table. Abruptly the male *Paradisaea minor*, Lesser Bird of Paradise, lights on her bare shoulder. Simon halts for a moment to stare down. The Lesser Bird of Paradise cocks its head to gaze back at him. The iris of its eye is a clear lime yellow. "The chair is wobbling, Simon," Ashley says.

"It's all right."

"It's too old to stand on like that—"

"I'm sure it's quite reliable."

"Would you like me to hold it for you?"

"No, please don't get up."

"I can't live here forever without lifting a finger."

"You can hardly believe you've lived here forever," he says. Her hyperbole sometimes stings his sense of exactitude. Simon believes that politeness is simply one variation of accuracy.

"No," she says. "I mean that you shouldn't have to do all the work for both of us."

"I do precious little more than I would for myself alone," he says. He tinkers with the light bulb. He is reluctant to twist it the rest of the way in, fearing that when he does she will get up, disturbing the Lesser

Bird of Paradise. He has not had nearly enough time to observe it. He is pleased to see that the curved barbs of the long white tail feathers are utterly free of lice. Snowy, neat, and separate, they fall between Ashley's shoulder blades, brushing the back of her chair. Before she came, he had sighted only blackbirds, sparrows, and an occasional nightjar or marsh hen—nothing that excited his professional interest. After Michael had gone, and she had been in the house only two weeks, Simon found ferns unfurling like sea horses from the cracks between the floorboards, and brilliant feathers strayed into his pockets. He had retrieved his old pair of binoculars from the back of a closet shelf, dusted them off, and taken to wearing them around his chest, where their cool remembered weight balanced like a second, steadier heart.

The Lesser Bird of Paradise's tail feathers flick in agitation. It shifts to keep its balance while Ashley lights a cigarette. Its wings slant forward, the feathers extending in a dovetailed curve. It holds this pose, stiff with ardor or apprehension, within a haze of slowly rising cigarette smoke. "Simon, aren't you done yet?"

"Done." He dusts his palms against his trousers. "Stay like that, would you?"

"Why should I?"

"I was thinking what Michael would give to see you like this."

"Oh? What would Michael give?"

"His right arm," Simon says. "Willingly."

"I'm not as sure as you are," she says. "He hasn't written for nearly two months. The last letter he wrote was from Cuzco. He was sitting at a café table, reading 'A Farewell to Arms' and drinking espresso. He said that 'A Farewell to Arms' wasn't as good as he remembered."

Simon gives the bulb in its socket a final, extraneous twist, proving—he hopes—his extreme care. He intends it as a sort of reproof. Ashley inhales cigarette smoke; the lesson is lost on her. He climbs down from the chair and drops the old bulb into the paper bag below the sink.

"I suppose you think it's silly of me to want to go somewhere in all this snow," she says.

"Not necessarily," he says carefully. "A great deal of valuable information was exchanged at faculty parties even in my era."

It is one of their problems: they often begin to apologize at the same moment, and abandon the attempt out of a sort of mutual embarrassment. She twists the cigarette out in a small, violent spiral in the bottom of the ashtray and sees him watching. "Maybe I ought to give up smoking for one of my New Year's resolutions," she says.

"Excellent idea."

"There's a big difference, you know, Simon. You were famous in your era. Of course people courted you and told you things. You and McPherson discovered the birds of paradise—"

"That's inaccurate, as you very well know."

"It must have been *extraordinary*—to observe their courtship in the rain forest when you knew no one had ever seen anything like that before. Michael thinks you've never quite gotten over it."

"Michael believes in getting over things."

"And you don't?"

"Sometimes not. There are certain things I wouldn't want to get over."

For a moment, he observes her: the thin shoulder, the shading of the eyelids, the glimpse of vein in her wrist. The Lesser Bird of Paradise seems frozen on her shoulder; only its golden eye blinks. Ashley lights a second cigarette, after tapping it against the kitchen table. She does not seem surprised to have caught him staring; she simply stares back. Then she rises to turn on the light, and the Lesser Bird of Paradise— startled, the wings doubling back toward the body, its nape suddenly dimming into shadow—takes flight, and swerves around a corner of the refrigerator and down the hallway. She sits back down and awkwardly crosses her legs. Simon has never seen her in high heels before. He is almost certain that they are not the sort of thing a young woman ought to wear into the snow. He strains to remember Anna's shoes; his only memory is of something sullen, with a pinched tongue and bone buttons. He dismisses it hurriedly. He thinks of Ashley as a glorified tomboy, her beauty all unwitting. It pains him that she would suddenly display the fine curve of her instep in such a precarious black shoe. He leans against the counter and looks away from her, out the window. In the light from the kitchen, the falling snow is dense and uneven. It seems to pause in its downward slant several inches above the ground, as if balked by the warmth the earth still casts upward.

"The snow's not even sticking," she says.

"It's beginning to stick." He feels suddenly irritable.

"The driving should be all right for a while longer. It's really not all that far from here."

"I haven't seen the lights of a single solitary snowplow," he says. "This is the very worse sort of weather to do any driving in. They don't consider a storm like this serious enough to get off their bums and start plowing. You'll hear them out about midnight, not before."

"Fine," she says. "A little after midnight, after everyone's kissed everyone, I can come home. It's New Year's Eve, Simon."

"I don't need to be told what night it is." He unscrews the lid of a jar of Skippy. It is creamy peanut butter instead of chunky, and Ashley likes chunky, but it is not his fault. He did the best he could.

In the 7-Eleven—the one store he found open when he went out earlier that evening—an old woman had been sweeping things into a ragged net shopping bag hanging by a string from the crook of her elbow: chocolate milk in pint-size wax cartons; a dented box of Count Chocula breakfast cereal; chocolate-covered graham crackers, Oreos, and Pepperidge Farm Milanos; Hershey's chocolate bars; chocolate Santa Clauses in parchment-thin red-and-silver foil, left over from Christmas; one yellow and one brown bag of M&M's. Scanning the shelves, she chose a can of cat food and dropped it into her bag with the other things. Simon was watching. The old woman lifted her bag and rattled it provocatively at him, as a triumphant hunter might display a rabbit by its heels. "You're lucky you're not old," she said.

It confused him. "I'm as old as you," he said.

"You are?" She frowned. "I must say you hide it pretty well. I myself don't stand a chance. The cat wears me down. Morning, noon, and night, nag, nag, nag."

"I am old," he had said, for the second time that week, and, in the cramped aisle below the glimmering fluorescent lights, it had suddenly come true.

In the street outside the 7-Eleven, cars slid by, fans of brown slush rising behind each wheel. Crossing the street warily, Simon observed how small and crooked his house looked, its steep Victorian roof the only old-fashioned angle in a block of condominiums whose right angles and massive slabs of pebbled cement offer insufficient habitat for even a sparrow. As Simon watched, a Count Raggi's Bird of Paradise flew slowly across one of the upstairs windows of his house. Simon balanced the paper bag in the crook of his elbow and withdrew a small notebook from his jacket pocket. It was already getting colder, and his fingers ached around the bitten pencil stub. *"Paradisaea raggiana,"* he wrote crookedly. " ♂. Spectacular!" He crossed the last word out as unprofessional. He must learn to be harsher with his own lapses. The *Paradisaea raggiana* was yellow-crowned, black-breasted, with an astonishing tail of pale-apricot plumes; he could not refrain from doing a small dance step on the icy curb. Two boys were watching him from the far corner. One of them bent and scooped a stone from the gutter. He was wearing a Darth Vader face mask. Simon thought suddenly of the Papuan New Guineans who had tattooed crescents of blue ink above the bridges of their wide noses and their flat, feminine cheekbones. The young tribesmen had had something of Darth Vader's faceted, unblinking menace. The stone caught Simon squarely between the shoulder blades. He put the pencil away and tucked the notebook securely into his pocket. He felt absurdly lucky to have made a sighting from outside the house—*P. raggiana!*—and at such an unlikely hour. "Crazy man, crazy man, lives his life in an old tin can!" One of the voices was muted by the face mask. A lucky throw, Simon thought. He loped stiffly homeward, the brown paper bag under his arm.

He takes saucers from the cupboard; he puts one peanut-butter sandwich in the unchipped saucer and deposits it gallantly in front of Ashley. "Look, Simon," she says, "we need to air our differences." He nods. He likes anything to do with air, or light. His only objection to New Guinea had been that the light in the rain forest seemed sifted, rare, and inaccessible. If he and Anna had aired their differences, perhaps she would not now be in a condominium (in her letters to Michael she calls it, affectionately, "the condo") in Miami Beach, on a narrow balcony far too high above the sea. He and Ashley have solved other problems. What had particularly dismayed her, in the beginning, was his habit of using up several jars of Vicks VapoRub in a week. She burned small wands of sandalwood incense to rid the living room of the damp, tropical taint that Simon secretly loved. He had agreed, with some reluctance, to use Vicks VapoRub in the bathroom, in modest amounts, and only on those afternoons when she is teaching.

There are still problems, although Simon considers them minor: Ashley gets telephone calls, mysterious and prolonged, quite late at night. Simon wakes in his narrow bed to the single *ching* of the receiver as she lifts it, catching it before the first complete ring. She must whisper, the telephone cradled to her jaw, facing the corner where he leaves his overshoes—an old man's pairing, toe to toe, as if a ghost stood anxiously inside the foyer. Who telephones her? He can't make out a word. McPherson used to stand amazed when Simon would pinpoint the location of a single Magnificent Bird of Paradise on a distant ridge. *"Ca cru cru cru,"* Simon would mimic, for McPherson's benefit. "He's a musical little bastard. *Diphyllodes magnificus*, in extremely good form, north by northeast, at an elevation of perhaps two hundred and fifty feet above the forest floor." "Damn," McPherson would say. "Can you really hear the bloody thing from this far away?" Who telephones her, and why does she talk so long? This ache within his rib cage, he reasons, must be a sort of paternal jealousy. It does not ease until, sometimes an hour later, she replaces the telephone receiver and—this time with cunning quiet—climbs the creaking stairs to her room.

"Simon," she says. "I've been under certain pressures—*professional* pressures, I won't bore you with them—lately, and they sometimes make me feel slightly claustrophobic. I know you've seen signs of it. I've been losing my temper entirely too often."

"I always take it with a grain of salt."

"A grain of salt the size of Antarctica," she says. She studies the smoke, which sifts toward the ceiling. "You've been very patient with me, and I've liked living here, but I dislike the feeling that you are watching over me. It's not something you're obligated to do, and it must be exhausting for you, and I sometimes find it distracting."

"Distracting?"

"Distracting."

It is, he thinks, a gentle word, more introspective than "annoying," less specific than "bothersome." He has seen her do worse, with less provocation. He looks at her with renewed admiration as she stands, brushing the front of the black dress. His sandwich, untouched, rests in the chipped dimestore saucer painted with thistles. She has left only her crusts. "I ought to get going," she says. "The Fiat will probably stall on me, and I don't want to be too late. Can I ask you something?"

"Ask," he says.

"I especially don't want you to stay awake all night long because of me."

"Why?" he says. "Do you think I've nothing better to do?"

In the hallway she lifts her coat in a clatter of empty hangers, ignoring his question. He has intended for years to clean out the closet; lying on the floor is an ancient umbrella of Anna's, dusty and tightly furled, which Anna somehow overlooked. Ashley shrugs on the long blond coat and turns the collar up against her chin. Nervously, with a stilted grace he attributes to her high heels, she crosses the kitchen and hugs him. "Simon, you're thinner," she says, her cheek against the front of his shirt. "You're getting to be only skin and bones."

NOT A GOOD GIRL

PERRI KLASS

Perri Klass was born in Trinidad and grew up in New York City and
Leonia, New Jersey. She attended Radcliffe College, majored in biology, moved to San Francisco and did graduate work in zoology at the
University of California, Berkeley. She spent a year in Rome, doing
research on mosquitoes and malaria and writing a novel, and then
returned to Cambridge. She is presently in her second year at Harvard Medical School, and teaches expository writing at Harvard. Her
stories have appeared in *Mademoiselle*, the *Antioch Review*, and the
Berkeley Fiction Review. This is the second year a story from Perri
Klass has been chosen for *Prize Stories: The O. Henry Awards*.

Men nowadays can be very strange, if you ask me. I went to bed with
one I had just met when I was up in Boston for two days. This is not
something I do ferociously often, jump into bed with men I've just
met. In fact, for the last six months or so, I haven't jumped into bed
with anyone. Not that I've been celibate on principle, or anything like
that. It's just that I've been pretty busy lately.

This man I went to bed with in Boston was a graduate student in
biochemistry at Harvard who had come to my seminar, the first of the
two I was going to give. (You would never say, would you, "the man
with whom I went to bed"? I suppose the whole phrase has its roots in
such a cute, euphemistic view of things that it has to be kept schoolgirl-
ish and ungrammatical.) Anyway, he was a graduate student in my
field, which is immunology. That, of course, lends itself easily to crude
sexual analogies, since it is concerned with the body's defenses against
foreign intruders, but never mind all that now. I didn't take any particular notice of him at my seminar, except when he asked a reasonably
intelligent question. Then he turned up again that evening, when the
people who were "hosting" me took me to an Italian restaurant; there
was a big group of junior-faculty types and graduate students, including

Copyright © 1983 by The Condé Nast Publications Inc. First appeared in *Mademoiselle*. Reprinted by permission.

this one, Eric. After dinner, which was extremely so-so and which seemed to leave everyone feeling a little discouraged, my hosts wanted to take me out drinking, but I said I thought I would just go back to the hotel, and Eric said he had a car and would drop me off. In his car I was conscious of our different clothes, me in my give-a-seminar outfit, blazer and wool skirt and stockings, Eric in very worn corduroy pants and a workshirt frayed at the cuffs. We stopped for a traffic light, he put his hand, ragged cuff and all, on my stockinged knee, and asked perfectly straightforwardly if I wanted "company for the night." As simple as that. I considered for a minute, maybe less, aware that I wanted his hand to travel further up my leg, and said okay, appropriately nonchalant.

I could not possibly have been more than four or five years older than he, though, of course, there was that infinite spiritual distance between still-in-school and out-of-school-and-working. Still, I was inclined to put his lack of romantic finesse down to his callow youth. I don't mean the come-on in the car; that seemed to me very acceptable and even sweet and disarming. And of course I wasn't expecting genuine romantic feeling and wouldn't have welcomed it if it had materialized, but once we were in the hotel room, I was less than thrilled when he kissed me and said, "Well, why don't you take your clothes off?", then started to pull off his own. It would frankly have done more for me if he'd unbuttoned even one or two of the buttons on my shirt. He did switch off the light, which might have indicated a romantic awareness of the full moon coming through the window, but more likely just meant he wanted the conventional darkened room. Anyway, we had sex on the professionally large and accommodating hotel double bed, in the romantic silver splash of the full moon.

It just knocked me out how good he was, which shows that she who doesn't expect much is sometimes richly rewarded. But then, afterward, when we were exchanging bits of information to give our mutual nakedness some small base of intimacy (how we had no boyfriends, girlfriends, husbands, wives, how much he respected my work, that kind of thing), he said to me, "Women nowadays can be very strange, if you ask me." And he went on to tell me that women nowadays expect men to be gentle and tender but still to go on filling all the traditional male roles, by which he meant, for example, expecting the man to get out of bed and investigate noises in the night. I was protesting halfheartedly that I personally could imagine nothing worse than being left alone in bed to listen to night noises, when it occurred to me that this "complaint" was Eric's way of letting me know how sensitive he was, that he took seriously what he thought were feminist expectations of men, at least seriously enough to complain about them. A scientist who truly cared about his human relationships. I felt, with some irritation, that we had omitted all the traditional first-night trappings; there had been no false tenderness, no ersatz romance, and neither had there been any hard-bitten bedpost notching. Eric and I seemed to have skipped emotionally to some point later on in a relationship (and not a very appealing relationship), when sweeping generalizations about "men" and "women" were just another way of attacking each other.

But I didn't want to worry about any of this. Isn't the point of a one-night stand that you get off on the novelty and the adventure without having to worry about the other person?

In any case, it didn't turn out to be exactly a one-night stand. It turned out to be a two-night stand, though something should be said about the day between the two nights. I was supposed to go visit some labs, but it was a beautiful morning, and as Eric was driving me past the Boston Common, he suggested that we stop and enjoy the sunshine. So we got out of the car and went to the Public Gardens. I sat on Eric's wool lumberjack jacket which he had spread for me in deference to my costume, stockings again, and a different wool skirt and a different shirt, the same blazer. He, of course, was wearing exactly the same clothes he had worn the day before. I was feeling tension about the seminar I had to give that afternoon, and mindless pleasure in the sun and the smell of the earth, and I had half-forgotten the details of Eric's after-sex conversation, except that something about it had been faintly disagreeable. I also retained somewhere, between my legs perhaps, the impression that the preconversation sex had been distinctly agreeable. Overall, though, I was finding Eric, today, rather less attractive than I had the day before.

Mentally, I redesigned him, giving him truly curly hair instead of vaguely wavy tendrils, making him taller and thinner to entitle him to his awkwardness, while knitting his body more carefully so that the awkwardness would be more superficial. Though, in all fairness, I had to admit that he hadn't been the least bit awkward in bed. Just then, he put his arms around me and kissed me. I let him, first amused, then aroused, though I don't really believe in making out in public. Soon, we had gotten each other pretty thoroughly worked up, and then without any apparent reason, certainly nothing as definite as anyone's orgasm, we slacked off and began to relax. I began thinking about my seminar again. Then, three boys, who apparently had been watching us climb all over each other, began to call things out at us, encouraging us to finish what we had started. They couldn't have been more than ten years old, maybe less, and they were all three small and thin and pale and should have been in school. One of them carried an enormous portable radio, a ghetto blaster, as they say, though they were as white as Eric and I. After a moment, when they still hadn't gone away, Eric got to his feet and ran toward them, running with rather surprising grace, for someone engaged in such an awkward and ridiculous bit of behavior. I supposed that his motive was simple irritation and a desire to protect me from the jibes of these children, but he must have realized almost immediately, finding himself running across the grass, that he could only look sillier and sillier. The children retreated, slightly scared but triumphant in having provoked him, and he gave up the chase, veering around in a would-be-casual semicircle, as if he had just been running a little ways to work off his exuberance at the feeling of spring in the air.

Needless to say, I was not fooled. I was annoyed with his silliness and more annoyed because I had just discovered a run in my stocking, which I attributed to our making out. Now, I would have to stop at a drugstore sometime before my seminar and replace the stockings. Again I felt, watching him lope shamefacedly back to me, that we were somewhere deep into a relationship, maybe someone else's relationship, certainly not mine. The man making a fool of himself in public, attempting to defend his woman's honor against the onslaughts of smart-ass ten-year-olds. Someone else's relationship, someone else's man.

I might not have slept with Eric again if my second seminar had not gone so exceptionally well. I had been much more nervous about this one than the first, since I'd given the first one many times before. The second seminar, though, explained my very recent work, including work still in progress. I felt vulnerable and a little unconvinced about some of the material, but it went almost devastatingly well, the applause at the end was genuine, and the questions had a slightly awestruck air, even the challenging questions, the ones that were meant to suggest major gaps in my thinking. I had no trouble with the questions. And I felt that one reason it had gone so well was Eric's presence; I was showing off particularly for him and also trying to intimidate him and dazzle him and so on. And so then I felt a little in his debt; also I enjoyed the tentativeness of his offer: "Do you want me to come with you tonight?" It was much more tentative than you would expect, considering that I had slept with him the night before. It took us out of the middle of all those other relationships.

Once again, things turned out very well in bed, and we were both satiated and asleep at 2:30 in the morning, when the phone by the bed rang and it turned out to be my friend Eleanora, calling from New York to say she'd broken my big blue platter. Eleanora and her husband lived two floors up from me, and I had given her my key when I left for Boston and asked her to feed my cat. She had had company that night and had needed a big serving platter and had taken mine and broken it while she was washing it. Then she cried and drank steadily, until she was drunk and miserable enough to call me at the hotel in Boston.

She was crying over the phone. Don't cry, it doesn't matter, I told her, aware that it mattered, that I would not forgive her. I had not told her she could take the platter. Eleanora, I kept saying, why are you carrying on like this, it doesn't matter, I'll buy a new platter. The rhyme was becoming a refrain. Eric was awake and had turned on the bedside lamp. The sight of him was reassuring; he was calm, and we were not emotionally mixed up with each other. I wanted to hang up on Eleanora and see if Eric could get it up again. I was angry about the platter and angry with myself for caring about the platter, and angry with Eleanora for having judged me so correctly that she knew I would be angry about it.

I'm so messy, she was saying. Everything I touch turns out to be a mess. My life is one mess after another. After the platter broke, she had a fight with her husband, a plump and pompous man. He had gone to sleep without forgiving her, she told me, and she was in the living room, with, I assumed, an empty bottle of Southern Comfort in front of her. I know Eleanora's tastes. Why did you have a fight, I asked wearily. Eric was lying back against his pillow, watching me, looking a little surprised. Eleanora said something incoherent, dinner had not gone well, things had not come out right, important guests. For heaven's sake, Eleanora, I said, this is right out of some TV sitcom when the husband's boss comes to dinner. Don't take it so seriously. But then I had to listen to a long speech about how awful her life was and how I couldn't understand. I had no husband, after all. Immunology. Fancy hotels.

Are you alone? she asked suddenly. Well, no, as a matter of fact, I'm not, I said. But it's okay. By which I meant, go ahead and keep me on the phone, we were only sleeping when you called, the sex was over and done with. Immediately, Eleanora's voice took on a giggly quality. She assured me that she hadn't meant to interrupt, that clearly I had more important things to worry about than a broken platter. I'll tell you all about it when I get home, I said. Eric raised his eyebrows; I shrugged. You just bet you will, Eleanora giggled, I'm not going to let you off without a full description. And she said good-bye in high spirits, so I guess I really did manage to do a good turn and cheer up a friend in distress.

I explained a little to Eric, feeling he deserved it. He seemed a bit off balance. It was the sudden awareness of my real, tangled life, which he did not know anything about, in which he had no place. He had asked me all the wrong questions, it seemed—did I have a husband, a boy-friend?—and should have asked, instead, if I had a cat and if I had a friend named Eleanora who broke things.

"What's your cat's name?" he asked me, after I explained why Elea-nora had the key to my apartment; then, after I told him, he said, "You have a cat named Carmen?" I wondered if he thought that was a ridiculous name, if he would, after all, turn out to be some kind of kindred sensibility, so I said, "Someone else named her," leaving him free to make fun of the name. But he had no particular opinion; he had perhaps begun to wonder who had named my cat—an ex-lover, some-one I used to live with—and I thought of telling him that my little sister had chosen the name; giving me one of her own cat's kittens, she had thought to please me, knowing I like music. I didn't say it. Instead, Eric and I investigated and discovered that he could indeed get it up again, though, to be honest, it took him so damn long to reach orgasm that I lost interest. But I kept my eyes wide open; it is very bad man-ners to fall asleep in such a situation.

As if in return for his unexpected glimpse into my life, he offered me a confidence the next morning as he drove me to the airport to catch the air shuttle to New York. He told me that sometimes he was afraid he wouldn't be able to write his dissertation. All I could say was that I was sure he would be fine. I wondered whether he actually would be fine and whether I would see his name on articles or run into him in the future at scientific meetings. "Can I ask you something?" he said. I nodded. "If we lived near each other, would you have an affair with me?" I was silent too long to make it convincing before saying that we'd certainly give it a try, didn't he think? Fortunately, we got to the airport very soon after that and, instead of letting him park, I just got out in front of the terminal and kissed him good-bye and escaped.

Later, on the plane, I was thinking about all the little pieces of far-advanced and none-too-pleasant relationships that I had sensed between myself and Eric. I was wondering what my two-night stand might have to teach me; in science, of course, you have to learn from your experiments, and one valuable lesson is that you can never control all the variables. It can be scary when an experiment gets out of hand, and back at the airport, I'd had the distinct feeling that Eric was ready for all sorts of complications. I suspected there was something to be learned from this interlude with him about the nature of entanglements that occur between lives, the extremely fine line between no relationship and all relationships. And then suddenly, I began to smile to myself, almost to giggle, because it occurred to me that Eric had wanted to follow this experiment to wherever it might lead us, but that I had prevented it. I'd kept it to something more like a seminar—short, controlled, ending neatly on schedule. But it had been educational, I decided; it's hard to learn major lessons in quick little seminars, but they can serve to expose you to new ideas, to start you thinking. The most important thing about seminars is that they should surprise you a little. You shouldn't know, walking in, exactly how you'll feel walking out. And if, in addition, you enjoy them while they last, then you have to consider them successful, I suppose.

THE STORY HEARER

GRACE PALEY

Grace Paley lives in New York City with her husband, writer Robert Nichols. She is the author of two collections of stories, The Little Disturbances of Man *and* Enormous Changes at the Last Minute.

I am trying to curb my cultivated individualism, which seemed for years so sweet. It was my own song in my own world and, of course, it may not be useful in the hard time to come. So, when Jack said at dinner, What did you do today with your year off, I decided to make an immediate public accounting of the day, not to water my brains with time spent in order to grow smart private thoughts.

I said, Shall we begin at the beginning?

Yes, he said, I've always loved beginnings.

Men do, I replied. No one knows if they will ever get over this. Hundreds of thousands of words have been written, some free-lance and some commissioned. Still no one knows.

Look here, he said, I like middles, too.

Oh yes, I know. I questioned him. Is this due to age or the recent proliferation of newspaper articles?

I don't know, he said. I often wonder, but it seems to me that my father who was a decent man—your typical nine-to-fiver—it seems to me he settled into a great appreciation of the middle just about the time my mother said, Well, Willy it's enough. Goodbye. Keep the children warm and let him (me) finish high school at least. Then she kissed him, kissed us kids. She said, I'll call you next week, but never did speak to any of us again. Where can she be?

Now I've heard that story maybe 30 times and I still can't bear it. In fact, whenever I've made some strong adversary point in public, Jack tells it to grieve me. Sometimes I begin to cry. Sometimes I just make soup immediately. Once I thought Oh! I'll iron his underwear. I've

Copyright © 1982 by Grace Paley. First appeared in *Mother Jones.* Reprinted by permission.

heard of that being done, but I couldn't find the cord. I haven't needed to iron in years because of famous American science, which gives us wash-and-wear in one test tube and nerve gas in the other. Its right test tube doesn't know what its left test tube is doing. Oh yes, it does, says Jack.

Therefore I want to go on with the story. Or perhaps begin it again. Jack said, What did you do today with your year off? I said, My dear, in the late morning I left our apartment. The *Times* was folded on the doormat of 1-A. I could see that it was black with earthquake, war and private murder. Clearly death had been successful everywhere but not —I saw when I stepped out the front door—on our own block. Here it was springtime, partly because of the time of the year and partly because we have a self-involved block-centered street association which has lined us with sycamores and enhanced us with a mountain ash, two ginkgoes and here and there (because we are part of the whole) ailanthus, city saver.

I said to myself, What a day! I think I'll run down to the store and pick up some comestibles. I actually thought that. Had I simply gone to the store without thinking, the word *comestible* would never have occurred to me. I would have imagined—hungry supper night time Jack greens cheese store walk street.

But I do like this language—wheat and chaff—with its widening pool of foreign genes, and since I never have had any occasion to say *comestible*, it was pleasurable to think it.

At the grocer's I met an old friend who had continued his life as it had begun—in the avant-garde—but not selfishly. He had also organized guerrilla theater demonstrations and had never spoken ill of the people. Most artists do because they have very small audiences and are angry at those audiences for not enlarging themselves.

How can they do that? I've often asked. They have word of mouth, don't they? most artists peevishly will reply.

Well, first my friend and I talked of the lettuce boycott. It was an old boycott. I told my friend (whose name was Jim) all about the silk stocking boycott which coincided with the Japanese devastation of Manchuria and the disappearance of the Sixth Avenue El into Japanese factory furnaces to be returned a few years later—sometimes to the very same neighborhood as shrapnel stuck in the bodies of some young New Yorkers of my generation.

Did that lead to Pearl Harbor? he asked respectfully. He was aware that I had witnessing information of events that had occurred when he was in grade school. That respect gave me all the advantage I needed to be aggressive and critical. I said, Jim, I have been wanting to tell you that I do not believe in the effectiveness of the way that you had the Vietnamese screaming at our last demonstration. I don't think the meaning of our struggle has anything to do with all that racket.

You don't understand Artaud, he said. I believe that the theater is the handmaiden of the revolution.

The Valet you mean.

He deferred to my correction by nodding his head. He accepts criticism gracefully since he can always meet it with a smiling bumper of iron opinion.

You ought to know more about Artaud, he said.

You're right. I should. But I've been awfully busy. Also, I may have once known a great deal about him. In the last few years, all the characters of literature run together in my head. Sometimes King Ubu appears right next to Mr. Sparsit—or Mrs. . . .

At this point the butcher said, What'll you have young lady?

I refused to tell him.

Jack, to whom, if you remember, I was telling this daylong story, muttered, Oh God no! You didn't do that again.

I did, I said. It's an insult. You do not say to a woman of my age who looks my age, what'll you have young lady. I did not answer him. If you say that to someone like me, it really means What do you want, you pathetic old hag?

Are you getting like that now, too? he asked.

Look Jack, I said, face facts. Let's say the butcher meant no harm. Eddie, he's not so bad. He spends two hours coming to New York from Jersey. Then he spends two hours going back. I'm sorry for his long journey. But I still mean it. He mustn't say it anymore.

Eddie, I said, don't talk like that or I won't tell you what I want.

Whatever you say honey, but what'll you have?

Well, could you cut me up a couple of fryers?

Sure I will, he said.

I'll have a pork butt, said Jim. By the way, you know we're doing a show at the City College this summer. Not in the auditorium—in the biology lab. It's a new idea. We had to fight for it. It's the most political thing we've done since *Scavenging*.

Did I hear you say City College? asked Eddie as he cut the little chicken's leg out of its socket. Well, when I was a boy, a kid—what we called City College—you know it was CCNY then, well, we called it Circumcised Citizens of New York.

Really, said Jim. He looked at me. Did I object? Was I offended?

The fact of male circumcision doesn't insult me, I said. However, I understand that the clipping of clitorises of young girls continues in Morocco to this day.

Jim has a shy side. He took his pork butt and said goodbye.

I had begun to examine the chicken livers. Sometimes they are tanner than red, but I understand this is not too bad.

Suddenly Treadwell Thomas appeared at my side and embraced me. He's a famous fussy gourmet, and I was glad that the butcher saw our affectionate hug. Thought up any good euphemisms lately? I asked.

Ha ha, he said. He still feels bad about his life in the Language Division of the Defense Department. A year or two ago Jack interviewed him for a magazine called *The Social Ordure*, which ran five quarterly issues before the editor was hired away by the *Times*. It was a fine periodical.

Here's part of the interview:

Mr. Thomas, what is the purpose of the Language Division?

Well, Jack, it was organized to discontinue the English language as a useful way to communicate exact facts. Of course, it's not the first (or last) organization to have attempted this but it's had some success.

Mr. Thomas, is this an ironic statement made in the afterglow of your new idealism and the broad range of classified information it has made available to us?

Not at all, Jack, it wasn't I who invented the expression "protective reaction." And it was Eisenhower, not I, who thought up (while thousands of hydrogen bombs were being tucked into silos and submarines) —it was not I who invented Atoms for Peace and its code name, Operation Wheaties.

Could you give us at least one expression you invented to stultify or mitigate (Jack, I screamed, *stultify* or *mitigate*, you caught the disease. Shut up, said Jack and returned to the interview).

Well? he asked.

Well, said Treadwell Thomas, I was asked to develop a word or series of words that could describe, denote any of the Latin American countries in a condition of change—something that would by its mere utterance neutralize or mock their revolutionary situation. After consultation, brainpicking and the daydreaming that is appropriate to any act of creation, I came up with *revostate*. The word was slipped into conversations in Washington; one or two journalists were glad to use it. It was just lingo for a long time. But you have no doubt seen the monograph *The Revostationary Peasant in Brazil Today.* Even you pinkos use it. Not to mention Wasserman's poetic article, "Rain Forest, Still Water and the Culture of the Revostate," which was actually featured in this journal.

Right on, Treadwell—as our black brothers joyfully said for a couple of years before handing that utterance on for our stultification or mitigation.

Still it's true Thomas could have gone as far as far happens to be in our time and generation, hundreds of ambitious jobless college students at the foot of his tongue on Senior Defense Department Recruiting Day, but apart from cooking a lot of fish he has chosen to guffaw quite often. Some people around here think that guffawing, the energetic cleansing of the nasal passage, is the basic wisdom of the East. Other people think that's not true.

Which reminded me as we waited for the packaging of the meat, how's Gussie?

Gus? Oh, yeah, she's into hydroponics. She's got all this stuff standing around in tubs. We may never have to go shopping again.

Well, I laughed and laughed. I repeated the story to several others before the day was over. I mocked Gussie to Jack. I spoke of her mockingly to one or two strangers. And the fact is, she was already the wave of the future. I was ignorant. It wasn't my ocean she was a wave on.

In fact, I am stuck here among my own ripples and tides. Don't you wish you could rise powerfully above your time and name? I'm sure we all try but here we are always slipping and falling down into them, speaking their narrow language though the subject, which is how to save the world—and quickly—is immense.

Goodbye Treadwell, I said sadly. I've got to get some greens.

The owner of our grocery was hosing down the vegetables. He made the lettuce look fresher than it was. Little drops of water stood on the broccoli heads among the green beady buds and were just the same size.

Orlando, I said, Jack was walking the dog last night at 2:00 a.m. and I was out at 7:00 a.m. and you were here both times.

That's true, he said. I was.

Orlando, how can you do that, how can you get to work, how can you live? How can you see your kids and your wife?

I can't, he said. Maybe once a week.

Are you all right?

Yes. He put down his hose and took my hand in his. You see, he said, this is wonderful work. This is food. I love all work that has to do with food. I'm lucky. He dropped my hand and patted a red cabbage. Look at me, I'm a small businessman. I got an A&P on one side, a Bohack on another and a fancy International full of cheese and herring down the block. If I don't put in 16 hours a day I'm dead. But Mrs. A., just look at that rack, the beans, that corner with all the parsley and the arugula and the dill, it's beautiful, right?

Oh yes, I said, I guess it is, but what *I* really love are the little bunches of watercress—the way you've lined the carrot bin with them.

Yeah, Mrs. A., you're O.K. You got the idea. The beauty! he said and went off to take three inferior strawberries out of a perfect box. A couple of years later—in the present, which I have not quite mentioned (but will)—we fought over Chilean plums. We parted. I was forced to shop in the reasonable supermarket among disinterested people with no credit asked and none offered. But at that particular moment we were at peace. That is, I owed him $275 and he allowed it.

O.K., said Jack, if you and Orlando are such pals why aren't all these strawberries ripe? He picked up a rather green eroded one. I invented an anthropological reply. Well, Orlando's father is an old man. One of the jobs Orlando's culture has provided for his father's old age is the sorting of strawberries into pint and quart boxes. Just to be fair, he has to hide one or two greenish ones in each box.

I think I'll go to bed, said Jack.

I was only extrapolating from his article in the final issue of *The Social Ordure*—"Food Merchandising, or Who Invented the Greedy Consumer." I reminded him of this.

He said politely, Ah . . .

The day had been too long and I hadn't said one word about The New Young Fathers or my meeting with Zagrevsky the Pharmacist. I thought we might discuss them at breakfast.

So we slept, his arms around me as sweetly as after the long day he had probably slept beside his former wife (and I as well beside my etc. etc. etc.). I was so comfortable; our good mattress and our nice feelings were such a cozy combination that I remembered a song my friend Ruthy had made up about ten years earlier to tease the time, the place, us:

oh, the marriage bed, the marriage bed
can you think of anything nicer
for days and nights of years and years
you lie beside your darling
your arms are hugging one another
your legs are twined together
until the dark and certain day
your lover comes to take you
     away   away   away

At about 3:00 a.m. Jack cried out in terror. That's O.K. kid, I said, you're not the only one. Everybody's mortal. I leaned all my softening strength against his skinny back. Then I dreamed the following in a kind of diorama of Technicolor abstraction—that the children had grown all the way up. One had moved to another neighborhood, the other to a distant country. *That* one was never to be seen again, the dream explained, because he had blown up a very bad bank, and in the dream I was the one who'd told him to do it. The dream continued, no —it circled itself widening into my very old age. Then his disappearance made one of those typical spiraling descents influenced by film technique. Unreachable at the bottom, their childhood played war and made jokes.

I woke. Where's the glass of water, I screamed. I want to tell you something, Jack.

What? What? What? he saw my wide-awake eyes. He sat up. What?

Jack, I want to have a baby.

Ha ha, he said. You can't. Too late. A couple of years too late, he said and fell asleep. Then he spoke. Besides, suppose it worked, I mean suppose a miracle. The kid might be very smart, get a scholarship to MIT and get caught up in problem solving and god-almighty it could invent something worse than anything us old dodos ever imagined. Then he fell asleep and snored.

I pulled the Old Testament out from under the bed where I keep most of my bedtime literature. I jammed an extra pillow under my neck and sat up almost straight in order to read the story of Abraham and Sarah with interlinear intelligence. There was a lot in what Jack said— he often makes a sensible or thought-provoking remark. Because you know how that old story ends—well! With those three monotheistic horsemen of perpetual bossdom and war: Christianity, Judaism and Islam.

Just the same, I said to softly snoring Jack, before all that popular

badness wedged its way into the world, there *was first* the little baby
Isaac. You know what I mean: looking at Sarah just like all our own old
babies—remember the way they practiced their five little senses. Oh
Jack, that Isaac, Sarah's boy—before he was old enough to be taken out
by his father to get his throat cut, he must have just lain around smiling
and making up diphthongs and listening, and the women sang songs to
him and wrapped him up in such pretty rugs. Right?

In his sleep, which is as contentious as his waking, Jack said Yes—but
he should not have been allowed to throw all that sand at his brother.

You're right, you're right. I'm with you there, I said. Now all you
have to do is be with me.

THE LOVE CHILD

HELEN NORRIS

Helen Norris has lived most of her life in Alabama, where she grew up on a five-hundred-acre farm outside of Montgomery. She received A.B. and M.A. degrees from the University of Alabama and completed further work at Duke University. For thirteen years she taught English at Huntingdon College in Montgomery but resigned to return to writing. She has published two novels, and a third novel will appear in 1984 from Zondervan. She has published eight short stories in the past year. She is the first recipient of the newly established Andrew Lytle Award for Fiction, for "The Love Child." Ms. Norris has one son.

The wind was brawling out of the north when they told her she had to move. Her son Sam, who was getting gray and stout, and his tall wife Ardis, who dyed her hair the color of peanut brittle, came down from Memphis to tell her, leaving their children with a neighbor overnight.

She was seventy-six. She had lived in her house for fifty years and she refused to leave.

"Mama, they're going to put a highway clean through your house. You wouldn't like that, Mama. Would you want the cars running straight through your living room?"

"Yes," Emma said. She was always difficult when they talked to her like a child. Then she said, "I never gave my consent. They couldn't do it without my consent."

"Mama, they can. How could you live all your life and not know that? The Government can do anything it wants."

So they moved her to a little farmhouse on the outskirts of the town. They bought it for her with the money the Government gave them for her own house in town. And they added some, or so Sam said. Because this house was better built and would last for years. "I don't need one that will last," she said. But they didn't listen. It had ten acres of land

Copyright © 1983 by Helen Norris. First appeared in the *Sewanee Review*, Vol. 91, No. 2 (spring 1983). Reprinted by permission.

that stretched back from the road, with a lot of underbrush that needed clearing and trees and a pond with fish that moved like shadows through the feathers of green scum.

"I don't need all this," she said, looking at it from the back porch with her head wrapped in a brown scarf.

"You'll get used to it, Mama. It's a good investment."

She knew they meant that when she died they could sell it at a profit. They expected her to die, she thought. And very soon. But if she thought that, she was wrong: She found they were expecting her to live. After all the work of birthing, raising, nursing, grieving, they wanted one thing more.

Meanwhile in the new place she lasted out the winter, beat it down into the ground. Actually it seemed to disappear into the trees and lie in wait on the other side of the hill. Oh, she hated winter, always had. But it was better in the town, with Mrs. Ellis coming in for coffee. And Mr. Greer, the postman, stamping through the slush and ringing her bell. And the boy from the grocery blowing into his hands, Effie Higgins' boy . . . The days were draughty, noisy with the wind, but they were full of faces she could wave to from her window if she felt like waving. You get older and the world is changing and you hardly know yourself except for people who have always known you and you can see it in their faces who you are. Then you know.

Here the days were long and soaked with rain and all her past, and no one was coming in or passing by. Even the rain was different, blowing now from the left instead of the right. She took off her steel-rimmed glasses and stared at her face, all blurry, in the mirror. It's what I'm like inside, she said. I don't know who I am. I'm blurred inside.

But the spring brought Sam and Ardis. They had called the night before. She watched them drive up and get out. They had with them one of their three children, who was staying in the back seat of the car. She saw her grandchildren so seldom that she wasn't sure which one it was.

"Is that Todd or Steven? Bring him in. Or show him the pond in back."

They looked at one another. "Mama, we have to talk to you first." And they followed her in and got right to the point. "Mama, it isn't . . . Mama, it's Cissie's child."

Cissie was her grandchild, the daughter of her own child Rachel, who had died a dozen years ago.

"Cissie?" she said. "Cissie had a child? I never heard a word of Cissie's wedding."

"Mama, there wasn't any wedding. She was fifteen and she ran off. We took her in when Rachel died and did the best we could. You know we did. We raised her like our own."

"Cissie ran away and had a child? At fifteen?" She was trying to see the polished skin, the green eyes, the fluffy hair of Cissie. "Why are you telling me this now? I can't help what she did. Young people now, they're not the way we were."

"We didn't want to worry you, because we didn't know where she was. And then she came back, and she brought this child . . ." They were looking through the window at the pond. "We've kept him through the winter. But we have our own."

Her voice was full of wonder. "Why isn't Cissie keeping him?"

"Mama, Cissie's found a man who wants to marry her. She wants to start all over. We can all see that's the best . . . But we have our own three children. Mama, we've brought him here."

After a while she asked, "You've brought him here to stay? For how long, Sam?"

"Oh, a while. Just a while." By the way he said it she knew it was forever, for the rest of her days.

"I'm too old," she said. "I'm seventy-six."

"He'll be good for you, Mama. Give you something to live for."

"You mean to die for. I'm too old," she said again. And her age loomed dark before her like a tunnel through the mountain. Their faces were strangers' faces. "I'm not the same," she said. "When your father died . . ."

"Mama, that was eighteen years ago. And you have your health."

"Something broke . . ."

"Mama, that was eighteen years, and life goes on."

"Mine didn't." She was being difficult again. But when she was difficult they looked at her as if they knew who she was. And then she knew herself.

They stood up, and Ardis stayed with her while Sam went to the car and brought the child. He was very small, with Cissie's fluffy hair and ice-green eyes. He looked up at her for the merest flash of time and then away.

"Ethan," Ardis said, "this is your own great-granny. Uncle Sam was her little boy."

Sam said, "He knows he's staying."

Her voice fought through the tunnel of her age. "How old is he?"

"He's four . . ." His voice was lowered. "Cissie says he was born July the ninth. You might want to do a little something. We'll send a box."

Then Sam got the suitcase with his clothes and a small box with his toys. And they were gone, their Buick eating through the new oak leaves and out into the warm spring sun and down the road.

He was still looking through the window long after they had disappeared. She sat down in a chair and stared at his back in a green striped T-shirt that all but covered his short pants. He was so still and small that she could almost believe he wasn't there. She was dazed and weary. She was trying to think about him and where she would put him and what she would fix for him to eat today and tomorrow and all the days of her life. She thought of all the questions she should have asked Sam.

And so she was given Cissie's love child, as her grandmother would have called him, to have and to hold. The black woman who came to work for them a thousand years ago on the farm where she was born would have said Cissie "found" him.

It was all the same. However made or found, he was given her to keep. So she kept the child. But the strange and chilling fact of their life was that he never looked at her and never spoke. At first she thought him shy, so she talked in a soothing voice of her children when they were young—Sam and Jamie and Rachel—and of her own childhood. He gave no sign of hearing. He sat or stood with vacant eyes on the floor or on the trees and sky or on his brown hands which were peppered with small warts. She took one of his hands in her own. He did not draw away. "My brother used to have some little lumps like these. I made them go away. Would you let me try to make yours go away?" Slowly, almost absently, he drew his hand from hers.

He ran and played in the yard, but when she was near he seemed to move in his sleep. He did as he was bidden. He went to bed when he was told. He ate what she cooked for him. She tried to win him round with her baking, which she had almost forgotten how to do. He ate the sweet muffins and the cookies silently, then walked away.

He was smaller than he should be for his age, she thought. Cissie had been small. His skin was fair, a little freckled, his nose always pink and peeling from the sun. His hands brown and dotted with the colonies of warts. A rim of insect bites just below his short pants. His hair was pale silk, like Cissie's hair, with bits of leaf or a feather clinging. But his eyes were really not Cissie's at all. They were more like the water at the edge of the pond, gray shading into green and back into gray. But not like the water, for if you looked into them you didn't see yourself. You were never there. Sometimes there was a flicker that moved out of sight, like the fish in the pond that were always just leaving wherever they had been. He was as tight as a nut inside a hard shell. He never came out. He never let her in.

At first she was a little amused at his tightness, then a little dismayed. And then there was a cold hard stone in the center of her breast. Like a question it was. Perhaps it was fear.

To put away the fear or whatever it was, she took to singing to him in her low rusty voice the songs of her childhood about animals and games. When she sang he grew still as a rock, and sometimes his eyes swept in passing her hands or her dress. But never her face. She began to feel faceless. So as not to feel voiceless she needed to talk to him. She needed to sing. And she watched for the slightest sign that he attended to anything at all except a request to go to bed or to eat, to go out or come in, to dress himself or wash . . . When she made a request a kind of pale hardness, translucent like porcelain, would appear in his face. His mouth would move slightly as he pulled on his lip. He seemed to be asleep. But he always obeyed.

Soon after his coming she took his toys from the box and arranged them on top of the cedar chest below the window in the room she had given him. Some of them were toys he must have had since he was very young: a small brown bear with one green eye. A cord with colored spools. A yellow truck. A dozen blocks. A plastic duck. Some soldiers still attached with wire to the card on which they came. A box of crayons. A picture book to color. She placed them in a row on the chest. Then she put his clothes from the suitcase in the chest of drawers.

When she passed his room next, she saw that the toys were back inside the box and the clothes were in the suitcase. She left them there.

The strangest thing of all was that she never heard his voice. Sometimes at night she awoke and thought that he had called. She lay still and listened. She had only dreamed his voice. It was strong and high-pitched. It was Jamie's voice. Even when awake, she thought of Jamie as little, because she had never seen him growing old, getting gray like Sam.

She tried not to think. She unpacked her boxes full of things from the old house. A lot of them were strange to her away from their places on the tables and shelves. She couldn't recall the flowered china bowl. Where did she get it? Where had she kept it? She went on with the unpacking as if she hoped to find herself wrapped in old paper in one of the boxes.

She came across two small harmonicas, both a little rusted, that had belonged to Sam and Jamie. She tried them out in secret, and then she placed one in the pocket of her apron and one on the table in the dining room. In a day or two she heard what she was waiting for. When she was in the kitchen there came the voice of the harmonica—one note sustained, a long pause, and then the same note three times. She took the mate from her pocket and blew an answer. She held her breath to listen. There was nothing. After a moment she looked into the dining room. He was gone and the harmonica was on the table where she had placed it. She grew to believe that she had dreamt its sound.

She tried to read the magazines that came in the mail, but words meant nothing any more. Words got in her way. Sometimes she stroked the dried-out skin of her arms with the coarsely woven cloth of her long cotton sleeves. Or she held her face with both hands. Or she moved her legs deliberately when she walked across the room. Or she drank the well water that tasted of moss, holding it in her mouth till it slid down her throat and into her bones and she shuddered with the cold. I'm here. I'm alive.

But the trees outside were more alive and full of growth, their balled leaves bursting into hands and fingers. The weeds and grass shot up around her porch, crowding the steps as if they wanted to come in. At night the long tendrils of wisteria were scratching at her window—all of it alive, more alive than herself. All of it knowing itself and who it was. She was canceled by the spring. It was worse than the winter.

She might have willed herself into the world if only Ethan had known her.

She waited one night till Ethan went to bed. When she was sure he was asleep she rang up Sam in Memphis. Ardis answered.

"There's something I need to know," she said, "about the boy . . ." She could feel that Ardis was waiting, tapping her long teeth with the nail of one finger as she liked to do. "Can he talk? I mean he hasn't said a word . . ."

"Mama, he's probably shy. When he gets used to you . . ."

"I mean does he know any words?"

"Any what?"

"Any words. Does he know any words?"

There was a silence. She thought she could hear the click of Ardis' teeth.

"Mama, he's almost five. Let me put it this way: he knows as many words as Steve and Todd."

She waited for a moment, enduring the impatience at the end of the line. "Tell Sam I called."

She thought more and more about her house in town. She dreamt of it at night. And in her dreams she walked from room to room touching the things that had made her who she was—the fireplace, the mantel, the lattice doors, the kitchen windows overlooking the trees, the wall of bricks where the porch had been extended when her husband was alive, the sill where Rachel sat when she painted her pictures of the shed in vivid colors, a different color every time, rusting out the screen where her jar of water spilled. She had never really believed the house would not be there. Or the street with its lacing of sycamore boughs . . .

She put Ethan in the car, the ancient Plymouth that had taken her away from her house, and drove into town and straight to her street. It was indeed gone or soon would be. The bulldozers were prowling the devastation like prehistoric monsters. Her house, when she found it, had gone to rubble, the boards heaped and broken, the chimney crumbled in upon itself, the hearth place buried.

It was the scattered chimney that broke her heart. She had a strange guilty feeling that if she had not deserted the house it would still be alive.

The child beside her was standing up to look at the machines. "That used to be my house," she said. He gave no sign of hearing. If only she had some one to share it with. Mrs. Ellis had gone away to live with her daughter in another state. Mr. Greer the postman would not be coming round. She did not know about the rest. They seemed to her dead. She went on talking. "Your mother used to come and visit when she was your age. Such a pretty little girl. She always played in the swing . . ."

She gave it up and cried a little. He did not seem to notice. She drove them away. Mrs. Ellis had a niece with a child who couldn't love. She said he couldn't belong to them, only to himself. When Mrs. Ellis talked of him she shook her head from side to side and smoothed the dress on her knee. He would never be right. There was a name for it, but Mrs. Ellis could never remember what it was. She drank a second cup of coffee; still she couldn't remember.

The sun was growing hot. The air was still. For three whole days Emma mourned for the house and for her crumbled life. Tears swam in her eyes, blurred the figure of Ethan and the field that shimmered in the late spring heat, but dried on her lashes before they fell. The tears were a comfort and still they were a shame. They seemed to be tears from a long time ago that had welled and waited for the coming and the bleak indifference of Ethan.

She shook herself free. She called Mr. Hagan at the grocery store and got a man to come and cut the weeds with a scythe. She paid him five dollars. She asked him if he knew of a dog for sale. He looked off across the field and spat into the grass and did not reply. But the next day he brought her a puppy with short amber hair and long wilted ears like dried autumn leaves. She did not know what kind it was, perhaps a mixture of breeds, possibly a stray, found like Ethan. Its name was Bean.

She hired the black man to make Ethan a swing from a tire in the shed and hang it from the sweet gum outside the kitchen. While she worked she watched Ethan swing by the hour with the puppy beneath him running back and forth, leaping and nipping at the boy's bare feet. His bark was short and mocking. Sometimes she could hear a faint murmur as Ethan bent to the dog. Was he talking to Bean? Or was it the low, chiding music children make for animals? She listened with a kind of hunger in her stillness, till she was dizzy with being in the body of the dog, running back and forth beneath the voice of the child.

Once while he was swinging a bee stung Ethan. She had never heard him cry. She thought at first it was Bean. She ran to the child and searched his body till she found the swelling on the side of his arm. She pulled out the stinger and smeared the wound with baking soda. He held his breath and turned away his head. She spoke to him in soothing tones, telling him not to worry, that the hurt would go away. She held him lightly and touched his hair with her lips. He smelled of earth and leaves and puppy. It was so much like holding Jamie that she grew a little weak. But Ethan stiffened in her arms. She felt his will against her voice and her arms, her lips on his hair. She let him go. How could he be so strong for so long? How could he never need her?

It was as if she held captive a wild sort of bird or some creature of a species she had never seen before. But in a strange way she herself was the captive. She was deeply at his mercy. She took to seeing him in all the corners of the house. Even when she knew that he was swinging in the yard or throwing stones into the pond, she would seem to catch a glimpse of him just beyond her vision when she entered any room. As if he dwelt in all of them, always, forever, and never knew that she was there.

But the child was real enough. A lively glow was in his face when he chased the speckled chickens that had come with the house and nested in the shed. She forbade him to approach the edge of the pond except when she was near. But, standing away from it, he had learned to fish with a pole for the green feathered scum and roll it into balls and toss it at the hens. His legs were always freckled from assaults of insects and scratched with the briars in the underbrush. While he ate his food before her at the table in the kitchen, he smelled of dust and puppy and the tire swing. Even after Bean was gone he smelled of puppy . . .

It was around the first of June that she saw him from the house leaning over something at the side of the road. She knew at once what it was. Without seeing she knew. She hurried to where he knelt to the small crumpled dog. He was touching its nose and its long wilted ears. She was thankful that the car had not mangled or bloodied it. There was only a small wound at the side of the head, but it was quite dead. She dragged it by one foot into the ditch. "Go to the house, Ethan. Bean has been hurt." But he did not stir.

The sun was hot and final. After a time she left him and waited on the porch. She rocked and would not see the buzzards circling in the sky. But her mind grew giddy with their wheeling and troubled with shreds and patches from the day Rachel died. At last she saw a black man passing down the road, and she offered him money to bury the dog in the woods behind the house. While Ethan stood and watched, the old man found a bit of wire, tied Bean to her shovel, and dragged him down her walk. The shovel full of Bean bounced and chimed on the gravel, so light it was. Past the pond and down the field he pulled the shovel behind him in a stately walk. She watched the buzzards follow and Ethan follow.

"Come back," she pled. But the child kept going, running to keep up. She could not bring herself to follow. She stood beside the pond and waited in the sun. She felt old and weak. It was time to make lunch, but she stood with eyes fixed on the small running figure, waiting for the trees to swallow him up. "Watch out for the boy," she called to the man; but he could not have heard, so faint was her voice.

Suddenly before they reached the trees Ethan stopped. Then he turned and started back. She followed his return every step of the way. She searched his face when he neared, but there was nothing to see. No grief or terror or interest or wonder. Just nothing at all. He began to gather sticks and throw them into the pond.

Later he did not seem to remember. It was as if Bean had never been, never come or gone. But she mourned for the dog; she couldn't say why. As if she mourned for herself. She saw in her mind his shallow grave in the woods, his wilted ears filled with moss and crumbling into loam.

She had always taken Ethan with her when she drove the mile down the road to get her groceries at the crossroads store. She left him in the car. It must have been a week after Bean was killed. While she was inside she suddenly heard the sound of voices in the yard. Grant Eris, who pumped gas, was talking to Ethan and Ethan was talking back. Words poured from the boy. She listened in wonder. His voice was strong and high-pitched exactly like Jamie's, the way it was in her dream. She went to the screen door and looked out. They were talking about a fish that Grant had caught and threaded on a branch and now held up to Ethan.

She was deeply stirred. And lurking in the shadow of the airless country store, she grew confused and could not remember the items she had come for. She could not face the boy and surprise him in the act. So she waited inside, faint with the spice-and-honey smell of snuff and the sour-pickle smell and the pungent odor of the spray for flies, pretending to read the labels on the packages and cans. When the voices grew still she summoned the courage to open the screen door where the flies clustered singing and drive away with Ethan through the summer heat.

She thought of telling the boy that she had heard him talking. But she feared the reproach in her words or her voice. So she said nothing to him. But his speaking filled her with a mounting shame. Ethan could talk to others but not to her. It made her glad that she had moved away from town and that her friends were gone, and that she could live alone with the silence between herself and the child.

His silence made her know what she didn't want to know—that the silence of the others had grown with the years. It had come so slowly, year by year, whenever they died or moved away. She could almost pretend that it wasn't there. Like snow it was that seldom came, but once it fell on the town all day, all night, till little by little it filled her world and stifled her steps and the sounds she knew. You can bear the hush if it's slow . . . if it's slow. But then Ethan came, driving his silence like a wedge through hers, making her hear how still it was, making her lose her way in the snow.

Gradually she spoke less and less to Ethan. For she dreaded the stillness that followed her words. And the feel of being wasted and withered away. She could not forget the sound of his voice when he talked to Grant Eris. She heard it in her sleep. Once in her dream he touched her eyes, her lips, her hair. But she could not be sure if it was Ethan or Jamie . . . She woke to her weeping.

Now she talked to herself when she worked about the house. She talked about the years when her husband was alive. One year most of all when they were alone and they brimmed with the shadow and sweetness of life, when he would walk through the door with the gladness in his eyes that was hurtful to see, so fragile it was. And dear little Rachel, pretending to be blind with her eyes crushed tight, groping in the dark to find your face and laugh. She talked about nursing one child or another, the grace of its delicate hand on her breast, the shape and the silk of its golden head. She talked about the past. She was afraid of losing it. She rang up Sam and Ardis but they never answered.

Then she talked to herself about her past with Ethan. She returned in her mind to the day Sam brought him. She longed to go back and begin again. One day, while the boy was playing in the yard, once more she put his clothes away in the drawer. She emptied the old cedar chest of its linens and put his toys inside. She placed the box that had contained them on a shelf of the closet that he could not reach.

The next afternoon she found them again in the box on the floor of his room. His clothes were back in the shabby suitcase. For the first time she noticed the label on the side of the box. It read: T. Sherman, Atlanta, Ga. She examined the suitcase then. In the upper right corner inside the lid was penciled the name of Mrs. Harold Gant and then a Spartanburg address. It came to her suddenly with the force of revelation that Cissie had farmed him out with others—who knew how many?—before he came to Sam and Ardis. Like a seed the fact had lain here all along. And now it was pushing through the crust of her heart. She remembered the inked initials R. M. in the tail of his T–shirts. She searched for one and found it, with its faint smell of puppy in spite of all her washing. She stroked the canvas-covered suitcase. It was sticky with soil. She lifted his clothes mechanically and folded them again and put them back inside.

Crouched on the floor, her stiff old joints beginning to pain her, she stared at the room with the eyes of the child. Never would he call a room his own. Or a dog his own. Or a person his own. It was this that made her think that in four years of life he'd learned a terrible thing. Something that had taken her a lifetime to learn. Fourscore years and ten and she was still learning: You give yourself to others and they take your bits and pieces and you disappear.

She was staring down into the clothes she still pressed with her hand. Each garment was separate and alive with his will. His will against her and against this room. She shut the lid upon it. He would never be like her—dependent on another to tell him who he was. Or a house to tell him. He would be himself from the day that he entered her presence, not knowing her or needing her or needing her room or her drawer or her chest. Ethan was contained in his own small body and in the shabby suitcase that had been another's and in the box for his toys that had been another's too.

She got up with effort. The pain in her legs would go away in a while. She stood looking down at his toys in the box. The bear with one eye was head down among the rest. A child who couldn't feel, one who couldn't belong? No, he wasn't like the child of the niece of Mrs. Ellis. He had tried to belong and had given up belonging. When they moved him yet again, he was packed and ready. The soldiers in his box were still wired to the card. If the chimney crumbled he'd survive untouched. There would be no separations to tear a heart he'd never given. She could envy him for that.

And yet she mourned for him. Beside his bed she sat in the chair, where she had once held Jamie, and rocked and mourned, slipping her hand along the blue cotton quilt, mourning for her own lost self and for him. The sparrows were quarreling in the eaves outside. She could smell the four-o'clocks in the bed below. The sun was slanting through the airless room. It lay along the floor and across her knees. She held it in her lap and watched her rocker slice it into wedges of light . . . shadow and light.

She was afraid of what he knew. He was older than she. It was why she went on rocking the sun in her lap, knowing he was out in the yard beyond, swinging beneath the tree as she was rocking in the room he'd never taken from her. She could hear the iron chain rubbing against the branch of the sweet gum tree. She rubbed her face and arms. She measured her motion to the rhythm of his swinging, willing herself to be enough . . . enough.

At length she got up and went to where he was, but leaving a part of her rocking in the chair. She placed herself before him. Slowly he stopped swinging. But he did not look up. He sat suspended in the tire between heaven and earth. She made the part of her that rocked in his room come to join her in the yard. And she felt that she was swaying before him even now.

She couldn't talk of love. She wasn't sure that she loved him or would ever do so. Or that he understood what love was.

"I am your own grandmother. Look at me," she implored. "Ethan. Please." Her hair had come undone from the motion of the chair. She felt it about her neck and the side of her face. He was looking at the ground. It seemed to her that all the ones she had loved, all her own children, were shrunk into the figure in the circle of the swing and now could deny that she had ever been. But all she really knew was that his will was more than hers.

She knelt to him then, her knees bruised by the bare packed surface of the earth, her hands gripping the tire. "Ethan. Ethan. I have no one left but you." She could smell the faint odor of the puppy still alive in the dust. "I used to have Sam, but he married Ardis and moved away from me and hardly ever comes back. He has Todd and Steve and Gloria, but I hardly ever see them." She stopped for a while. "I have another boy named Jamie who lives in California, but he has a sick wife. She lives in a wheelchair, and so he never comes back. Not ever, Ethan. I had a little girl named Rachel and she grew up and had your mother. But she died, Ethan. Like Bean, you know. So she never comes back. And I had a husband, Ethan, the way Ardis has Sam. But he died too." After a time she said, "And so he never comes back."

She held the swing tightly to keep from falling. "There is nobody in the whole world I can have but you . . . You don't even have yourself unless you have somebody else . . . They gave you to me, and they gave me to you. I belong to you, Ethan. And you belong to me. And I will never give you back. If Sam and Ardis came and tried to take you I wouldn't let them. I would lock all the doors. And if they broke them down I would hide you. And if they found you I would take your hand and run with you across the field and through the trees and over that hill. And if they caught us I would fight them. I would fight my own son. I'm old but I am stronger than anybody knows." Her legs were numb. She felt that she was sinking through the ground before him. "If your own mother came I would fight her too. I would tell her . . . I would tell her you belong to me. Nothing could take you. I would never give you back." Her voice was trembling. Her hands were locked and trembling on the rim of the tire. She could scarcely speak for the violence in her throat and chest. "I will never die and leave you. I promise not to die. And when you grow bigger you can help me not to die." Swaying, she took his face between her hands. "Will you help me not to die?"

She searched his face. He was staring without expression past the trees beyond the hill. The toes of one foot were making scratches in the dust.

She stood up in anguish. Then she walked away. He's a child who can't belong. He can't feel . . . He's a child who can't love. God help me, she said.

God help me because I meant every word that I said. God help me because without him I am losing myself. I'm nothing. I'm lost.

She stumbled toward the pond and walked along beside it. The gnats and waterflies were picking at its surface. She fell kneeling to the face below her in the water. A breeze she could not even feel was stirring it, blurring it into the face in her bedroom mirror without her glasses on.

She closed her eyes, and when she opened them his face was close to hers. His hand was raking the water, shattering their faces into arcs and fragments till they seemed to tumble like her fallen chimney, crumbling into nothing. Like drowning it was. She wanted to turn and leave him, for he was lost too. But she could not move.

And then the water stilled. The shards and slivers mended into faces. They stared at one another down below. Slowly his hand in the water was moving toward her in the depths. It touched her hair. It passed across it, tracing the way it fell in coils against her neck.

She held her breath. She willed herself into the woman in the mirror. And then she could feel his groping hand, seeking in the water her living face.

Her tears fell. Like waterflies they pricked the surface of the pond.

FOR JEROMÉ—WITH LOVE
AND KISSES

GORDON LISH

Gordon Lish is the author of the novel *Dear Mr. Capote*. He has published three anthologies of short fiction—*New Sounds in American Fiction, The Secret Life of Our Time,* and *All Our Secrets Are the Same*. For some years he was fiction editor of *Esquire;* since that time he has been an editor at Knopf. "For Jeromé—with Love and Kisses" will appear in *What I Know So Far,* a Holt, Rinehart & Winston collection of Mr. Lish's short stories.

Jaydeezie darling,
dear cutie fellow,
my wonderful son Jerome,

You will do me a favor and answer me this question, please God it should not be for you too much trouble to do it. So you will take all of two seconds and you will tell me, Jerome, since when did you hear of a civilized person which gets rid of a perfectly good unlisted and then goes and gets another one on top of it? Also, darling, assuming you could see your way clear to fit it into your busy schedule, you will inform me as to the whys and wherefores of how come the same aforementioned individual couldn't exhibit the simple courtesy to first communicate to his own father the particulars with regard to the necessary digits. So this is asking too much, Jerrychik? I mean, first and foremost your father wants your assurance he is not causing you too big a perturbance. Listen, you will be a sport and you will take two seconds and you will list for me the reasons for this behavior. Because to tell you the truth, pussycat, in my personal opinion I think your father is entitled to hear an explanation.

I am waiting, darling. God willing, you will go into private confer-

Copyright © 1983, 1984 by Gordon Lish. First appeared in *The Antioch Review*. Reprinted by permission.

ence with your heart of hearts and think it over and advise me as to your decision. So you could do this for me, cutie fellow? Because I your father am meanwhile sitting here on pins and needles expecting. Make yourself a promise that in a voice which is calmness itself you will pick up the telephone for the sole and exclusive purpose of advising your father whether you decided in your mind if this is the behavior of a civilized person.

Meanwhile, who could help himself but to think along the lines of a certain possible conjecture? So plunge a dagger into my breast for giving serious consideration to the following theory, but are we dealing here with a situation where the party of the first part says to himself, "The phone rings and I pick it up, it could be the party of the second part trying to communicate with me, but could he do it if I get another new unlisted?"

So go ahead and plunge a dagger, Jerome, because what I just told you is more or less along the lines of your father's personal thinking. And may I inform you, darling, that the father who is doing this thinking is also the same father who two seconds ago only wanted in his heart of hearts to say hello to you and wish his cutie fellow Happy High Holidays?

Sonny boy, I will tell you something. You got my permission to stab me in a vital organ for passing comment, but I want you to hear with your own two ears my appraisal of the foregoing situation. Because the answer is it's not nice. Jerome, when I see behavior like this, I have to say to myself it is not nice. And thank God I still got the strength in my body to say it. But don't look at *me*, Jerome—because your father did not make the rules, even if the rule is it's definitely not.

And so long as we are discussing the philosophy in this particular department, Jerome, I will tell you something else. Objectively speaking, in my personal opinion your whole area code should be ashamed of itself to have an operator that's got the unmitigated gall to say to a senior citizen get lost. Because in so many words, darling, this is just what the snip up there in 603 said. For shame, Jerome, for shame! And to a person of your father's years and age.

Are you listening to me, darling? To your own flesh and blood, a total stranger says get lost! So tell me, boychik, this is what they teach them in your area code? Or did she get some coaching from a mutual party of our acquaintance who at this juncture I your father will leave unnamed? In so many words, take a walk? I want you to tell me, Jerome, what kind of a person says take a walk to the father of the child?

Because I hope I do not have to remind you that the father who heard these words said to him is also the same father who would lay down his life for his cutie boy, please God I should only be alive and well to do it when you got nothing better planned and you decide in your mind it's time to ask.

Look, darling, if God makes a miracle and you find the strength to call me, who knows, maybe you could afford to take an extra two seconds to give me the figures on what it costs you in so many dollars and cents to get an operator to talk like this to a person of my advanced years, never mind if I told her it was an emergency and also that the party in question is my very own child. Listen, would the woman divulge the first digit? You are down to her on your hands and knees, but is this a normal area code with a single shred of human decency?

Boychik, I am sitting here and I am thinking certain thoughts to myself. So are you interested in the nature of your father's current thinking? Because the answer is if a certain person wants to be a hermit, well and good—then let him go live where they don't have an area code to begin with. But barring this contingency, I say that so long as you continue to maintain your permanent residence in 603, I think that I your father have a perfect right to be informed as to the rest of the particulars after these three digits!

Tell me, darling, did you ever stop to consider all of the ramifications of the situation we are dealing with here? So stop to think and tell me what if, for instance, it was a question of in sickness or in health? I want you to think about this, Jerome. I want you to consider it very carefully. They come in here and they shoot your father in the head. So like any normal person, I rush to the telephone to call you up and tell you the news. But what is the upshot in the situation we are considering? What is in this case the net result? Believe me, your father didn't have to go to college to describe to you the net result. Because the answer is it's some snip up there in 603 which says to me when I am bleeding to death in so many words get lost!

Okay, so don't excite yourself, Jerrychik.

I promise you, all is forgiven, all is forgotten. And besides, it was only for the sake of argument I said it could be a question of in sickness or in health. So far they didn't come in here yet and shoot me. All right, you never know, but so far they didn't. Meanwhile, thank God it was only a question of hello and good-bye, my sonny boy should live and be well. I give you my written guarantee, Jerome, this is all your father had scheduled for the agenda, Happy High Holidays and hello and good-bye. In two seconds flat, the whole deal would have been over and done with, and you would have lived to tell the tale.

So go pick up a hammer and bang me on the head with it because your father was going crazy to hear his sonny boy's voice. Cutie guy, you know what? I only hope and pray I am alive to see the day when vice versa is the case. Please God, Heaven should make a miracle and your father should live that long, you won't have to worry, his number is in the book. Believe me, you would not have to talk yourself blue in the face, Jerome. You would not have to stand on your left ear and dance a jig and then hear my particular area code say to my son, "That's cute, that's nice, now take a walk."

So what is it now, darling?
First, it was your own room.
Next, it was your own business.
So now, in the final analysis, season after season, it's what?
Sonny boy, can your father give you a piece of his personal advice? You promise you wouldn't excite yourself if your father talks to you from the bottom of his heart of hearts? Because I am here to tell you, darling, sometimes your father does not know if he dares to open his mouth with you. But who can breathe with this on my chest, such a burden it's like a big stone? So go get a hammer and hit me with it, but meanwhile it is on your father's chest and he's got to get it off.

Sweetie boy, you know what it means where it says enough is enough? It means you do not go overboard! It means whatever the department, it gets handled accordingly. Because there comes a time in every life when enough is definitely enough. And you know something? Your father did not have to go to college to tell you this is the rule. But go look it up for yourself, it's there in black and white. You name me the department, the answer is you don't go overboard, the rule is enough is enough. Like with the woman who goes up to the judge, for instance, you heard about this, Jerome? So this woman says to this judge, "You'll give me a divorce," and the judge says back to her, "At your age you want a divorce? You are how old, ninety, ninety-five?" And the woman says to him, "Ninety-seven last July." So the judge says to her, "You come to me now, ninety-seven last July?" You hear this, Jerome? That judge says to this woman, "Why come to me now, a person who could any instant drop dead?"

Jerome darling, I want you to know what this woman said to this judge. Sweetheart, are you listening with both ears? She said to this man, "Because enough is enough."

This is wisdom, darling. I don't have to tell you, this is wisdom. Granted, you are a genius in your own right. But even a genius could live and learn. Even a brilliant man like that judge could. Believe me, Jerrychik, that woman didn't have to go to college and study at the feet of no Einstein to teach that judge what it's all about. And the man was an educated man, Jerome. But just ask yourself, did he or did he not have a lot to learn?

Boychik, this is your father's advice to you from your father's heart of hearts. In words of one syllable, darling, there comes a time when you have to say to yourself enough is enough. But let's face it, who am I to open my mouth and try to teach a genius like yourself? Listen, just because I am the father and know from bitter experience, does this make me entitled to tell you what it's all about? Forget even that I am the elder, Jerome. Forget even that I as your father would jump off the highest building for you. It still doesn't give me the right to come along and spell out the facts of life for a person who is a genius, even if it just so happens he doesn't know which end is up.

But meanwhile, boychik, your father knows what he knows, and he didn't wait around for some professor to come along and spell out the facts of life. You name me the subject, Jerome, every college in the world will tell you there is one rule that is first and foremost, and for your information it's the one which says enough is definitely enough. Granted, a genius has a perfect right to think to himself, "I am a genius and I just discovered a subject where the rule is enough is never enough." You think your father doesn't understand this, Jerome? You think your father doesn't realize that with a genius the brain gets all balled up and it says to itself, "I just found a subject where all bets are off"?

So just for argument's sake, sweetheart, let's consider this particular situation. Because your father is willing to go along with you and consider the question from all sides. Like just suppose I pick a subject off the top of my cuff and we go ahead and examine it like two civilized adults. So how about for instance *PRIVACY* maybe? Let's for instance consider a person who says to you he has got to have his *PRIVACY* or else. So for two seconds, Jerome, you and your father will make believe that this is our subject, *P-R-I-V-A-C-Y.*

Now tell me, darling, did your father know the one to pick? Because don't worry, Jerrychik, this subject your father could put his hands on it for you *blindfolded* even with his eyes shut and the room is pitch-black. Not to mention he could also spell it for you backwards and sideways and meanwhile tell you it still comes out the same thing, which is *G-E-T L-O-S-T*. But God forbid your father should dare to spell for a person who is a genius and is supposed to know how to spell for himself.

Listen, pussycat, you don't have to stand on ceremony with me, I promise you. Go ahead, whenever you're ready, I'm ready. Go get a hammer or a dagger, whichever it wouldn't be too big of an effort for you to get. Believe me, sweetheart, as a genius and as a brilliant child, you got a perfect right to go ahead and get whatever pleases you. I say God willing you could even spare the time to get up and go look for it, maybe you could lay your hands on a red-hot poker and put out both my eyes with it if this is what will make you feel better. Because you know what, Jerome? Your father just heard himself mention the subject of privacy, so he doesn't deserve whatever you decide in your mind is the worst punishment.

Maybe you should call the FBI, Jerome.

So call the FBI because your father had the gall to talk to you from the bottom of his heart of hearts.

Do you hear me, Jerome? I am waiting for whatever punishment in your brilliant opinion would be the one I couldn't take. Because if just breathing your father makes such a loud noise you couldn't hear yourself think, all you got to do is pick up the telephone and tell them you want to report me. So you'll call the G-men instead of the FBI if the FBI answers and they tell you right this minute they're so busy they couldn't take the case.

Listen, Jerome darling, I want to give you every assurance your father would not blame you for one instant if you went and got another new unlisted on top of the one you just got. But why knock yourself out, darling? Use your common sense. You think your father would stand by and let you have to go all the way down to the telephone company and wait around to all hours until they get good and ready to inform you as to the ins and outs of your new digits? Believe me, cutie guy, you only have to ask and your father will spare you all this heartache. Because even if with just my mouth breathing, it's so loud you couldn't bear it, forget the phone company, all you got to do is speak up. Do you think I your father would deny you one shred of your happiness for one single instant? So why hesitate? A signal is all your father asks for. You wouldn't even have to lift a finger if the racket the blood in my veins makes happens to constitute such a terrible perturbance to your privacy you don't get the peace and quiet to be a genius. You could wink, darling. Lifting a finger, I definitely don't recommend it. Who knows, you might strain something—it's not worth it to take a chance. One wink, boychik, and all your worries will be over. One wink will be perfectly sufficient—believe me. Because your father will take it from there, your father will do all the running, whereas you yourself could just sit back and relax and forget it. Don't worry, you wouldn't even have to give me a whole wink if you decide in your mind you don't feel like it. Darling, you could give me maybe a mini-wink if this is your decision. Because I guarantee you, sweetheart, one mini-wink and already your father will be racing up the stairs of this building, hoping and praying in his heart of hearts the management didn't put no fence around the roof. So I apologize, Jerome, your father when he moved in didn't have the foresight to go take a look in the first place.

But do I make myself clear, darling? Answer me, it is not going in one ear and out the other? Because I want you to know that your father could not kill himself fast enough if this is what it takes to make sure his sonny boy gets every last ounce of all the bliss he's got coming to him. But I ask you, pussycat, solitude? Are you telling me forever and forever solitude and seclusion is what it takes? Because I am willing to learn, sweetheart, so tell me. So show me where it says solitude and seclusion is the same thing as happiness, and meanwhile one peep out of anybody who adores you to pieces is such a tragedy you couldn't stand it. In black and white, Jerome, show me where this is written. Because as dumb as your father is, he is still keeping an open mind. But until you get ready to show me, in the interim don't excite yourself, darling, your father just gave you his solemn promise. If a telephone call or a postcard or a letter is such a tumult for you that you couldn't take it, even if it's only for hello and good-bye and I hope I didn't disturb you, then relax, pussycat, don't worry, one mini-wink from you will settle the whole affair. Do you hear me? One mini-wink and your father will be only too happy and glad to make you a present of his own dead body. And you know what? You wouldn't even have to thank me for it if you're too busy being a hermit and a genius.

Are you listening to me, boychik? Are you paying strict attention? Your father is not talking just to hear himself talk. Because I can't rest for a single solitary instant until I make sure in my heart of hearts you heard me. Listen, maybe you should write it down as to the fact that your father is ready and willing to go to his grave in case his presence here on the earth doesn't give his boychik all the privacy he needs. Also, make a note that a full wink is utterly uncalled for. A little wiggle of the eyelid like you are maybe just thinking of winking but are altogether too tired to do it, I promise you your father will run next door to another building if, God forbid, it turns out that this one here got a fence on the roof. Sweetheart, I only hope and pray the upshot is I don't have to keep you waiting. As God is my judge, I'm sorry, but at my years and age, a fence, who knows, maybe I couldn't climb over it and meanwhile there's nobody up there waiting to give me a boost. But even if the next building it's the same story, don't worry, darling, there's buildings up and down the block, and your father will just keep looking until something works out.

This, sweetheart, is my solemn promise to you. And all I got to say is that I am down on my hands and knees thanking God that your father still got the strength in his body to give you his sworn statement in writing. But, believe me, Jerome, if in all these years this is what you needed, you only had to say so. Because it's just like with the man who goes to get the suit. So he says to the tailor, "You'll make me a suit— whatever it costs, it costs, I want the best, so don't worry." And the tailor says to him, "Okay, I'm sparing nothing. The cloth I'm getting special from Borneo, the thread I'll have made up in China, and for the buttons I am thinking in terms of this yak they got in Turkey, buttons from the horns of that yak." So the man says to the tailor, "This sounds to me like a wonderful suit, so when can I get it?" and the tailor says to him, "A production like this, from here and from there, everything made up to order, we're talking six, eight months *minimum.*" So the man says, "Six, eight months! How can I wait six, eight months if I got a bar mitzvah this Saturday and I was thinking of wearing the suit?"

Jerome darling, would you like to listen with your own two ears to what that tailor said to that man? Because this is what he said to him. He said, "You need it, you'll get it."

So do I make myself clear, Jerome? Why stand on ceremony? You'll wiggle your eyelid a little and in two seconds your father will take himself right out of the picture.

Meanwhile, who knows, maybe I am jumping to too many conclusions. Maybe 603 wasn't working right because of the High Holy Days, such a strain all of a sudden on the electricity. Let's face it, you got sons and daughters galore calling all day down here from all the different area codes, and meanwhile your father is the only person who is calling in the opposite direction, maybe I got some kind of funny hookup and it wasn't even 603 in the first place! But be this as it may, you still do not say go get lost to a person when he is asking you a perfectly civilized question. Listen, darling, please God they don't get fired up there in 603 and come down here to 305 looking. Because I can tell you, with a mouth on them like the one your father heard, they don't hire you so fast in this area code. Not even if you got in your pocket the personal recommendation of a genius!

Jerrychik sweetie, it's forgotten and forgiven, so let's forgive and forget it. Meanwhile, it's the High Holidays again, so is this the right time for bitterness and recrimination? Sweetie boy, it's water under the bridge. So let's do ourselves a favor and change the conversation. It's a fresh start, boychik. So what if it's another whole year down the crapper and everything is still under par at your end of the bargain? You think your father is keeping score with regard to the question of who sends who cards and letters, never mind who doesn't even place a simple phone call? So big deal if everybody else in 305 is getting. You think I don't know I don't have the right to expect a little decency and consideration when it could always happen you might get a rupture from lifting the wrong pencil? Listen, perish the thought that your father should even look twice at a mailman. Why kid ourselves? Who remembers what one of them even looks like anymore, it's been so many years since your father had the pleasure.

Listen, darling, before you forget, with your own two hands you better check around for the nearest blunt instrument. Because I hear myself talk to you and what is it but criticism after criticism? Promise me, Jerome, you won't spend too much money. So long as it's good and heavy, go ahead and make the investment and then give it to me right between the eyes or on the back of my head, whichever you decide in your mind is more convenient. Because here I am, writing to bring you High Holiday greetings, and what am I bringing you but recrimination after recrimination in spite of my honest intentions. And even if it's all for your own benefit, Jerome, I still say shame on me, shame on me! Look, when you get through with the blunt instrument, you should leave instructions for them to put your father in the gas chamber and keep him on bread and water. No leniency, Jerome—your father didn't earn in his lifetime one iota! The gas chamber and then the rubber hose, Jerome, even this is still too good for a person of my caliber.

Sonny boy, can you find it in your heart of hearts to wipe the slate clean? Because so far as your father is concerned, from this very instant it's a whole new ball game. It's like we're starting from the outset, okay? Whatever I said, promise me, darling, you erased it. I mean, it just occurred to me you maybe sent a little something but you forgot about the zip code. A genius like you with so much on his brain, so who's got room in a thing like that for so many extra numbers? So ask yourself, you leave off the zip code, do the morons deliver? Believe me, you're just lucky if they don't also come after you to your own personal address and tear you limb from limb.

It's the truth, Jerrychik—nothing is these days what it used to be, not in any shape, manner, or form. It's not like it was in the old days. Tell me, darling, you remember how it was in the old days when you were at the top of the heap and your father was down here up in the penthouse? So guess who is in the penthouse now. Because the Allen people is the answer! And after them, it's the Krantzes which is second on the list to get in there. But in the good old days, it was all different. These days, maybe you got the right idea, a hermit. Believe me, don't think your father hasn't considered. I look at it the way it is these days and I have to say to myself, "Sol, maybe we should all go live where the operator hears they are looking for you and she tells them whoever they are, forget it, take a walk."

These days, Jerome, it's things of every description, and just a fraction of it is enough to make your father vomit. Go look if you don't believe me. Like even in the kindergarten the teacher says to the children it's milk time, take out your milk and drink it. But, lo and behold, nowadays there is always one child which wouldn't touch it. So the one I have in mind, his name is Arnold, and the teacher says to him, "Arnold, drink your milk." But how does Arnold answer this woman? You wouldn't believe this, Jerome, but he says to her, "I wouldn't drink the goddamn milk."

This, Jerome, is how in this day and age a child answers. So I don't have to tell you the teacher goes right to the telephone and she calls the child's mother and she says to this woman to come over. So when the woman gets there, the teacher says to the mother, "I want you to hear this," and then she says to Arnold, "Arnold, drink your milk."

Jerome, as I live and breathe, this is how the child answers her back the second time. He says to her, "Not only I wouldn't drink the goddamn milk, but you could also shove it up your tookis."

Did you hear this, Jerome? Can you in all your born days believe it? So you know what happens next? Darling, that teacher turns to that mother and she says to the woman, "Did you hear what your son just said?" Jerome, I am ashamed to say it, but that mother turns to that teacher and says to her, "Sure, I heard him—fuck him."

Sonny boy, this is what today's world is. Don't worry, boychik, your father noticed. But speaking of the subject of mothers, Jerome, I just remembered something. Because maybe you called to say hello and I wasn't here to answer. So even if you called at night, it could have happened, darling, your father not here to pick it up because of a certain Mrs. Pinkowitz, and I am not ashamed to admit it.

I know I don't need to remind you that your father is a grown man, Jerome. In case you didn't realize, your father is an adult. So as a grown man and as an adult, excuses I don't have to make to anyone, a certain resident of 603 included. Sonny boy, these are the facts of life, and it wasn't your father which invented them.

So now you know. So it was only one night, but now you know, so sue me, so call Clarence Darrow and sue me.

Listen, Jerrychik, between father and son, honesty is the best policy, this is my personal opinion. So it's speaking along these lines, darling, that it is time to come to the subject of Gert Pinkowitz. Do I make myself crystal clear, Jerome? Because even in my health and my years, I thank God that romance is not totally out of the picture. But first and foremost, Jerome, your father is the type of person who gives comfort where comfort is due. Now you take the creature previously referred to, for your information this is a person with enough heartache for an army. If you can believe it, darling, even worse than your father, this person suffers and suffers. Not in all your born days could you even guess! But who knows, maybe I already told you what a svelte and adorable creature Gert Pinkowitz is, not to mention that she is also an individual which could give your father cards and spades when it comes to the question of how much agony a human being could stand at the hands of their own flesh and blood. And guess what, boychik—just like your own personal father, it's a son which is the source as to where every last shred of Gert Pinkowitz's tragedy is coming from.

Tell me, sweetheart, did you ever think you would live to see the day when I your father would run smack into such a terrific coincidence? Listen, I know it's a small world, but a thing like this is definitely unbelievable—right here in this same building a creature just like your father which also got a son who you could die from.

But who knows if I already made mention? Maybe I did or maybe I didn't in a prior communication. On the other hand, darling, since I didn't write to you the day before yesterday, then I have to say to myself, "Sol, face facts, you didn't." Because when you stop to consider the arithmetic, boychik, it's only twenty-four hours since the woman first set foot on the premises and established her residence in this building.

So okay, sweetie darling, your father has been seeing a certain svelte person, it is nothing to be ashamed of. So what if it is a whirlwind romance? You think I can't see where the arithmetic speaks for itself? Meanwhile, it couldn't be avoided, two creatures which are both available and got so much agony in mutual.

This is fate, boychik. This is what it means when you ask them for the whys and the wherefores and they say to you it's fate and you could stand on your left ear but you couldn't avoid it. Like with the fella who says to his brother, "So go to Miami and don't worry, I promise you I'll watch the cat, it'll be all right, in its whole life the cat wouldn't get better looking after." So the brother who's so crazy about his cat goes to Miami, Jerome, and when he gets there, the first thing he does is he picks up the telephone and he calls his brother which is still in New York and he says to him, "So how's the cat?"

Listen, Jerome. Because I want you to hear how the brother in New York answers the brother in Miami when he says to him, "The cat's dead."

So naturally it's a long silence with no one talking. And then the brother in Miami says, "You're some brother I got! I ask you how's the cat, and you answer me, bing bang, the cat's dead! What kind of a way is this to say a thing to a brother, bing bang, the cat's dead? Believe me, you should learn how to say a thing when a person asks you a question —not just bing bang, no preliminaries, no fanfares, the cat's dead! Next time somebody asks you, you say you took the cat up to the roof for a little breath of air and she got a sniffle and you got her in bed and in a few days, please God, she'll be up and around as good as new. So then when I telephone back in a couple of hours to ask you what's what with the cat, you say to me, well, there's complications, you're getting in a specialist, but with God's help she will pull through—not no bing bang, no overtures, the cat's dead! So when I call again to check with you what the specialist said, this is when you say to me you never know, there's no guarantee, the cat you had to rush to the hospital two seconds ago and even with the top men in medical science, lo and behold, the cat passed away. This is how a brother speaks to a brother, not bing bang, the cat's dead!"

So the brother that's in New York, Jerome, he says to the brother in Miami, "Look, I'm sorry, next time I'll know better, I promise you." So this is when the brother who is in Miami says to the brother in New York, "Forget it. So it's only a cat. Meanwhile, more important, how's Mother?"

Jerome darling, are you listening to this? Did you hear when the brother in Miami says to him, "So meanwhile how is Mother?" Now pay attention, darling, because I want you to also hear what the brother in New York says to the brother in Miami, because this is what he says to him verbatim. He says, "Mother?" He says, "Well, I'll tell you, Mother I took up to the roof for a little breath of air."

This is fate, boychik—this is fate and there is no two ways about it. So between your father and Gert Pinkowitz it's the same story—it's fate whichever direction you look at it from. And don't kid yourself, two individuals in our situation, it couldn't be avoided.

Okay, so at this point everything is still in the dating stage. But even with Romeo and Juliet themselves, you had to have your dating stage before it got around to this and that and the other thing. Believe me, your father is a patient man, Jerome—thirty-six hours, forty-eight hours, for a living doll like this, a person so svelte, your father could make an exception and wait to count his chickens.

But for some things, sweetheart, patience is already beside the point, patience wouldn't make the big difference.

Sonny boy, Jerome darling, do me a favor and listen to me—because your father is here to tell you that in certain departments not even the patience of a saint would do the trick.

So call the G-men, Jerome. And if the G-men wouldn't give you total satisfaction, then maybe you could get somewhere with the Supreme Court or the Food and Drug. Darling, just so long as you know your father couldn't help himself, he has to speak up. *Enough is enough!*

So first you will take your time and decide which one you want to call to come and get me. And in the meanwhile, your father gives you his promise, he wouldn't budge from this very spot. Also, I wouldn't even put up a fight when they come with the handcuffs.

Jerome, I am giving you every assurance, darling, your father will go quietly, he wouldn't even begin to make a fuss.

But if you are asking me to keep my mouth shut when it comes to the question of the envelope, from the bottom of my heart of hearts, I am sorry, Jerome—but this I could not promise you, not even if they made a law.

Cutie fellow, pussycat, stop to ask yourself—your father gets to the end of this letter, what comes next? Because the answer is the envelope. So just like it was first the cat and then the mother, here is another one where it is a question of fate and you couldn't avoid it. Sonny boy, you leave off the zip code and they don't deliver. So ask yourself, how much leeway does your father get, could he leave off two thirds of a person's whole name?

No, he couldn't. But also could your father write it any different from how he has been writing it all these years and years?

Darling, this is a question you don't need your father to answer.

Just so you know in advance that I your father tried to give this question every last ounce of consideration. But meanwhile, Jerome, the answer is forget it with this J.D. thing—because even if they made a law, not on a bet could your father ever do it! You hear me, darling? Not even if the G-men took the case and came down here with all their badges. Not even if the Supreme Court said to me, "Sol, it went nine to nothing against you, so for life it's Leavenworth, forget it."

Jerrychik, your father is an old man. But whatever the future holds, he would spend every minute of it in chains before he would go along with you on what you did to your wonderful name.

Listen, kiddo, you could go to Woolworth's and you could buy thumbtacks. Darling, you could even buy carpet tacks if this is your particular preference. So go ahead and buy whichever variety that pleases you and come stick them in my elbows. Okay, so if the elbows don't interest you, I'll give you a choice, you can choose the kneecaps instead. So choose the kneecaps, Jerome. Believe me, if this is what you decide in your mind, then this is what you decide in your mind— kneecaps, your father wouldn't for two seconds stand in your way. Tell me, boychik, are you getting the picture? Because the picture is this, Jerome—in every last department your father is only too happy and glad to go along with you, but this J.D. thing you did to your name, this he could never get used to! This thing here is where he has to draw the line!

I'm sorry, sweetheart, but J.D. I couldn't go along with, not even if they came down here with their handcuffs and shot me down like a dog. Because by me, darling, the name you were born with, you could go ahead and ask anyone, they'll tell you it is a symphony of music to the most discriminating of ears.

I promise you, sonny boy, you could go to the ends of the earth and you still couldn't improve on it. Just to listen to it! So are you listening? *Jerome David.*

Now tell me that's not the last word when it comes to a symphony of names.

But a thing like J.D., Jerome, since when is a thing like this a name?

Cutie guy, you want to kill your father with this thing of J.D., then go ahead and kill me with it. But meanwhile don't ask me to write it on the envelope. Because if this is what you are asking, darling, then you are asking for what your father could not give!

Stop to think, pussycat. Promise me you won't excite yourself and you will stop to think for all of two seconds.

So first of all, answer me the following question. There isn't a thoroughfare called Jerome in the Bronx? As thoroughfares go, it's not one which down through the ages is a thoroughfare that is famous and respected?

So is this a simple question? And does a person have to be a genius to give it a simple answer?

Sonny boy, take my word for it, when the city fathers sat down to pick a name, they didn't say to themselves, "So let's pick a shtunky one for this one here."

Okay, I admit it, so maybe it was the borough fathers which sat down. It's still the same principle. Believe me, darling, right here in the Sunshine State, where I your father bring you High Holy Day greetings from, on Lincoln Avenue they got a Jerome Florists. On Lincoln Avenue, darling. So am I talking about a first-class thoroughfare? Look for yourself, as big as life, a Jerome Florists. And it's not just here or there, darling—because it's *Lincoln* Avenue, not to mention also a corner location!

But listen, a father does not know a son? I need all of a sudden a mindreader to tell me what's in my sonny boy's head? So arrest me because I happen to know my own child. Tell them to come and lock up your father on bread and water in Death Row because I happen to be an expert on my sonny boy's brain. Meanwhile, you can stand on your left ear but you cannot change the rule that says it takes a father to know a son. Jerome, they could come and cut off both my arms.

They could chop me up in little pieces. But I your father am here to tell you, a father knows a son.

Guess what, darling. Are you listening to me, Jerome? To the fathers of this world, a son is what is eating your heart out—and you don't need no Walter Winchell to come along and give you this particular news.

But don't think I don't know I should learn to keep my mouth shut. Believe me, Jerome, they should come and cut your father's throat from ear to ear until he learns to bite his tongue. Lincoln Avenue—I had to go ahead and say Lincoln Avenue. So does a father have to go to college to find out what is in his sonny boy's head? Don't kid yourself, Jerome, your father can hear every last word you are thinking. Does a father know a son? I guarantee you, darling, your father could quote you your exact phraseology, word for bitter word.

"So how come they didn't name me Lincoln?"

Boychik, tell me the truth, was that verbatim? Open your heart of hearts to me and tell me, did your father just quote you every single word?

Don't tell me the answer because I know the answer. And you know why, Jerome? Because a father knows a son! And you know what else, darling? The more brilliant the brain of the child, the more you cannot please him—not even if you did a dance and stood on your left ear.

Kiddo, this is what your father knows. You could talk yourself blue in the face, but this is what your father knows.

Oh, but you really got a lot to complain about, Jerome—a father which gave you a gorgeous name and then has the gall to write it down on an envelope instead of something it makes him heartsick to even mention out loud. Believe me, I never saw a boy with more to complain about. But don't kid yourself, sonny, it's no picnic for me neither. I promise you, all I need is an excuse and I'll show you it's a subject I couldn't drop fast enough. But so long as you didn't give me an excuse yet, it couldn't hurt to mention a few comparisons.

Like take, for instance, a certain Mrs. Roth who lives in this building. So tell me, darling, does she have a relation who is a Philip or a P.? Or look instead at the Bellow people who got such a nice ocean view on ten. Ask yourself, do they have a second cousin named Saul or a second cousin named S.? The Malamuds on six, a one bedroom facing front, we're talking in this case about a Bernard in the family or a B.?

Please God, darling, you stopped and took a good look at these questions, and then you answered each and every one of them from deep down in your heart of hearts.

But now we come to your father, Jerome. Do you appreciate what I am saying to you, Jerome—now we come to your own flesh and blood? Who is *also* a resident of this building! Who *also* has to live with these people! Who *also* has to answer to them! And what, pray tell, is the question?

Jerome, the question is, "J.D., Mr. Ess—what, please be so kind, is a J.D.?"

Cutie guy, pay attention—down here in 305 a Saul they heard of, a Philip, a Bernard. But since when did somebody in 305 ever hear of a J.D.? Stop to think, boychik. Because in this building this is the question your father has to answer to morning, noon, and night. And you know for how many years now? Day in and day out, you know for how many?

This is why I say to you, Jerome, thank God for Gert Pinkowitz. This is why I have to say to you thank God for the heartache she's got with her own kid, because for your father it's a lesson to see there's those that got worse—even if I wouldn't wish it on my worst enemy.

Twenty-four hours, Jerome, the woman is in the building only twenty-four hours, and already the gang of them found better to talk about!

But believe me, I don't wish the woman ill. For Gert Pinkowitz, your father's got nothing but hearts and flowers. It's just I couldn't take it no more—J.D. this and J.D. that, years and years, day in and day out, the whole building couldn't leave you in peace. Besides, darling, svelte as Gert is, the woman is made of iron. Of *iron.*

Listen, Jerome, forget Gert Pinkowitz for all of two seconds. Because your father requires your utmost attention. Cutie fellow, will you give me your very utmost? Because it is time for your father to go down on his hands and knees to you again and beg you to please in your heart of hearts reconsider.

Jerome, listen to me, where does your father live, which building?

Since years and years ago when he moved down here, has he ever for one instant lived in a different residential?

All right, so what would you call this place—a building like any other building?

Jerome, don't make me have to remind you.

Sweetheart, we are talking the Seavue Spa Oceanfront Garden Arms and Apartments. So do you need reminding which is your father's residential? Because for how many years now have I been telling you, but do you ever listen?

Other children listen, Jerome. The Allen kid, Woody, *he* listens. *Philip* listens, *Saul* listens—and for your information, so does *Bernard!* Believe me, Jerome, everybody in here, they got a kid which they can count on to listen—the Krantzes do and the Plains do, and so do the Sheldons and the Friedmans and the Elkins and the Wallaces and the Segals and the Jaffes and the Barretts and the Bernsteins and the Halberstams! And notice that I am not even mentioning the Robbins family and their Harold, and the Potoks and their Chaim. You think the Wouks don't have a Herman that listens?

The Mailer people, their Norman *listens.*

The Kordas got a Michael, and *he* listens!

The Apples with their Max, the Michaels people with their Leonard, the Stones with their Irving—every last one of these children is a child which listens!

And did I even get to the Markfields and the Richlers and the Liebowitzes? Ozick, you think this is a girl which doesn't listen? The Charyns, you heard of the Charyns? So they also got a child which listens—and his name is *Jerome* and not no J., into the bargain!

Jerome darling, I didn't even begin to scratch the surface yet of who's who in the Seavue Spa Oceanfront Garden Arms and Apartments! But answer me, is there a single solitary one of them which doesn't have a relation in the literature business? And exclusive of the exception of your father and Mrs. Pinkowitz, tell me if it's not a kid which doesn't take to heart what you say to him and *listens!*

In the whole building, they all got what to listen to them—all except your father and Gert Pinkowitz, all except her with her Thomas and me with my J.D., the two big geniuses which wouldn't listen!

And look at who I didn't even discuss yet—not to mention the Millers and the Hellers and the Ephrons and the Kosinskis! Do the Paleys have a Grace? So tell me, Jerome, does the girl listen?

The Olsens got a Tillie, and the Golds got a Herbert, and the Uris family, they got there a wonderful, sweet-natured boy, a Leon—but what else do they have which your own father doesn't have?

I will answer you in words of one syllable, Jerome. Because the answer is *a child which listens!*

Jerome darling, your father is hoarse from screaming. Even though your father is writing and not talking, Jerome—I promise you, your father has just lost his voice from the screaming. So call the Justice Department, your father had to shout. Because to make himself heard with you, who could talk like a civilized person?

Darling, sonny darling, lean close, open your ears up wide, I couldn't speak no more above a whisper.

So who is in the penthouse here when it used to be your father who was up there? And you know the answer why?

Because they got a child which listens! And you know what, Jerome? His name's not no W. Allen neither!

But far be it from me your father to pass comment. After all, your father is only your father, Jerome. He is only the person which has to live here with these people and answer to them. He is only the person which has to face these people day in and day out because in his particular area code you don't get away with saying to the whole wide world, "Go take a walk."

Jerrychik, sweetie boy, is it asking too much for you to look into your heart of hearts and try to see what is going on down here from your father's side of the standpoint? Do I live in the Seavue Spa Oceanfront Garden Arms and Apartments or do I live in the woods in a tree? And as to this residential, Jerome, we're talking from one floor to the next what? Are we talking people which got kids in cloaks and suits, or are we talking people which got kids in books?

The works, Jerome—the cream of the crop of the literature business is right here in this very building, and I want to remind you that it is your father, and not you, which has to live with them!

But did you ever stop to think, "For my father, considering that he is a person of his age and his years, I, Jerome David, am going to ask myself what is it like to live in a setup where everybody's got somebody in the business?"

Darling, your father will put two and two together for you and answer you with one word. Are you ready for this?

C-O-M-P-A-R-I-S-O-N-S.

Comparisons, Jerome. Notice, like *privacy,* your father can also spell this one too. And, believe me, it comes out the opposite of GET LOST.

So you are not a genius in your own right and I got to draw for you a diagram? You need me to write down for you Saul this and Saul that,

Phillie this and Phillie that—not to mention Woody, Woody, Woody morning, noon, and night?

You could live to be a thousand, Jerome, you still wouldn't see any letup. But meanwhile does your father ever get to get a word in? Does he have Jerome this and Jerome that the way he used to have in the old days when guess who lived in the penthouse? But God forbid the facts of life should be brought to your attention. So stick a spear in me and break it off in my ribs because your father has the nerve to plead with you for your attention when it is the facts of life which is the subject on the table. Boychik, you know what it means where it says the facts of life? It means somebody has to live with them. So just for argument's sake, darling, between the two of us, guess which one got elected to do it!

Listen, in 603, let's not kid ourselves, so it's no big deal to walk around with two initials. Even three or four, maybe up there in your area code they still wouldn't look at you cross-eyed. But in 305, Jerome, I hope I don't have to tell you, they find out you got a kid who calls himself J.D., you couldn't live long enough, you'll never hear the end of it. Meanwhile, who's complaining? Believe me, I know I got plenty to be grateful for. Because when you hear what Gert Pinkowitz has got with *her* kid, you'll see why your father is only too happy and glad to sit down and count his blessings.

But you'll promise me, boychik, you'll reconsider? Because this is all your father asks of you, two whole seconds of heartfelt reconsideration. Darling, I am down on my hands and knees to you asking. God forbid in all my life I should ever ask again. Please, darling, if you hear me even thinking to ask, you'll run out and get railroad spikes and hammer them into my shins. But meanwhile, for all of two seconds, Jerome, I am begging you to sit down with yourself and like a civilized person you will go into conference with your heart of hearts and you will say to yourself, "For my father's sake, who would let me hammer even rusty railroad spikes into his shins for me, I, Jerome David, am going to think this question over and change my spiteful ways."

Cutie sonny, what your father is asking you can ask anybody and they will tell you it is not too much to ask. Look, you'll let your better judgment be your guide—and whatever you decide in your mind, just remember that your father knows you will be a good boy and come to your senses and decide the right thing. And if I ever utter one more word in this department, may I inherit the Waldorf-Astoria and drop dead in every room.

By the bye, sweetheart, you'll never guess what the Roth woman said to me last week. Because when she said it to me, right away your father said to himself, "I can't wait to tell the sonny boy what this woman is saying to me, please God he will go along with his father's thinking and realize that you never know where wisdom is going to come from next." So here is the quote. Jerrychik, you'll listen closely and you'll tell me what you think of this quotation. She said, "Mr. Ess, tell me, did you ever stop to realize that when he stood up and had to swear on a stack of Bibles, they said to him, 'Do you, Dwight David Eisenhower,' and so on and so forth? But pay attention, they didn't say to the man no D.D."

Darling, you can't argue with what the woman said. Believe me, I myself stood there and said to myself, "You know, Sol, this woman is speaking the truth—it's right there in the history books in black and white."

Believe me, Jerome, this is wisdom. So whatever the source, I say you've got to hand it to the woman, she spoke wisdom pure and simple, and you don't look a gift horse in the mouth. But if you couldn't bear to hear it, Jerome, if even history isn't good enough for you, then tell them to come down here and take my shoes off and make your father jump on broken glass. All right, I grant you, you didn't decide yet in your own mind that you want them to swear you in as the President of the United States. This your father grants you, this much your father acknowledges. But the principle is still the same thing, Jerome—don't kid yourself, in every way, shape, manner, and form it is still the same principle.

Cutie fellow, sweetie fellow, boychikel mine, go back to the gorgeous name your father gave you and you wouldn't have to hold your breath for the world to be your oyster all over again. This is my written guarantee to you, Jerome. Get rid of this J.D. thing, and I promise you, you'll feel like a brand-new person. And don't think that in two seconds everybody won't notice. Before you know it, they'll all be singing your praises just the way they used to, the whole gang of them in the literature business, not to mention their families and relations. Believe me, darling, they'll all be saying to themselves, "God love him, he's some terrific kid, that kid, look how he did the right thing and made his father happy."

Pay attention, boychik, they are definitely not no dummies, these kids that also went with you into the literature business. And even if there's plenty of them your father looks at and has to say to himself, "That one there, to tell you the truth, I don't see what they see in him," even the worst of them your father can tell you they still got a head on their shoulders and are only too willing to take off their hat to a person which does the right thing when it's a question of his father's wishes. Are you listening to me, sweetheart? They'll hear what you did, and even the Allen kid will step aside and tell you to go back up to the top of the heap again. All it takes is for you to show them you made up your mind to be a serious person with a serious name that makes sense to decent people.

Your father is speaking to you without favoritism, Jerome. Your father is speaking to you the way a Solomon would speak to you if the man was alive to tell you himself. Your father does not play favorites, Jerome. Believe me, your father does not give you one shred of credit you don't deserve. So when he tells you all you got to do is go back to being Jerome David again, your father is giving you his honest appraisal. Darling, please give me some credit for intelligence! Your father doesn't give a person his honest appraisal until he's weighed all of the whys and wherefores. Phillie, Saul, Bernie, and the rest of them, they'll hear what you did and they wouldn't be able to get out of your way fast enough. Are you listening, Jerome? Because I am taking into consideration not just exclusively these youngsters and the Allen kid but also your other top people in this building, which if you look up on sixteen just under the penthouse, you're talking the Robbins family and the Krantz family and the Sheldons. But meanwhile ask yourself, darling, in the case of the aforementioned, is it S. or is it Sidney? Is it J. or is it Judith? And Harold you could ask anybody, it's Harold!

You see what your father is saying to you, boychik? So do me a favor and don't make me repeat myself. Tomorrow morning, first thing, it's a clean slate, okay? Believe me, your father can hear them already, it's such a shout in my heart, it's such music in my ears. "Say hello, everybody, to Solly's terrific cutie guy, Jerome David, a new person!"

And another thing, darling—don't kid yourself, the King of Sweden is no dumbbell neither. Ask anyone. You ask anyone, Jerrychik, they'll be only too happy and glad to tell you the King of Sweden didn't just get off the boat. Go ahead, ask anyone, and they'll tell you the man is paying very close attention to who writes down his name on his book like there's something in it he is proud of and who puts down a name like the whole deal from start to finish was just a lick and a promise. Believe me, the King of Sweden comes along and sees a thing like just

J.D., you think the man can't draw his own conclusions? Cutie guy, you could cut out my tongue for telling you—but your father didn't have to go to college to know the King of Sweden has got eyes in his head, the man could add up two and two. So the man sees where it says you didn't have the heart to put your whole name down, just don't be surprised when he says to himself, "This one here, he's not fooling no King of Sweden nohow!"

But don't look at *me*, Jerome. I promise you, the King of Sweden can see for himself. I told you, I your father did not make the rules, not even the ones which is secondary.

So tell me, sweetheart, the plots I sent you last time, did any of them work out for you? So if in your opinion nothing looked good to you, don't worry, I already got a couple a dozen new ones from keeping my eyes and ears wide open in the card room. Listen, in just my regular Wednesday game there's Charlie Heller, Mort Segal, and Artie Elkin, and between the four of us, believe me, we could fill a whole library from top to bottom. By the bye, darling, I want you to guess what Mortie said to your father only two days ago. Because as God is my witness, Jerome, the man said to me, "Sol, do the child a favor and tell him to get rid of it. My Eric, for instance, he *added*, he didn't take away. So the boy wants a little flourish, a little trim, he *adds* a letter and gets Erich, whereas he meanwhile doesn't let three perfectly good letters go altogether to waste." So Mortie says, "Go tell your kid he could add a thing maybe, like a little trim something over an *e*, whereas David he could make Davidorf—it's up to him. But the principle is you *add*, Sol, you don't take away."

Sonny, to tell you the truth, your father in his own mind never thought of this before. So for what it's worth, boychik, I your father am passing along to you a mere possibility, you don't have to hurry up and make a decision. But to your father's way of thinking, the name Jerome with a little trim on the top of it is definitely not the worst idea in the whole world. So who knows, the King of Sweden might even get a kick out of it. Because if you ask me, the man must have looked at the name Saul and he said to himself, "This here is a name which looks a little skimpy to me, a little fixing up here and there couldn't hurt it. But meanwhile I don't have to put up with just an S. Meanwhile you can see this Saul has got his heart in the right place."

Darling, the upshot of this I don't have to remind you. A medal. Thousands and thousands of dollars and a medal.

Be smart, Jerome. Listen to what Mort Segal says. You *add*, you don't take *away*. Believe me, maybe the man's got nothing but an Erich, but he knows whereof he speaks.

Which reminds me, sweetie boy—before I get to the subject of your father and his new excitement in life, it just this instant dawned on me to tell you that I noticed it's another year but what's what with you and "Merv Griffin?" Cutie fellow, if I have said it to you once, I have said it to you a million times, no business and no pictures is bad enough but no "Merv Griffin" you definitely can't get away with!

You know what you are, Jerome?

Because the answer is you are your own worst enemy!

All right, no pictures is a fact of life your father is learning to live with. So forget pictures. You don't want to have a picture, then don't have a picture. So maybe a genius doesn't have to have a picture. Only days ago I said to Murray Mailer, I said, "Murray, believe me, when you are a genius in your own right, then you will know you don't need a picture." I said to the man, "Listen, Murray, I myself am not questioning if your Norman is a genius. I am just saying if you are one, then you know you could live without pictures."

Jerome, I wouldn't even begin to tell you what the man said to me. But at the Seavue, do they ever give you the least little consideration? Jerome, the man stands there and he says to me, "Sol, this fella Einstein, like with the hair and the sweater and the popeyes? The man wasn't a genius? So tell me, Sol, how come you know what I'm talking about? You met him? You sat down to a meal with the man and broke bread with him? You saw a *picture*—wherever you looked, you saw a *picture*. But pardon me, my friend, I forgot—your kid with the initials is a bigger genius."

So please God Murray Mailer should live and be well, Jerome, but from him, I guarantee you, your father does not need a history lesson. Meanwhile, I say you cannot discount the man totally. Believe me, darling, in this world, whatever the source, a person tells you something you never heard before, then you got to sit down and think it over and give that person credit. So it's the truth, darling, and in my own mind I never stopped to think about it before. But am I ashamed to admit it? So all right, Einstein was a big genius, the biggest—but even him, the biggest genius, he had a picture here, a picture there, pictures, pictures, pictures.

Believe me, sonny boy, I as your father am not holding Murray Mailer up to you. But meanwhile the man knows wherefrom he speaks.

Sweetheart, I want to speak to you as your own father, an individual who does not play favorites. Jerome, you know what? You got on you a face like an angel! Do you hear me, Jerome? An angel!

But if a picture is for you such a trial and tribulation, then I say forget it, darling, you don't have to knock yourself out for no Murray Mailer's benefit, not to mention the millions and millions of fans who would get down on their hands and knees to you to thank you for one single solitary exception.

Believe me, Jerome, I am washing my hands of the whole subject. You don't want a picture? Then don't have a picture! On the one hand no picture, and on the other hand a name like J.D. when that's not a name which makes any sense to anybody down here, these are things that are killing your father, but he never said he couldn't learn to live with them. Whereas the question of no "Merv Griffin," Jerome, *this,* for your information, is a whole different question altogether!

Jerome darling, answer me this. Do I have to tell you what goes on down here when it's four o'clock in the afternoon at the Seavue Spa Oceanfront Garden Arms and Apartments? Answer me, Jerome, I didn't tell you enough times already?

Jerome, it is four o'clock, and where is everybody suddenly running? From the card room, from the pool, from everywhere in sight, where are all these hotshots in such a hurry to get to?

Because the answer, Jerome, is "Merv Griffin!"

You don't believe me, go take a look in their apartments. You could look for yourself if you wouldn't take your father's own word for it. Four o'clock, where are they? They're looking to see who's the lucky family who's got his child on with Merv today and who's the poor shnooks which doesn't!

So stop to think, Jerome—did your father ever once have the pleasure?

But far be it from me to utter one word when it comes to your own father's peace of mind and happiness. Believe me, Jerome, first and foremost, your father is not an individual who asks for himself. So think, Jerome—if not for myself, then who am I asking for?

Darling, please, do me a favor—go into conference with your heart of hearts and ask yourself how you could ask your father such a question when you already know the answer. I promise you, when you know, you know, and you do not require a father to sit down and draw you a diagram. Like the woman who hears the telephone and she goes to pick it up. Did I tell you about this, Jerome? This woman, she goes to pick it up and she says, "Hello?" Just like any normal, civilized person, Jerome, the woman says, "Hello?"

So there's a man there on the other end, Jerome, and I want you to hear what this man says to this woman—because, as God is my judge, he says to her, "I know what your name is and I know where you live and I know you can't wait for me to come over there and tear off every stitch you got on you and throw you down on the floor and do to you every filthy dirty thing I can think of."

You heard this man, Jerome? You heard what this man said to this woman? But now I want you to hear how this woman answers him. Because this is what she says to him, "Darling"—she says—"so you know all this from just hello?"

Jerome, did you hear every word that woman said to that man?

So do me a favor, darling, and don't ask your father any questions when the answer is something you already know.

Sweetheart, I am going to give you some quotes that will interest you —word-for-word verbatim.

Gus Krantz: "So, Mr. Ess, you tell me your little one is too *sensitive* for 'Merv Griffin,' he couldn't go on there and make a little *intelligent* conversation? Tsk, tsk, Mr. Ess, we all under*stand*, believe me. When a child is too *sensitive*, who is it it's always a *tragedy* for? Believe me, Mr. Ess, my heart goes out to you, because for the father it's *really* a tragedy. A mother, she could maybe *live* with it, but a *father*?"

Burt Bellow: "With my own eyes I noticed, Mr. Ess, maybe J.D. stands for a girl and she wants to keep it a secret? Listen, you'll tell your daughter to talk to Merv, the man will figure out an angle. Meanwhile, God love her, ask her if she heard about my Saul, a medal and thousands and thousands of dollars."

Cutie guy, don't excite yourself. So there are worse quotes than the ones I just told you, but does your father even listen? I promise you, I hear it, and it goes in one ear and out the other.

Who listens to these people with their Merv Griffins and their Merv Griffins!

But meanwhile it is the principle of the thing which to I as your father is interesting. And, Jerome, in case you didn't already figure it out for yourself, the principle is it is either "Merv Griffin" or forget it!

Granted, for years in memoriam I tried to shield you with my own body. Granted, what your father has had to go through for you a million fathers couldn't go through. And I also grant you it's still not half of what this woman Gert has got with her high and mighty Thomas. But, Jerome, darling, be a nice boy and make an exception. So what's the big production? You'll pick up the telephone and you'll call the man and you'll say to Merv you thought it over in your mind and you are ready to make an appearance.

Boychik, would your father begin to ask you if he saw even the slightest alternative? So tell them to strap me down and turn on the electricity, your father is asking for your own benefit!

Sonny sweetie, they could go ahead and give me all the volts they got, but your father still wouldn't hesitate to tell you all it takes is a little intelligence even when a person is a genius. But does this mean that to his dying day you haven't got your father's vote? Jerrychik darling, your father will go right down the line with you to his last breath regardless. Meanwhile, ask yourself, is it fair that you who are the child should never meet your father halfway—when he is your father and your elder and would die for you if this is what you demanded? So answer me, for your own father you couldn't sit down with Merv for all of two seconds and make a little civilized conversation? Bing bang and it's over and done with, you can pick yourself up and go back to your 603 and meanwhile your father in his mind could go to his grave in peace and quiet and contentment. Because I want to ask you a question, Jerome. Tell me, so how do you propose I'm supposed to answer these people year in and year out when they come down the next day to the card room and they say to me, "Tsk, tsk, Mr. Ess, we watched and watched, but we didn't see no J.D. on 'Merv Griffin' "?

You want another quote, Jerome? I tried to shield you with my own body, darling, but you want another one?

Okay, here is one from Artie Elkin.

"Tell me the truth, Solly, it was a cut-rate nose job and the girl couldn't ever again show her face in public? Listen, my Stanley is very close to certain very big doctors. You want me to give him a call and see what maybe could be done for her if you know the right people?"

Jerrychik, this is what your father has to live with, quotes like this morning, noon, and night. Whereas one word from you, and it's a whole new ball game. Pay attention, Jerome—you'll call up and say, "Merv, look, I haven't got all day—the answer is yes, so when do you want me?"

So you'll tell them to kill me and bury me alive under boulders,

Jerome, but first you'll do this for your father. Because I am here to tell you, boychik, maybe Gert Pinkowitz is made of iron, but your father definitely isn't.

So the Everest Mountain should fall over on me for remarking, but when they put your father together, darling, they made a mistake and used flesh and blood.

Do you hear me, Jerome? I couldn't take it anymore, every weekday all my life no "Merv Griffin" and meanwhile your father keeps watching and waiting, please God his sonny boy will get some sense in his head and someday see the light!

You want me to quote you Artie Elkin again? Because what the man said to me only this morning you wouldn't believe it unless you heard it for yourself—so I want you to hear this, Jerome, because, believe me, you'll appreciate. Are you listening? The man said to me, "Sol, as to your J.D., did I miss her or didn't I? Four-thirty, four-forty, was she on there or wasn't she? Because maybe I left the room at the inopportune point of departure when I had to go see a man about a dog in the toilet. So was she or wasn't she? Even with the nose, maybe the girl took her chances? So tell me, Sol, what is the terrible verdict?"

Pussycat, what will it cost you to pick up the phone and tell Merv you'll make an exception? As your father, am I or am I not entitled to a civilized answer?

Enough privacy for two seconds, Jerome! It wouldn't kill you! It's only "Merv Griffin!"

Jerome, I have to whisper again, I'm so hoarse from all this screaming. Darling, pay attention, we are talking about a wholesome show for the entire American family. So did you hear me? Please, you'll sit down with the man, you'll say hello and good-bye, take a look at my face—and then you'll get up and walk away on your own two feet, and I promise you, you'll thank me for every minute of it, and so will all of your fans from coast to coast in every direction.

Okay, so you don't have to give your father your answer this very instant.

You need to think it over in your mind, then go ahead and think it over in your mind. So in the morning, your decision will be your decision, and you'll call Merv and advise the man accordingly. And don't forget to tell him to send you a round-trip ticket.

You know what, Jerome? Tonight, after I finish this letter, when your father finally puts his head on the pillow and says his prayers, I am going to thank God that with regard to the simple question of "Merv

Griffin" my sonny boy and I have had a meeting of the minds and the subject is all settled. And I promise you, I wouldn't even say boo to Artie Elkin and the rest of them beforehand. The gang of them should only be looking and not be ready for it when you walk out and Merv says, "Ladies and gentlemen, have I got for you the cream of the crop of the literature business!"

Jerome, I'll tell you something which just between you and your father will be our little secret. Artie and the rest of them, who wishes these gangsters ill? But when a certain person walks out and sits himself down to converse with Merv, every hoodlum in this building will drop dead! From one floor to the next, right up to the penthouse, all the big shots will grab their kishkas and keel over. And you know what? Your father wouldn't blame them.

So call the Chinese Army and tell them to come and stick knitting needles under your father's fingernails, but this is what I am telling you. Even up in the penthouse with their Woody, they'll have to get the undertaker!

So the plots, Jerome, tell me, did you see anything there? Because since you're going on Merv, it couldn't hurt to ask the man what he thinks of this here plot as against that one. Believe me, Jerome, the man knows. The man didn't just get off the boat, darling. Pay attention to your father—you ask Merv an intelligent question, he'll be only too happy and glad to give you the benefit of his wisdom.

The man knows the business, Jerome. Are you listening to me? Believe me, the man didn't get where he is giving bad advice. Listen, Jerrychik, you open your heart of hearts to Merv and, I promise you, you won't be sorry. The man knows whereof he speaks. Besides, does it ever hurt to ask? You'll show him the plots I sent you and then you'll sit down with him and you'll listen to him and you'll see what the man thinks. And meanwhile whichever ones he says to you, "Jerome David, these are the ones I want you to get rid of," don't forget to send them back to me, and your father will be a sport and make a present of them to Gert Pinkowitz.

Who knows, maybe God will make a miracle and the woman could get somewhere with one of them with her own kid.

Sweetheart, I didn't tell you yet what the story is in that department, did I? Believe me, I know you got a lot on your mind. Just getting ready to go back to your old name and go on Merv, I realize that this is plenty for the current agenda. But meanwhile, Jerome, when someone comes along who is suffering worse than you are, then you should always sit yourself down with that person and listen to their story—because I'll tell you something, you never know what you could learn from it. Like the furrier who calls up his travel agent and he says to him, "Look, I'm sick to death of the usuals, give me what you got in the way of the Joneses couldn't keep up with it," and the travel agent says to him, "Well, what do you say to a couple of weeks on a slave ship?" So the man says, "A slave ship? What's a slave ship?"

Jerome, the travel agent answers him like this—he says to the man, "A slave ship, a galley ship—you never heard of a galley ship?" And the man says, "Sure, I heard of a galley ship. Next time you're talking a galley ship, *say* a galley ship. So tell me, this season the right people are cruising on a galley ship? Then book me a galley ship, first class."

So the next thing you know, Jerome, it's time to go get aboard, and the man and his wife of forty years, they go down there, and they get on board, and it's gorgeous.

Darling, your father is here to tell you, this was some gorgeous ship this man and his wife got on. Service like this you never saw in your life. Hand and foot, they couldn't wait on you fast enough. So the man and his wife, they're in there in their stateroom and it's so gorgeous they can't believe it—when meanwhile here comes this terrible knocking on the door. And who is it, Jerome? Because I am here to tell you, it's this individual maybe seven feet tall, and he says to the man, "You Goldbaum?" So Goldbaum looks at him, seven feet tall, naked all over, these muscles, Jerome, such muscles. So Goldbaum looks and he winks and he says, "I'm Goldbaum."

Well, darling, this big naked man says to Goldbaum, "If you're Goldbaum, then it says here it's your turn at the oars." Do you hear this, Jerome, the *oars?* And the fellow is looking at this list he's got and he says, "Nathan Goldbaum, right?" So Goldbaum says to the man, "Oars?"

Jerome, this is when the big naked man gives Goldbaum a grab and pulls him out into the hall and he says to Goldbaum, "Fucking right, oars!"

Jerome, would you believe this? In all your born days, would you believe with your own ears what is happening here? Because they take Goldbaum down there into the bottom of the ship and they tear off the clothes he's got on his back and then they put these chains on his legs and they make him sit down and with all the other men he's got to pull on these oars until the ship is rowed all the way out of New York

Harbor! But this is nothing, Jerome, nothing! Because meanwhile there's all these big fellows walking around and they're hitting Goldbaum and the rest of them such smacks. With whips!

Whips, Jerome!

Well, I don't have to tell you, it takes maybe two, three days to row out there—and in all this time, darling, did Goldbaum get one drink of water? Forget water! Not even a piece of *fruit,* Jerome. Hitting with whips, *this* is what Goldbaum and the rest of them got!

Meanwhile, okay, they get the ship rowed out there and the big fellow comes over and he gets the chains off Goldbaum and he has to pick him up and *carry* the man, this is the condition which Goldbaum is in!

But listen, darling, even in this condition, like a dead man, I want you to ask yourself what Goldbaum is thinking to himself when the big fellow is carrying him back to his stateroom like a rag which is no good for nothing.

Jerome darling, do you want me to answer you?

The man is *starved,* Jerome, the man is dying of *thirst!* And *bleeding!* Believe me, I don't have to describe to you the blood, it would make you sick if I told you just the half of it, how much blood Goldbaum already bled all over himself.

But meanwhile, Jerome, what is Goldbaum *thinking?*

Jerome darling, I want you to hear this. Because even in his condition, God love him, Goldbaum is thinking to himself, "So what do you tip a fella like this?"

Did you hear this, Jerrychik? "What do you tip a fella like this?" Did you hear every word of what Goldbaum is thinking?

So this is why I say to you, darling, it never hurts to listen to the other person's pain and suffering. Believe me, Jerome, whatever the source, you could always learn something when you pay attention to the other fellow's aggravation. Even from Merv Griffin, you could learn, for instance. Because don't think the man hasn't been through plenty in his own right.

But on this earth, darling, even taking into account your own personal father, there is *nobody* what got the heartache and aggravation that you could even begin to compare with the heartache and aggravation of Gert Pinkowitz.

Look to the child, Jerome. This is what your father says to you, look to the child. Because if you want to see what is killing a mother or a father, don't look for a truck, don't look for a bus—unless you know it's the child which is driving it.

But listen, would you ever hear one word of bitterness from the woman's own lips?

A *saint*, Jerome—the woman is a living saint! Believe me, kiddo, every last word I your father had to pry out of her because wild horses couldn't get this woman to talk and tell you what's what with her high and mighty Thomas.

You know what, darling? In my personal opinion, the entire human race should get together and take off their hat to this wonderful creature.

And I'll tell you something else, boychik. Thank God this is a person made of iron. Of *iron!* Because with flesh and blood you couldn't live with what this woman's got to live with. I as your father look at this creature and I say to myself, "Sol, even with the agony you are suffering at your own child's hands, this is nothing when you stop to compare it to the agony of a person like Gert Pinkowitz!"

This is what your father says to himself, Jerome. Every time I even *look* at the woman, this is what your father in his own mind has to say to himself.

On the other hand, who could overlook the similarities? I mean, when I look at what this woman has her hands full with, you think I don't say to myself, "Sol, when you consider your own heartache and aggravation, you don't notice the terrific similarities?"

Jerome, believe me, darling, whoever said it's a small world, the same person could go ahead and say it a thousand times and he still wouldn't be saying it enough.

Number one, Gert tells me her Tommy is a brilliant boy. So even if I am in no position to pass judgment, let's give the woman credit. Like my own Jerrychik, Gert's Thomas is another genius, this much I am willing to acknowledge even if the Robbins woman, who has her own Harold, says to your father she's read the Pinkowitz's boy's books and every word in all three of them she could take it or leave it.

Okay, so it's a free country, the Robbins woman is entitled to her own personal opinion, maybe the woman knows whereof she speaks. But meanwhile, so long as Gert Pinkowitz tells me the child is a genius, then the child is a genius—even if Dora Robbins wants to look your father in the face and maintain as to the contrary.

But, Jerome, I ask you, when did the boy last do a little business? Because the answer is don't ask. Not for seasons and seasons. So listen, maybe in your lifetime you ran across another individual where this particular situation is the case?

Meanwhile, what's the next thing?

No *pictures*, darling! Just like with somebody else your father happens to be acquainted with, no pictures, not even a snapshot in the newspapers—plus no "Merv Griffin," no "Merv Griffin" neither!

But wait a minute, Jerome, wait a minute, the similarities I'm not even finished with yet. Listen. Because is the name which the boy's mother sat down and gave him good enough for this ungrateful child? Like somebody else who is associated with your own father's personal acquaintance, is it?

Only *worse* than you, Jerome. Worse!

Believe me, worse isn't even the half of it. Because with you, darling, maybe there is a certain degree of rhyme or reason. But with the Pinkowitz kid? With him we're talking a whole different ball game altogether. With him we're talking it's all the way out of the whole total picture!

Myself, boychik, when I heard it, when the woman is on the premises only an hour already, you could have blown your father over with a feather. The woman does not even have one stick of furniture moved in yet! Do you hear me, Jerome? Not one stick! But meanwhile this is how heartsick she is—the woman is so heartsick she's got to say to the moving man she's sorry but not for another instant could she stand the strain and the aggravation, would he please leave everything sit while she goes and sees who her new neighbor is and gets this off her chest. And do you know *why*, darling? Because if the woman does not talk to somebody in the next two seconds, then she is going to have to scream or take a pill. And meanwhile I don't have to tell you a pill she can't take since so far they didn't unpack the first thing yet, not even the box with her emergencies.

Jerome, I know I don't have to draw you a diagram, it is I your father who is the individual next door.

This is how small the world is, Jerome—you turn around and the next thing you know you are the person next door!

Sweetie guy, you could go ahead and send hoodlums. They could bring brass knuckles down here to get me with, but your father wants you to know one thing. In this world, Jerrychik, even if you couldn't believe it, there are worse things than what you did to your name when you made it J.D., which, by the way, even President Eisenhower himself didn't think was such a hot idea—but, all right, go ahead and look up the history on it for yourself.

I promise you, boychik, you go listen to Gert Pinkowitz with her Thomas, you'll hear and you'll hear plenty—a child which comes into this world with such a gorgeous name and then has the gall to turn around and change it the instant they come along and say to the boy, "Pinkowitz?"

All right, so the child wanted to make a good impression. So, darling, your father will tell you what happens when all you can think of is making a good impression. Because if you remember Goldbaum, then you'll know who your father is talking about when I tell you the man's son comes home with a *blonde*.

A *blonde*, Jerome, as your father lives and breathes, the man's son comes home with a *blonde*.

But meanwhile Goldbaum couldn't learn to live with it? And also his wife of forty years couldn't learn to do likewise?

So they make a meal, Jerome. Are you listening to me, darling? Mrs. Goldbaum, God love her, she makes a meal. And right off to begin with she puts soup on the table. And the blonde, Jerome, the blonde who only wants in her heart of hearts to make a good impression, she says, "Oh, God, is this soup wonderful, is this delicious soup, never in my life did I have such a bowl of soup!"

This is what the girl says, Jerome. So are you listening? The blonde says, "This soup, such a wonderful soup—so tell me, everybody, what is it, what is it?"

Darling, Mrs. Goldbaum shouldn't answer the girl?

Believe me, Jerome, Mrs. Goldbaum you never met maybe, but let me tell you that this is a civilized person.

So to make a long story short, she says to the blonde, "Matzoh ball soup, we call it matzoh ball soup."

Darling, verbatim, this is how Mrs. Goldbaum answers.

But the blonde, Jerome, are you remembering *her?* This blonde which in her heart of hearts only wants to make on these people a good impression? Because I want you to hear what she says as a consequence of she only has the best of intentions.

You're listening, sweetie boy? Was your father born yesterday because he's taking it for granted you are listening? Because this blonde which I am referring to, this is what the girl says to Mrs. Goldbaum, and I am quoting you, sweetheart, every single *word.* She says, "Holy

Mother of God, it sure turns out better than when they make it from the matzoh's shoulder."

Good impressions, Jerome—this is the aggravation they give everybody. But Mrs. Pinkowitz's Tommy, all the child can think of is how to make a good impression. And forget just a T. for Thomas. *Worse*, I'm telling you. Worse by a long shot.

Believe me, Jerome, the sin you did to your name the instant your father's back was turned, it's nothing by comparison. Even the woman herself would tell you if you asked her. Because I your father asked her, and she answered me, "Solly, Solly, what your child did to you when he made it J.D., take my word for it, it's a blessing by comparison. A blessing, Solly, a blessing!"

Cutie fellow, it should only fly from your father's lips to God's two ears when I say to you in all honesty, "The nerve of some children!"

Okay, so send bullies to knock me down and steal my last red nickel, but your father, Jerome, is no stranger to what a child can do to a parent. So my heart shouldn't go out to this woman who's got a Thomas just like I've got a Jerome, only worse if you could actually believe it?

Darling, the woman has *tears* in her eyes when she says to me, "Solly, sit down, dear heart, because I want you to get yourself ready for the shock of the century."

Sonny boy, I am telling you they could have come in here and blown your father over with a feather when the woman told me what she told me. To take a gorgeous name like Pinkowitz and get cute with it? What kind of a child is it which does a thing like this? So if the boy had to have two syllables, what's so wrong with Pincus? But Pynchon, darling, this is a name which makes no sense from every angle!

So whoever heard of a name like Pynchon?

Tell me, Jerome, this is a name for a serious person? Believe me, darling, your father is willing to learn. There's an area code somewhere with a name like that they wouldn't all look at you sideways?

So the child could take Thomas and put a little trim on the top of it and also make a good impression!

This is why I say to you, Jerome, you have to give comfort where comfort is due. But I promise you, boychik, in this case it's a pleasure, the woman is a living doll, so svelte it would break your heart. And

meanwhile, I promise you, it's no trouble. I hear the creature crying her
eyes out, it's such an effort to run next door? So maybe that's where I
was if you called last night and your father wasn't here to pick up.

So you called, darling? Tell me, you really called?

You know what, Jerome? I say you used the brains God gave you and
you waited for when they knock the rates down and it wouldn't cost
you no arm and a leg just to say hello and Happy High Holy Days to
your father.

Tell me, sweetheart, did I guess the right answer?

Save your breath, I guessed.

Listen, you think a father does not know a son?

Don't worry, boychik, when all is said and done, a father knows a son
—even with no pictures and a name he could never warm up to. But
Merv, Jerome, Merv you promised me you'll get busy and take care of.
Because I'll tell you something, darling. If you will pay attention to me
with both ears, your father will let you in on a big secret.

You remember when years and years ago you sat yourself down and
you wrote about this woman who's so fat and all day long she sits on
her porch and listens to the radio? Darling, I'm going back years now,
but do you remember? So because this creature was so lonely and also
dying and so forth, it was you yourself which said, please God, the
people on the radio should all get together and do for her their utmost,
since what's the woman got in the whole wide world except the people
which talk on the radio?

Sweetheart, sonny boy, I don't have to tell you it was you yourself
which said this with your own two lips. So don't make a federal case,
Jerome—the difference is your father got a *television*. Are you saying to
me it's not the same principle?

Please, darling, for your father, and so please God you wouldn't have
to contradict yourself, be a sport and go on "Merv Griffin."

But if it is so important to you that it has to be a fat woman which is
listening, and if your own father's suffering is not enough for you,
Jerome, then do it for Gert, darling, do it for Gert.

So all right, Gert Pinkowitz is *not* so svelte! So your father told a
little fib, send G-men and put him in a prison.

The creature is *dieting*, Jerome. Did you hear me? Dieting! So between you and me, did she get anywhere yet? So sue me, the woman's
not skinny!

I'm telling you, darling, this woman is so fat it would break your heart just to look at her—and all I got to say is thank God 305 is her area code and you'll never have to see.

Boychik, are you listening? So you're already the most wonderful son in the whole wide world, no arguments. Your father admits it, there never was a better boy. Now go be an angel on top of it, Jerome—for a woman who is fat and is in agony and is also a saint, tell Merv Griffin here you come for Mrs. Gertrude Pinkowitz.

Love and kisses
from your adoring father,
and also Happy High Holidays!

P.S. Did I tell you about Goldbaum is passing away? The same Goldbaum which went on the slave ship, Jerome, the man who has the son with the *blonde?* So he's on his deathbed, and it's good-bye and good luck, I didn't tell you already?

But all right, Goldbaum's an old man, he's got no complaints, that's it and that's it. So did I tell you, Jerome? Because I want you to hear with your own two ears what happens next when the man says to his son which is sitting with him, "Kiddo, you've been a wonderful kid, from you in my whole life long your father has never had nothing but absolute joyousness, so good-bye and good luck and here is a kiss."

And the boy, Jerome, he says to Goldbaum, "Well, you have been a great pop, Daddy, and we'll miss you a lot." And Goldbaum answers him, he says to his son, "Forget it, when that's it, that's it, and it's time to call it quits."

So this is when the man shuts his eyes and lays back down again, he's ready to pass away. But then the next thing you know Goldbaum opens up his eyes and he's giving the air these little sniffs.

Are you paying attention, Jerome? The man is sitting up, and with his nose up in the air he's going like this, darling—sniff, sniff. So then he says, "Tell me, sweetheart, is Mama in the kitchen?"

And the boy answers him, he says to Goldbaum, "Mama is in the kitchen, she's making chopped liver in the kitchen."

Do you hear this, Jerome? "Mama is in the kitchen, she's making chopped liver in the kitchen."

So this is when Goldbaum says to him, "Look, darling, you'll be a sweetheart and go into the kitchen and for your father you'll come back here with a little taste, and please God, I only got a couple of seconds, so you'll hurry."

Jerome, did you hear each and every word of this? What Goldbaum said to his son, you heard? Because I want you to hear how his son answers the man. Even if you couldn't believe it with your own two ears, your father wants you to hear.

As God is my judge, darling, the man's child says to him, "I can't, Daddy, it's for after."

Did you hear this, Jerome? "It's for after." With these very words the child answers his father, "It's for after."

Jerome? Sweetie boy, are you listening to me? There *is* no after! Now God bless you and let this be a lesson to you.

MAGAZINES CONSULTED

The Agni Review, P. O. Box 229, Cambridge, Mass. 02238

America One, 55 Washington, Ipswich, Mass. 01938

Antaeus, Ecco Press, 1 West 30th Street, New York, N.Y. 10001

Antietam Review, 33 West Washington Street, Hagerstown, Md. 21740

The Antioch Review, P. O. Box 148, Yellow Springs, Ohio 45387

Apalachee Quarterly, P. O. Box 20106, Tallahassee, Fla. 32304

Arizona Quarterly, University of Arizona, Tucson, Ariz. 85721

Ascent, English Dept., University of Illinois, Urbana, Ill. 61801

Asimov Science Fiction Magazine, 380 Lexington Avenue, New York, N.Y. 10017

Aspen Journal of the Arts, P. O. Box 3185, Aspen, Colo. 81612

The Atlantic Monthly, 8 Arlington Street, Boston, Mass. 02116

The Black Warrior Review, P. O. Box 2936, University, Ala. 35486

The Boston Globe Magazine, Boston, Mass. 02107

California Quarterly, 100 Sproul Hall, University of California, Davis, Calif. 95616

Canadian Fiction Magazine, P. O. Box 46422, Station G, Vancouver, B.C., Canada V6R 4G7

Carolina Quarterly, Greenlaw Hall 066-A, University of North Carolina, Chapel Hill, N.C. 27514

The Chariton Review, The Division of Language and Literature, Northeast Missouri State University, Kirksville, Mo. 63501

Chicago Review, 970 East 58th Street, Box C, University of Chicago, Chicago, Ill. 60637

Christopher Street Magazine, Suite 417, 250 W. 57th Street, New York, N.Y. 10019

Commentary, 165 East 56th Street, New York, N.Y. 10022

Confrontation, English Dept., Brooklyn Center of Long Island University, Brooklyn, N.Y. 11201

Cosmopolitan, 224 West 57th Street, New York, N.Y. 10019

Cottonwood Review, Box J, Kansas Union, University of Kansas, Lawrence, Kans. 66045

Crazyhorse, Department of English, University of Arkansas at Little Rock, Ark. 72204

Cumberlands, Pikeville College, Pikeville, Ky. 41501

Dark Horse, Box 9, Somerville, Mass. 02143

December, P. O. Box 274, Western Springs, Ill. 60558

The Denver Quarterly, Dept. of English, University of Denver, Denver, Colo. 80210

Ellery Queen's Mystery Magazine, 380 Lexington Avenue, New York, N.Y. 10017

Epoch, 254 Goldwyn Smith Hall, Cornell University, Ithaca, N.Y. 14853

Esquire, 488 Madison Avenue, New York, N.Y. 10022

Event, Douglas College, P. O. Box 2503, New Westminster, B.C., Canada

Fiction, c/o Dept. of English, The City College of New York, New York, N.Y. 10031

Fiction International, Dept. of English, St. Lawrence University, Canton, N.Y. 13617

Fiction Supplement, San Francisco Review of Books, P. O. Box 5651, San Francisco, Calif. 94101

The Fiddlehead, The Observatory, University of New Brunswick, P. O. Box 4400, Fredericton, N.B., Canada E3B 5A3

Forms, P. O. Box 3379, San Francisco, Calif. 94119

Forum, Ball State University, Muncie, Ind. 47306

Four Quarters, La Salle College, Philadelphia, Pa. 19141

Gargoyle, P. O. Box 3567, Washington, D.C. 20007

Georgia Review, University of Georgia, Athens, Ga. 30602

Grand Street, 50 Riverside Drive, New York, N.Y. 10024

Green River Review, Box 56, University Center, Mich. 48710

The Greensboro Review, University of North Carolina, Greensboro, N.C. 27412

Harper's Magazine, 2 Park Avenue, New York, N.Y. 10016

Hawaii Review, Hemenway Hall, University of Hawaii, Honolulu, Hawaii 96822

The Hudson Review, 65 East 55th Street, New York, N.Y. 10022

Iowa Review, EPB 453, University of Iowa, Iowa City, Iowa 52240

Kansas Quarterly, Dept. of English, Kansas State University, Manhattan, Kans. 66506

The Kenyon Review, Kenyon College, Gambier, Ohio 43022

Ladies' Home Journal, 641 Lexington Avenue, New York, N.Y. 10022

The Literary Review, Fairleigh Dickinson University, Teaneck, N.J. 07666

The Little Magazine, P. O. Box 207, Cathedral Station, New York, N.Y. 10025

The Louisville Review, University of Louisville, Louisville, Ky. 40208

Mademoiselle, 350 Madison Avenue, New York, N.Y. 10017

Malahat Review, University of Victoria, Victoria, B.C., Canada

Manhattan Plaza News, 400 West 43rd Street, New York, N.Y. 10036

The Massachusetts Review, Memorial Hall, University of Massachusetts, Amherst, Mass. 01002

McCall's 230 Park Avenue, New York, N.Y. 10017

Michigan Quarterly Review, 3032 Rackham Bldg., University of Michigan, Ann Arbor, Mich. 48109

Mid-American Review, 106 Hanna Hall, Bowling Green State University, Bowling Green, Ohio 43403

Midstream, 515 Park Avenue, New York, N.Y. 10022

The Missouri Review, Department of English, 231 Arts and Sciences, University of Missouri, Columbia, Mo. 65211

Mother Jones, 607 Market Street, San Francisco, Calif. 94105

New Directions, 333 Sixth Avenue, New York, N.Y. 10014

New England Review, Box 170, Hanover, N.H. 03755

New Letters, University of Missouri-Kansas City, Kansas City, Mo. 64110

New Mexico Humanities Review, The Editors, Box A, New Mexico Tech., Socorro, N.M. 57801

The New Renaissance, 9 Heath Road, Arlington, Mass. 02174

The New Republic, 1220 19th Street, N.W., Washington, D.C. 20036

The New Yorker, 25 West 43rd Street, New York, N.Y. 10036

Nit and Wit, Box 14685, Chicago, Ill. 60614

The North American Review, University of Northern Iowa, 1222 West 27th Street, Cedar Falls, Iowa 50613

Northeast Magazine, 179 Allyn Street, Suite 411, Hartford, Conn. 06103

Northwest Review, 129 French Hall, University of Oregon, Eugene, Oreg. 97403

Ohio Journal, Department of English, Ohio State University, 164 West 17th Avenue, Columbus, Ohio 43210

Ohio Review, Ellis Hall, Ohio University, Athens, Ohio 45701

Omni, 909 Third Avenue, New York, N.Y. 10022

The Ontario Review, 9 Honey Brook Drive, Princeton, N.J. 08540

Operative, Box 686, Old Chelsea Station, New York, N.Y. 10113

The Paris Review, 45-39 171st Place, Flushing, N.Y. 11358

Partisan Review, 128 Bay State Road, Boston, Mass. 02215 / 552 Fifth Avenue, New York, N. Y. 10036

Perspective, Washington University, St. Louis, Mo. 63130

Phylon, 223 Chestnut Street, S.W., Atlanta, Ga. 30314

Playboy, 919 North Michigan Avenue, Chicago, Ill. 60611

Playgirl, 3420 Ocean Park Boulevard, Suite 3000, Santa Monica, Calif. 90405

Ploughshares, Box 529, Cambridge, Mass. 02139

Prairie Schooner, Andrews Hall, University of Nebraska, Lincoln, Nebr. 68588

Quarterly West, 312 Olpin Union, University of Utah, Salt Lake City, Utah 84112

Redbook, 230 Park Avenue, New York, N.Y. 10017

San Francisco Stories, 625 Post Street, Box 752, San Francisco, Calif. 94109

The Seneca Review, P. O. Box 115, Hobart and William Smith College, Geneva, N.Y. 14456

Sequoia, Storke Student Publications Bldg., Stanford, Calif. 94305

Seventeen, 850 Third Avenue, New York, N.Y. 10022

Sewanee Review, University of the South, Sewanee, Tenn. 37375

Shenandoah: The Washington and Lee University Review, Box 722, Lexington, Va. 24450

The South Carolina Review, Dept. of English, Clemson University, Clemson, S.C. 29631

The South Dakota Review, Box 111, University Exchange, Vermillion, S. Dak. 57069

Southern Humanities Review, Auburn University, Auburn, Ala. 36830

Southern Review, Drawer D, University Station, Baton Rouge, La. 70803

Southwest Review, Southern Methodist University Press, Dallas, Tex. 75275

Story Quarterly, 820 Ridge Road, Highland Park, Ill. 60035

The Spoon River Quarterly, P. O. Box 1443, Peoria, Ill. 61655

Story Quarterly, P. O. Box 1416, Northbrook, Ill. 60062

The Texas Review, English Dept., Sam Houston University, Huntsville, Tex. 77341

The Threepenny Review, P. O. Box 335, Berkeley, Calif. 94701

TriQuarterly, 1735 Benson Avenue, Evanston, Ill. 60201

Twigs, Pikeville College, Pikeville, Ky. 41501

Twilight Zone, 800 Second Avenue, New York, N.Y. 10017

University of Windsor Review, Dept. of English, University of Windsor, Windsor, Ont., Canada N9B 3P4

U.S. Catholic, 221 West Madison Street, Chicago, Ill. 60606

The Virginia Quarterly Review, University of Virginia, 1 West Range, Charlottesville, Va. 22903

Vogue, 350 Madison Avenue, New York, N.Y. 10017

Washington Review, Box 50132, Washington, D.C. 20004

The Washingtonian, 1828 L Street, N.W., Suite 200, Washington, D.C. 20036

Webster Review, Webster College, Webster Groves, Mo. 63119

West Coast Review, Simon Fraser University, Vancouver, B.C., Canada

Western Humanities Review, Bldg. 41, University of Utah, Salt Lake City, Utah 84112

Wind, RFD Route 1, Box 809, Pikeville, Ky. 41501

Wittenberg Review of Literature and Art, Box 1, Recitation Hall, Wittenberg University, Springfield, Ohio 45501

Woman's Day, 1515 Broadway, New York, N.Y. 10036

Writers Forum, P. O. Box 7150, University of Colorado, Colorado Springs, Colo. 80907

Yale Review, 250 Church Street, 1902A Yale Station, New Haven, Conn. 06520

Yankee, Dublin, N.H. 03444